THE OTHER SIDE OF GOODNESS

Also by Vanessa Davis Griggs

Forever Soul Ties

Redeeming Waters

Ray of Hope

The Blessed Trinity Series

The Truth Is the Light

Goodness and Mercy

Practicing What You Preach

If Memory Serves

Strongholds

Blessed Trinity

Published by Kensington Publishing Corp.

THE OTHER SIDE OF GOODNESS

VANESSA DAVIS GRIGGS

Kensington Publishing Corp.
http://www.kensingtonbooks.com

DAFINA BOOKS are published by

Kensington Publishing Corp.
119 West 40th Street
New York, NY 10018

ISBN-13: 978-0-7582-7358-1
ISBN-10: 0-7582-7358-4

First trade paperback printing: August 2012

10 9 8 7 6 5 4 3 2 1

Printed in the United States of America

Dedicated to
Danette Dial, Terence Davis, Cameron Davis,
Arlinda Davis, and Emmanuel Davis

Acknowledgments

I remain ever thankful to God, who chose me and continues blessing me beyond measure. To my loving mother, Josephine Davis, and father, James Davis Jr.: It's been such a privilege and an honor to call you my parents, having your love and support all of these years as we celebrate this God-given journey called life. I am truly blessed!

To my husband, Jeffery: Thank you for your unwavering support as I walk in my calling. To my children, Jeffery, Jeremy, and Johnathan: Each of you are a gift from the Lord and have blessed my life in your own special way. To my grandchildren, Asia and Ashlynn: You two truly light up my world! Danette Dial, Terence Davis, Cameron Davis, Arlinda Davis, Emmanuel Davis, Cumberlan Davis, and all of my aunts, uncles, cousins, nieces, and nephews: I'm grateful for family and the memories we continue to create.

Thank you, Selena James and Kensington Publishing, for continuing to believe in me and what God is giving me. I'm grateful for friends who've been in my corner a long time now: Bonita Chaney, Rosetta Moore, Vanessa L. Rice, Zelda Oliver-Miles, Linda H. Jones, and Shirley Walker. Pastor Michael D. McClure Sr., I appreciate your prayers and belief that great things are on the horizon for me. Ella Curry of EDC Creations, thanks for all you do!

To those of you who bless me by choosing my books and spreading the word about what I do: I love you so very, very much! Because of you and your support, I'm able to continue doing this. And to those of you who are new to my books: I pray you enjoy this read and you're moved to pick up more. To my Facebook friends who read my books and status messages: Thanks for the love. I definitely feel it! As always, I adore hearing from you! You can find me on the Web at: www.VanessaDavisGriggs.com.

Chapter 1

Woe unto him that saith unto his father, What begettest thou? or to the woman, What hast thou brought forth?

—Isaiah 45:10

"You are *not* the father!" The words reverberated through the mid-November 2009 Alabama air like the sound of a thin sheet of tin after being struck by a heavy metal object.

Twenty-seven-year-old Paris Elizabeth Simmons-Holyfield couldn't hold back her feelings and immediately jumped to her feet. "Yes! Yes! I knew it! I knew it!" she said as she danced her five foot eleven inch self around in a small circle. "*Now* what are you going to do? Huh? Huh? Oh, yeah, you're looking *real* stupid now, aren't you? Oh, no. Don't you dare fall on the floor crying now. You knew *good* and *well* he wasn't the father of your baby! What is this, the fourth guy you've said you were 'one thousand percent sure' was the father? And now you're looking crazy, wanting somebody to feel sorry for you? Well, you're getting *exactly* what you deserve! Exact—"

"What on God's green earth is your problem?" fifty-year-old Lawrence Rudolph Simmons said, his deep voice booming as he looked on with a clear scowl of disapproval on his face.

Paris had spun around as soon as she'd heard the first word come out of his mouth. The six foot one inch tall, one-hundred-eighty-pound man always had that effect on her.

Thirty-three-year-old Andrew Holyfield shook his head as he smiled, showing off deep dimples that, since he was a little boy, had garnered attention. "That's your daughter for you."

"Hi, Daddy." Paris grinned as she scurried over to her father and softly planted a kiss on his cheek. "What wind brought you here this time of the day?" She then pivoted to her husband and gave him a peck on his lips. "Hi, honey. I didn't even hear you two come in."

"Of course, you didn't," Andrew said. "You were too deep and hooked on your favorite little show."

"It's not my favorite show." Paris walked over to the black Italian leather sofa, picked up the remote control, and clicked the television off. "I only watch that show for educational purposes." She tossed the remote control back onto the sofa.

Andrew chuckled. "Yeah, educational purposes, all right. 'You *are* the father.' 'You are *not* the father.' 'The lie detector says you were *not* telling the truth.' 'The lie detector says . . . she was telling the truth.' " Andrew shook his head. "Educational purposes indeed."

"Well, some of these women are a trip and a half. Airing their personal business like that, and all of it on TV to boot. Bringing some man on the show, claiming he's the father of their baby when they know who they slept with and when. Although I *will* admit that some of these women have slept with quite a number of men in the same month, a few of them on the same day." Paris shook her head. "It's crazy. Then there are the guys who know they were with them, talking about that child can't possibly be his because the baby doesn't look anything like him. Like children have to look exactly like the father to be fathered by them. Calling the poor innocent child ugly, only to learn that the child really *is* his." Paris chuckled.

"And you can make fun of me all you want," she said. "But I like to study people. I can pick out the ones that are the fathers and the ones that are lying about it, just like that." She snapped her fingers. "You know I also took a semester of psychology in college. I love trying to figure out what people are really thinking and doing, and their reason behind it."

"If I recall correctly," Lawrence said, tilting his head slightly, "didn't you fail that course and ended up dropping it altogether instead of retaking it?"

Paris tilted her head in the opposite direction from his as she smirked. "Daddy, I told you what an awful professor Ms. Booth was. That woman just *didn't* like me." Paris widened her light brown eyes as she spoke. "If you want the real truth: Ms. Booth didn't care much for *you*, so she ended up taking her dislike for *you* out on *me*."

Lawrence shook his head. "Always an excuse. When it comes to you and trouble, it's always someone else's fault. It's never anything that you may have done."

"Well, that was not an excuse. She also didn't care for me because I was the third runner-up beauty queen at the college pageant and she was merely this homely old maid of fifty who was likely never going to find a man who'd ever want her."

Andrew laughed. "Both of you are something, if you ask me. You're like two peas in a pod. You two are so much alike that you never seem to get along or openly agree." Three inches taller than his wife, he rubbed his perfectly trimmed goatee as he grinned lovingly at her.

"Well, you didn't answer my question," Paris said to her father, ignoring her husband's comment. She began to run her fingers through her freshly permed, mid-length, wavy-styled, dark brown, medium-auburn-highlighted hair, tossing it a few times as she did. Catching her father's disapproving stare, she quickly stopped.

Her father had made it abundantly clear, countless times in fact, just how much he hated when women did things like that. He'd said they were *more than* aware of what they were doing (most of them merely being flirtatious instead of nervous as Paris often used as her defense to him), and that it was unladylike and unbecoming of a *decent* Christian woman.

Lawrence nodded, as though he was thanking her for saving him the trouble of having to correct her *yet* again. "My son-in-law and I came here to discuss a few of my legal woes. You know there are people who don't want to see me reelected to the Alabama State House of Representatives, so they're coming up with anything they can find to try and take me down this time around. That's what good opponents do."

Paris strolled back over to her husband and threaded her arm through his. "Well, you can't find a better lawyer than my dear husband here, that's for sure."

"Well, your *dear* husband doesn't seem interested in handling my most recent possible problem. So maybe you can help me convince him." Lawrence trained his eyes hard on Andrew.

"I told you, Pops," Andrew said. "There's not much I can help you with. Our firm would be facing a huge conflict of interest if I were to take you on. The other man involved—"

"Is a liar and a cheat, among other things I'll not say in the company of a lady." Lawrence eased down onto the sofa.

"He's talking about Rev. Walker," Andrew said to Paris. "That's the other guy someone in our firm is already representing on the opposite side."

"Marshall Walker, the pastor of that church so many flock to, or at least they *used* to flock to before that other preacher, George Landris, arrived in town. The authorities are trying to say that me and William Threadgill are involved in some kind of bribery scheme or something with Walker." Lawrence waved the thought away. "They picked him up and charged him last Friday or Saturday. This is just something the Democrats are trying to cook up, trying to tie me in to his misdoings to derail me and my candidacy. They're just upset, and likely desperate right about now."

"Can you blame them for being upset?" Paris said. "Everybody I know who's heard you switched parties is boiling mad. I've never voted for a Republican before *in my life*. But now that you've switched, in midstream I might add, I'll either have to vote Republican this time around, vote against you, or not vote at all."

"I'm still the same person I was before I decided to switch parties," Lawrence said, looking up at his daughter. "But you, of all people, know the district I represent has become much whiter now and, despite our racial advancements—perceived or otherwise—this is *still* Alabama, the heart of *Dixie*. A lot of folks that moved out of the area years ago are moving back, in droves now—"

"And they're driving the prices up so high that the black

folks can't afford to stay or move in," Andrew said with a few nods.

"Please don't get Andrew started," Paris said, grinning slightly. "You know at heart my husband is the poor man's lawyer. He loves to fight for the downtrodden and the broken who, most times, are *so broke* they can't even afford to pay his fee. So he gives of himself, pro bono if he has to, to represent them. Too many of them, if you ask me, which is the *exact* reason we're not more well-off than we are."

"We're doing just fine. I make enough to take care of my family," Andrew said. "I just see how unfair the system can be. Lady Justice may be blind, but her hearing lately has been overcompensating for her loss of sight. Enough so, when certain defendants speak and sound black or have a hint of a foreign accent or are just plain poor, she somehow knows who they are without having to see their faces."

Andrew uncoupled Paris's arm from his and took a step away from her. "Do you know how many innocent folks are behind bars because they couldn't afford a high-powered or, heck, merely a *decent* lawyer who could have gotten them *at least* a *fairer* trial? While some rich person gets off by saying they didn't steal the thing . . . that they were merely 'borrowing it' or forgot to give it back to the salesperson after trying it on. You find one who goes to rehab for the drugs he was caught *using*, while another goes to jail, getting ten years for the same or for having a small amount of another type in his possession."

"Well, I'm not concerned about anybody except me right now." Lawrence scooted back against the sofa. "And having this new legal thing possibly hanging over my head is no joke, either. The Tea Party movement appears to be picking up some steam, especially in some areas and especially now that we have a president of color. I figured by switching from the Democratic Party to the Republican Party and co-opting some of the Tea Party's rhetoric about being taxed enough already and the need for smaller government, I can more easily get reelected."

"Selling out," Andrew said as he sat down in the wingback chair across from Lawrence.

"No. It's called doing what you need to do to survive,"

Lawrence said. "That's the problem with folks: They don't know how to adapt, how to be nimble and change when the situation calls for it. People get set in concrete and don't know how to move. Sure, I could stand on past principles and talking points that have worked beautifully for me in the past, but that may not get me reelected this cycle. And if I don't get reelected, then I won't be able to help *anybody*."

"So you're saying you're just faking it," Andrew said.

Paris sat on the arm of the chair where Andrew sat. "I think Daddy is just saying that if he doesn't change his tactics, he won't be in a position to help anyone at all. Daddy's been in politics for ten years—"

"Eleven," Lawrence corrected her.

"Okay, eleven years." Paris nodded. "He knows the system, knows how to get at least *some* things done."

"So you *really* think black folks are going to vote for you as a Republican?" Andrew's look was serious and stern. "You honestly think that?"

"Yeah." Lawrence crossed his legs and leaned back with a grin. "Many of them feel they know me and my record regardless of whether there's a *D* or an *R* behind my name. Some will vote for me just *because* my name is familiar to them—that's the power of name recognition. Folks will vote for a name they've heard of when their choice is between that name and an unknown one. Then there are those who will vote for me just *because* I'm black and they'd rather see a black man win regardless of which team he's on. And last, there are the Republicans who loyally vote strictly for the *R*s and, most likely, won't have a clue what color I am. And it won't hurt when I play up my beliefs on social issues, emphasizing how much I'm pro-life, absolutely against abortion, and that I'm willing to fight for the principles they care most about."

Paris began to rub the wavy hair on top of Andrew's head. She couldn't help but think about their children and how beautiful they were going to be when they had them. How could they turn out to be anything but beautiful if they inherited their father's good hair and looks combined with hers?

That's if she could just manage to get pregnant and have children.

"Would dinner happen to be ready yet?" Lawrence asked Paris.

"No."

"Then why don't you go cook us something," Lawrence said. "And make enough for William Threadgill. He should be arriving any minute now. We three have business to discuss, and since I missed eating lunch today, I'm really hungry."

"You mean cook as in use the stove?"

Andrew, who had snickered a little when Lawrence asked if dinner was ready, was full-out laughing now, although he was trying his best to hold it down as much as possible.

"What's so funny?" Paris said to Andrew—her hand off his head now.

"Your daddy started it," Andrew said, trying to smother his laughs that were still managing to escape as giggles. "I'm sorry; I couldn't help myself."

"What?" Lawrence asked, looking from one to the other. "What's the problem?"

Andrew shook his head as he tried to keep his laughter from starting up again.

"He's laughing because I rarely ever cook. We generally go out for dinner or we call in for something to be picked up or delivered," Paris said. "I wasn't planning on cooking anything today."

"So exactly what *do* you do at home all day?" Lawrence asked.

Paris stood up. "I have my own things to do. I have various interests that require my attention, just like you two."

"She watches television pretty much all day," Andrew said, then grinned.

"I do not." Paris gave him a disapproving look to emphasize her words. "You're not here so you don't know what I do all day. And I assure you, I do a lot more than watch television."

"Yeah, that's right. She divides her time between the computer and her precious little CrackBerry, oh I'm sorry; I meant to say BlackBerry. No, no, wrong again. She has an iPhone now, her new play-toy. And what's that hot new thing on the Internet this cycle? Facebook! Yeah, that's right . . . Facebook. Her big thing used to be MySpace, but it's been replaced by another lover. And let's not forget about her have-to-have, much-needed therapy," Andrew said.

"Therapy?" There was clear alarm in Lawrence's voice. "What therapy? What's wrong? Now, Paris, you know if the media gets wind of this—"

"Retail therapy," Andrew said. "I'm talking about her retail therapy. Isn't that what you call it?" Andrew looked at Paris, who didn't respond, before turning back to his father-in-law. "She has to go shopping to take her mind off all the depressing things she sees and hears on television and that comes across on the Internet. You know, all of those 'devastating, distressing things that are happening all around the world,' like poverty, all of those poor and starving folks in the world, the daily reported civil unrest around the globe, and let's not forget those poor animals they show on TV in need of a good home. According to my dear wife, the only way she can feel better about all of these things after witnessing them is to go shopping."

"I'm sure this can't be true," Lawrence said. "I certainly hope it's not. Paris's mother and I raised her to be a productive member of society . . . to serve others. Paris, you could be spending time at a church or shelter, helping to feed the hungry, showing just how much our family truly cares about others."

"Daddy, I'm twenty-seven years old, twenty-eight in another eight months. I'm not a child anymore that you can mold into what you want me to be. I have a husband; we have our own home. I get to decide what's best and right for me."

"In other words: I can't tell you what to do anymore?" Lawrence said with a slight frown.

"Now, Daddy, I respect you. You just need to learn to respect me. I'm all grown up now. I'm not your little girl anymore." Paris bit down on her bottom lip.

"Oh, now, you'll *always* be my little girl." Lawrence grinned. "And I'll always be your daddy. And speaking of family and little girls, exactly when do the two of you plan on having children?

Your mother is ready to be a grandmother. And being a grandfather would certainly look good on my political brochures. There's nothing that says to the voters how much you care than letting them know you're not only a parent but a grandparent. And a child or two would definitely give you more than enough to do to keep you busy around the house, Paris."

"Daddy, is that all you ever care about? How something might benefit your political aspirations?" Paris asked.

"For now it is. That's why it's important for your mother to put on the right face for the public." Lawrence leaned forward. "That's why you, your brother, Malachi, and little sister, Courtney, must be on your p's and q's at all times, representing our family with the highest level of degree. Proverbs 22:1 tells us that 'a good name is rather to be chosen than great riches.' Our name is a brand now. And we have to protect it. So I don't need any of you doing anything that could embarrass or derail me, and *especially* not during this campaign cycle. I plan on winning my upcoming reelection. And I don't need any problems popping up. That's why I made sure I got that large ballroom last week for that campaign rally I had."

"We know, Daddy. Stay on our p's and q's. You've drilled that point home to each of us enough. Oh, yeah, and I heard all about that underhanded ballroom acquisition," Paris said. "That was *so* wrong of you on so many levels."

"Says who?" Lawrence pulled his body back as though he was shocked by her words.

"Mom, for one."

Lawrence waved her words off. "Your mother is such a softie. She'd give away everything if I'd let her."

"Well, to be fair," Andrew said, chiming in. "From what I heard, you did manage to somehow finagle that ballroom away from an elderly man's one hundredth birthday celebration after his family *clearly* had it reserved months before you ever thought about having anything there. That's the way I heard it, anyway."

Lawrence stared hard at Andrew, then released a quick smile. "All's fair in love and politics. If you can do it and get away with it, and it doesn't physically hurt anybody, what's the harm in the end? I happen to know folks who can make things happen. What is it the young ballers say? Don't hate the player; hate the game."

Lawrence then looked at Paris. "And your mother talks too much, as do you. Some things aren't meant to be repeated. With that being said, now get on in the kitchen and fix me and your husband something to eat. As I said, we have some business we need to attend to, and *I* am starving."

Paris smiled slightly, the way she did when she was completely under his rule and didn't care for what he was saying but knew it was best to just go along with him to get along, until the right opportunity presented itself. "Sure, Daddy. Whatever you say."

She went into the kitchen, opened the drawer where she kept a stack of various restaurant menus, pulled out the menu to the Italian place she used whenever she wanted Italian food, and called in an order.

She hung up the phone and grinned. "Sure, Daddy. Whatever you say."

Chapter 2

For though I be free from all men, yet have I made myself servant unto all, that I might gain the more.
—1 Corinthians 9:19

Paris's father's words about her having children had stung more than he knew. Her mother would have known, because the two of them had just talked about it two days ago. But her father was always too busy to care about anything that had to do with his family unless it was something that somehow fit with his political ambitions. She'd been trying to get pregnant for a little over four years now, desperately trying for the past two years, with no results.

Andrew really wanted children. He *really* wanted them. And he was good with them. He'd become more insistent about it lately, making comments about how they weren't getting any younger. Early in the year, he'd expressed how he was thirty-three, and before he knew it, he'd be forty.

"I don't want to be an old man trying to keep up with our children," he'd said. "I'd like to enjoy them while I'm able, and not in my forties, or worse, fifties when they begin elementary school and close to seventy when they graduate high school."

When he'd first conveyed his desire for them to start their family, it had come because Paris had been putting off getting pregnant until they'd been married for a year or two. She hadn't wanted to be like many she'd seen who'd gotten married and found all of their time as a couple lost in the demands of raising children. After two years, she'd discontinued doing anything that would keep her from getting pregnant—fully expecting she'd be like those who immediately got pregnant. Boy was she wrong! And since she hadn't told Andrew she wasn't doing anything to keep from getting pregnant, he'd merely thought she just still didn't want children yet.

So he'd ramped up his rhetoric, kept up his petition for them to get started.

Paris knew she should tell him that she wanted to have a baby just as much as he did, but seeing that there was now possibly a problem (and believing she might be the one *with* the problem), she didn't let on. She decided she would just let it be a surprise when she *did* finally conceive. It had been only in the past two years that she'd told Andrew she wanted to start a family, and only this year had she suggested they both see the doctor to find out why they hadn't made a baby yet.

Andrew went to the doctor, and just as Paris had suspected, there didn't seem to be any reason coming from him as to why she hadn't gotten pregnant. Andrew was so great about it. He played it down when he saw how devastated hearing this affected her. He told her things like, "Don't be so hard on yourself. We just started really trying about a year ago." And, "You know half of the fun of getting there is getting there." He, of all people, knew how Paris could be and how much she liked to get *what* she wanted *when* she wanted it. He also knew she was spoiled.

But since Andrew hadn't known she'd been trying for four years instead of the one he was aware of, he didn't know there was a really bad problem and everything pointed in her direction.

The delivery guy showed up forty minutes after she placed her order. He'd come to the back door and knocked as instructed. Normally, Paris would have told Andrew the food was there so he could come in and fix his own plate. But she knew her father didn't play that *at all.* Her father believed women should fix a man's plate. Since she didn't cook (that often anyway) and her father had turned up his nose about that, she decided it was best to just fix their plates and take it to them to keep her father from even knowing that she'd ordered in.

She went into the den to see if they were ready. William Threadgill, her father's forty-nine-year-old best friend and chief of staff, was there now.

"Hi, Paris," William said as soon as she entered and he'd looked up and seen her.

"Hi," Paris said, looking at him only briefly before directing her attention to her father. "The food is ready."

"Well, that was fast," Lawrence said. "I hope it's real food and not some sandwich or somebody's helper you threw together."

Andrew snickered. Paris threw a hard look his way. She knew that *he* knew she'd merely ordered in. Andrew cut off his snickering, then smiled as he winked at her. She couldn't help but smile, no matter how much she hadn't wanted to.

"You can bring it in here," Lawrence said. "There's no need in you going to the trouble of setting up the dining room table just for the three of us. We can eat in here while we finish up."

Paris nodded, then grinned. "No problem." She was glad he'd said that, since she'd had no intentions of setting up the dining room table. It was enough to have to put the food on a plate, deciding what was too much or not enough for each man. But to have to set plates and utensils as well as dirty up extra bowls just to put it on the table? No way.

She turned to William. "Would you like something to eat as well?"

William smiled. "Why, yes. Thank you, Paris."

Paris wanted to roll her eyes at William but held back. William was always so polite and respectful to her when he was in her father's and husband's presence. Nothing like he could be when it was just the two of them. She even hated how he said her name: Pa-ris. *Dirty old man.* She went back to the kitchen to fix three plates.

William and her father had been friends since before she was born. He was truly her father's best friend, his right-hand man, and now his chief of staff in the world of politics. Most folks knew that before they could ever get to her father, they had to get past William. And William was a silvery sly fox. He didn't care about how he looked to others or what they thought about him. So much so that Paris was convinced that was why he was allowing his hair to go gray while her daddy dyed his, which caused William to look older than her father even though he was a year younger than him.

On the other side, her father claimed he dyed his hair because he had to maintain his image, being that he was a politician and always in the public's eye and all. He argued that people judged public figures harshly on their looks. They liked their male politicians to be tall, with deep manly voices, and good looks were always a plus. Politicians needed to have firm handshakes and know how to work a crowd, yet still be effective when it came to being one-on-one.

But Paris also knew that Andrew was right when he'd said she and her father were like two peas in a pod. She, of all people, hated to admit that at times, because her father had some nasty (some might even call them downright borderline narcissist) qualities about him. However, she considered that she—like her father—was merely confident in who she was, what she wanted out of life, and that somehow in the end, she would find a way to get it.

She decided it was best to put the three plates on a tray to carry into the den. Doing that would save her a trip. She just had to be careful not to drop the tray with all of its contents or pour the plates onto the floor if she somehow tilted the tray the wrong way. *I could definitely not be a waitress or a maid,* she thought as she maneuvered her way out of the kitchen into the den with the tray of full plates. She was practically holding her breath as she walked. *No way!*

"That looks good," Lawrence said as she methodically made her way over to the coffee table, trying to figure out how to set the tray down around their stuff.

Paris couldn't believe how little help she was actually getting from the men (including Andrew) as she tried to situate the tray, finding she first had to move some of their things lying on the table out of the way. Managing to do it without any assistance, Paris stood up straight and waited on someone to acknowledge what she'd just accomplished.

"Are you planning on bringing us something to drink?" Lawrence asked Paris. "I'd like some cola if you have any."

"I'll get it," Andrew said, immediately jumping to his feet.

"It's okay," Lawrence said. "Paris can get it. She doesn't mind." He looked up at Paris. "Do you?"

Paris forced a smile. "Of course not. That's what I'm here for. Right, Daddy? To serve."

"No," Lawrence said in a tone lower and more serious. "It's *not* what you're here for. I just thought you appreciated the fact that we're all in here working hard on something important and you wouldn't mind helping out the best way you could."

Andrew went over to Paris and placed his hand in the small of her back. Paris nodded, then smiled. She received the message from both men. Her father was telling her that she didn't have a job outside of the house and that she really didn't do all that much to help out around the house (having someone who came and cleaned for them), so the *least* she could do was the *least* she could do. And Andrew was telling her to let this go and not to pay her father much attention. That he loved and appreciated her, and that their guests (mainly her father) would be out of their house soon enough, so just chill out for a little while longer.

Paris went to the kitchen and returned with three glasses of cola. The three men were eating now and didn't even notice she'd returned with their drinks. Noting this, Paris was careful not to disturb their conversation.

"That woman called again," William said. "She's persistent, that's for sure."

"Again?" Lawrence asked. "Well, does she have money she wants to donate to my campaign?"

"It doesn't appear to be the reason that she's calling," William said. "Mattie told me that she's called every single day, a few times twice a day even, for the past week. Mattie is positive that it's the same woman, and for some reason, she insists on speaking to you and only you. She won't leave her name or a message. Just asks when you're expected to be there and that she'll just call again later. Mattie said she showed up at the office yesterday still refusing to give her name. After about forty minutes of sitting there, she told Mattie that she couldn't wait any longer and left."

"Mattie is good at protecting me," Lawrence said. "She knows how to keep folks away from me." Lawrence began to chuckle. "She's almost as good at it as you are. And she's so convincing . . . so believable sounding."

"Well, I spoke to that woman today myself on the phone. I'd told Mattie if she called again to transfer her to me, if I was available. I was trying to make her think I was you so I could find out why she was trying to get in touch with you. She didn't fall for it. The mystery woman maintains it's imperative that she speaks with you; she claims it's a matter of life and death. She let me know, in no uncertain terms, she doesn't plan on divulging why she needs to see you, except to you, and only to your face. I have to give it to her; she's a bold one, that's for sure."

"Well, most folks believe their minute problems *are* a matter of life and death." Lawrence shook his head slowly. "But you say she's called for an entire week? And from what you and Mattie have gathered, she doesn't sound like she's interested in contributing financially to my campaign? Because you know now that I need some large donations."

"When I asked if I could be of assistance, going as far as to tell her that I was the person who had your ear, she wouldn't tell me a thing. Just that she had to speak with you, she was running out of time, and that it was a matter of life and death and asked if someone could tell her when she could meet with you." William picked up his drink and took a swallow, then set his glass back down.

"She said she will only say what she has to say to you," William continued. "Man, I'm going to be honest: It looks like she's not going to give up what she wants with you to anybody *except* you. At this point, she even has me curious as to what this is about. You know that I'm generally pretty good at breaking down even the best of them. But this woman is a tough nut to crack; she's not budging."

"Yeah, and you also know there are a lot of crazies out there who would love nothing more than to do me harm," Lawrence said. "We have to stay on guard."

"I know that. But honestly, she doesn't sound crazy at all. In fact, she has this really sweet, pleasant voice . . . really silky. But then, the women with the sweet, sexy voices are usually nothing like what they sound on the phone when you finally get to see them in person." William shuddered, then happened to glance at Paris, who was quietly standing in a corner out of the way.

Paris knew he'd realized they were talking about things he, at least, would prefer she not be privy to. Her father must have picked up on it as well, since he, too, was now looking at her. That conversation officially came to a screeching halt.

"Paris, this is some awesome food here," Lawrence said, pointing his fork at his plate. "I didn't know you could cook like this. Your mother needs to get your recipe for this lasagna. It's fantastic!"

Paris stepped out of the shadowy corner and came over to where they sat. "It's takeout, Daddy. You know I didn't cook that. I didn't have time to cook anything like that."

"Now how was I supposed to know that?" Lawrence put a forkful of food into his mouth, chewed, swallowed, then began to speak again. "Your mother never orders in and she whips up things like this, this fast and good, all the time."

Paris smiled. "Of course, Daddy. Of course."

Paris knew her mother didn't always cook what they ate when her father thought she was "whipping up" something. In fact, it was her very own mother, Deidra Jean (Long) Simmons, who had taught her to order takeout when she found herself in a pinch. But that was her mother's secret, and she certainly wasn't about to clue her father in.

She most certainly was not.

Chapter 3

Now some are puffed up, as though I would not come to you.

—1 Corinthians 4:18

The twenty-seven-year-old woman sporting a black V-neckline pantsuit with wide pant legs and modest-sized gold-looped earrings sat patiently outside of Representative Simmons's office. Mattie Stevens, Lawrence Simmons's secretary, refused to go to lunch and leave the woman unattended in the office. The woman disclosed when she arrived that she wasn't planning on leaving until Representative Simmons returned.

Mattie had informed the woman, who had been polite in her insistence to speak with Representative Simmons no matter how long she had to wait this time, that she wasn't sure exactly *when* he'd be back. But Mattie knew he was scheduled to return sometime before lunchtime. William had mentioned they would be back by then because he had a lunch date he couldn't miss. The two had gone in the same car. Of course, Mattie didn't tell the woman (whose age she had deduced to be around twenty-seven) that—hoping she would do as she'd done before and not stay longer than forty to fifty minutes.

Lawrence and William had gone to meet with a large donor. Mattie had managed to call William and let him know (using coded words since the woman was sitting there at the time) that the mysterious woman was there in the office. They both felt she likely wouldn't hang around long. But when he called two hours later to let her know they were on their way back, the woman was still there.

Thirty more minutes passed. The woman suddenly got up and, without saying a word, left. She didn't even respond back to Mattie's cheery "Good-bye" and "Have a nice day!"

William and Lawrence returned to an empty office.

"I guess Mattie went to lunch," Lawrence said.

William looked around. "Yeah, it looks that way. And it looks like that woman she said was here is gone as well. But you know Mattie wouldn't dare leave with someone here, not if she can help it. And especially not someone she's uncomfortable with. Mattie has real trust issues, specifically when it comes to strangers outside of your office."

Lawrence stopped at Mattie's desk and picked up the messages she'd stuck in the large, gold paperclip holder she still used for the messages she knew he would likely have to write down anyway. Lawrence unlocked and opened the door to his office, then turned back to William. "This has been a good day, wouldn't you say?"

"Absolutely!" William said. "And that was a nice donation, really nice. And to think: You didn't even have to sell your soul in order to get it."

"Yeah," Lawrence said. "Just had to make a few promises I may or may not, in the end, be able to keep. So, William, what's on your agenda for the rest of the day, besides your hot lunch date with your wife?"

"Oh, my wife ended up canceling on me," William said. "She sent me a text right as we were riding up on the elevator that she wasn't going to be able to make it." He held up his cell phone. "But it's just as well. Lately, she and I haven't had many nice things to say to each other. It seems like she's always upset with me about something or another. You know how it is."

"I do know that. So does that mean you're free for lunch now?"

"Yeah. You want to go grab something?"

"Sure," Lawrence said. "But let me take care of a few things first." He held the messages up in the air. "I have a few folks that I have to get back to right now. You know: You snooze, you lose. It shouldn't take but about ten . . . fifteen minutes at the most."

"That's fine. I'll just wait out here for you. I have a few calls I need to make while you're doing that." William sat down with his cell phone out as Lawrence stepped into his office and closed the door.

Five minutes later, a woman walked into the outer office area. William was just finishing up his call.

"Hi there," William said to the woman as she sat down two chairs away from him as though she were merely returning back to her own home.

He couldn't believe how gorgeous she was. Her hair, reaching down to her back, was the most beautiful loose tresses he'd ever seen. She didn't appear to be wearing much makeup. If she was, he definitely couldn't tell it. Her beautiful brown mocha-colored skin was flawless. Her lips were accentuated with a burgundy color that glistened from a touch of lip gloss placed just right. Her eyelashes were long and absolutely hers. And the outfit she wore couldn't have fit any better had it been tailor-made right on her body.

She gave a quick smile. "Hi," she said. The sound of her voice, to William, was positively angelic.

"Are you here looking for anyone in particular?" William asked. "The secretary is out right now, most likely at lunch."

"Yes, I see. And, yes, I *am* waiting on someone in particular," the woman said. "Do you work here or something?"

"Well, kind of," William said. "I mean I work here, but not *in* here. Perhaps I can be of some assistance."

She shook her head. "Unless you're Representative Simmons, which I can tell you that you're not, then, no; I don't believe you can be of any assistance to me."

"Well, now, I do work for the representative. I'm sure I can help you." His eyes scanned her from her head to her neck in a flirtatious-like way.

"I'm waiting for him to return. You wouldn't happen to know if he's back yet, would you?"

"I'm sorry. Where are my manners? I haven't properly introduced myself." He stood up and went over to her. "My name is William Threadgill. And you are?"

"Waiting on Representative Simmons," she said.

William chuckled. "Hold up. You've called here before. In fact, I've spoken to you on the phone once." He nodded. "Yeah, your voice is coming back to me."

"Yes," the woman said. "I've called many times before. I've been here before as well. Representative Simmons appears to be a hard man to catch up with."

"As you can imagine, he's a very busy man. Out there fighting for and trying to do the work and the will of the people. And in these days of high unemployment and uncertainty, he's working extremely hard. It *is* difficult to catch up with him. That's why he has such a fine staff in place." William sat back down, this time in the chair right next to her, and crossed his leg. "I'm his right-hand man. I'm certain if there's something you need, I can ensure that it gets done, that's if it's something Representative Simmons can do. I, at least, can pass the information along to him. You can trust me; he does."

She gave him a curt smile. "I agree. He does have quite a competent staff. So far, all of you have managed to keep me at bay this week. I've concluded either he's really busy or he's a pro at getting rid of the people he doesn't care to be bothered with."

"Well, the district he serves is quite large now," William said. "I'm aware that almost everyone would *personally* like to speak to him if they could. But that's not humanly possible. So if you'd just tell me your name and what you need, I promise I'll see what the two of us can do. You have my word."

She shook her head. "I appreciate the offer, Mr. Threadgill. But I'll just wait for Representative Simmons."

"Call me William. Look, Mrs."—he tilted his head slightly—"or is it Miss?"

She smiled as she slowly shook her head. "It's Miss."

"All right. That's a start," William said. "We're making progress here. Miss, let me be frank with you. You're likely not going to get to meet with the representative. Not because he doesn't want to, it's just a difficult thing to arrange. I'm his chief of staff. That means when you talk to me, it's just like talking to him. In fact, it's difficult for people to get to talk to me, but here you are." He grinned. "So why don't you tell me what you need and let me see what I can do. I promise I want to help you." His eyes again scanned her face, then began to roam downward.

"Listen, Mr. Threadgill. I appreciate you for being so nice in offering yourself up as you sacrificially are. But I have to speak to Lawrence Simmons and I'm not leaving here until I do," she said. "Now, I know he's due back into this office at some point today. I overheard his secretary on the phone telling someone that he would definitely be back in the office today. So I'm going to sit right here until he returns." She crossed her arms and sat back hard against her chair.

"You know I *could* call security," William said.

She uncrossed her arms and looked at him. "And tell them what? That a taxpayer is here to speak with Representative Simmons and you don't happen to care for her being here?"

William scratched his head. "No. But if you're a threat . . ."

She laughed. "So you're trying to say that I'm a threat?"

He laughed. "No. But you can't threaten to stay in a place where you've been asked to leave."

"You asked me to leave? That's funny; that's not what I was hearing coming from your mouth. Listen, Mr. Threadgill, this is the people's place." She stood up. "*Our* money pays for this place. It's not Representative Simmons's office nor is it yours, or his secretary's, for that matter. I have just as much right to be here as any of you. I'm not threatening anyone; I'm not a danger to anyone. I have requested to speak with Representative Simmons, and all I've been getting for my troubles from this office is the runaround. Believe me, I do have another option other than coming here and being put through what all of you are putting me through. And when Representative Simmons hears what I have to say, I dare say he'll thank me that I've been this persistent in seeing him instead of doing what I could be doing at this point."

William stood up. "So is this something personal?"

She looked at her watch. "Could you please find out how much longer it might be before Representative Simmons is due back here?"

"Listen, I was just about to head out to lunch. Why don't you and I go get something to eat? I take it you do eat lunch, don't you?"

"I'm not interested in lunch. I have to talk to Lawrence Simmons, and I'm running out of time! So if you really want to help, then get on your cell phone and call him or text him, whatever you need to do, and see if you can't make that happen! Can you do that? Can you?"

"Calm down. There's no reason for you to raise your voice," William said.

"Yes, there is!" She stomped her foot. "And I will *not* calm down. I'm tired. I took off from my job today just so I might *somehow* catch up with Lawrence. And I don't have time to play these silly games with you or anyone else for that matter. I know he's due to be in his office today. I heard his secretary confirming it. So you get in touch with Lawrence and you tell him that Gabrielle Mercedes . . . Booker wants to talk to him—"

"Gabrielle?" William said, stepping closer to Lawrence's closed office door. "So your name is Gabrielle. What a beautiful name. Gabrielle Mercedes *Booker.*" He was speaking loud now, loud enough for Lawrence to hear him. "And you want to see Representative Simmons today."

"Yes!" Gabrielle said. "I know his daughter Paris." Gabrielle was also speaking louder, as though she knew that the man she wanted to see might be on the other side of the door listening. "Paris and I were roommates for a couple of months back when we were eighteen. Representative Simmons will remember me."

The door to Lawrence's office suddenly swung open. Lawrence smiled. "Well, hello, there." His eyes were on the woman in the office. "I thought I heard voices out here." He pivoted to William. "William." He said his name as though there was more to what he was saying than just saying his name.

William nodded slightly. "Representative Simmons, this is Gabrielle Mercedes Booker. I happened to have found her out here waiting to see you."

Lawrence walked past William and straight to Gabrielle. "How nice. You've come by to see me. Well, as you've likely noted, it's lunchtime around here. And my dedicated secretary is away. I suppose it's a good thing that William came along when he did. We wouldn't want you sitting out here all by yourself." Lawrence extended his hand and gave her a firm handshake, the way he did with all whose votes he hoped to secure.

"I didn't realize you were in there," William lied. "I was sitting out here waiting on Mattie to return when Gabrielle walked in. We've been sitting out here chatting away."

"Well, our doors are always open," Lawrence said. "We're here to serve. And the only way we can do that is to be available to the people we were elected to serve, as much as is humanly possible, of course." He smiled and leaned in toward her. "Gabrielle Booker." He smiled. "So what can I do for you?"

"I need to speak with you," Gabrielle said. "Privately, if you don't mind." She glanced at William, who wore a mischievous grin on his face now.

"You know, I'm sure Representative Simmons would love to speak with you," William said. "But don't you have an important meeting you have to attend?" William said to Lawrence. "In fact, that's where I thought you were."

Lawrence looked into Gabrielle's eyes. "I'm okay," Lawrence said, not taking his eyes off hers.

"But, sir," William said. "I don't think you should miss this meeting. It really could have *detrimental* effects."

Lawrence looked at William, instantly dropping his smile. "I told you, William. It will be okay." Lawrence went back to his office door and held it open for Gabrielle. "Please, please. Come in," he said to Gabrielle.

"Then I'll just come in with the two of you," William said, realizing that Mattie wasn't there, and at this point in the political cycle, this woman—who although said she knew his daughter—showing up looking all beautiful and tempting could very well be a ploy to take Lawrence down.

Lawrence allowed Gabrielle to enter. "William, I *said* we'll be all right. Now, why don't you head off to that meeting I was scheduled for and hold things down until I get there."

"Are you sure?" William said, not speaking of the fake meeting, but referring to him being alone in his office with this dish of a woman. "Are you sure this is what you want to do?"

Lawrence smiled, then winked at William. "Yes. I'm sure."

Lawrence closed the door and turned around. "Gabrielle, it's good to see you again." He gave her a quick hug. "It's been a long time. My, my. You've certainly grown up since the last time I saw you." He motioned for her to sit down in one of the two chairs that faced his desk, then walked around to the other side and sat down. "So, to what do I owe this pleasure?" He leaned in.

Gabrielle took a deep breath and released it slowly. "Look, Lawrence, I'll just cut to the chase. It's about your daughter. She's in serious trouble. And it's come to a matter of life and death at this point. Your daughter desperately needs your help. And if she doesn't get it, she's going to die."

Chapter 4

What will ye? Shall I come unto you with a rod, or in love, and in the spirit of meekness?

—1 Corinthians 4:21

Lawrence eyed Gabrielle hard now. Yes, she was even more beautiful than the last time he'd seen her, which had to be almost ten years ago. She was eighteen when he met her, the same age as his daughter Paris. In fact, she'd just turned eighteen, at the end of May, if he recalled correctly. He remembered how Paris had allowed Gabrielle to come and stay with her after Gabrielle's aunt and uncle, who were her guardians at the time, put her out following her having graduated from high school and turning eighteen. Gabrielle stayed with Paris for a few months. Paris had turned twenty-seven back in July so that would be a little over nine years ago.

But Gabrielle and Paris had parted ways, and not at all on friendly terms. Paris never told him exactly why the two of them had fallen out, but it had been just as well as far as he was concerned. He'd met Gabrielle when he'd dropped in unexpectedly to the apartment he was paying for. That's how he learned what was going on.

Gabrielle Booker had seemed a nice enough young lady, although Paris hadn't told him she was staying there before his visit. Gabrielle had endured a hard life; that much was clear: her mother, having been killed by her own father; him sentenced to prison for her murder. This three-year-old child having to go live with her father's sister and husband along with their four children, feeling every single day like she wasn't wanted or loved, to then be put out on the streets with nowhere to go for no good reason. Gabrielle *certainly* had lived a hard-knock life.

Lawrence wasn't sure how Paris and Gabrielle had become friends, or more to the point, how they had become friends enough for Paris to open up her door and share her apartment with her. But to his surprise, his daughter had.

At first he hadn't been happy about it. After all, he was the one footing the bill, and here were two people essentially living off him for free. But, of course, Deidra, with her compassion for others, made him see how selfish he was being and the message he was sending his children when he acted that way.

"You keep telling our children it's about serving others, but then you don't walk the talk," Deidra had said. "You tell folks how much of a Christian you are, deacon at our church, but is your life demonstrating God's love? Lawrence, how much more is it really going to cost you to allow that child, and, yes, she's still a child just like Paris is still our child even though she's almost eighteen and all grown up. What more, Lawrence Rudolph Simmons, will it cost you if that child stays there with Paris until she can get on her feet?"

Lawrence knew Deidra was right. And she'd used his full name, which meant she was a bit put out with him about this. The young woman indeed needed somewhere to stay. And it was a two-bedroom apartment. What harm would it do to allow Paris to share it with a friend in need? *That's what Christians do, right?* And Deidra was indeed a good Christian, more Christian than him as he was still a devout WIP—Work in Progress.

Lawrence had met Deidra Jean Long back when they were in college. He absolutely noticed her, but she didn't appear impressed by anything about him. He was tall and athletic; some folks expected him to end up playing professional basketball. She was short and petite, a book worm who most felt was going to make the most wonderful teacher. After Lawrence was able to convince her to go out with him one time, more on a dare, they discovered that they were practically made for each other. He'd never before been so impressed with a girl.

"Smitten" is what his grandmother had called him. "Sprung" was the word most of his guy friends used.

Deidra was not only brilliantly smart, but when she let down her hair from the old-fogey chignon or single French braid down the back and removed those old-fashioned black-plastic-rimmed glasses, she was knockout gorgeous. Every guy was trying to get after her then. But by then, it was Lawrence who had captured her heart.

The two of them married straight out of college. And before they could even get settled as man and wife, nine months later Paris Elizabeth Simmons made her entrance, screaming onto the scene. And she'd continued to scream for attention ever since.

Lawrence was already fascinated with politics in his high school and college days, where he was on the student council. There was just something about feeling like you could effect change from the inside out that interested him. He wanted to be the one to possibly make someone's life better. He knew what it was to struggle. He knew what it was to try to find a way to first get into college, then to make it all the way through. His family had neither the money nor the means to send him. So he had worked hard for everything he'd gotten. If he went into politics, he felt he could bring some ideas that might make the next generation's life a little better than his.

But power can corrupt. It was like a shiny object being dangled before you to take your focus off what you were intending to do. And that's where Deidra came in the most with Lawrence. She was the one person who could bring him back to earth when he started getting too far out there. And as much as there were times Deidra really got on his nerves, he loved her for keeping it real with him, or as the young folks would say, "Keeping it one hundred."

Paris had befriended Gabrielle a little over nine years ago. Now here Gabrielle sat before him telling him that his daughter was in trouble. But he'd just seen Paris yesterday at her house. And Paris talked to her mother pretty much every single day. So how would someone like Gabrielle know she was in trouble when none of them had heard anything about it?

Lawrence politely smiled at Gabrielle. A smile tended to soften the words when you were essentially about to call someone a liar. "I didn't know you and Paris were still talking, let alone still friends," he said.

"Paris?" Gabrielle said. "I haven't seen or spoken to Paris in over nine years. Not since that day she told me to get out of her apartment and never come back."

"Oh, I'm sorry," Lawrence said. "I thought perhaps you two had talked. So how do you know Paris is in trouble?"

"It's not Paris that's in trouble," Gabrielle said, adjusting her body better in her chair.

"Well, I'm pretty sure you can't be talking about my daughter Imani. That girl practically runs from trouble. When she sees trouble coming, she turns and sprints in another direction."

"I'm not talking about Imani, either." Gabrielle swallowed hard. "The daughter I'm speaking of that's in trouble, the one who desperately needs your help or she's going to die . . . is my and your child. I'm talking about Jasmine . . . essentially, *our* daughter."

Chapter 5

That I might make thee know the certainty of the words of truth; that thou mightest answer the words of truth to them that send unto thee?

—Proverbs 22:21

Lawrence began to shake his head. "So that's how you're going to play this, I see. Okay, who sent you?"

Gabrielle frowned. "What?"

"I want to know who put you up to these shenanigans." Lawrence stood up. "Who sent you here and how much are you being paid?"

"Nobody sent me and nobody is paying me to come here," Gabrielle said, standing now as well.

Lawrence walked around his desk to her. "Is someone threatening you or something? Does someone have something over your head and that's why you're here doing this? Is it about money? Do you need money that bad that you would come here and lie like this?" He was standing right in front of her face now. "Tell me why you're here spewing this nonsense!"

"If you'll go back and sit down, I'll calmly explain everything. Look: We don't have too much more time left. And we really don't have a lot of time to waste."

"What is this 'we' business? I'm not in whatever little scheme you're cooking up here. Do you have a recording device on you or something? Is that why you're in here lying?" He nodded. "You're just trying to set me up so you can take something to my opponent. I get it. I say something here and you leak selective parts to the media to make things appear like there is something going on when it's not."

"Lawrence, please. Go back and sit down and let me explain. I promise this will all make sense when I'm finished."

"No. What I *want* is for you to get out of my office." He pointed at the door. "Now! Or I'll call someone to escort you out!"

Gabrielle could see just how angry he was getting. She'd seen him like this once before. The day she'd told him that she was pregnant and she didn't want the abortion he told her to have. He'd reacted almost the same way he was acting now. But she wasn't that scared little eighteen-year-old who didn't have a clue of what to do. And this wasn't about her. It was about an eight-year-old little girl who possibly wouldn't see nine if Gabrielle didn't succeed in doing what she could to help her.

"Did you hear what I just said?" Lawrence was leaning in even closer now. "I told you to get out! Now if you force me to have to call someone, I'm prepared to do just that!"

"Not until you hear what I have to say!" Gabrielle shouted back, causing him to take a step back away from her. "And I'm not going to stop until you know everything. So I can tell it to you here, behind closed doors, with just me and you. Or I can tell it to the world. But I *will* tell it! And I *will* be heard! It's that important. Now, go take your seat and hear me out. Or stand if you like. At this point, I don't care."

Lawrence stood with a clenched left fist. To Gabrielle, it appeared not so much that he wanted to hit her, but more like he was using his balled-up hand to hold on to something he felt he was losing.

Gabrielle acted like she wasn't afraid at this point, but inside she was trembling. "Are you going to sit down, and we talk rationally without the yelling and screaming, or what?" Gabrielle tried hard to keep the corners of her mouth from quivering. "I'm sure you don't want to be the cause of anyone overhearing us on the other side of that door."

Lawrence nodded, sat back down in his oversized leather chair, and stared hard at her. "All right. Say what you have to say."

Gabrielle eased down into her chair. She placed one hand over her face. This was much harder than she'd thought it would be, but this had to be done. She took her hand down and released a sigh. "Do you remember those last few times you and I saw each other?"

"Yes. So we don't have to bother going over that again," Lawrence said.

"Yes, we do. I told you that I was pregnant."

"Yeah, and I told you that I didn't believe that even if you were, the baby was mine," Lawrence said.

Gabrielle couldn't believe, even after all these years, how much it still hurt that he'd said that. She held her head up and looked boldly right back at him. "Well, whether you believed it or not, I *was* pregnant, and it *was* by you."

Lawrence's grin now was slightly sinister. "The operative word being 'was,' " he said. "Because the last time I saw you, I gave you money to . . . *take* care of it. I never actually admitted to being the father of your baby. But I was gracious enough to give you enough money to help you during that time of need. And *this*"—he sucked in air as he raised a fist into the air before slowly releasing his breath as he gently brought his fist down and allowed it to rest on his desk—"*this* is how you repay me and my family's, both Paris's and my, kindness shown to you."

"Lawrence, please don't attempt to rewrite history. Yes, Paris was nice enough to let me come and stay with her. But if you want to know the real reason why she did it, it was mainly because she wanted someone to keep the apartment clean without having to pay them to wash her clothes and cook, which honestly, for me, was no different from where I'd left. So, no, I didn't mind. And I didn't have and never *have* had a problem with paying my way, which is precisely why, as hard as it was to get it, I also paid her half the rent those two and a half months I stayed there."

"Actually, my daughter had pity on you and was trying to do something noble for someone who *obviously* is nothing more than a scam artist trying to get over on anyone foolish enough to fall for your sob story. You see I know for a fact that Paris didn't take one thin dime from you for rent. And you know why? Because *I* paid the rent and all of the utility bills and for all of the groceries there. So my daughter wasn't in need of any help from you, not when it came to paying any of the bills over there."

"Listen, Lawrence, I didn't come here to discuss or rehash what may or may not have gone down between me and Paris."

"Yeah, that's right. You came to try and take me down or shake me down with your deceit and, otherwise, lies."

Gabrielle laughed. "You want to talk about deceit and lies. Do you really want to go there with me?" She pulled her body back and set her face hard. "I'm talking about *you* now. You know Mr. Blissfully Married, Proud Father of Three, Servant of the People, Deacon of the Church Simmons. A man of virtue and integrity who thought it was all right to sweet-talk, then sleep with an eighteen-year-old girl. Oh, let's just come totally correct here: a just-*turned* eighteen-year-old girl who, as far as you knew or was concerned, was friends with your then eighteen-year-old daughter. And let me remind you that this was not once, not twice, but three times. So you can't say it was something that just happened in the moment. Those next two times were deliberate."

Lawrence let his head drop slightly before looking up and pressing his hands to his face. He removed his hands. "I was wrong. Okay? Is that what you want to hear? Is that why you're sitting there saying all this other stuff about some child that you *know* is not true?"

"Wait? Are you talking about the baby I was carrying that you claim couldn't possibly be yours? You know, the baby that caused you to call me out of my name because you were sure I had to be sleeping around, which, as I told you back then, I was not. I was a virgin, and you know that."

"All right. I was wrong to have said those things to you as well."

"Lawrence, I didn't come here to torture you or to try and get you to apologize to me. I let go of all that a long time ago," Gabrielle said. "And I truly forgave you after I gave all of my hurts over to the Lord after giving Him my life."

"So you're telling me that you're a Christian now?"

"Yes, I am a Christian. I am a follower of Jesus."

Lawrence smiled. "That's wonderful. I'm happy for you. Welcome to the family of Christ. I guess that makes us sisters and brothers now."

Gabrielle nodded one time. But she wasn't finished with the conversation they were already having; she wasn't going to let him skillfully change the subject. "You gave me money to get an abortion. I didn't ask you for any money to do that."

"I know you didn't. But I felt it was the least I could do to help out."

Gabrielle let out a single laugh, but not because anything was funny. "Are you serious?"

"Yes, I'm serious. How were you going to provide for a baby? You could barely provide for yourself. And other than at my daughter's at the time, you didn't even have a place to live. What on earth would you have to give a helpless baby? So you did what was best for you and the baby and got rid of it. I'm aware as a Christian, it doesn't seem right. But it was the humane thing to do . . . for both of you."

Gabrielle shook her head. "You know, you really are a piece of work. And you want to boast about how you're pro-life working to protect the unborn."

"My past is my past. What I did or believed in the past is not where I am now. From a pro-life standpoint, yes, I was wrong to have aided you in destroying a life. But my views have changed since that time. I'm a fighter of life."

"Well, you know what? I'm glad to hear you are now 'a fighter of life.' Because that's what I'm doing in your office right this minute: I'm fighting for a life that's not had a real chance to live very much yet. Lawrence, I didn't have the abortion," Gabrielle said. "Aren't you proud of me? Even as a sinner, without knowing how or why, I made the right decision. I let our baby live."

Lawrence stood up, placed both fists on the desk, and leaned on them as he spoke through tightly clenched teeth. "Stop . . . saying . . . *our* . . . baby!"

"What? You don't want to hear about the baby I didn't abort?"

He shook his head, then stood back straight.

Gabrielle stood up. "I had the baby, Lawrence—a little girl. And I got to hold her for a few minutes before a woman came in and took her away. I gave her up for adoption, Lawrence."

For the first time since Gabrielle began this part of the conversation, the corners of Lawrence's mouth turned up into a slight smile. "So you're telling me that you didn't have the abortion and that you gave your child up for adoption?"

"Yes."

"Then it sounds like everything worked out," he said. "So why are you here putting me through all of this?"

Gabrielle eased back down and swallowed hard a few times. "Because our child, the child that you and I created together, needs a bone marrow transplant or she's going to . . . die."

"What?" Lawrence flopped down. "A bone marrow transplant? Or she'll die?"

"Yes, Lawrence. When I decided to have her and give her up to be adopted, I moved on with no intentions of looking back. Yes, I've made some bad decisions along the way, but I've also made some good ones."

"Well, that would apply to all of us," Lawrence said with humanness.

"Yeah." Gabrielle looked down, then up at Lawrence. "I won't go into each and every detail here. Earlier this year, I received a call from the adoptive mother."

"Does she know about me?"

"No. I've not told anyone about you. They tested me to see if I was a match to be a donor."

Lawrence looked into Gabrielle's eyes. "Were you?"

Gabrielle wiped her eyes as tears began to fall. "I wasn't. That's why I had to come find you. Otherwise, I wouldn't be here right now."

Lawrence leaned over and handed her the handkerchief he kept in his suit coat pocket. Gabrielle wiped her eyes. "So what are you wanting from me?"

"A blood relative has a better chance of being a match in this case."

"So you're asking me to see if I'm a possible match?"

Gabrielle dabbed at her eyes. When she saw that his handkerchief had his last name embroidered on it (not just his initials as most do), she almost laughed. "Yes. I'm asking you to see if you're a match. The medical personnel and adoptive mother have things set up so that no one will know who the donor is, if that's what one prefers."

"Well, that's a good thing, I suppose. Giving who I am, the last thing I need is for something like this to get out. My political opponents could bury me alive with this information—the fact that I *could* have a child outside of my marriage."

"Not could . . . technically speaking, you do."

"According to you," Lawrence said.

"You know what, Lawrence? You are more than welcome to have a paternity test done. In fact, I would welcome it. If you like, I can even have it initiated."

Lawrence stared hard at her. "You would do something like that, knowing how it might affect my political career?"

"Lawrence, there's an eight-year-old little girl who, in about four months, will turn nine. That's if she gets the bone marrow transplant she desperately needs to make it to nine. We're talking about her life. Do you get that at all? I know it was your intent for me to get rid of her before she got here. Well, I didn't. And she's here now. So if you think for one minute that I care more about your political career than the life of that child . . ." Gabrielle shook her head slowly as she smiled and frowned at the same time.

"Lawrence, I'm going to tell you something. There was a time in my life when I wasn't saved. That person didn't always do the right thing. She wanted to be nice to everybody but quickly learned not everyone out there played by those same rules. What you're looking at right now is the other side of Goodness." She was somewhat making a play on the name of Goodness and Mercy she'd once gone by. "Please don't make me have to go back. Because I'll tell you, on that other side, I learned how to fight and fight dirty if I had to. And I *will* fight if I have to, when it comes to this little girl's life, I promise you: I'll fight if forced. Don't force me to have to go to the other side."

Lawrence swallowed hard; she saw it as his Adam's apple rose and fell several times. "And what if I'm not a match? Then what?"

Gabrielle stood up to leave. "Then what? Well, from all I've been told, the best matches are usually a sibling. I don't have any more children; you do. So if it turns out that you don't match, I pray you come up with a way to see if any of your other children might be. Because as I just told you: I'm not going to merely sit back and allow this child to die. Not if there's anything I can do to help her." Gabrielle started for the door, then turned back to a now standing Lawrence. "I promise: I'm not trying to hurt you or mess things up for you. I'm not. And if we can come up with a way for all of us to accomplish our goals on this, I'll be happy to do what I can from my end."

Mattie opened the door, stepped inside, and stared at Gabrielle. "I *thought* I heard voices in here," she said. She then turned to Lawrence. "I'm sorry, Representative Simmons. I thought you were at lunch."

Gabrielle smiled as she walked back over to Lawrence. "Oh, I almost forgot." She pulled a blank square piece of paper off a pad on his desk and picked up the pen stuck in what appeared to be an inkwell. She wrote something and handed him the paper. "Here are my phone numbers so you can easily get in touch with me. I look forward to hearing from you, sooner, rather than later. Thanks." She then turned and walked toward the door. "Bye-bye, Ms. Stevens," she said as she passed by her. "And *do* have a nice day!"

Chapter 6

When I heard, my belly trembled; my lips quivered at the voice: rottenness entered into my bones, and I trembled in myself, that I might rest in the day of trouble: when he cometh up unto the people, he will invade them with his troops.

—Habakkuk 3:16

William walked into Lawrence's office as Mattie merely stood with a befuddled look on her face.

"What's going on?" William asked Lawrence.

"Mattie, you can go," Lawrence said.

Mattie nodded, then promptly exited, closing the door behind her.

"Why are both you and Mattie looking like that?" William sat down in the chair Gabrielle had just vacated. "Both of you look like you just saw a ghost or like somebody just died or something."

Lawrence slowly took his seat behind his desk. "I don't know what's with Mattie except her possibly hating that Gabrielle managed to get in here despite her valiant efforts to keep her out."

"And you?"

"Me?" Lawrence said, shaking his head slowly. "I might possibly *be* in better shape *had* I seen or heard a ghost instead of what just transpired here."

William leaned in. "Okay. Spill it."

Lawrence dropped his head, then sheepishly looked up. "That *woman* that was here?"

"Yeah?"

"Gabrielle . . . Well, I think she's possibly going to be the source of some major problems for me."

William nodded. "Exactly what I thought was going to happen. That's why I didn't want to leave you in here with her by yourself. So what kind of possible damage control are we talking about here?"

Lawrence stood up and walked over to the window behind him. He gazed out, then turned back to William. "This one is going to be pretty substantial. Especially if what she says is even *partly* true."

"Well, whatever it is, I'm sure we can make it go away. Between the two of us, we're pretty resourceful." William leaned back. "And with her knockout looks, no matter what she tries to accuse you of, we can always turn it back on her. I'll have her looking like a gold digger before the night is over good. And you *know* how people, especially women, hate a good-looking woman like her trying to get something out of a man. All we have to do is use that stacked body of hers and her beautiful face against her."

Lawrence shook his head. "She tells me she's a Christian now."

"Aren't they all?" William snickered. "Then the horns and the fork show up, and bam! You're done. The devil made me do it."

Lawrence sat back down. "She claims there's a child."

William sat back against his chair seemingly unfazed. "A baby, huh? You and her?" He laughed. "And she really believes she can make something like that work? I thought we had a real problem. What's for lunch?"

"Not a baby, a child—an eight-, almost nine-year-old child."

"Almost nine, huh?" Lawrence laughed again. "You're talking about that woman that just left here? Gabrielle *Mercedes* Booker? Oh, I know what the Mercedes stands for—homegirl is trying to get *paid*!"

Lawrence nodded, but not because he agreed with everything William had just said.

William continued. "We're talking about the woman who

says she was once friends with your daughter Paris?" William grunted. "The one that looks like she's barely twenty-five?"

"Well, she's twenty-seven, same age as Paris."

"And she really thought she could just come up in here and threaten you with something like a child? A child she's claiming is almost nine?" William shook his head as he chuckled. "Well, sir, I suppose I've heard just about everything now."

"William, I'm telling you: She's going to be a problem."

"Not with *that* lie she's not. We'll bust her before she can get started good with something like that," William said. "Although I will admit that it does have some possible political fallout woven in there. Her putting something like that out in the public is damaging, even if it's *not* true. She would have done better though to have a younger baby she was trying to blame on you. But it's not like I've not had something like this to have to squash before. You remember that woman, about three years ago, who claimed you were the father of her child and threatened to go public if you didn't pay her to keep quiet?"

"I remember her."

"You remember that she was lying through her teeth. But she thought you would pay her hush money just to not have a scandal on your hands to deal with. When I finished digging up stuff on her and presenting her with those facts, she was giving money to *you* and your campaign to keep *her* business under wraps." William nodded. "I'll just put my folks on this little lady, and we'll shut down this noise right now. Gabrielle Mercedes Booker picked the wrong money tree to try and shake."

Lawrence leaned in. Placing a hand over his fist held up by his elbows, he set his chin on it. "William, this situation is a tad bit more complicated than the past situations have been. And this woman has let me know that she's willing to fight if she has to."

"So she's willing to fight. I'm trembling in my boots. Well, tell her to bring it! Apparently, she's never come against anyone like me and you. Let the games begin!"

"She says this eight-year-old child is in need of a bone marrow transplant. She's merely trying to find a matching donor for the child. That's it."

"Well," William said. "There are ways to go about accomplishing something like that without trying to blackmail a government official for help. I hope you let her know you weren't falling for this type of extortion, no matter *how* noble the cause."

Lawrence sat back against the chair and stared up at the ceiling.

William leaned in. "Hold up." He held his hand up in the air. "Is there some *remote* possibility this child really could be yours?"

Lawrence swiveled his chair away from his desk slightly. "It's possible. I don't believe it's true though. But I'm not going to sit here and tell you there's no possible way." He turned back and faced his friend.

William cocked his head to the side. "*You* were with *her*? Some nine years ago? You slept with a girl who is young enough to be your daughter? A girl who was your daughter's friend? What was she . . . eighteen years old at the time? And you *slept* with her?"

"Can you keep it down," Lawrence said, glancing at the closed door.

"Mattie's not out there trying to listen in on you. Mattie worships the ground you walk on. She thinks you can do no wrong."

"But still, I don't want any of this to get out," Lawrence said.

"Okay, so do you want to tell me everything so I'll know how to proceed in cleaning this mess up?"

"Do I *want* to tell you everything?" Lawrence chuckled a little. "Not really. Needless to say, looking back on it, it wasn't one of my finer moments in life."

"Would you rather we go someplace where we can talk more freely? Because I need to know what we're up against if I'm going to make this go away," William said.

"Yeah. I'd feel better talking about this someplace other than here." Lawrence stood up. "So you haven't had lunch yet?"

"No," William said. "You know good and well I wasn't leaving here until I knew that woman was gone and that you hadn't messed up somehow."

"Then let's go get a bite to eat and we can talk on the way."

* * *

Lawrence and William were in the car. Lawrence told William how his daughter had opened up her apartment to this young eighteen-year-old named Gabrielle Booker when she had nowhere else to stay. He'd met her when he was over there checking up on Paris. He'd been immediately struck by her innocence and beauty. The next time he stopped by, Paris wasn't home and Gabrielle was there alone cooking dinner. She'd politely asked if he cared for anything to eat and he'd accepted.

The two of them talked while they ate. He learned about her mother having been killed by her father and her having witnessed the whole thing when she was almost four years old. Her father was still serving time for the murder. Gabrielle had then been sent to her aunt's house where it was apparent she was mistreated. He'd picked up in their conversation that something had happened with her uncle trying to molest her, if he hadn't molested her. But she'd quickly gotten off that topic when she'd veered in that direction.

Lawrence had felt somewhat sorry for the young woman. It was obvious she was talented; and she didn't have a shortage of dreams and goals. He'd started out trying to see what he could do to help her get into a college. He'd known of certain programs available and felt she could get into a college with someone championing her cause.

He ended up sleeping with her the third time he saw her. Sure, he'd felt bad about it after it was over. But there was just something about this young vibrant woman who was not only beautiful outside but inside as well. He'd promised himself he wouldn't allow that line to be crossed again. But being with her that one time was like having been introduced to a drug he thought he was strong enough not to get hooked on, but soon found out just how wrong he was. He couldn't think of anything else *but* her. And he wanted to be around her . . . to be *with* her.

He'd taken precautions after that first time they were together. But she must have gotten pregnant on that first time. She'd told him as soon as she suspected she might be pregnant, some three weeks after the first time. He'd insisted she go to the doctor to be positive. He quickly learned she was indeed going to have a baby.

His first instinct had been to deny the baby was his. After all, here was this young eighteen-year-old beauty that turned heads merely by inhaling and exhaling. Surely, she had to have some young stud she was also being romanced by. She had to. He figured she'd merely pinned the baby on him because he was stable and could provide not only for the baby but her if she needed him to.

But Paris (unaware that he was fishing for information about her roommate) had confirmed that Gabrielle wasn't talking to anyone, at least not anyone Paris was aware of. But then, Paris was into only herself, so she likely wouldn't notice if Gabrielle was talking to anyone or not.

Following that, his strategy had been simple. Be supportive of Gabrielle and give her whatever money she would need to make this go away. He would then help get her into a college so she could go on with her budding new life. What he hadn't counted on was her not wanting to have an abortion. She'd been firm about that in the beginning. But he was a new person in politics. He was a deacon at his church. So he knew how to get people to do things they didn't always want to do while making them think it was their idea.

But Gabrielle was not having it. She wanted the baby and she was planning on keeping it. Lawrence hadn't wanted to do it, but he pointed out the obvious: She didn't have anywhere to live, so how on earth could she take care of a helpless little baby that would be depending solely on her? She'd made the comment that he could help her. That's when he decided it was time to get tough with her.

"I'm not going to be around to help you take care of a baby," he'd said. "I have a wife and a family. I love my wife dearly. I'm not going to do anything to jeopardize my marriage."

"But you already have done something," Gabrielle said with tears in her eyes. "I'm pregnant! And it's your baby."

"Yes, I know you're pregnant. But that was an accident. Neither you *nor* I meant for that to happen." Lawrence could see how much his words had hurt her. But he felt if he stayed strong, she would get it and agree to have the abortion.

"Do you really want to bring a child into this world that's not completely wanted? Do you? Is that fair to the child? And if you can't financially do for that child, isn't it being selfish to do something that cruel to him or her?" Lawrence said. "Sometimes you have to deny yourself and do what's right for another. Don't you think?" he said.

He'd come at her from every angle he knew how. He'd been nice, offering to pay for everything. He'd even given her some extra money. Sure, he'd been mean by telling her he didn't want the baby, going as far as letting her know that he didn't truly believe the baby was really his. And that if she pursued trying to pin this baby on him, he would fight her until it was proven one way or the other. And should she take it all the way to a paternity test, he would let everyone know how she had thrown herself on him. Dropping hints that he may have been intoxicated at the time it happened and he didn't really know what he was doing.

He'd said things to Paris about Gabrielle, trying to set things up just in case he and Gabrielle ended up going the distance with the baby situation. A week into all of this, Paris put Gabrielle out. He never found out what happened between the two of them that caused the blowup; Paris said she didn't want to talk about it. He wondered if she'd found out about him and Gabrielle. He was able to breathe a slight sigh of relief when it became more certain that Paris's putting Gabrielle out had nothing to do with him and their little secret.

He was just glad that, before Gabrielle left Paris's apartment for good, she'd pretty much acquiesced. He'd given her money for the abortion and extra to make up for any work time she would lose. She had to have the abortion, now that she was without a place to live. After Gabrielle left Paris's place, he didn't hear anything more from her following the three calls she made to him that day for help. He *had* hoped she would call after she was settled somewhere else and let him know she was okay.

But until this very day, when she'd shown up at his office and he discovered it was her and not some crazy woman determined to talk with him, as Mattie and William had portrayed her to be, he hadn't known even that she was still alive.

He'd been overjoyed to see her again, even more beautiful than some nine years ago. He wasn't quite sure what he thought as he gazed upon her. Was he hoping to pick up where they'd left off, minus the baby, of course? Was he just glad to know that she was all right after not knowing what had happened to her after she left Paris's apartment and rid herself of the baby she was carrying?

But there she was, sitting in front of him telling him that she hadn't aborted the baby. Instead, she'd given the baby up for adoption. She was saying that their baby was still alive. Gabrielle was telling him that he had a child out there he hadn't even known existed, and that *this* child . . . a little girl named Jasmine, was now dying . . . that she needed a bone marrow transplant. And Gabrielle wasn't asking him to acknowledge the child, only to do what he could to help save her life. That was all.

Lawrence had tried, in the beginning, to have this child's life aborted. The question now: Would he sit back and allow her to die now?

Chapter 7

Thou hast consulted shame to thy house by cutting off many people, and hast sinned against thy soul.

—Habakkuk 2:10

"Okay," William said after Lawrence filled him in on everything. "So what do you want to do?"

Lawrence looked over at William, then played with his hands. "I don't know. Gabrielle says all she wants is for me to be tested to see if I'm a match as a donor."

William nodded. "That's it?"

"Yes."

"She's not trying to get more out of you than that?" William asked. "Maybe a little something for her troubles?"

"I didn't get that at all from her," Lawrence said. "She genuinely seems to care about this child."

"Do you really think the child is yours? That's, of course, if there really *is* a child?"

"I don't know. I don't know if she's telling the truth about there being a child. But honestly, what she said to me registered as being true. Although, for whatever reason, she says she's willing to fight me all the way if she has to, to help save that child's life."

"But you said she gave the baby up for adoption," William said as he pulled into the lane for valet parking.

"That's what she told me."

"If that's the case, then why is she the one coming to you for help? I mean, unless it was some weird kind of an adoption, she shouldn't even be in the picture." William opened the door and handed the valet the key to his car. Lawrence got out and closed his door. They walked to the restaurant door and stepped in.

"Your usual spot?" the hostess asked.

Lawrence smiled. "Please." The two men followed her to his booth where they usually sat off the beaten path. "Thank you," Lawrence said to her. She nodded to him with a smile.

"She likes you," William whispered as he glanced at the redhead who had just seated them as he slid into the booth seat across from Lawrence. "She's never that nice to me when I come in by myself."

"Maybe she just knows how to take care of politicians and the clientele that takes care of them."

"Maybe," William said. "Okay, now back to that problem at hand. Now that I know what I'm dealing with, I'll get my folks on it, checking into things with Miss Booker, and see what all we can turn up."

"How long will it take?" Lawrence asked. "She's not giving me a lot of time. She says the child is dying and we don't have much time to lose."

"You know my people move fast." William pulled out his cell phone and began texting. He laid the phone down on the table. "Already working on it," he said with a smile. "Already working on it. All right, Miss Gabrielle Mercedes Booker, let's see what you got."

"Are you ready to order, or do you need a few more minutes?" the waitress asked.

"Oh, I'm ready!" William said, rubbing his hands together and looking over at Lawrence, who also nodded he was ready as well. They ordered and the waitress left.

"What am I going to do?" Lawrence said. "What if this goes public?"

"Just chill out. Let the master do his work. My folks are on this. We'll find out all about this woman as well as her claims. If there's no truth to what she's saying, we'll bust her and shut her down before you can say, 'Next stop is the U.S. House of Representatives.' "

"And if there is some truth?"

"Well, in my years of doing this, I've yet to find a person who didn't have their own Achilles' heel. All I know is that I'm going to do whatever it takes to ensure she doesn't mess up all of our hard work on this campaign."

"As well as my marriage . . . and my family," Lawrence said.

"Yeah. Don't worry; we'll do what we need to do to protect your career, your marriage, *and* your family."

Lawrence nodded. "Yeah. Deidra's not going to buy too many more times that these women are just lying on me. She's not a fool now, not by any means."

"Deidra loves you. She knows the game out there. She knows how women are. You don't have to worry about her, that's even if she ever hears about this. Which, if I'm as good as I think I am, she won't."

Lawrence nodded and took a few swallows of water. He set the glass back on the table. "You're a really good friend. You and I have been through a lot."

"Yes, we have," William said. "And we're not through with going through yet, so don't go getting all sentimental on me."

William's phone made a ringtone sound. He picked it up and looked at it. The waitress came with their food and began placing their plates on the table.

"Looky, looky," William said with a grin as he read what was on the screen of his phone. "Now *that* didn't take long at all!"

"Do you need anything else?" The waitress looked from one to the other.

"I'm good," Lawrence said.

"Steak sauce, please. Heinz Fifty-seven." William held his phone in his hand as he spoke. "I like mine a little sweet and saucy, not too vinegary, although I can handle a *little* bite."

The waitress turned her nose up slightly at William. He released a small giggle.

Lawrence wasn't sure if William was laughing at what he'd just said to the waitress or what he was reading on his phone's screen.

The waitress left.

"Good news?" Lawrence asked.

"Here you are," the waitress said, setting the bottle down in between the both of them. "Anything else?"

"No, I think I have *everything* I need right about now," William said, still gazing at the screen.

"Thank you," Lawrence said to the waitress, who left after a quick nod and a smile at him. Lawrence bowed his head and said a quick prayer of grace over his food. He looked at William, who was still grinning. "So, are you going to share or what?"

William set the phone back down on the table and smiled as he bowed his head all of two seconds, then began cutting into his T-bone steak. He put a piece of steak in his mouth. "Gabrielle Mercedes Booker, who now legally goes by the name of Gabrielle Mercedes, works at that church with that pastor named George Landris. You remember Pastor George Landris, don't you? He's the one I told you blew me off in that little deal I was trying to broker with him and his church earlier this year. You know Mr. High and Mighty who apparently thought he was too good to get down in the ditch with us—"

"Okay, so she works at a church with a pastor you still *obviously* have beef with."

"*We* have beef with," William said. "We. Whatever I do in the name of you and your office is for us as an organization."

"Yeah. And *us* as an organization are now in a mess with that other preacher, who has, among other things, IRS problems and is on schedule to be prosecuted, potentially implicating us in some of his *mess* along the way."

"I told you not to worry about that," William said. "I'm good at what I do. And I know how to cover my tracks. Rev. Marshall Walker may go down, but you don't have to worry about us going down with him."

"Is that why you were so happy reading the information that just came in? You think Gabrielle can help with this other situation you've been working on?"

"Oh, no." He put another piece of steak in his mouth and chewed, then took a swallow of his water with lemon. "Gabrielle Mercedes Booker aka Gabrielle Mercedes has just given us something I believe we can deal with her on."

"And that is?"

"And that is that Gabrielle Mercedes Booker aka Gabrielle Mercedes, reportedly, at least from my sources, was once an *exotic* dancer . . . or in plainer terms, a stripper who went by the name of *Goodness and Mercy.*" William smiled.

"Goodness and Mercy?" Lawrence said.

"Yes. Goodness and Mercy. The woman who showed up at your office trying to push you into some kind of a corner has her own past she might not want exposed to the whole world. Especially not on the level you and I can take it. And believe me: I will *decimate* her. I'll totally and unsympathetically *decimate* her. And anyone else who may remotely be important in her life as well, if I have to." William shook some steak sauce on his steak and placed another piece in his mouth. "This is so good! Just the way I like it: well done, a little sweet and saucy, with a slight bite."

Lawrence wasn't sure if William was referring to his steak with the steak sauce or the information he now had on Gabrielle.

Chapter 8

Woe unto him that giveth his neighbor drink, that puttest thy bottle to him, and makest him drunken also, that thou mayest look on their nakedness!

—Habakkuk 2:15

Gabrielle went home, lay across her bed, and cried. She couldn't believe how badly things had transpired. When she'd gone to Lawrence's office, she wasn't quite sure what she would say or how she would bring up what she'd ultimately gone to his office to do.

From the beginning, she never intended for any of this to have happened. Not her getting pregnant, and especially not being with a married man, let alone a married man old enough to be her father.

Lawrence Simmons had been so different the first time she met him. He was so caring and he listened to her. He was Paris's father—a man that loved, provided for, and protected his little girl. Something she couldn't help but admire and wish she had in her life; something she honestly had never had. Paris had been nice enough to let her move in with her when she discovered from another friend that Gabrielle had nowhere to stay after her aunt and uncle put her out for no good reason. She and Paris had never even been friends, remotely or otherwise. So she was surprised when Paris approached her about coming to stay at her place until she could get on her feet.

As it turned out, Paris was a bit of a slob when it came to housekeeping. Gabrielle didn't mind cleaning up after her and all her friends that came over. In fact, it felt like being at home for Gabrielle, since she'd always been the one to clean up after everyone at her aunt Cee-Cee's house. Paris never included her in the things she did, whether at the apartment or outside of it, which was also fine with Gabrielle, since she didn't care for all of it anyway. And when Paris was gone (which happened a lot), she had the apartment all to herself. She could twirl around the room and dance at will like no one was watching, which, of course, no one was.

Paris's father showed up one day when Paris wasn't there. He knew who she was; he'd met her earlier and checked her out. She'd just finished cooking and offered him something to eat. The two of them had a great time laughing and talking. He then asked her what she wanted to do.

"Excuse me?" Gabrielle had said.

"With your life," Lawrence said. "What would you like to do? Do you want to go to college? Are you looking for a full-time job? And if so, doing what?"

At first she thought he was telling her she couldn't stay there, essentially living off him and his daughter. She worked a temp job. The pay wasn't much and work was inconsistent, but so far it had been enough to cover her share of the expenses.

Lawrence refined his question. "What would you do if you didn't have to worry about whether you were paid or not?"

That was easy. "Dance," she said with a huge smile. "I would dance."

He tried to get her to dance for him, but she wouldn't. A few days later he just "happened" to stop by again, and again, Paris wasn't there. This time, he brought Chinese food and two bottles of Moscato d'Asti. She'd never had wine before (she wasn't of legal age to drink). But the glass he poured for her didn't taste anything like she thought it would. It was sweet and fruity, so she drank more than she probably should have. But then again, he'd kept refilling her glass.

"Dance for me," he'd said again. "Let me see you dance. Come on. Do what you love."

So she danced. And she was like the wind. Dancing was her place of refuge. It was where she could always go and be completely free.

That night was the first time she'd ever been with a man. And he had been so wonderful after it was over. So when he showed up the next time (again when Paris wasn't there), she was already falling for him. And again, they slept together. Three times they were together, and apparently one of those times produced a baby.

She thought when she told him that she was pregnant he would step up and do the right thing. That's when she saw a totally different man. A man that was not all that loving *or* caring. He was mean and he said some horrible things to her. He indicated that he thought she was someone who did nothing but sleep around with whatever man that came along.

But she wasn't like that. She hadn't cared about men and dating at the time. Well, maybe there had been this one guy at school she'd liked, but that never really went anywhere. She'd cared only about dancing and trying to figure out how she could do what she loved for the rest of her life. She missed Miss Crowe so much, even more right then. Gabrielle had no one she could talk to, no one to confide in, no one who could guide her in the right direction. She was all alone.

She definitely couldn't talk to Paris about this. Gabrielle thought she'd have time to sort everything out. But Paris changed on her and told her she had to leave. She didn't even know what she'd done to make Paris become so upset with her all of a sudden. Gabrielle was pretty sure that Paris's father hadn't told her about the two of them. Lawrence had all but let her know that he didn't want the baby she was carrying, even if it was his, which he maintained that it wasn't. He'd given her money to "take care of it" and some extra to, what she now believed, make her completely go away. Immediately after Paris told her to get out, she tried to call him a few times, hoping he might drive her someplace. But he wouldn't take and didn't return her call.

It was never her intent for Lawrence to know she hadn't aborted the baby as he'd instructed . . . had given her money to do. Instead, someone she barely knew saw her, picked her up off the streets, invited her to stay at his home, giving her time to think. Shortly, she found her way to a place for soon-to-be mothers in predicaments.

And had everything gone as planned, she would have given the baby up for adoption (which she had) and the baby would have grown up in a good and loving home with good and loving parents and had a great life. From all she could tell from these past months of talking to Jessica Noble (the woman who adopted her baby girl) over the phone, the little girl was indeed loved. But the adoption should have been the end of it. Unless and until, of course, the child had wanted to find her biological mother and sought her out. Which in that case, her baby girl would be eighteen and an adult.

But things weren't going as planned, not at all. The eight-year-old was in life-threatening danger and time had almost run out. Her doctors weren't optimistic that she would even make it to see her ninth birthday on March thirtieth unless a matching donor was found and soon.

A bone marrow transplant seemed easy enough, at least from the donor's standpoint. You found someone to match. Marrow was taken from the donor using a special needle under general anesthesia (the hip bones were said to be rich in marrow stem cells) and the donor was on his or her way. The one who went through the most was the one receiving the transplant. So much advance preparation and all of the things that had to be done afterward. But if the receiving body didn't reject the transplanted cells taken from the spongy tissue found inside of the bone, in a matter of four to six months, the patient was completely healed. That sounded simple enough.

But Gabrielle had quickly learned that black folks weren't so hot on being donors, even when they don't have to be dead to do it. She'd been tested, but found not to be a good match. That's why she'd gone to find Lawrence. He was Jasmine's biological father, and maybe he would be a good match. And if not him, she'd been told that siblings had an even greater potential of being the best match of all. Lawrence had three children (that she knew of). She didn't *really* want to involve his children, but if that was the only option left besides merely allowing the child to die without them doing everything they could to save her, she was willing to go there.

Gabrielle picked up the phone to call Zachary. She was so

upset with herself at how things had gone today. She sat there with the dead cordless receiver in her hand as she reflected on how all of this had honestly begun in the first place.

She was living with her aunt and uncle because her father had killed her mother and she had nowhere else to go. She hadn't had a say-so about where she would live at the age of close to four. Her uncle had come on to her several times after she turned seventeen, even as much as coming into her room when everyone else was in bed asleep, attempting to kiss her and touch her in his own sly way. After he came on more forcibly, she'd told her aunt Cee-Cee. Nothing was done. When it happened again, she told her again. The next thing she knew, her aunt was telling her that as soon as she graduated from high school and turned eighteen (which would be in a few months) that she would have to find someplace else to live because she couldn't stay there. Her aunt acted like what happened to her had been her fault, her doing, instead of her scumbag husband's.

And as though things couldn't have been worse already, during that same time, Miss Esther Crowe (the only person in the world who had ever shown her love, kindness, and compassion, and would most certainly have opened her door to her if she had needed a place of refuge) had gone to see about her relatives up north. Miss Crowe was in an accident and she never returned to Alabama. There was no one to tell Gabrielle what had happened with her. And for the longest, she was certain Miss Crowe was dead.

She met Zachary Wayne Morgan, who turned out to be Dr. Zachary Wayne Morgan or Dr. Z, as many of his patients called him, who turned out to be the nephew of Miss Esther Crowe, who ended up taking her to see the woman who had made such a gigantic difference in her life. Gabrielle began to cry.

The phone started to ring, even as she held it, causing her to jump. Looking down at the caller ID, she started smiling.

"Hi there," she said, quickly stifling her sniffles so he couldn't hear them.

"What'cha doing?"

"Thinking."

"Thinking? About what?"

Gabrielle smiled. "You, for one."

"Good things, I hope," Zachary said.

She let out a sigh loud enough she was sure he heard it. "Some." She sniffled.

"Hey? Why do you sound like you're crying?" Zachary asked with concern.

"I'm okay."

"Gabrielle, what's wrong?" His voice escalated slightly.

"I finally got to see somebody today I've been trying to catch up with, and I didn't act at all in the way that I should have. I didn't act like a Christian, that's for sure. I don't know what happened with me."

"Who did you see?" Zachary asked.

Gabrielle hesitated for a moment. She hadn't told Zachary everything just yet. Sure, he knew about the baby she'd given up for adoption. He knew she'd been tested to see if she was possibly a match for the bone marrow transplant. He also knew she hadn't been a good match and how extremely disappointed, but not deterred, she'd been about the news. He'd asked her about the father of the baby. But she could tell he'd been averse to even go there with her.

Here they were, having agreed to make a go of it as a couple. Leslie Morgan, Zachary's mother, was not fond of the idea, and that was putting it mildly. Leslie had made that *more* than clear. But she'd also told Gabrielle it was nothing against her personally. She'd said she really liked Gabrielle as a person. Leslie just felt that Gabrielle had too much other baggage she didn't want ending up in her doctor son's closet.

But Zachary had been able to convince Gabrielle that it was their lives to live and their decision to make and not his mother's or anyone else's for that matter. Gabrielle understood that Zachary's mother was merely looking out for him and his career as an up-and-coming doctor. How could Gabrielle ever be upset with a mother who loved her child so much that she would put herself out there to protect that child no matter who else it might hurt? Leslie knew she would likely draw her son's wrath when she said something, even if all she was doing was trying to protect him from her.

When Zachary had asked Gabrielle about the baby's father, she didn't tell him much. Only that she was going to see if she could locate him and speak to him. She wasn't exactly sure what all he'd taken from that. Still, Zachary had been considerate enough not to push her for any more details than she was willing to give.

But the truth was that she didn't have to *find* the baby's father. She knew exactly who Jasmine's biological father was and pretty much where she could find him. However, getting to him would be another matter entirely. Maybe that's why she had come off the way she had today with Lawrence. His staff had given her such a runaround. For a man whose job it was supposed to be to represent the people, he wasn't so easily, or readily, accessible to their voices.

Her intent had never been and was not now to hurt him. That's why she'd insisted on speaking to him and only him. Her plan was simple: tell Lawrence what was going on, and he, being sympathetic to Jasmine's plight, would voluntarily, unprompted, agree to be tested to see whether or not he was a match. Prayerfully, he would somehow be the donor Jasmine needed without anyone ever having to know any of the details. And if he turned out like her, and wasn't a match, that he would somehow involve his children to see if one of them might be. If one was, they would donate the marrow, and that would be that. Everyone could go back to their respective lives, without anyone's life being *completely* disrupted. And Jasmine would *have* a life to live.

Jessica Noble would continue being Jasmine's mother and the only family Jasmine would know, just as things were right now. Lawrence would be the politician on his journey toward reelection. And she would be . . .

What would she be after all of this?

"Gabrielle?" Zachary's voice broke through her wandering thoughts. "Are you there? Are you okay?"

She was really crying now and hadn't even realized it. And before she could stop herself, she let out a loud wail.

"Okay, I'm coming over!" Zachary said. "I have a few more patients to—"

"No, I'm all right." She took in a deep breath and tried with all that she had to pull herself together. "Zachary, I'm okay." She said it as convincingly as she could. She forced a smile hoping it would alter her voice's tone. "Really. I'm all right. See?"

"Are you sure? Are you sure you're all right?"

She nodded as though he could actually see her. She continued the fake smile; it was working. "Yes. I'm okay. I'm fine. Just a momentary breakdown, but I'm fine now."

"Well, you're not fine, because if you were fine, you wouldn't have broken down like you just did. I can come over as soon as—"

"No, you stay there and take care of your patients. I'll be okay. It's just hormones," she said. "You know how emotional hormones can make folks. And then everything else I'm thinking about. You know how it is."

"Well, if you're sure you're okay."

"I am." She shook herself. Her voice was steady and strong, reassuring. "I'm fine."

"Okay. But when I leave here, I'm coming over to see you."

She nodded. "That will be fine. I'll see you then."

She hung up and began to sob loudly. "God, please help me. I don't know what to do. I know I didn't handle myself with Lawrence the way You would have desired for me to. I lost my temper. I know that Your Word says to be angry but to sin not. Well, I missed it. I even went so far as to threaten him. But it's because I just don't know what to do. Please guide me in the correct way. I know this is not my battle alone, that You've already got this. And, God, I know I have to tell Zachary everything. But what's he going to think when he hears the rest of it? So far, he's been wonderful. But it's starting to look like as soon as I've disclosed one secret part of my life to him, another secret part pops up. Maybe his mother is right about me. Maybe I'm not the right person for him. Maybe the things in my life are too toxic and will be the very thing to ruin his. Please, God, I'm lost down here. I just need You to tell me what to do. What should I do? Please tell me. What? What do I do?"

Chapter 9

Yea also, because he transgresseth by wine, he is a proud man, neither keepeth at home, who enlargeth his desire as hell, and is as death, and cannot be satisfied, but gathereth unto him all nations, and heapeth unto him all people.

—Habakkuk 2:5

Lawrence went home after his lunch with William.

"Hi, honey," Deidra Simmons said with a puzzled look on her face as soon as he cleared the doorway. "What are you doing home so early?"

Lawrence smiled, then kissed his wife on her cheek. "Can't a man come home early to be with his beautiful wife?"

She tilted her head, almost looking at him sideways. "Yes, a man can, but you hardly ever do."

He grinned a bit. "I can see I've really fallen off my duties. It's obvious that I have a lot of work to do. When my wife starts to give me the third degree about coming home early, I must be *really* bad off."

"No, now, don't go get it twisted. It's not that you can't come home like this. It's just . . . it's been a long time since you've been home so early in the day. That's all I'm saying. In fact, it's generally pretty late in the evening." Deidra ran one hand down the left side of her smooth, slicked-down, just-tinted, auburn brown hair.

"I see you got your hair done today," Lawrence said.

Deidra pulled back slightly, then grinned. "You noticed?"

"Of course, I noticed." He laughed. "Wow, I'm not believing you today. So what's going on with you?"

"Nothing. I was thinking about asking you the same thing. It's just . . ."

"Just what?" He came over to her and grabbed her around her waist, rocking her from side to side.

She smiled. "It's just you never ever notice when I get my hair done."

Lawrence smiled. "Oh, I notice. I just don't always say anything. But it looks nice, *really* nice." He took a hand and smoothed down the side she had been playing with a minute ago. "I mean . . . *really* nice."

She was grinning now. "So, you still haven't told me."

His kissed her softly on her lips. "Told you what?"

She sucked in her bottom lip as though she was tasting it before she spoke. "Told me what brings you home at this time of the day."

He grinned big. "Oh, I'm looking at the reason right now," he said. "I was thinking about you and just how much you actually put up with *because* of me and who I am in this state. And the next thing I knew, I just had to come home and wrap my arms around you. So sue me."

Deidra blushed, her light skin showing patches of glowing red. "Is that right?"

"That's right, Mrs. Deidra Jean Long Simmons."

"You don't have to say my whole name."

He raised his eyebrows several times in a playfully flirty way as he smiled. "I know. I just love having your name on my lips. Deidra Jean Simmons, my wife. My beautiful, loving wife Deidra Jean . . . my Dee."

Deidra pulled away. "Okay, did something happen today? Are we in financial trouble and you're trying to figure out how to tell us that things are about to get rough around here?"

He grabbed her and pulled her back into his arms. "Nothing happened except it hit me just how much I love you and how little I've shown you of late."

"Okay," she said with a touch of skepticism. "But, Lawrence, *you* know that I know *you*. And usually when you start acting like this, it's because of some function you want me to go to with a lot of stupid stuff that tends to come along with it. And I'm telling you right now: I'm not about to squeeze into some dress you've decided I have to wear that's way too small for me just because you want to impress some big donor with deep pockets—"

Lawrence broke away and turned from Deidra. It had been the word "donor" that had affected him. When he'd said and heard the word "donor" before now, it had always been in the context of money. His world revolved around obtaining donors. But today, his past had walked boldly back in the door. And his past had brought with her the word "donor" on her lips, only for a completely different cause.

"Honey," Deidra said with a frown on her face. "What's the matter?"

He snapped out of his daze and forced a smile. "Nothing's the matter."

"Well, you were starting to look sick there for a minute. Are you having problems finding donors?"

He kissed her on her lips again. "Nothing for you to concern yourself with. Whatever problem I have with donors is my problem and mine alone."

Deidra laughed. "Your problems are never yours and yours alone."

"I know: You and I are in this together—"

"Oh, I wasn't talking about me this time. I was referring to William. You and William are practically joined at the hip. Lately, I've thought about finding a doctor who can surgically separate you two. William knows more about what's going on with you than I do."

"That's not true," Lawrence said.

"Yes . . . it *is* true. But you know what: We've had this discussion too many times, and I already know that nothing I say or do will make any difference. So I'm resigning myself to keeping my nose out of that side of things and stick with our home and our children."

"That's the only job that really matters to me anyway," Lawrence said. "So, where would you like to go tonight?"

"Say what? Go tonight?"

"Yes, where would you like to go?"

"You mean as in me and you? Alone? Together?"

He laughed. "Yes, me and you . . . alone . . . together. You know: like a date."

Deidra laughed as well. "Oh, it's been so long since you and I have done anything that wasn't for show, I don't even know if I even remember how to act with just me and you alone and nobody gawking at or scrutinizing us."

"Again, I can see that I have much work to do here at home. So you decide where you want to go. And wherever and whatever it is, it's you and me tonight."

"Okay." Deidra smiled, but with a hesitancy. "Lawrence, are you *sure* everything is all right? Are you sure? You're not keeping anything from me that I need to know, are you? This isn't the calm before the storm is it? Because if it is, I'd rather know now so I can be prepared. I don't want you wining and dining me tonight, and tomorrow the levee breaks and washes me out. You know this would not be the first time . . ."

"I know. And I told you that I was sorry about that time after it happened. I hated you had to go through all of that, but you also know that I have a huge target on my back, more so now that folks think I'm a sellout, a traitor to my race, just because I decided to become a Republican. It's open season on me; there are folks out there who want to take me down. Folks will be fabricating all kinds of lies. And you of all people know how hard it is to disprove a negative . . . something that's not true."

Lawrence took Deidra's hand. "Deidra, I've told you: You're the only woman for me. Those other women who come after me or claim that I was with them or that I did something inappropriate: They're lying and they're jealous, plain and simple. They want what you have, and they'll go to whatever lengths they have to in trying to take what you have away from you. Well, we're stronger than anything out there that might try and come against us. What's the scripture that we stand on as a family?"

" 'No weapon that is formed against thee shall prosper,' " Deidra said. "I hear what you're saying, Lawrence. But it doesn't help watching you flirt with all of those women like you do."

"Those women don't have anything I want other than their

votes, spreading the word to others about my political platform, and possibly their money. That's it! What they give to my campaign becomes ours. Yes, I may want their money; I'm not going to lie. But you, my dearest, have my heart. You always have and you always will own my heart. And no lying female is going to come between us; I don't care *how* compelling her story might be. I don't care what kind of proof she claims she is able to produce. I don't care how much she may bark that I wined and dined her, then misled her into thinking there was more to us. I just need for you to stick by me no matter what folks may say or put out there. No matter what lies you hear, you have to promise me that you'll always hear me out before you believe what you hear. Okay?"

Deidra nodded.

"I keep telling you, Dee. We're going somewhere. You know we're doing a great work in the community and for our state. My next move is going to be a run for our nation's Congress where I can really have an impact. But you know what they say: To whom much is given, much is required. People think that only means that once you get, you have a greater responsibility to give back and do. But you and I know that before some things are given, much is required. I've been in politics for almost twelve years now. You and I both know how things work around here. Folks will build you up just to take you down. The media will sensationalize anything just to have something to fill up their twenty-four-seven so-called news channels that have become mostly entertainment chatter. We know the deal. I'm just saying that things are likely going to intensify even more so now. I'll dare not tell you that a storm isn't in the forecast. I'm just telling you that *should* it hit where we live, we're going to ride the storm out together—you and I." He grinned and began to sing the chorus of Rick James's song "You and I."

Deidra nodded again, but this time with a huge grin. "I love you, Lawrence."

He smiled back. "And I love you, Mrs. Lawrence."

Chapter 10

O Lord, how long shall I cry, and thou wilt not hear! Even cry out unto thee of violence, and thou wilt not save!

—Habakkuk 1:2

Gabrielle's phone rang. She was still lying across the bed crying. At first, she considered not answering it, but decided she should at least see who was calling. It just might be Lawrence calling to tell her he was ready to do the right thing. She looked through blurry eyes at the caller ID and hurriedly pressed the TALK button.

"Hi," she said as opposed to her normal "hello." She knew who this was and precisely what was being called to discuss.

"Did you find him?" Jessica Noble asked, getting straight to the point. "Did you get a chance to talk to him yet?"

Gabrielle didn't quite know how to answer that question. She also knew that neither of them had time to play games. "Yes, I found him. And, yes, I was able to talk to him." She paused, trying to think of what to say next.

"And—"

Gabrielle had kept Jessica informed as much as she could about what she was doing from her end to help Jasmine, Jessica's daughter (in truth, Gabrielle's biological child). Jessica and the hospital team were all searching diligently in conjunction with the donor bank for a possible match. Gabrielle and Jessica both knew that their best efforts would be in locating Jasmine's biological family to see if any of them might possibly be a good match. At this late stage, they'd given up on a perfect match; a mere good match would give Jasmine a fighting chance. They'd already determined that Gabrielle's HLA markers (the six markers used to determine how viable a match a person was) were not enough to count as even a *good* match.

After that, Gabrielle had resolved to get in touch with Jasmine's biological father. Besides Gabrielle, no one else in the world knew the identity of the father. When she told both Jessica and Zachary that she was trying to get in touch with him, they most likely assumed she'd have to locate him first, that's if she even knew who the father was. Neither of them had said it aloud, but she felt they were thinking it, especially since it seemed to be taking her so long.

But she knew who the father was and where to find him. She'd called to talk with him as soon as she'd learned she wasn't a match. Still, she couldn't very well tell Jessica it was taking her so long because she wasn't having much success getting in to see an Alabama House Representative, having been put off by his local office here in Birmingham. Oh, yes. And by the way: He's the biological father of your daughter.

"Gabrielle? Are you still there?" Jessica said.

"I'm here." Gabrielle looked toward the ceiling, then back down. "And he's thinking about it."

Jessica's voice practically exploded. "He's *thinking* about it?"

"Calm down," Gabrielle said softly. "Yes. He's thinking about it."

"My little girl is dying and he's *thinking* about it? Nobody is asking him to pay child support or anything. He doesn't ever have to let it be known that he fathered her. Did you tell him this? That he can be tested and a donor anonymously."

"Yes, I told him. But he's just now hearing about all of this. This news is slightly blindsiding him."

"Well, Jasmine doesn't have time for him to process his thoughts or feelings about whatever may have taken place in the past. He needs to go and get tested at least to see if he's possibly a match." Gabrielle could hear Jessica crying now.

"I know," Gabrielle said. "Please don't get upset. I believe God is going to work all this out."

Jessica released a short laugh. "There was a time when I used to believe that. In the beginning, I did. But how much more am

I supposed to take? Tell me: How much more does God want from me? He took my husband and now He's about to take—"

"No," Gabrielle said. "Don't speak those words. Don't even allow those words to come out of your mouth. Jessica, Jesus came that we might have life and life more abundantly. Then there's Satan, who comes to steal, kill, and to destroy."

"So what are you saying? That Satan was the one who took my husband? And that it's Satan trying to take my little girl now?"

"If you want to go there, then, yes, that's what I'm saying." Gabrielle was still learning about God and His Word as well as things in the Bible.

Pastor Landris had just taught on this subject. And one of the things he'd said was that in Job 1:21 when Job said, "Naked came I out of my mother's womb, and naked shall I return thither: the Lord gave, and the Lord hath taken away; blessed be the name of the Lord," that Job was incorrect in his assessment. Pastor Landris explained that the account as listed in the book of Job is correct. But Job's statement concerning the Lord giving and the Lord taking away was not the correct conclusion. In truth, Satan had been *allowed* to come at Job. God removed the hedge of protection that kept Satan out. But Satan had been the one to take away from Job.

"Okay, whatever," Jessica said in a clearly dismissive tone. "Right now, I really don't have time to talk about God. I just need to do whatever I can to help my little girl."

"With all due respect, God is the one who can help her," Gabrielle said. She didn't want to get into an argument with Jessica. Not at this time, not at this point. She didn't want to upset her, knowing that right now her mind had to be all over the place. Jessica wasn't thinking or talking clearly. "Jessica, we need to be speaking what we desire and to keep believing and trusting God."

"Whatever it takes to save Jasmine's life, I'm willing to do that. I'd give my own life if God would just spare hers. I promise I would."

"I understand," Gabrielle said. "But trust that right now God is working on Jasmine's behalf and He's already worked it out. I don't know how it will be done, but I believe God *will* do it. I do."

"So does that mean you believe Jasmine's biological father is going to go get tested?" Jessica asked. "Does that mean that if he's not a match, he'll have his children tested, if he has any, to see if any of them might be a match?"

"I can't answer those questions at this point. I'm just praying that God will move in the way we need Him to move. That God will touch hearts—"

"And if God doesn't?"

Gabrielle was crying but trying not to let Jessica know that she was. "Let's just keep our thoughts on what we desire, okay? Are you familiar with the scripture that talks about whatsoever things are true, pure, lovely, and of good report, that if there be any virtue, and if there be any praise, to think on these things? Well, let's just think on these things for now. Let's think on the good we desire. Jessica, I believe God is going to bring Jasmine through this. I honestly and truly do. I have faith."

"I hope God does," Jessica said. "I'm just so beat up at this point. I don't know anymore. My husband died. Jasmine is deathly ill. I have my own health issues. And what should be a simple thing, just like it was after you learned Jasmine needed your help, is turning into just more waiting, more anxious moments, and more having to pray." Jessica was crying now, too. Gabrielle could hear her sniffles as she spoke. "I just feel so alone. It's like I'm all by myself. It's just so hard!"

"Well, you're not alone. God is with you."

"Yeah, but God created us to have people down here to help us through things. And right now, I don't have anybody. That's a fact. I have no family left. And right now, at this moment, the only person Jasmine has left in this world is me."

Gabrielle considered what Jessica said. "Well, you have me. And if you ever need someone to talk to, a shoulder to cry on, someone to lean on, someone who's pulling for both you *and* Jasmine, then I'm here. I don't mind . . . if you need someone."

"Seriously?"

"Yeah."

"So if I were to ask you to come here to the hospital and sit with me, would you? Knowing that, should things go the way we desire them to, that after this is all over, we all will go back to our respective lives? Knowing that Jasmine is the child you gave up for adoption . . . the child who likely won't even know she was adopted at least for a few more years down the road? You're saying you would be there for me now, knowing all of this will most likely come afterward?"

"Jasmine doesn't know she's even adopted?" Gabrielle hadn't ever thought about this. She didn't know what she thought now because she hadn't been forced to ever think about the child she'd given up all those years ago.

"No, she doesn't. My late husband and I had many discussions on when might be the appropriate age and time to tell her. We decided to wait until she was old enough to understand everything and to appreciate how much we truly love her, in spite of her being adopted, and truthfully, how incredibly *much* her birth mother loved her to make the sacrifices as she'd done."

Gabrielle's tears were flowing really fast down her face now. But she was determined to hold her voice steady. "And here we are."

"Yes, here we are. Praying and doing all that we can to be sure she lives to see her ninth birthday. It's just not fair." Jessica stopped speaking, then released an audible sigh. "Listen, I'm going to get off this phone. But if you should hear anything . . . anything at all, will you please—"

"I'll call you the moment I know something from my end. I promise."

Gabrielle hung up after saying good-bye. She picked up her Bible off the nightstand and began to turn the pages. She couldn't remember where that scripture was. "God, please bring it back to my remembrance. Help me find that scripture."

She fanned the pages, stopped, then scanned down the page. *Nope, not it.* She allowed the pages to fan past again. When it stopped, she again scanned the page. *Nope.* Again, she let the pages fall from her thumb, then she stopped and scanned. There it was; the scripture she had just referenced to Jessica. Philippians 4:8. She began to read. "Finally, brethren, whatsoever things are true, whatsoever things are honest, whatsoever things are just, whatsoever things are pure, whatsoever things are lovely, whatsoever things are of good report; if there be any virtue, and if there be any praise, think on these things."

Gabrielle looked upward and closed her eyes as she thought, *Whatsoever things are of good report. I believe God. I believe.*

Chapter 11

Their horses also are swifter than the leopards, and are more fierce than the evening wolves: and their horsemen shall spread themselves, and their horsemen shall come from far; they shall fly as the eagle that hasteth to eat.

—Habakkuk 1:8

Deidra brought the telephone over to Lawrence. "It's William." She handed the phone to her husband. "Should I hold off on finishing getting dressed for this evening?"

Lawrence smiled. "No. I told you that we're going out, and *nothing* and *no*body is going to change that." Lawrence held the phone in his hand. "So you just go right on and finish getting all dolled up for your man. This won't take long."

Deidra looked at him as though she didn't believe him. Lawrence could understand why she would feel that way. This wouldn't be the first time he'd stood her up for a night out on the town after receiving a call from William.

"Go on now, baby. Go on and finish getting ready."

Deidra walked out of the bedroom and into the master bathroom. As soon as Lawrence was certain she was out of ear- and eyeshot, he scurried out of the bedroom and down the stairs into the den.

"What's up?" he said to William, barely above a whisper.

"I have some good news and some better news," William said.

"Better than what you already told me earlier today at lunch?"

"Oh, yes. Now you know we have the best folks around working on our behalf. Of course, you also know that I don't trust cell phones when it comes to discussing most of our business.

That's why I had to wait until I was home and could call from my landline to your landline."

"It's *that* good?"

"Oh, it's that good! Do you want to hear the long version or the short?" William said.

"Give me the short version. Deidra's upstairs getting ready for our date, and the last thing I want is to be late in taking her out, especially during these obviously contentious times."

"Okay. The short version is Miss Goodness and Mercy is dating an up-and-coming doctor named Zachary Morgan. And my sources tell me the good doctor is trying to get his clientele up and going. Of course, you know that in starting up his business, he's incurring quite a bit of debt. Then there's Miss Gabrielle's family."

"She has a family? But I thought she was single—"

"I'm talking about her aunt Cecelia and uncle Dennis Murphy and their four delightful grown children."

"There's something on them that we can use?" Lawrence asked.

"If we need to. Although my sources tell me that the relationship between them may be strained at the moment. Looks like Aunt Cee-Cee has gotten herself into a bit of a jam by forging a signature and embezzling money that didn't belong to her."

"Aunt Cee-Cee," Lawrence said with a bit of nostalgia. "If I recall correctly, she was the one that put Gabrielle out on the streets with no place to go. I don't know how much Gabrielle will care when it comes to them."

"Lawrence, Lawrence, Lawrence," William said as though he was saying his friend just didn't get it. "When have I ever come at a thing from merely one angle? I can use the aunt's situation, believe me. Cecelia Murphy is being charged with stealing. She needs a good lawyer or it's very possible she's on her way to jail. Now tell me: What do you think our helping her out would be worth to her? Huh?"

"Well, if possible, I'd like to keep the list of folks involved in whatever we do down to as few people as possible. I don't like it when you get too many players. It's a sure recipe for problems down the road, and I don't need any more problems than I already have. Let's just see if we can get Gabrielle to go away and be done with it." Lawrence glanced at his watch. "Listen, I need to get off this phone. I don't want to do anything to disappoint Deidra. Not at this point."

"So I have the okay to proceed on this matter?"

"Go with the one that's the least messy and will meet up with the least resistance. I'd like to nip this before it ever gets a chance to bloom."

"All right; I'll get my folks right on it. You know that my people's horses are swifter than the leopards and fiercer than the evening wolves. When I dispatch them on a prey, they fly like a hungry eagle in a hurry to feast."

"Just make sure when they're done, we're not left with more of a mess to clean up than what we started with," Lawrence said. "I've seen your people's handiwork; they can be quite brutal."

"Hey," William said. "You either want it done or you don't. There's no in-between."

"Fine, William. Do what you need to do and just keep me updated. But not tonight," Lawrence said. "Tonight, I'm turning off my cell phone and focusing on making things right with my wife. I can already see we're going to have a long road ahead of us to this next election. I don't need to have to deal with a wife with an attitude to boot." Lawrence looked up and saw Deidra walking into the room. "And speaking of my beautiful wife," he said, hoping she hadn't heard any of what he'd just said. "I have to hang up now. This vision of beauty just entered the room."

Lawrence clicked the END button. "Baby, you look absolutely stunning!" He walked over to her, scanning her up and down as he took note of the V-neckline, black and white, silk, bold-abstract-print, belted dress. "How did I become so blessed that God would even allow me to be able to behold such beauty this close? Huh? Tell me. And tell me who designed that dress that's fitting you all *over* the place? Uh-uh-uh."

Deidra smiled. "Oh, so you like this? I'm glad to hear that. It's a Venus flytrap by Emilio Pucci. It cost a little over two grand, and that was the on-sale price." She did a quick twirl as she smiled. "I just came to let you know that I'm ready."

"Yes, ma'am. *That* you are. But the question is: Am I ready? Because I can already see that I'm going to have to fight off the men from staring at you tonight. Wow! Let me run the phone back upstairs, get my jacket, and we'll be on our way." He started out of the room, turned back to his wife, then kissed her. "Wow!" he said. "Look at *my* baby. Nothing *but* the best, on the best, *for* the best!"

Deidra giggled. "Boy, you are so silly."

"I'll be right back." He ran upstairs, returned the phone to its base, put his jacket on, checked himself in the dresser mirror, then smiled. "Thank You, God. I can see things are already looking up!"

Chapter 12

For the stone shall cry out of the wall, and the beam out of the timber shall answer it.

—Habakkuk 2:11

"What's wrong?" Zachary asked a crying Gabrielle as soon as he arrived at her house and she answered the door. She'd been crying a lot these past four hours. And she still hadn't heard a word back from Lawrence.

"I need to go," Gabrielle said.

"Go where?"

"To the hospital. Jessica just called. She's falling apart. She asked me to come to the hospital. She's never asked to see me before. She and I have never really met in person, except for that one time when she came and took the baby out of my arms. I didn't even look at her that day; I don't even know what she looks like. This has to mean things are taking a turn for the worse for Jasmine. I don't know if I can do this. I can't let her see me crying like this."

"Then I'll take you," Zachary said.

"No. I don't think that's a good idea. Jessica wants as few people knowing what's going on as possible."

Zachary gathered Gabrielle up by her shoulders. "I'm going with you. Understand?"

Gabrielle timidly nodded. She was glad he wanted to go with her. She didn't know what to say to a mother who had possibly just been told her daughter was taking a turn for the worse and time was running out. It had just been hours ago when the two of them spoke and she told Jessica she was there if she needed her. She didn't really think Jessica would take her up on her offer, and definitely, not this soon.

"Zachary, before we go . . . there's something I need to tell you."

"Okay. But if you like you can tell me on the way."

"No. I need to tell you here . . . right now. Because after I tell you, you just may decide that you don't want to have anything more to do with me. And if that's the case, then I'll be the first to understand."

Zachary smiled. "Nothing you can tell me will make me feel like that. So what is it? What's going on?"

Gabrielle looked up, closed her eyes, opened them, and looked at Zachary with a nervous smile. "It's about Jasmine's birth father."

"Yeah?"

"I told you that I went to see him."

"Yes."

"Well, I didn't tell you everything. And I need to tell you. I don't want there to be any secrets between us. And since I botched it so badly with him when I saw him, things just might get ugly."

"So, is this guy a gangbanger or something?"

Gabrielle shook her head. "No, not a gangbanger."

"Then he's no credible threat."

"I don't know about that," Gabrielle said. "His name is Lawrence."

Zachary smiled. "Lawrence, huh? You don't hear of many black men named Lawrence these days. Lawrence. I *assume* he's black. Is he? Not that it matters."

"Yes, he's black. And his name is Lawrence Simmons."

Zachary nodded. "Okay, Lawrence Simmons, like that congressman's name of Lawrence Simmons, the one that's made the news lately after he switched from the Democratic Party to the Grand Old Republican Party. He defends his actions by saying he's now with the party of Lincoln. Only Lincoln did something that benefitted people of color. The Republican Party these days could *give* a flip."

She briefly cast her eyes downward. "Not *like* that Lawrence Simmons . . . is."

Zachary frowned. "Excuse me? Come again?" He tilted his ear toward her.

Gabrielle nodded, then leaned her head back before straightening it to look into Zachary's eyes. "Jasmine's birth father *is* Representative Lawrence Simmons."

Zachary jerked his upper body back. "Whoa!" he said one octave lower. "You're kidding me, right?"

"Nope. I'm not kidding you."

"But he's sort of old, isn't he? He has to be close to fifty. I mean . . . he's old enough to be your father."

"Yes . . . he *is*."

"And you're telling me that you and him—"

"Yes. Me and him. I'd just turned eighteen at the time."

"But how . . . how did something like that even happen?" Zachary held up both his hands as though he was surrendering. "I'm sorry, that's really none of my business." But the look on his face said otherwise.

"I told Jessica, when she called me earlier today, that I'd spoken with the father."

"Wow. You have to give me a minute to process this." Zachary walked away from Gabrielle. "He appears to be such a wonderful family man, spouting off all that family-values stuff, claiming to be a Godly man, deacon of his church for over twenty years, a man of integrity. And you're telling me that Mr. I Love My Wife and Family, 'my wife and I have been madly in love for the entire twenty-nine years of our glorious marriage' had an affair with you some nine years ago?" He looked at her.

She stepped up to Zachary. "You say that as though you don't believe me?"

"No." He gathered Gabrielle by her shoulders. "No. Of course I believe you. I'm just trying to process all of this." He let go. "You say you saw him earlier today?"

"Yes."

"I can imagine how *that* conversation most likely went. The man is up for reelection. Word on the street is that he's pretty much done for. Something like this getting out will bury his chances of being reelected for sure. He was already so desperate that he switched to the Republican Party. A black man running as a Republican is hard enough. But a black man in the south running as a Republican is . . ." Zachary shook his head. "Let's just say me and those traveling in my circle are all scratching our heads on this one."

"Lawrence didn't believe me. But then, I did do something that gives him plenty of a reason to doubt me at this point."

"And that would be?"

"Lawrence had wanted me to get an abortion. He thought I'd gotten rid of the baby. So you can imagine what it was like for him to have me show up telling him that not only didn't I get rid of the baby, but that she's now eight . . . close to nine years old and in desperate need of a bone marrow transplant—"

"And him taking the test to find out whether he qualifies as a possible match could surely expose him as suspect to having fathered her."

"No," Gabrielle said, shaking her head slowly. "I told him the way for him to do this without him ever being exposed, just like any other anonymous donor can do. I told him that. Zachary, I'm really not trying to hurt him. I hope you know that's not the type of person I am."

"Oh, I know that." He shook his head. "And I didn't mean to imply that you were."

"All I want is to get Jasmine the help she desperately needs. And poor Jessica is about to completely lose it. I'm not sure what kind of faith she had going in, but she certainly sounds like she's given up on God at this point. That's a dangerous place to be."

Zachary moved closer to Gabrielle and lovingly cupped her face. "And what about you? How are *you* holding up through all of this? This has been a lot for you to process and deal with."

Gabrielle stepped away from Zachary so he wouldn't be able to look in her eyes when she spoke. "She's not my child. She's Jessica's. I gave my child up. I gave up my right to care when I signed her over to them."

Zachary grabbed Gabrielle's wrist and turned her back toward him. "And you still love her. And it's okay. In fact, I would wonder what's wrong with you if you didn't."

Gabrielle began to cry. Zachary held her. "Yes. I love her," Gabrielle cried. "And I don't want anything to happen to her. I don't want her to die, Zachary. But I don't know what else I can do to help her. I . . . don't . . . know . . . what . . . to . . . do!"

Zachary continued holding Gabrielle. "It's okay. I understand."

Gabrielle looked up at him. "Do you? Do you really? Do you understand that I love her so much and I'm afraid she's going to die if I don't do all I can to help her?"

"Yes, I do."

"And do you understand that I practically threatened to go public if Lawrence doesn't do what he can to at least try and help her?"

"You didn't threaten him, did you?" Zachary looked worried. "Tell me you didn't threaten him."

"Well, in a backhanded way, I suppose it might have come across that way."

"That wasn't a good thing to be doing. He *is* a government official, you know."

Gabrielle pressed her lips tightly together. "I know. But I lost it. I asked God to forgive me because I didn't come off as the best example of a Christian with him. But he was trying to deny the baby could even *possibly* be his. I told him he's welcome to take a paternity test if he doesn't believe me. I told him he can donate the marrow anonymously if he turns out to be a match. I don't want to expose him on this. But I also know that I could care less about his reelection bid if that's all that's holding him back from doing what he can to help save Jasmine's life. I just want to get Jasmine the transplant she needs. That's it. Maybe I'm just being selfish. I don't know. It's been hours since I told him and I haven't heard a peep from him. Nothing. I've called his office again and left several messages, but . . ."

Zachary held Gabrielle tightly in his arms.

"I'm okay," she said, trying to push loose. "I'm okay."

He continued to hold her tight.

"I'm okay," she said. "Really. I'm okay. She's not my child. She's not. She belongs to somebody else. She's Jessica's little girl. I'm just . . . I'm just—" Gabrielle broke down completely. "Oh, Lord! Please help me! I don't want her to die! I don't want her to die! I don't want . . . my child . . . to die! God, please don't let my baby die!"

Zachary kept his arms tight around her, holding on to her as she crumbled to the floor. He wouldn't let go.

Chapter 13

According to the word that I covenanted with you when ye came out of Egypt, so my spirit remaineth among you: fear ye not.

—Haggai 2:5

We need to go to the cafeteria," Gabrielle said to Zachary as she clicked off her cell phone, after having just spoken to Jessica. They strolled through the automatic opened doors of Children's Hospital. "Jessica says she'll meet me there. I'm so nervous. We've talked on the phone since my part in this began, but this will be our first time officially meeting face-to-face after close to nine years."

"Okay," Zachary said, leading the way. They made their way to the cafeteria.

Gabrielle looked around. The place was empty of patrons. "She's not here yet. I guess we can just sit and wait on her to get here."

Zachary led Gabrielle over to an empty table away from possible traffic of folks. "She can see us when she comes in easy enough over here."

They sat down. A minute later a man and a woman came in together. The woman stopped, looked over at Gabrielle, then tilted her head as though she was trying to figure out who Gabrielle was.

"That woman looks familiar," Gabrielle said.

"Do you think that's Jessica?"

"No, I'm pretty sure it's not Jessica. Jessica will be much older. That woman staring our way looks to be around my age."

The woman with auburn-colored hair strolled over to where Gabrielle and Zachary sat. "I'm sorry," she said. "Please forgive me for interrupting. But you look so familiar to me. I'm trying to figure out why I know you."

Gabrielle nodded. "You look familiar as well."

"My name is Paris."

"Paris?" Gabrielle stood up. "Paris Simmons? I'm Gabrielle."

"Gabrielle Booker? Oh, my goodness!" Paris hugged Gabrielle. "It's been ages! How have you been? I've thought about you so many times and wondered how you were doing. You look *so* good. Oh, my goodness! Look at you!"

Gabrielle tried to not lose her smile. She could just imagine Paris must have wondered what had happened to her . . . especially after she put her out on the streets with nowhere to go and not enough time to find a place. "I've been just wonderful, thank you very much."

"Oh, my goodness! Gabrielle, you look absolutely amazing. Wow!" Paris continued to smile as she looked at Gabrielle. "Oh, my! Where on earth are my manners? This is my husband, Andrew Holyfield. He's a really successful lawyer. I'm Paris Simmons-Holyfield now, with a hyphen. I went with the hyphenated thing. You know how it is these days. Have to keep my identity attached to my roots." She turned to Andrew. "Honey, this is an old friend from way back: Gabrielle Booker."

"Actually, it's Gabrielle Mercedes," Gabrielle corrected her.

"Oh, you got married!" Paris said with a grin as she looked at Zachary still sitting at the table. "Congratulations! It looks like you snagged a good one."

"Oh, no. I'm not married. I just dropped the Booker as my last name and went with my middle name as my last."

"Oh," Paris said as she turned up her nose before quickly recovering with her Miss America–like smile.

Andrew extended his hand to Gabrielle. "I'm pleased to meet you," he said.

Gabrielle looked at him. She knew Andrew already. But she decided if he wasn't going to say anything, she wouldn't, either. "Likewise." Gabrielle then turned to a now-standing Zachary. "This is Zachary Morgan."

Zachary extended his hand to Paris first. "Hello. Nice to meet you."

"Charmed," Paris said with a cheesy grin.

Zachary tugged his hand out of Paris's firm grip and shook Andrew's hand. "Nice to meet you."

Andrew began to nod his head a few times like a bobblehead doll. "You're *Dr.* Morgan, aren't you?"

"Why, yes, I am."

"You're a doctor?" Paris said, her smile fading slightly. "So are you two in consultation right now? Did we interrupt you while you were working? I am *so* sorry! I walked in, saw someone I thought I knew, and I just came barging over—"

"We're not in a consultation," Gabrielle said.

"Then how do you two happen to know each other? Do you work for him or something?"

"No," Zachary said. "This beautiful smart woman is the love of my life. And if I'm successful at all, I hope to someday convince her to be my wife." Zachary placed his arm around Gabrielle and looked lovingly down at her.

Gabrielle wanted to hit Zachary after that last statement, a playful hit. Nothing violent. She almost laughed out loud, but managed to keep it to a blushing smile. She knew Zachary was laying it on thicker than he had to. He must have picked up on Paris's snarky, covert jabs at her.

Paris put her smile back on her face. "Well, we didn't mean to intrude. We're here to visit a friend's little boy. I saw you over here and couldn't help but think that I knew you from somewhere. I'm sure you know how that can be. I didn't want to be wondering about it for the rest of the night. So I just made my little way over here and at least thought I'd find out if we knew each other or not, and if so, from where."

"Well," Gabrielle said with a smile, "now you don't have to wonder. It was great seeing you again, Paris. And Drew"—Gabrielle quickly realized she'd called him by the name she always called him and hurried to correct, hopefully masking her error—"*And*rew, it was nice meeting you."

Andrew grinned a little. Gabrielle knew it was because she'd called him Drew and that had to have brought back some memories. He used to always grin when she called him Drew, since only one other person (that she knew of other than her) called him that. "Nice meeting you both."

Paris looked at Andrew first, then Gabrielle with a slight scowl, before turning on her pageant smile, as Gabrielle called that particular phony smile that anyone with half of a brain could tell wasn't the least bit sincere.

"Yes, it was really nice meeting you, Dr. Zachary Morgan," Paris said. "Tell me: Are you an OB/GYN? I may be looking for someone soon. Andrew and I are about to start our own little family."

"No, I'm not. I'm a burn specialist. But I can certainly recommend someone, should you need me to," Zachary said.

"Do you have a business card?" Paris asked.

"Of course." Zachary reached in his pocket, took out his card holder, and handed her one of his gold, embossed cards.

Paris smiled. "Thanks." She turned to Gabrielle and leaned in to hug her without getting too close. "It was really good seeing you again. And I'm so excited that things are going so well for you." She released Gabrielle, grabbed her by the hand, and squeezed it. "I really *am* happy for you!" She shifted her eyes to Zachary and grinned, her way of letting Gabrielle know she had indeed snagged herself a real hunk . . . a true prize. "You know, Gabrielle, I should get your number as well. Maybe we can have lunch or something. You know, catch up."

Gabrielle knew this was all a mere act. Paris had no desire to hang out with her and Gabrielle knew it. And if she were to follow through, it would be only to get more information out of her on the real deal going on between her and Zachary. Still, Gabrielle wanted to show that she held no grudges . . . that she'd forgiven Paris for the way she'd treated her, just the way Christ admonished all people to do. She reached inside of her purse, pulled out a business card, and handed it to Paris.

Paris looked at the card. "You work at a church?"

"Yes."

"You're the *director* over the dance ministry at Followers of Jesus Faith Worship Center? Over there with Pastor George Landris? I've never been, but have said I was going to visit there someday. I hear he's a powerful minister leading a powerful ministry."

"Yes, Pastor Landris is. And Gabrielle is the director of the dance ministry," Zachary said. "And she's doing an awesome work for the Lord herself."

Gabrielle looked at Zachary. The look in his eyes softened her words even more. "Thank you, Zachary. I appreciate that."

"So does this mean you're saved now?" Paris asked. "I mean, people can work in a church without being a member of that church or having given their lives to Christ. I know plenty of folks doing just that. It's all about the paycheck."

"Yes, I'm saved now. I gave my life to Christ on January 4, 2009. And I'm totally sold out for the Lord."

"Wow. You know that just proves the power of God. I know when I was trying to tell you about Him, you didn't seem interested in hearing me at all. It didn't matter what I said, you weren't hearing me and you weren't listening."

Gabrielle wanted to tell her it was because her actions didn't line up with her words. She'd seen plenty of so-called *talking* Christians—those who could talk the walk. She just hadn't met too many *walking* Christians—those who walked the walk and the talk. Gabrielle hadn't grown up totally devoid of church. She'd gone to church plenty of times as a child. Her family was what some folks called CME attendees—they went to church for Christmas, Mother's Day, and Easter. CME. Gabrielle knew *about* God, at least that He existed. It wasn't like she'd never been exposed to church, church folks, or those who called themselves Christians prior to moving in with Paris for that brief time. But it wasn't until she hooked up with Pastor Landris and that great ministry that she began to *know* God . . . to form a relationship with Him and not just know *about* Him.

A woman who appeared to be in her late forties, maybe early fifties, came over to Gabrielle. "Excuse me," the woman said. "But I'm looking for Gabrielle Mercedes."

"Listen," Paris said. "We're going to run. Gabrielle, it was great seeing you again. Dr. Morgan it was *really* great meeting you." Paris and Andrew left.

"I take it you're Gabrielle," the woman said. She looked so tired.

"Jessica?" Gabrielle said.

"Yes. So finally, we meet again." Jessica nodded, then immediately, as though she could no longer hold her own body in an upright position, she slowly lowered her body into the chair.

Chapter 14

Now therefore thus saith the Lord of hosts: Consider your ways.

—Haggai 1:5

"I apologize. I don't seem to have much energy left these days. Just making my way down here seems to have taken a lot out of me," Jessica said.

Gabrielle and Zachary sat down as well. "You don't need to apologize," Gabrielle said. "I understand. You're dealing with a lot."

Jessica nodded.

"Thank you for agreeing to meet me here. I realize this was short notice and unexpected."

"No problem," Gabrielle said. "This is Dr. Zachary Morgan. I hope you don't mind that he came with me."

Zachary took Gabrielle's slightly shaking hand and looked at Gabrielle. "Actually, I insisted."

Jessica looked at Gabrielle first, then to Zachary. She smiled. "So this is your doctor friend you told me about? The one who helped you better understand what was going on with my Jasmine." Jessica nodded. "I don't mind at all. It's what my late husband would have done had it been me. It's good to have someone who cares so much." Jessica took in a deep breath and slowly released it.

Gabrielle swallowed hard. "How's Jasmine?"

Jessica shook her head slowly. "Not so good." Jessica's mouth trembled as she tried, unsuccessfully, to form a smile. "But she has such a great spirit about all of this. She does all she can to make sure I'm not sad or worried. I try not to let her see me get down, but you know, I have my moments and can't help myself." Her smile faded. "It's so frustrating to sit back and have to watch her go down like she's been doing and not be able to do anything about it." Jessica smiled again. "I don't know what I did to have been blessed with such a beautiful little girl. But I want to thank you so much, Gabrielle, for the gift you gave to me and my husband. If you only knew . . ."

Gabrielle felt tears begin to puddle up in her eyes. She didn't want to cry in front of Jessica. She was supposed to be here to support her. It was just . . . she'd never considered how her actions would play out all these years later. She'd known she didn't want to get rid of the baby she was carrying. But she equally knew she couldn't take care of a child, not at that stage in her life. No family. No help. No place to call home. So she'd opted to give her baby up for adoption and could hope only that the family where the child would end up would love and take good care of her. As she sat here before Jessica, she was able to see that her child had truly gotten that and so much more. Even before she'd known about God and prayer, God had been looking out on her behalf.

Zachary squeezed her hand. He then reached over and took Jessica's hand and squeezed hers as well.

"It's so hard when you're all by yourself," Jessica said. "It's hard."

Gabrielle didn't want to pry, but Jessica had been the one to open the door. "So you don't have any family to support you? None?"

Jessica shook her head. "My husband was an only child as was both his parents. His father died two years after his mother, seven years after he and I married. I grew up in foster care, shuffled from one home to another, not really knowing who my parents were. I knew what it felt like not to be wanted. After his parents died, all my husband and I had were each other." Jessica began to chortle a little. "My husband and I had planned on having this big old family. We were going to have a house full of children." She primped her mouth. "But things didn't quite work out the way we'd planned. For whatever reason, I just couldn't get pregnant. So we decided to look at adoption. I knew from firsthand experience how many children were out there in need of a loving home." Jessica took her hand out of Zachary's.

Zachary continued holding Gabrielle's. "You're right about that," he said.

"My husband and I weren't even going to be choosy about the age of the child we would be blessed with. We went through all of the necessary steps to get our names on the waiting list. And, lo and behold, if we didn't get a call about a newborn baby." Jessica looked at Gabrielle and smiled. "Your sweet, little beautiful baby girl with a head full of black curly hair. Of course, we didn't want to get our hopes up too high just yet. We'd heard heartbreaking stories about birth mothers who changed their minds within the allotted period after signing the papers. But when I was allowed to come into your hospital room, and you released that sweet little baby girl into my arms, oh, my goodness—" Jessica placed her hand over her heart.

Gabrielle began to nod, then wipe tears that were now rolling down her face. Zachary went and got napkins and handed them to her. Gabrielle dabbed her eyes. "She *was* a beautiful baby, wasn't she?"

"She most certainly was." Jessica reached over and grabbed hold of Gabrielle's free hand. "And she has grown into an even more beautiful little girl."

Gabrielle nodded continuously.

"Would you like to meet her?" Jessica said, her hand now squeezing Gabrielle's.

Gabrielle grabbed her hand and squeezed it back without even thinking about it. It had been more of a reflex at the surprise question. She had agreed in signing the papers that she wouldn't see the child she'd given up until and unless the child wanted to find her after the child turned eighteen. Of course, things changed when Jasmine got so sick and needed a bone marrow transplant. But even then, she and Jessica had agreed that if she *had* been a match, she would donate what was needed, and things would go back as they'd been. Now, here Gabrielle was, sitting face-to-face with the woman she'd handed her baby over to, and she was being asked if she would like to meet her. Although joyful about meeting her, Gabrielle now knew that the situation with Jasmine had likely become dire.

Gabrielle couldn't even find her voice now to give Jessica an answer. She nodded quickly, fighting back her tears. She sucked in a deep breath and released it slowly. Yes, she would like to meet her . . . to see her again. Yes, she would love to gaze into her daughter's eyes again.

"Well," Jessica said, not waiting on a verbal answer from Gabrielle, who was wiping away tears. She used the table to help her push her body to a standing position. "Then what say we go and make the introduction. The only thing . . . I'm not going to tell her who you really are to her. She doesn't need to know that at this point."

Gabrielle was already on her feet. She nodded in agreement. "That's fine. You and I can just be old acquaintances . . . new acquaintances . . . whatever you want to call me or tell her."

Jessica gave a quick nod. "We still must consider our ways. But at this point, Jasmine needs all the love, support, and positive energy she can get. I may not know much about you at this point, but I know that you love her. She may not know that you're her birth mother, Gabrielle, but I believe she'll feel something special when the two of you meet again."

Standing as well, Zachary grabbed Gabrielle and hugged her. "It's going to be all right," he whispered. "It's all right, in the name of Jesus."

Gabrielle nodded, took a deep breath, then released it with a slow quiet sigh. She was going to see the child she hadn't seen in exactly eight years, seven months, and nineteen days.

Chapter 15

For thus saith the Lord of hosts: Yet once, it is a little while, and I will shake the heavens, and the earth, and the sea, and the dry land.

—Haggai 2:6

"So, where do you know Miss Gabrielle from?" Paris said as soon as she and Andrew stepped back into their house. She'd pretty much given Andrew the silent treatment from the hospital to the door that led from their garage to their kitchen. It had been relatively easy to be silent since they'd gone to see their friend's child and stayed only fifteen minutes after leaving Gabrielle. Paris detested going to hospitals to visit anyone. And it was even worse visiting children, because the parents usually sat looking sad and the children were too sick to interact with at all.

"Who said I know her from anywhere?" Andrew headed straight to the refrigerator, opened it, and looked inside.

"There's nothing in there," Paris said. "I don't even know why you bother looking. I need to buy groceries, but you know how much I detest grocery shopping."

"Yeah," Andrew said. "I know. I asked you if you wanted to stop anywhere on our way home tonight."

"I heard you. But in case you didn't notice: I wasn't talking to you."

"Yeah, I noticed." Andrew went over to the drawer with the restaurant menus in it and opened it. He pulled out the stack. "So, what do you feel like eating tonight?"

"I don't *feel* like eating anything. What I *want* is an answer to my question."

"I gave you an answer." Andrew let the menus he wasn't interested in fall onto the counter. "How about Indian tonight?"

"How about you answer my question about Gabrielle?" Paris stomped over and snatched the menus he still held out of his hand. "I saw the way you two exchanged looks. It's just like it was when she was living with me that time."

"Oh, the two of you lived together at one time?" Andrew laughed a little. "Who knew? You two definitely don't appear to be anything alike, not enough to live together."

"And you would know that *how*?" Paris put her hand on her hip. "Because you certainly wouldn't be able to determine what she's like just from that brief how-de-do we just had."

"How-de-do?" He tapped her on her nose. "You are so cute. Now, what do you have a taste for? Because you know it's going to be another forty-five minutes to an hour before whatever we order arrives. The sooner I call it in—"

"I don't care about any food right now!" She slammed the menus she held in her hand onto the counter. "I would like a straight answer from you. It's obvious you and Gabrielle know each other. I'm just interested in knowing from where?"

Andrew picked up one of the menus he'd let fall to the counter. "You like Chinese food, so I'll just order Chinese."

"My goodness! Are you even listening to me? I'm telling you . . . this is just like it was when she stayed at my apartment that time. I don't know why she has to always want whatever I have. It's pitiful that her pathetic little life is so miserable that she has to find a way to drink from the same fountain I draw my water from."

"Paris, why don't you stop being so dramatic? You're always making a garden out of a seed." Andrew went over to the cordless phone and took it out of its base.

"And you are always so corny when you think you're being clever. You stole that from the sermon our pastor preached the other Sunday when he was talking about making a garden out of a seed in his series on sowing and reaping. But I'm telling you, Andrew: I saw the way the two of you looked at each other." Paris snatched the phone out of his hand. "And what was that slipup of your name she made and thought nobody caught? Yes, I most certainly caught it, *Drew*!"

"You're tripping for real now." He gently took the phone back from her. "If you don't want anything to eat, then I'll just order what I want." He stopped a second. "On second thought, you know what? Since I'm going to get what I want, I think I'll go get myself a real hamburger . . . and some onion rings." He set the phone back in its base.

"Don't you dare leave! We're in the middle of an argument and we're not finished yet."

He walked over to her and softly kissed her on her nose. "Yes . . . we are. You've put me on the stand. You've cross-examined me. Now you need to rest your case, Counselor, and stop this nonsense before you end up saying something you're likely to regret later."

Paris stomped her foot down hard. "I hate you! Do you hear me? You make me sick!"

"Okay," Andrew said. "I'll pick you up something while I'm out."

"I mean it, Andrew. If you leave now, then don't bother coming back tonight."

"French fries for you," he said as he walked toward the door that led to the garage. "And no mayo and no onions on your burger. You hate onions. I'll be back shortly."

"Andrew! You come back here! Do you hear me! You'd better not leave!"

Andrew closed the door behind him. She heard his car when it cranked, the garage door as it went up and down when he left.

"Ugh!" Paris yelled. "I hate you!" She threw the menus at the kitchen door, found Gabrielle's business card in her purse, tore it up, and threw it in the trash. She then marched up the stairs to her bedroom, flung herself onto the bed, and yelled again, "I *really* hate you! Sometimes!"

Chapter 16

Ye have sown much, and bring in little; ye eat, but ye have not enough; ye drink, but ye are not filled with drink; ye clothe you, but there is none warm; and he that earneth wages earneth wages to put it into a bag with holes.

—Haggai 1:6

After scooting out of the taxi and paying her tab, Paris walked quickly to the side door. She thought about using her key, but decided it was too much trouble to look for it and easier to just ring the doorbell. Pressing the lighted button, she waited a minute before pressing the button again. Not even thirty seconds later, she was pressing it repeatedly—one right after the other. "Come on!" she said as she pressed the doorbell button again and again.

The side door that opened into the garage before the door that opened to the kitchen flung open. Fifteen-year-old Courtney Imani Simmons (who everybody called Imani) now stood with one hand on her hip and an attitude to match. "I was coming! You didn't have to live on the doorbell."

"Well, it was taking you too long," Paris said to her little sister as she brushed past her and headed for the opened door that led right into the kitchen. "Where's Mom?"

Imani closed the outside door, walked through the kitchen door, and closed it behind her. "She's out . . . on a date."

Paris stopped, turned around, and looked hard at Imani. "Out on a date? A date with whom?"

Imani walked on ahead of Paris and sat down on the barstool at the kitchen counter. "With Dad."

Paris stood next to her sister. "Dad who?"

"Girl, stop acting. Dad took Mom out to dinner and who knows where else."

"You're talking about *our* dad? So what kind of political function did he drag her to *this* time?"

Imani smiled. "Oh, it was nothing political. They went on a *date* date . . . just the two of them. Well, at least that's what Mom told me it was, right before she left."

"Well, you and I both know that if Dad took Mom anywhere, it wasn't to anything that she cared about. He never takes her anywhere unless it somehow benefits him or his objective." Paris went to the refrigerator and looked inside.

"Why do you always come over here raiding our refrigerator? Do you *ever* have any food at your own house? Besides milk, cereal, and eggs, that is."

Paris took out a pan with a roast in it. "Why don't you mind your own business? I have just as much right to eat here as you do."

"No . . . you don't. You have your own house. You're grown, remember? At least, that's what you say when anybody tries to tell you something you don't like or care to hear. So why don't you go grocery shopping and cook sometimes yourself instead of coming over here eating up all our stuff?"

Paris set the pan on the counter, then went back and retrieved the bowl of whole potatoes swimming in butter and fresh herbs. Her mother made the best potatoes. She took a dinner plate out of the cabinet. "Do you want any while I'm warming this up?"

"No." Imani took out her cell phone and started texting.

"You do know that it's rude to do that while someone is talking to you, don't you?" Paris put a few of the thinly sliced roast pieces onto the plate before scooping up two spoonfuls of potatoes.

"Well, it's not like you came over here to see me." Imani continued with her texting. "You came to see Mom and I just happened to be all you have right now." Imani carefully set her cell phone down on the brown granite countertop.

Paris put her plate in the microwave and pressed the QUICK START button to heat her food. She turned back to Imani. "So . . . how's school?"

"School's okay."

"Do you have a new boyfriend yet?" Paris stood by the microwave as she looked on at her sister.

Imani burst into a huge grin. "I know Malachi already told you."

"I haven't talked to Malachi in almost three weeks. Our brother is apparently too busy and too important to talk to me much these days." Malachi Everett Simmons was their twenty-six-year-old charmer of a brother. "You know with him being a business administration graduate with a master's degree who just happened to graduate at the top of his class, a highfalutin banker now, and lest we forget, God's gift to women—"

Imani laughed. "Oh, you're just jealous."

The microwave beeped. Paris took out her plate that had smoke rising from it and sat next to her baby sister. "Jealous of who?"

"It's jealous of *whom.* Not jealous of who."

Having forgotten her utensils, Paris got up and got a knife and a fork out of the cabinet drawer, then came and sat back down. "You're just like Dad; always correcting somebody." Paris bowed her head and said a two-second prayer.

"You know you didn't actually pray," Imani said. "I don't know why you're always pretending."

"You don't know what I did." Paris used her knife to cut the whole red potato into smaller pieces.

"I know that it takes longer than two seconds if you're really saying grace over your food."

Paris waved the now fork-speared potato at her sister. "Whatever, *Courtney.*"

Imani's countenance instantly changed from the smile she'd just had to a glower. "Don't you start, Paris! I'm not playing with you!"

Paris giggled. "What?" She speared another bite of potato, twirled her fork in a dance-like movement, then placed the potato in her mouth.

"Don't start calling me Courtney."

"Well, it *is* your name. Isn't it? *Courtney* Imani Simmons."

Imani stood up. "You and Dad really get on my nerves with that."

"What nerves?" Paris laughed. "You're not old enough to have nerves, at least not real nerves that count yet."

Imani started out of the kitchen.

"Hey! Where are you going? Oh, come back, Imani," Paris shouted after her. "I'm sorry!"

Imani stopped, but remained facing away from Paris.

"I'm sorry. Okay? I didn't know that was such a touchy subject with you." Imani tilted her head slightly but still kept her back to Paris. "Come on back over here and sit by me."

Imani turned around. "You promise you're not going to aggravate me anymore?"

"Well now, I can't promise you all of *that.* I mean, you *are* my little sister, and by that virtue alone, I'm sure I'll end up doing *something* that will aggravate you. But I promise not to play with your name like that if you feel that strongly about it. But why do you get so upset with being called Courtney? I mean: It *is* your name. And it's your real first name, not your middle name."

Imani walked back over to the barstool and sat down. "I'm just tired of Dad making my name into a political football. Ever since I've been born, everybody has called me Imani. But during this reelection campaign especially, Dad has decided I have to go by the name Courtney instead of Imani. How would you like it if someone were to tell you that you're now going to be called Elizabeth instead of Paris after we've called you Paris all of *your* life? Like your name isn't good enough. So now you have to go by a different one because your father is ashamed of you."

"Girl, Dad is *not* ashamed of you *or* your name." But Paris did know that her mother had wanted to name her little sister Imani and her father had wanted to go with Courtney. So as a compromise, they named her Courtney Imani, but agreed they would call her Imani.

"If he's not ashamed, then why, when he sends out his political stuff, does he list my name as Courtney instead of Imani? My friends don't have a clue *who* he's talking about. They tease me and ask if I'm really his child or worse: Does he have an illegitimate child he's acknowledging over me. It's embarrassing, I'm telling you. And it hurts. A lot."

Paris leaned over and hugged Imani. "I'm sorry. I understand better now why you're upset. But you see: Dad's under a lot of pressure this election time around. It's because of how much things have changed. He now has to appeal to the more *conservative* sector of the election population."

"You mean white people."

Paris pulled back a tad. "Well, you don't have to put it quite that blunt."

"But it's true. I overheard him and his little lapdog William talking about how the name Imani is just a tad *too* ethnic. Talking about Imani makes white folks uncomfortable and think about Kwanzaa, and Kwanzaa makes them think African, and African makes them think that they don't even want to give this person any consideration. So *they* decided that using the name Courtney instead of Imani will make *us* more acceptable to folks who might otherwise not be interested in voting for a black man." Imani leaned down and rested her chin on her fists propped up by her elbows. "Do you know how much hearing something like that hurts? I'm so tired of racism! I just wish folks would stop it! God hates it and everybody just needs to stop it!"

"I can imagine it hurts. But you shouldn't take what Dad and William do personal. That's just Dad being Dad." Paris put her last piece of potato in her mouth. "He feels like he's sown much but brought in little to show for it, even after all these years of serving in government. But if it makes you feel any better, Dad is making all of us conform to some kind of image he feels is acceptable. Me, I have to be the good supportive wife who's using her spare time volunteering to work in soup kitchens."

Paris got up, took down a glass, got crushed ice, and poured some soda from the two-liter bottle sitting on the counter. "Then there's Malachi who has to tone down his womanizing ways, or at least be sure he's not involved in some kind of dustup the news can use. Mom has to lose weight around this time, even though they go to more eating functions than ever. She has to be the perfect arm candy and keep smiling when she attends all of those stupid functions with all of those phony people that Dad drags her to. And you . . . you, dear little sister, sort of get off easy. You just have to stay out of trouble, which you should be doing regardless of what Dad is doing, and allow Dad to refer to you as Courtney instead of Imani for his campaign junk."

Imani laughed. "You're crazy."

"Yeah. That's probably true. But what do you expect? I've had to live this life a lot longer than you. And that, Imani, is why I keep telling you to get a good education and get away from this place as soon as you can. Oh, and try to get a scholarship so you can go to California or somewhere distant like that. Because I'll tell you right now, if Dad has to pay for your college, you're going to find yourself right here, just like me and Malachi had to end up doing. And you'll never escape."

"Well, you *are* an adult now. You have a husband. You could move anywhere you want."

Paris took a swallow of soda. "Yeah. And if you believe that, then I have an iPad3 I'd like to sell you for thirty-nine dollars."

"There's no iPad3. There's not even an iPad2 yet, although there's talk of it coming in a year or two, most likely in 2011." Imani went and got a glass, poured herself some soda, and sat back down.

"Oh, but it's coming. You see . . . that's why it's good to get in while the getting is good. You don't want to be like folks who earn money, then put their money in a bag with holes in it."

"Well, if I take you up on the iPad3 offer, that's exactly what I'd be doing: putting my money in a bag with holes. And one thing we Simmons girls can't be accused of and that's being stupid." Imani's cell phone began to sing.

Paris smiled. "And that's *just* why I'm here. Andrew apparently didn't get *that* memo. I'm *not* stupid." But Imani didn't hear any of what Paris said, not that Paris had said it for her to hear. Imani had already jumped down from the barstool and was talking excitingly, about what sounded to Paris as a lot to do about nothing, to one of her little girlfriends.

Chapter 17

Therefore the heaven over you is stayed from dew, and the earth is stayed from her fruit.

—Haggai 1:10

Lawrence and Deidra started walking toward the door leading to the house in thc garage. Deidra was giggling like a schoolgirl. Lawrence was acting like a guy who had just taken his best girl out on a date and was hoping to sneak some more time . . . some alone time, to be exact, with her and not get caught by her parents.

"Shhhh," Lawrence said. "You're too loud."

Deidra giggled some more. "Lawrence, this is our house. And we have every right to be as loud as we want."

"It's after midnight. I don't want to wake Imani up."

"I doubt very seriously that Imani's asleep this time of the night. She's more than likely either on her computer or on her phone."

Lawrence opened the door that led into the kitchen and quickly keyed in the numbers to turn off the alarm system. "I thought we told her she couldn't be on the phone after eleven."

"She's a teenager. If we're not here and she can get away with it, I'm sure there's a good chance she may be on the phone."

"Well, if she is on the phone, with all of the noise you're making, I'm sure she's off now." Lawrence turned toward his wife and grabbed her around her waist. "I had an amazing time with you tonight, Mrs. Simmons."

Deidra gave a coy grin. "I know. Maybe you should consider doing this more often."

He smiled. "Yeah. Maybe I should."

"And to think, the night is still young."

Lawrence leaned back a little and eyed his wife. "You don't say, pretty lady?"

"I do say, Mr. Handsome. The night is far from over. And I'm still young . . . at heart." Deidra laughed.

"Girl, don't be starting nothing while we're down here," Lawrence said. They made their way to the dark den. Lawrence stopped near the couch and kissed her softly. "What say you and I—"

"Mom? Dad? Is that you?"

Lawrence jumped and tried to see who was speaking, but it was too dark to tell. "Who is that?"

A body lifted up off the couch. "It's me—Paris."

Deidra turned on the lamp next to the couch. "Paris?" Deidra said. "What are you doing here?"

Lawrence wiped his hand over his face. "And on our couch?" He couldn't believe the mood had been changed, just like that.

Paris sat up straight. "I was waiting on you to come home," she said to Deidra. "I needed to talk to you."

Deidra went and sat down next to Paris. "Didn't Imani tell you where I was?"

"Yes, she told me. That's why I decided to wait on you to come back."

"Did Imani tell you that your mother and I went on a date?"

Paris turned to her father. "She did."

"So instead of here on our couch, shouldn't you be home with your husband?" Lawrence said.

Paris turned back to her mother. "Mom, I *really* need to talk to you."

Deidra tilted her head. "Did something happen between you and Andrew?"

"Again," Lawrence added with a touch of sarcasm.

Deidra gave Lawrence "the look." Lawrence nodded, but he was a bit upset that such a perfect night with his wife was ending like this.

"Mom, Andrew and I went to the hospital this evening—"

"Is Andrew all right?" Deidra asked with a bit of panic lacing her voice.

"Oh, he's fine. We just went there to visit a couple of friends' child. But before we went to see them, we stopped off at the cafeteria. You know, we were thinking they might like something from there. So we decided to stop there first and pick up a cup of coffee or something, you know. Although had Andrew listened to me in the first place, we would have stopped off at a *decent* place and bought some *decent* coffee—a nice latte, mocha, or frappe—and maybe a nice fresh pastry to snack on. Not that either of them, as it turns out, were really even coffee drinkers. But then again, they're more Andrew's friends than mine."

"Would you *please* get on with it?" Lawrence said. "We really don't need the full play-by-play account."

Paris let out a loud sigh. "I'm getting to it, Daddy. I just needed to set the stage."

Deidra was leaning in toward her daughter. "It's okay, baby. Just finish telling me what happened between you and Andrew that has you upset. It's getting late."

"Anyway, while we were in the cafeteria, we ran into someone I thought I knew. So I went over to speak and to refresh my memory of who it might be."

Lawrence was moving his head around, but not saying a word. He was clearly trying to coerce her to finish already without saying anything and having to receive another disapproving look from his wife, who was wearing the heck out of that dress.

"Mom, you remember that girl that lived with me a few months right after I graduated from high school? The girl whose aunt and uncle put her out on the streets with nowhere to go."

"Yeah, I vaguely remember her. I only met her once, you know. I can't recall her name though."

"It was Gabrielle Booker."

Lawrence froze. "Gabrielle Booker?"

"Yes, although she goes by Gabrielle Mercedes now. How corny is that?" Paris shook her head. "She says she decided to use her middle name for her last."

"So you ran into that girl that stayed with you that time?" Lawrence said.

"Yeah, you should remember her really well, Dad. Because you came over to the apartment and, in the beginning, ordered me to put her out. You said you weren't paying for that apartment for me to take in every stray cat I might find wandering the streets in need of a home."

Lawrence scratched his head. "So, what did she say today when you saw her? Did you talk to her? I mean, she must have said something to get you this riled up and have you over here sleeping on our couch?"

Deidra squinted as she looked at Lawrence. He knew she was wondering what was going on with him. He hardly ever had any input or comments when Paris brought her drama or problems to their doorstep.

Deidra patted Paris's hand. "I do remember now. She's the young lady you put out of your apartment without even a day's notice. So, was she still mad at you about that? Did she say something or do something that hurt you?"

"No. In fact: She couldn't have been nicer. It was as if what went down between us never happened."

"Then why are you *here*, instead of at home with your husband?" Lawrence asked. Both his hands were in his pants pockets now as he rocked back and forth.

"I'm *here* because of what happened when I introduced Gabrielle to Andrew. Or more to the point, what *didn't* happen when I introduced them," Paris said.

"Baby, can you just get to the real point?" Deidra said. "A point that makes sense."

Paris looked down, then back up. "I think the two of them know each other, Andrew and Gabrielle. I don't think I was introducing either of them to the other."

"And *what,* pray tell, would make you think that?" Lawrence asked. "I mean, you know how you are, Paris. You'll take something little and—"

"Lawrence," was all Deidra said in her that's-*enough* tone. He became quiet. "Paris, what makes you think the two of them know each other?"

"For one, the way Andrew was acting around her. Like he was trying hard not to let on that they knew each other. And she must have picked up on his cue and decided to play along with him. But she slipped up and called him Drew."

"Drew?" Lawrence said. "Nobody calls him Drew. Maybe she's just ignorant and didn't know how to say Andrew or misstated it. It happens you know. Or even worse: Maybe she knew it would bother you if she pretended to know him on a deeper level. When she was staying with you, she appeared to be a person who might go to any lengths to get what she wanted or to hurt someone she believed had hurt her."

"Well, if we're talking about the same young lady that *I* met," Deidra said, "she appeared to be a very sweet young lady. She certainly kept that place clean and she could cook. You told me that much yourself, Paris. I only met her once after we initially found out she was there. But whenever I came to see you, Paris, the apartment was always spotless. I knew you weren't doing anything to keep it that way, which became quite evident after you put her out."

"Mom, I didn't come over here to be reminded of how deficient I am. I came so you can tell me what I should do," Paris said.

"Do about what?"

"About Andrew lying to me, trying to act like he doesn't know Gabrielle when it's obvious that he does," she said to her mother. She then turned to her father, "And, Dad, for your information, Andrew's mother calls him Drew. And she's the *only* person I've ever heard call him that, so it has been used for him."

"Maybe Andrew grew up in the same neighborhood with her," Deidra said.

"If that's the case, then why won't he just tell me that? Why is he going to such lengths to keep this to himself?" Paris stood up. "And when I pressed him on it, he left me."

"He left you?" Lawrence said, clearly shocked by this revelation. "What do you mean, he left you? Paris, you know I have this campaign. I don't need any foolishness—"

"He didn't leave me like that, Daddy," Paris said. "So you don't have to worry about your precious little reelection campaign. It's great to see just how much you care about me and my husband when it comes to our marriage." Paris picked up her purse. "I'm sorry to have burdened y'all with my trivial problems and selfishly interrupted your lovely night. I guess Miss Drama Queen strikes again."

"You're *not* a drama queen," Deidra said. "You were just upset."

"Well, I'll just call a taxi to take me home and get out of your hair." Paris pulled out her cell phone and turned it on.

"You took a taxi over here? I was wondering where your car was," Deidra said. "Why didn't you drive your car?"

"Truthfully?" Paris said. "I wanted Andrew to be worried. I mean he walked out on me to go get something to eat! So when he came back, I made sure that I wasn't there. If I had driven my car, he would have figured I was over here and wouldn't have even checked to make sure. This way, he has to be worried." She looked at her phone and smiled. "See there. Just as I thought. Twenty-one missed calls, all from my dear little hubby."

"Paris, you really shouldn't be playing games like that," Deidra said. "What if something was to really happen to you one day? You'd be like the boy who cried wolf. Andrew has no way of knowing you were all right. And your father and I both had our cell phones off for the past few hours."

"Yep," Lawrence said, powering his back on. "It was part of your mother's deal tonight. No phones; no interruptions." Once the phone was up totally and he could see calls and messages, he said, "Andrew called me four times." He continued scrolling to see what other calls he'd missed. William had called three times even though he'd told him he was turning off his phone prior to him going out. It had to be important; Lawrence would need to check in with William as soon as he got a chance. All the others could wait.

"I think instead of calling a taxi, you need to call your husband, let him know where you are, and tell him to come get you," Deidra said.

"If I do that, then Andrew wins," Paris said with a slight whine at the end.

Deidra sighed. "This is not a game, Paris. You have a great

husband. Unless there's something you haven't told your father and I?" Deidra primped her mouth and waited.

"No, he's really a good man. It's just I'm so stressed these days. You know what I told you is going on with me. What if Andrew gets tired of waiting? What if he decides I can't give him what he wants and he decides to move on elsewhere?"

"Well, you coming over here and hiding out like this is not going to help the situation," Lawrence said. "And your mother is absolutely right about playing games. A marriage should be built on *t-r-u* squared: truth and trust. If you don't have those as a foundation, your house is built on sinking sand and will not stand when the storms of life come smashing through."

Paris nodded. "Okay. I'll call Andrew and tell him to come pick me up." Her voice was resigned.

"Good," Lawrence said. "And tell Andrew he and I need to talk as soon as he gets a moment."

"Dad, I don't need you getting into my personal affairs," Paris said.

"Who said it has anything to do with you or your personal business?" Lawrence said.

"Nobody."

"All right, then. Andrew and I have other things we talk about other than you. I was planning on calling him, but since you're here, you can deliver the message for me." Lawrence went over to the couch and pulled Deidra up. He put his arm around her waist. "For now, your mother and I have a date we need to finish. Set the security alarm on your way out and be sure to lock my door."

"Daddy!" Paris said with a pretend huff.

" 'Daddy' nothing! I promised your mother a night she wouldn't soon forget. And nothing and *nobody* is going to keep me from making good on that promise." He kissed Deidra, who was now clearly blushing.

Deidra gave Paris a hug before Lawrence pulled her away completely. "Call me tomorrow!" Deidra yelled as Lawrence whisked her out of the den. "Or better yet, I may be sleeping in, so I'll call you!"

Chapter 18

And the Lord answered the angel that talked with me with good words and comfortable words.
—Zechariah 1:13

Jessica had gone into the hospital room by herself. She instructed Gabrielle and Zachary to wait outside the door until she came back for them. Gabrielle looked up and said a silent prayer. This was the last thing she ever expected to happen. In a matter of mere minutes, she would be walking through that door and seeing the child she'd given birth to. It was hard to put into words what she was feeling right about now.

Zachary put his arm around her and gave her a quick hug. "Are you all right?"

Gabrielle nodded.

"Are you sure you want to do this now?"

She nodded again. How was she going to open her mouth to the little girl lying in there without crying when she could barely talk to Zachary without breaking down? But she had to hold it together. She had to. This was not about her; it was about a little girl, in a hospital room, who had been through a lot already. And whatever Gabrielle could do to help her through this, she was going to do it. *Lord, please give me strength to do what I need to do. Help me to be a blessing to both Jessica and Jasmine, in Jesus's name I pray. Amen.*

The door opened. Jessica smiled and nodded. "Come on in."

Three words: Come on in. Gabrielle stood frozen. She couldn't believe those three words would cause her to become so paralyzed. Zachary still had his arm around her waist. He helped her take that first step.

And there she lay. Gabrielle released a quiet controlled sigh. Zachary pulled her toward him one more time, then released her fully. She was on her own now.

Gabrielle put a big smile on her face. "Hi there," she said, her attention fully locked on a little girl who, although noticeably frail, remarkably possessed features she'd found in the few pictures she had left of her mother. Seeing this little person who favored her mother was almost too much for her. She hadn't expected this. She merely thought she'd see a little girl who held no reminders in particular, but would be a beautiful child, nonetheless. And she *was* beautiful. Even in a hospital bed with an IV hooked up to her and machines monitoring her, she was a beautiful child.

Then she heard the small, sweet voice. "Hi," Jasmine said. "How are you?"

Gabrielle gathered everything within her and pushed out the biggest smile she could find. "I'm just fine, thank you for asking. But I hear you're not feeling so hot."

"Oh, I'll be okay. I'm going to get better soon. Isn't that right, Mama?" Jasmine said, now looking at Jessica.

Jessica smiled, leaned down, and lovingly placed a kiss on Jasmine's forehead. "That's right, baby. That's right. Soon. You're going to be better real soon. We just have to keep believing. Good thoughts so we can have a good report. That's what my friend Gabrielle here told me just recently."

Zachary took a step forward. "Hi there, Jasmine."

"Hi there, sir," Jasmine's little voice said.

"Jasmine, these are the friends I was just telling you about. They wanted to come in and say hello."

"I know, Mama. That's Miss Gabrielle and Mr. Zachary." She acknowledged them with a smile.

Zachary walked over to the bed. He held out two fists crossed at his wrists, switching them with each syllable as he began to sing, "Alabama hit the hammer."

Both Jessica and Gabrielle opened their eyes wide and both let out a gasp. Gabrielle was surprised at hearing and seeing Zachary doing something like this.

Jasmine released the cutest little giggle. "You know that game?"

Zachary nodded. "So . . . Ala-bam-a, hit the ham-mer, high or low."

"If I pick the right one, I may go!" Jasmine said, taking over the song, then tapping Zachary's right fist that was crossed over to the left side.

Zachary opened his fist and presented an open hand to her.

"Yay," Jasmine said, clapping. "I picked the right one! Look, Mama! It's a piece of candy." She looked at her mother with pleading eyes. "Is it okay if I have it?" Jasmine's brown eyes almost seemed to twinkle as she smiled. "Please . . ."

"Well . . ." Jessica said with a smile as she looked to Zachary.

"It's okay," Zachary said it, first to Jessica, then to Jasmine. "You see, Miss Jazz, I just so *happen* to be a doctor."

Jasmine's face seemed to light up even more. "You are? For real?"

Zachary grinned. "Yes, I am. For real. I'm not exactly like the doctors that are taking care of you, but I'm a doctor, nonetheless. And I happen to know for a *fact* that it won't hurt you to have that one piece of hard candy. It's sugar free, but the neat thing about it is that it doesn't taste like it. Not at all. I used to give them to some of my favorite patients when I worked in the emergency room, and they loved them."

Jessica nodded her okay for Jasmine to have it.

Jasmine scooped up the piece of hard candy and hurried to untwist the clear wrapper. "Green is my favorite color," she said, carefully putting the piece in her mouth.

"Is that right?" Zachary said in a voice that sounded like it was created to speak to children her age. "If I'm not mistaken, I believe green is Gabrielle's favorite color, too. Isn't green your favorite color?" Zachary asked Gabrielle, who was still standing off to the side, out of the way, barely saying anything. He reached his hand out for Gabrielle to come closer.

Gabrielle smiled and moved next to Zachary. "As a matter of fact, green *is* my favorite color."

Jasmine suddenly burst into a laugh. "Dr. Zachary, let me see your other hand."

"What?" Zachary said, standing straighter.

"I said let me see your other hand."

"And why exactly do you want to see my other hand?"

"Okay," Jasmine said, her voice noticeably becoming weaker even though it was evident she was enjoying herself. "I tell you what. Hold your fists like you were doing before."

Zachary started laughing, but held his fists out as Jasmine instructed.

"Alabama hit the hammer, high or low. If you pick the right one, you may go." Jasmine looked at Gabrielle. "Miss Gabrielle, pick his left fist."

"Look at you," Zachary said, laughing. "You little cheat, you."

Jasmine giggled. She nodded at Gabrielle, who smiled and tapped Zachary's hand as her little friend instructed.

Zachary opened his left fist.

"I knew it!" Jasmine said. "I knew you rigged the game so I would win no matter which one I picked."

"So, not only are you a beautiful little girl, but you're smart, too."

Jasmine laughed, throwing her head back as much as her pillow would allow her.

Gabrielle stood lovingly looking at Jasmine, finding it hard to look away.

"That one's yours, Miss Gabrielle," Jasmine said.

Gabrielle took the piece of hard candy out of Zachary's hand. "Thank you, Miss Jasmine." She bowed slightly to Jasmine.

"You know, I think I like it," Jasmine said, her eyes trained on Zachary.

"What do you like? The candy?" Zachary asked.

"Yes, the candy, but that's not what I'm talking about."

"Then what is it that you like?" Jessica said, tears sliding down her face now.

"I like Dr. Zachary calling me Miss Jazz and I like Miss Gabrielle calling me Miss Jasmine. It's like our own little special system." Jasmine turned to her mother. "Sorry, Mama. You're just going to have to stick with Mama. I don't want to call you anything differently than what I've always called you. You're my mama."

"Baby, I wouldn't want you to call me anything other than mama, either."

Zachary put two fingers on Jasmine's wrist. "Miss Jazz, some folks call me Dr. Z. So if you want, instead of calling me Dr. Zachary, you could just call me Dr. Z."

Jasmine looked toward the ceiling as though she was thinking about his offer. "Let's see: Dr. Zachary . . . Dr. Z. Hmmm . . . Okay! I think I like Dr. Z."

"Great!" Zachary was still holding on to Jasmine's wrist in what seemed to be a medical thing. "Then Dr. Z it is," he said.

"This candy is really good," Jasmine said, sticking her tongue out with the green candy on the end of her tongue. "Thank you. It takes away the metal taste in my mouth. It's been so long since I've had anything good like this."

"Yeah, I know," Zachary said. "But having a treat every now and then is a good thing." Zachary released her wrist and gently patted her hand.

"Dr. Z?" Jasmine said.

"Yes, Miss Jazz."

"I wish you were my doctor. Not that the other doctors are bad or anything. But you're really nice. You have wonderful bedside manners."

Everybody laughed.

"Such a large repertoire you have. First the word 'system' and now 'bedside manners.' What do you know about bedside manners?" Zachary said.

Gabrielle smiled. "Yeah, Miss Jasmine. What do you know about that?"

"When you've been here as long and as much as I have, you learn this kind of stuff. Isn't that right, Mama?"

Jessica nodded. "That's right, baby. But you're also just a smart little girl."

"And brave, too," Gabrielle said. "I'm so in awe of you right now that I hardly know what to say."

"Is that why you're not saying much?" Jasmine asked.

"That and . . . I don't want to tire you out."

"I'm okay." Jasmine closed her eyes briefly. It was obvious she was getting tired since they'd come in.

"Well, they really do have to go," Jessica said. "So tell them thank you for coming by to see us."

"Thank you for coming to visit with me," Jasmine said, yawning. "Will you both come back again? Soon?"

Gabrielle looked to Jessica for the answer.

Jessica patted Jasmine's hand. "Yes, they will. I'm *certain* they'll be back."

"That's great," Jasmine said. "I'd really love that. I like both of you. You make being in here not be so bad. Hopefully, I'll get a donor soon, and I'll be *out of here*! Then maybe you can come and visit me at our house. We have a nice, *big* house." She flipped her hands outward in a large circle.

"I positively agree," Gabrielle said. "You'll get a donor soon. Well, we're going to go now. We'll see you later."

"Promise?" Jasmine said to Gabrielle.

Gabrielle nodded. "Cross my heart." She made a cross over her heart.

Zachary patted Jasmine's hand. "Before we go, Miss Gabrielle and I would like to pray for you. Would that be okay with you?" He looked at Jasmine, who smiled and nodded. He looked over at Jessica, whose hand was now covering her mouth and tears were in her eyes. She nodded her approval. Zachary took Jasmine's hand and prayed a short but moving prayer for her healing. "Amen," he said when he finished.

"Amen," both Gabrielle and Jessica said quietly.

"A-men!" Jasmine said louder than any of them.

Zachary laughed and patted her hand again. "See you later, Miss Jazz."

Jasmine giggled. "See you later, Dr. Z." She held her two fists crossed, up in the air. "Alabama hit the hammer, high or low. If you pick the right one, you may go."

"What?" Zachary said.

"Pick," Jasmine said, continuing to hold crossed fists up.

He tapped the left one.

"Nope," Jasmine said, opening the empty hand. "Try again."

Zachary laughed. "Try again? You only have two hands. You

know I'm going to pick the right one on my second try." He tapped her right fist.

Jasmine opened her hand. Zachary laughed, as did Gabrielle, then Jessica when they saw that in her hand was the empty candy wrapper.

Zachary took the paper and put it in the trash can. "Bye, Miss Jazz. We'll see you later."

"Bye," Gabrielle said, touching Jasmine's hand for the first time since she was a newborn, then quickly taking her hand away. She and Zachary headed for the door.

Jasmine waved at them. "Bye. Don't forget to come back to see me again soon . . . You promised." She closed her eyes. "You promised . . ."

Chapter 19

Make thee bald, and poll thee for thy delicate children; enlarge thy baldness as the eagle; for they are gone into captivity from thee.

—Micah 1:16

Zachary gathered Gabrielle by her shoulders after they stepped out of Jasmine's room. Gabrielle almost doubled over, but he held her up. "You okay?"

Gabrielle nodded. Zachary wrapped his arm around her shoulders and they made their way to the elevators. Gabrielle placed her hand over her mouth. She wasn't sure if she didn't clamp her mouth whether the loud cry she was holding in would escape. Zachary kept her close as they rode down. She stepped out of his arm when the elevator stopped and they got off.

Most of the way back to her house, she and Zachary were silent. Zachary had tried twice to strike up some form of talk, but must have quickly figured out that she wasn't in a place to talk right now. So he stopped trying.

"I'm okay," she finally said when Zachary parked his car in her driveway. "You don't need to come in."

Zachary turned off the engine, opened his door, and got out. Walking around to her side, he opened her car door and held out his hand. Gabrielle placed her hand in his and got out. Zachary held on to her hand as they walked to the front door of her house.

"Seriously," Gabrielle said as she took out her keys. "You don't have to stay. I'm fine. Really I am."

Zachary quietly took the keys from her trembling hand and opened the front door. Standing back, he allowed her to go in. Inside, she flipped on the light switch. He handed her back her keys, then closed the door.

"Thank you," she said barely above a whisper. "And thanks for going to the hospital with me." Gabrielle forced a smile, but couldn't sustain it as the corners of her mouth began to tremble.

Zachary looked at her with such loving kindness. He then pulled her into his arms and hugged her.

"I'm all right," she said, trying to break free from his secure embrace. "Really, I am." And before she knew anything or could stop herself, she was crying. "She's so sick," she said between her sobs. "Did you see how sick she is? She's not going to make it too much longer, not in that condition. But she's so beautiful in spite of how sick she is. My goodness, she's beautiful inside and out. And she's smart." Gabrielle cried even more. "Zachary, what am I going to do? Tell me: What do I do to help her? What?"

Zachary walked her to the den and eased her down onto the couch as they remained locked together. He simply held her as she cried. And after she calmed down, she touched the spot where her face had rested on him. "Look at your shirt. I got you all wet. There's a wet spot there now."

Zachary didn't even look down. He kept his eyes locked on hers. "It's okay. I have plenty of shirts." He touched Gabrielle's hair. "You are so beautiful. And caring. And smart."

Gabrielle primped her lips, then pressed them tight. "You were so wonderful with her tonight. I think she likes you."

"And I like her." He continued to pick up sections of Gabrielle's hair and let it fall, just to watch it fall it seemed.

"I'm not sure she likes me all that much," Gabrielle said. "I suppose I was more in shock than I knew I'd be. I couldn't believe I was standing there looking at a baby I actually carried for nine months, so grown up. Well, not grown up, but she's almost nine. And did you notice how tall she is already. If she keeps on at this pace, she's going to be tall enough to be a model. She's certainly beautiful enough—"

Zachary placed his finger on Gabrielle's lips and smiled. "You were fine, Gabrielle. She likes you. She does. I could tell that she does. It's just: I was the only male in the room, so there was no fear of competition to be had."

"Competition? What do you mean by that? There's no reason for competition. Jasmine doesn't have a clue who I am to her."

"Well, I happen to know that sometimes when women are around each other, there's a tiny bit of silent competition going on, whether they realize it or not."

Gabrielle shook her head and primped her mouth again. "Well, there's not."

"It's nothing bad. Okay, it's like this. Jasmine knew her mother was there. Then there you were, this beautiful woman she'd never met, walking into the room. Now, she wasn't consciously thinking about it in these terms, but *unconsciously* she was aware that if she gave you too much attention in a positive way, it *might* . . . keep in mind I said 'might,' have made her mother feel a little jealous."

"Oh, that's malarkey! The child is just eight years old. She's still innocent."

"Malarkey? Wow, that's a strong rebuke right there. I wasn't meaning anything by my statement except to say on an unconscious level, Jasmine didn't want her mother to think she was giving you more attention and love than her. That's all I'm saying here. She wasn't *consciously* thinking that."

Gabrielle turned her body more toward Zachary. "Oh, and the way you called her Miss Jazz . . . she loved it. That was so precious!"

Zachary reached his hands in his pockets, pulled his hands out as fists, and crossed them. "Alabama hit the hammer, high or low. If you pick the right one, you may go."

Gabrielle grinned, then tapped his right hand. He opened his hand and another green hard piece of candy was there. Gabrielle snatched it up, then quickly tapped his other fist.

"What?" Zachary said.

"Open that one," Gabrielle said with a grin.

"Why? You already picked the right one."

"Open it," she insisted.

He opened his left fist and began to laugh.

"You are such a cheater! Just like Jasmine said you were," Gabrielle said.

"No. Not a cheater. But I'm not beneath rigging the system a bit to put a smile on a beautiful face every now and then."

"That was so right tonight. How do you know that game?"

Zachary grinned. "Aunt Esther." He was referring to his aunt Esther Crowe.

"Miss Crowe taught you?" Just the thought of the woman who taught her to dance and showed her unconditional love when she felt all by herself, the woman she'd just only recently been reunited with, the woman she'd learned was aunt to the man she was now courting, brought a smile to Gabrielle's face.

Zachary chuckled a little. "Well, I don't know if I'd say she actually taught me. But she would have me and my other siblings sit on the steps and play that game with us. The first one to reach the top by picking the correct hand more times than the others was the winner. I guess you can say that even though it was a tame game that girls were likely to enjoy more than boys—"

Gabrielle hit him softly. "Zachary! That's sexist."

He laughed. "No, it's not. It's true. Boys like contact sports. Sitting on some steps with someone holding out two fists while singing a song, then telling you if you pick the right one you may go, is not exactly a true contact sport. But as I was *about* to say before I was so *rudely* interrupted: Even though it was a tame game, I enjoyed the principle behind it. If you choose right, you get to move up. If you choose wrong, you stay where you are until it's your turn again and you get to choose again. If you continue choosing correctly, you have a chance of winning in the end."

Gabrielle opened one of the candies she now held and put the green piece of hard candy in her mouth. She put the other one on the coffee table. "I saw you placing your hand on her wrist. You were checking her pulse, weren't you?"

Zachary nodded. "Yes. I was trying to see how she was doing.

Her pulse is weakening, that's for sure." He forced a smile. "I'm going to put in some calls tomorrow to see what I can do to help. We're not going down without a fight. And I'm also going to be tested to see if I might be a match for her. You never know until you try."

Tears welled up in Gabrielle's eyes.

"Now don't you start crying on me again. I'm not telling you this to have you crying on me. I just want you to know you're not in this alone. Jasmine's not in this alone. And whatever you need from me, I'm here for you, Gabrielle. Do you understand me? I'm not going anywhere I don't care how much you insist you're okay. And I'm not going to let you do this all by yourself. It's me and you, kid." Zachary said that last line like a line in a movie she couldn't recall.

She leaned over and lay inside of his open arm that rested on the top of the couch. He then wrapped both his arms around her and squeezed her even closer.

"You're really the greatest, do you know that?" Gabrielle said.

"I don't know about the greatest . . ." he teased. "But far be it from me to stop you when you're on a roll."

She popped her head up and looked at him.

"What?" he said. "What did I do?"

"I know what you can do to help me . . . to help Jasmine!"

"What? Name it and, if it's in my power to do it, it's done."

"Okay, but I need you to hear me out completely." Gabrielle readjusted her body better. "I've been trying to get back in contact with Lawrence. I haven't heard back from him. And even though it hasn't been long since I told him, we really don't have time to waste. Well, even now, his little snarky secretary keeps putting me off. I suppose Lawrence hasn't told her that I could bring him down or at least cause him some major problems if I want to. Anyway, when I call, she won't give me an appointment to see him, and even though I leave my name and number, I have a feeling she doesn't pass my messages along."

"Okay," Zachary said.

Gabrielle smiled. "So, what I was thinking is you could call and make an appointment. I bet she will schedule *you* to see him."

"Especially if I use the name Dr. Morgan and she thinks I'm interested in donating some big cash to his campaign."

Gabrielle's smile got even bigger. "You would do that for me and Jasmine?"

"Are you kidding? Woman, I would go sit in his office early in the morning and wait on him, for you."

Gabrielle leaned over and kissed him lightly on his lips.

Zachary began to nod as he looked into Gabrielle's eyes. "I would go down there early in the morning and sit there all day long if I have to, for you and Jasmine."

Gabrielle gave him another kiss on the lips.

"You know I would take a lunch with me and a sleeping bag and stay all night waiting for him, for y—"

"Okay, Zachary, I get it," Gabrielle said with a humongous grin. She kissed him again, but this time, it was a *real* kiss.

"I love you," he said. "I do."

"I know. And I love you," she said.

Chapter 20

Therefore the prudent shall keep silence in that time; for it is an evil time.

—Amos 5:13

Andrew looked up as his father-in-law made his way to the table at the restaurant.

Lawrence sat down. "Thank you for meeting me here."

"No problem. Although it's not often you take me out to eat."

"I needed somewhere we could go and talk without worrying about anybody listening in."

"And a public restaurant is the place you thought was best for that?" Andrew said with a chuckling laugh behind his words.

"This restaurant is the perfect place. I come here often when I want to discuss certain things and not be interrupted."

"So, I suppose you're upset about Paris and what happened with us the other night," Andrew said, leaning in slightly.

"Oh, I don't care about your and Paris's little tiffs. All married couples have them. But you know how Paris is. I tried to tell you that before you two got married. She's a bit 'high-maintenance,' as her mother likes to politely put it. I just call her a spoiled brat. But"—Lawrence held up his index finger—"she's *my* spoiled brat. And I don't want her mistreated or being deliberately hurt by *any*one in any way, and that includes by her husband."

Andrew nodded. "Well, I can assure you, I was at as much of

a loss for what was going on as you and Deidra were. I left to get us something to eat, and when I came back, she was gone. The car was still in the garage, but she was nowhere to be found. I phoned her friends; they all said they hadn't seen or talked to her in the past few hours. I called you and Deidra, but your phones went straight to voice mail, which with you, was a shocker, since you generally keep your cell phone on at all times."

Lawrence sat back against his cushioned seat. "That was mostly Deidra's doing. I wanted to give her a night out and her stipulation to go was that we had to turn off our phones completely."

"It was okay," Andrew said. "It was just, I did start to get worried after a few hours when I couldn't find her or anybody to tell me what was going on. I could just see *that* playing out on television. You know how the husband claims he went to do something and upon his return, his wife was missing. Then days roll by, and before you know anything, he's the main suspect or, as the authorities like to put it in the beginning, 'a person of interest' in her disappearance. There's no way I could have convinced anyone that I didn't have anything to do with Paris's disappearance had that turned out to be the case."

"Well, Deidra and I both stressed to Paris to not do anything crazy like that again."

"I appreciate that. I just hope she listens to you and her mother better than she listens to me."

A waiter came over to the table and took their orders.

Lawrence sat back in his seat. "Okay. Now what's this about you and some woman named Gabrielle Booker . . . Gabrielle Mercedes, whatever her name is, knowing each other prior to Paris introducing you the other day?"

Andrew laughed. It was a slightly nervous laugh. "Paris told you all that?"

Lawrence nodded. "She did." Lawrence steepled his fingers and leaned in. "So."

Andrew rocked his body a little before quickly stilling himself. "I'll tell you like I told your daughter: I don't know what she's talking about. It was like this: She and I go to the cafeteria to get something to eat because Paris hadn't cooked anything at home, so when we got to the hospital she was hungry. She wants to say we were going to get coffee for my friends, but that wasn't it at all. As soon as we walked into the cafeteria, she says she sees someone she thinks she knows and heads straight for this couple. Of course, I tag along behind her. It turns out the woman is someone she knows. Which I must confess was a relief to me, since Paris has been known to march me up and introduce me to an old boyfriend or two as though hearing that they were an item shouldn't bother me. Well, she and this woman used to be roommates or something once."

"I don't know if I'd call them true roommates," Lawrence said. "She gave this young woman a place to stay until she could get on her feet and find a place of her own after her folks apparently threw her out on the streets for no good reason and with nowhere else to go. It was a noble gesture on my daughter's part. And if I can be brutally honest here, a complete surprise to both me and her mother when she did it, since Paris has never been known for helping much of anybody out."

Andrew nodded. The waiter brought their food and began placing everything appropriately, momentarily putting a halt to their conversation.

Lawrence knew Andrew really couldn't argue with him on his assessment of Paris even if he disagreed, which Lawrence knew that he didn't. Andrew had apparently been struck by Paris's beauty and he couldn't see anything else lurking beneath. Lawrence had tried to tell Andrew that beauty was more than what could be found on the surface and that people should always dig deeper. Andrew told him he knew all that he needed to know when it came to Paris and that he loved her unconditionally.

Lawrence has never doubted Andrew's love for his daughter. They'd been together for eight years, married for seven. Lawrence knew that Andrew desperately wanted to have children. From what he could tell, Paris didn't until just recently. And Lawrence wasn't sure whether Paris really wanted children now or if she was saying that to string Andrew along. He knew his daughter. Manipulation and trickery were never beneath her.

"Thanks," Andrew said to the waiter when he finished.

"Can I get you anything else?" the waiter asked.

"Hot sauce," Andrew said. "I have to have my hot sauce with my chicken wings."

The waiter left and returned with a bottle of hot sauce.

"Anything else?" the waiter asked.

"We're good for now," Lawrence said, essentially dismissing the waiter.

"Thank you," Andrew said to him. The waiter then left.

Lawrence began to chuckle.

Andrew shook the bottle of hot sauce, then uncapped it and began shaking drops on his wings. "What's so funny?"

"I was just thinking of the stereotype you're helping to perpetrate. Got to have your chicken and, oh, yeah, by the way, my man, would you happen to have some hot sauce in the house."

Andrew didn't crack a smile. "I personally don't care what folks say *or* think about me. I like what I like, and if other folks don't like it, then it's *their* problem, not mine." Andrew sat up straighter. "Now, are you saying grace or am I?"

Lawrence smiled, then nodded. "Please. Be my guest."

Andrew bowed his head and said a quick prayer over their food. He then picked up a wing and began to devour it.

"So finish telling me about this woman . . . Gabrielle whatever her last name is."

"What's to tell?"

"My daughter believes you two know each other."

"Your daughter believes a lot of things. It never makes what she believes true."

"That's true. But you seem to be going to great lengths to give me lawyer responses to direct questions. So typical. Forever trying to be politically correct."

Andrew laughed. "You're the politician of the family. You're the one willing to sell out at any price if it will get you reelected. Now *that's* typical."

Lawrence leaned in and took a bite of his meatloaf. He chewed a few times, then swallowed. "I didn't ask you here to discuss me or my reelection efforts. I've heard and duly noted your objections to my reelection tactics. I know you completely disapprove of my switching over to the Republican Party. I know you don't like my pretending to embrace the Tea Party movement. But if this is what I have to do to be able to continue to serve the great folks of Alabama, then that's what I'm willing to do. If you can't find your way to vote for me, as you stated you wouldn't if I did this, then that's your right. But you know what they say: One monkey don't stop no show."

"Oh, so you're calling me a monkey now? You've been with the Republicans and the Tea Party all of two months, and you're already calling the black man a monkey."

"See, that's the problem with *you people.*" Lawrence grinned.

Andrew pretended to chuckle. "Oh, a good one: 'you people.' What's that? Racism One-oh-one. Now it's coming from my own, so I guess you can hide behind the fact that technically you can't be a racist against your own people. Yep. This is going to be an interesting election cycle for sure. And I am so not looking forward to it. I can already see the covert racial attacks. The dog-whistle sound bites that let those who think we don't know the whistle is being blown know that the hunt has begun."

Lawrence sat back and began to clap softly. "Lawyer One-oh-one mastered beautifully. Bravo, Counselor. Bravo."

Andrew wiped his hands on a napkin, then grabbed another one and began to wipe his mouth and his hands again. "What do you mean?"

"I know a diversion tactic when I see one. I didn't get this far in politics letting folks spit on me and tell me it's raining."

"Hey, I'm still eating over here. I can do without the visuals."

Lawrence nodded, then leaned in. "Now, I'd like a straight answer, if you don't mind. No more clowning around. Did you know Gabrielle Booker . . . Gabrielle Mercedes prior to my daughter introducing you at the hospital cafeteria the other day?"

Andrew's phone started playing a tune. Without even looking to see who it was, Andrew said, "That's your daughter calling me. Now, if I don't answer it, I'm sure she'll be coming to you to tell you something else that she knows *nothing* about. Like right now for instance, when she tells it, she'll be saying she called me and I didn't pick up because I was out with some woman, most likely, and I didn't want to interrupt our time together to answer my phone."

"Answer your phone," Lawrence said. "We have time. We're not going anywhere for a while." Lawrence continued to eat while Andrew talked to Paris.

Andrew placed his phone back in the holder on his belt.

"Is everything okay?" Lawrence asked when Andrew didn't say anything more.

"As you likely heard from my end of the conversation, I told her where I was and with whom. She wants me to bring her some takeout from here."

"Making sure you're really here, eh?" Lawrence said with a chuckle and a grin.

"I don't know. I just don't understand Paris. I've tried to give her everything her heart desires, but it still doesn't seem to be enough. It's like there's this big hole there and no matter what I do, I can't fill it."

"Well, I wouldn't stress myself out about it. That's just women for you. If you can figure out how to make them feel special enough days out of the week, and pretend you're listening when they talk, you have ninety percent of the battle won. The other ten percent, I guess you just have to give to God." Lawrence took a swallow of his soda.

Andrew nodded as he began looking around. "I guess I should order Paris's takeout so it will be ready by the time I'm ready to leave. She asked me to drop it off at the house before I go back to work." He shook his head.

"Yeah. And I just remembered: I have an appointment my secretary said I didn't need to be late for. It sounds promising. Mattie thinks he could be a big-money donor with the potential to bring in some others from his field."

Andrew got the waiter's attention, and he made his way over to their table. After Andrew gave him his takeout order, he turned back to Lawrence. "I know you think I'm trying to dodge your question about Paris's old acquaintance, ex-roommate, whatever you and she want to call her. But I'm going to say this to you even though I didn't say it to Paris. I'm really tired of defending myself every time she gets the notion that I'm looking at some woman we pass by on the street, accusing me of either wanting them or knowing them. It's gotten old. I respect you, Lawrence. But honestly, this is between me and my wife. And if you *really* want to go there, Paris thinks you and Gabrielle may have had eyes for each other. So, would you care to tell me about that?"

Lawrence almost choked on the meatloaf he'd just placed in his mouth. He quickly grabbed his soda and began taking swallows to try to clear his passageway.

"Are you okay?"

Lawrence nodded quickly, throwing up his hand to let Andrew know he didn't need him beating on his back. "I'm fine. I'm fine," he said.

After Andrew saw that Lawrence was really okay, he said, "I guess hearing that didn't go down too well with you, either. Now you know how I feel. You can ask me if I knew Gabrielle prior to seeing her in that hospital cafeteria. And I can ask you what the real deal was between you and your daughter's then eighteen-year-old roommate. You see how this could go if we fall into Paris's little world?"

Lawrence absolutely knew how this could go. He would say that Paris had quite an imagination and a flare for the dramatic. And Andrew would agree that his assessment is correct.

But still, Lawrence couldn't help but wonder if Andrew was keeping something from both him and his daughter when it came to Gabrielle. Was it possible the child Gabrielle claimed to have been pregnant with and didn't abort but instead gave up for adoption might possibly even be Andrew's? He was grasping now, he knew that. But it was still something to consider. He would get William and his people to see what they might be able to find out.

Discreetly, of course. After all, he didn't want to do anything that might upset his daughter's apple cart. Talk about drama—he didn't even want to think about that.

Chapter 21

That strengtheneth the spoiled against the strong,
so that the spoiled shall come against the fortress.
—Amos 5:9

"You got back in great time," Mattie said as Lawrence strolled back into the office.

Lawrence smiled as he stopped by her desk to pick up his messages. "Did you have doubts?"

She smiled coyly. "How long have I worked with you?"

"Mattie, is that supposed to be some kind of a trick question? You've been with me since day one."

Mattie nodded one time in a matter-of-fact way. "Sho' you right." Mattie pronounced the word "sure" as though she was saying "show," but only when she was alone with Lawrence. It was her way of acknowledging her roots, having grown up in the country, raised by a grandmother who didn't always speak perfect English, but whose heart was made of pure gold. A grandmother who would say "sho' 'nuff" when she wanted you to know that she was *more* than sure. Lawrence loved that about Mattie; how she could still easily transition between the two worlds. Mattie handed him his messages. "And don't you forget it. I'm one person you know will always have your back."

Lawrence quickly scanned through the five messages. "Sho' you right," he said with a laugh. "Well, you know where I'll be if you need me." He went into his office and closed the door.

* * *

Mattie was typing when the man first cleared the doorway. She couldn't help but grin. He was a nice tall "drink of water," as her grandmother would have said. Refreshing and *more* than pleasant on the eyes. *He'd better be glad I'm in my fifties and not a cougar like my friend Janice,* she thought. *Or I might give this twenty-year-old something a run for his money. Sho' you right!*

Mattie continued to smile. "Hi there. May I help you?"

He smiled back. "Why, yes. I'm here to see Representative Simmons. I have an appointment."

Mattie pretended to look at her appointment book even though she knew exactly who he was and what time he was scheduled. "You must be Dr. Morgan." She held out her hand for him to shake. Just as he was strolling toward her desk, her smile suddenly dropped.

Dr. Morgan shook her hand, but looked over his shoulder to see what had caused Mattie to go from a warm smile to a cold stare.

"I'm sorry," Mattie said, releasing Dr. Morgan's hand quicker than she had originally intended. "Can I help you?" she said to the woman who had come in.

The woman smiled. "Oh, I'm good," she said as she sat down as though the office belonged to her.

Dr. Morgan went and sat in the seat next to her. Mattie figured this woman had that kind of an effect on most men she came in contact with. Of course men would fawn all over her. Seeing them sitting next to each other, she could see the two of them being attracted. But she was going to fix this real quick.

"I'm sorry," Mattie said to the woman. "But the representative will not be able to see you today. He's quite busy and quite booked. When you called earlier, I told you as much. I'm pretty sure that was you I spoke with. I remember you and your voice from before. Your name is Gabrielle, isn't it?"

Gabrielle nodded with a smile and an assurance. "Did you happen to even tell Lawrence that I called?"

That really irked Mattie. The level of disrespect this woman was showing by calling Representative Simmons by his first name totally disrespected the office he held. Then attempting to make her look bad in front of this possible donor. Mattie figured this woman was merely trying to rattle her. But Mattie had tangoed with the best of them. She knew how to take off her heels, and she kept a jar of Vaseline in her top drawer, mostly to use when she was ashy or needed to moisten her lips. But if she had to grease down her knuckles and fight, she remembered how to do that as well.

No, Mattie, she said to herself as she stood and took steps toward Gabrielle. *Lawrence has told you that you can't be going alley on folks. Keep your cool. Handle your business in the professional way. Don't do anything to run this donor away.*

"Ma'am, I'm quite efficient at what I do," Mattie said. "But I'm sure you know that *Representative* Simmons is an immensely busy man. Now, I'll be glad to make an appointment for you. But I can already tell you that he's booked until at least the end of next week. And even with an appointment, you never know what emergency may pop up and cause the appointment to be canceled or rescheduled."

Mattie smiled. She knew Dr. Morgan had to be feeling quite special right about now. He'd called yesterday and had gotten an instant appointment for today. Mattie was sure that would possibly earn Lawrence some extra points with him. Powerful people love to feel they've been treated as such. He crossed his leg, locked his fingers in place around his crossed knee, and lifted his chin up even higher. *Yes, he was making a note of all of this, and she was* definitely *making an impression.*

Gabrielle leaned back comfortably. "It's okay. I don't mind waiting."

"Okay," Mattie said with a forced smile. "Suit yourself."

Mattie glanced at the clock on the wall and walked back around to her desk. She then buzzed Representative Simmons. "Your one thirty is here." She smiled at Dr. Morgan. "He's ready to see you."

Dr. Morgan stood up. Gabrielle Mercedes stood up as well. Mattie's smile grew bigger. *Thank You, Lord. She's going to leave. Because Lord, You* know *I didn't want to have to sit out here with her. Thank You, Jesus!*

Dr. Morgan walked toward the office door. Gabrielle was

right there with him. It dawned on Mattie that this little sneaky woman was trying to muscle her way in ahead of Dr. Morgan. *Oh, she's a slick one! But she doesn't know who she's messing with. I don't play that!*

Mattie quickly stepped out from behind her desk and before Gabrielle. "I'm sorry, but I was speaking to this gentleman here." She smiled at Dr. Morgan.

"Oh, I know," Gabrielle said.

"So, you can't go in there." Mattie positioned her body right in front of Gabrielle. She was prepared to physically stop her if she had to.

"Excuse me," Dr. Morgan said, his deep voice almost causing her to suck in air too fast for her body to process.

"I apologize for this. But this woman—"

"Is with me," Dr. Morgan said.

Mattie's upper body jerked back. "Excuse me?"

Dr. Morgan smiled, grabbed Gabrielle by her hand, and said, "This woman . . . she's with me. We're together." He pulled Gabrielle gently along with him as he opened the door.

As soon as the door closed, Mattie regained her composure and hurried back to her desk. She picked up the phone and pressed a button. "I need you to get in here. Now!" she said. "We have a slight problem!"

Chapter 22

Can a bird fall in a snare upon the earth, where no gin is for him? Shall one take up a snare from the earth, and have taken nothing at all?

—Amos 3:5

Lawrence was already standing when the donor Mattie had been so excited about walked in. He had his ready-to-receive-a-large-donation face on, but his smile quickly fell when his eyes fell upon Gabrielle.

Zachary marched up to his desk with his right hand extended. "Representative Simmons. Nice to meet you. I'm Dr. Morgan. Thank you for agreeing to see me."

Lawrence shook Zachary's hand firmly enough, although he continued to keep an eye on the woman with Zachary. "Dr. Morgan. Nice to meet you. What can I do for you?"

Zachary looked at the chairs positioned in front of the representative's desk. "Mind if we have a seat?"

"Oh, of course! Please, please, sit down, sit down." He glanced at Gabrielle, who wasn't smiling at all. "Both of you . . . sit."

Zachary waited until Gabrielle was seated, then he sat down.

"Gabrielle, how are you?" Lawrence said, trying to regain his obvious loss of footing.

She nodded without saying a word.

"So," Lawrence said, directing his attention to Zachary. "You're a doctor. Are you here on official doctor business? Something you need to talk to me about that has to do with legislation? Interested in donating to my campaign?" His chuckle with the last question was quite manufactured.

Zachary leaned in. "Look. I know you're a busy man. Your secretary all but made that much clear a few minutes ago when she told Gabrielle you were too busy to see her until possibly the end of next week. Funny thing though. Gabrielle has been calling to talk to you long before I picked up the phone yesterday and requested to see you. I seemed to have had no problem in getting on your schedule. So let's not play games, if you don't mind. What do you say?" Zachary sat back straight.

Lawrence chuckled a bit as he slowly leaned back into his black leather chair. "I can already tell we're going to get along splendidly," he said to Zachary. "But in Mattie's defense, let me assure you that she meant no harm in not letting me know of you trying to get in touch with me, Gabrielle." The last sentence was totally directed at Gabrielle.

"Then we all have an understanding here?" Zachary said.

Gabrielle glanced over at Zachary, then Lawrence.

Lawrence leaned in toward Zachary. "So, why are you here?"

"I suppose the question you really want to ask is: How much do I know?" Zachary said.

The door to Lawrence's office suddenly swung open without a knock or anything preceding. "Excuse me, sir. But I really need to speak with you. It's important," William said, taking strides toward Lawrence's desk, his long legs closing the distance in no time.

Lawrence held up his hand. "It's okay, William."

"Excuse me? But this really is—"

"It's okay. I got this. And whatever you have that's important, I'm sure it can wait until this meeting is over. In fact, I don't think we're going to be *too* much longer," Lawrence said, looking at Zachary as though he were expecting him to confirm that statement.

"But, sir, I have something I think you should see *before* you continue." William held out a red folder. Lawrence took it and glanced over it quickly, then nodded as he set the folder down on his desk. "Thanks. You may go now."

"Excuse me, but did you read it?" William's eyes darted from Lawrence to the two sitting across from Lawrence.

Lawrence nodded again. "I did, and I said: You may go." His voice was a bit more forceful this time.

After William left, closing the door behind him, Lawrence swiveled his chair a little. "Would you mind if I speak with Gabrielle alone?" Lawrence said.

"Oh, so *now* you're willing to talk to her. But when she was calling before, you and your office were blowing her off."

"Dr. Morgan . . ." Lawrence stopped a second. "Is it okay if I call you Zachary?"

Zachary hadn't given any of them his first name, not even when he'd made the appointment. He'd only said Dr. Morgan. "Zachary is fine. But just so you know: This is not about me. I'm here with Gabrielle. And as far as me leaving while the two of you talk, we can skip all that. Gabrielle and I are in this together. There's a sweet little girl who is not going to live much longer if she doesn't get the bone marrow transplant she *desperately* needs. This little girl doesn't have time for grown folks to be playing silly little games."

Gabrielle placed her hand over her mouth. Zachary glanced over at her. His words had come out harder than he'd meant, but he had to get Lawrence to see how dire the situation was.

"So, I guess you know more than I thought you did," Lawrence said. He looked at Gabrielle. "You told him everything? I'm talking about everything?"

"Yes," Gabrielle said. "So whatever he just brought you on me to try and get me to shut up, it really doesn't matter. You see, Lawrence, that's the thing about the truth and telling it: No matter what comes up, you've already handled it with the truth."

"So you're telling me that Dr. Morgan here knows all about your past? Every single detail of it?"

"I'm telling you that I haven't deliberately kept anything from him," Gabrielle said. "Now, is there something I didn't think to volunteer that may look like I'm trying to hide something? If you have something and it's true, I promise you that I won't be denying it. Not if it will help save this little girl's life," Gabrielle said.

Lawrence put his hand up to his mouth as he picked up the red folder. "So, you're saying that Zachary here knows all about your father? How your father killed your mother and tried to blame it on someone else? That he's in prison right now."

"Yes," Gabrielle said.

"And he knows all about your wonderfully conniving fraudulent aunt? It appears she's in a bit of trouble herself right now. Theft, huh?" Lawrence directed that question to Gabrielle. "Looks like dear Aunt Cee-Cee might be getting payback for all the hateful things she did to you, Gabrielle. Forging documents, stealing money that should have gone to your dancing education. Allegedly, I should say. Allegedly. Umph. Some colorful folks in your life, Gabrielle."

Gabrielle and Zachary just sat there, not commenting.

"You know, Gabrielle. I remember how good you were and just how much you loved to dance," Lawrence said. "For certain you could have used that money and the experience you would have gained from attending Juilliard. Now *that* was the real tragedy of all your aunt's *alleged* actions. Instead, you ended up at my daughter's place, kicked out and onto the streets by the very person who stole from you."

"Listen, I didn't come here for you to stroll down memory lane," Gabrielle said.

"I'm sorry. I was just thinking about how much you liked to dance, Gabrielle. And how, if these other things hadn't happened that obviously got you off track, you might have become a celebrated dancer instead of . . . a celebrated stripper."

Zachary rose to his feet.

"I'm sorry," Lawrence said, standing to his feet as well. "Don't tell me you didn't know she used to take off her clothes in a strip joint for other men for money?" He looked down at Gabrielle. "You didn't tell the good doctor about Goodness and Mercy? Gabrielle, do you have any idea how much the knowledge of something like that could hurt someone like Dr. Zachary Morgan, if that was to get out in a big way?"

"Let me tell you what I do know," Zachary said. "I know she might have done that in her past, but after giving her life to Jesus, her past is gone, pardoned, and her slate wiped clean. Gabrielle may have been Goodness and Mercy once upon a time, but because of Jesus and what Jesus did, she's now on the *other* side of goodness. She knows what it is to have her past cast into the sea of forgetfulness when it comes to our Lord and Savior Jesus Christ. It's just devils like you who are always trying to resurrect the past to throw it in folk's faces. But it's not going to happen. Not here; not today."

"I'm taking it that she didn't tell you about that part of her life and you're trying to cover it by directing your anger at me," Lawrence said with a smirk.

"Oh, she told me. She told me about that part of her life. And she told me all about the real you, and not those phony ads that promote you as Mr. Happily Married to the same woman for the past twenty-nine years who you've never cheated on, faithful deacon of your church for the past twenty years, loving father of three, man of integrity, who is pro-life and staunchly against abortion," Zachary said as he stood squarely staring at Lawrence. "Only thing about your lies about yourself is that Gabrielle can bust that entire narrative you've been heavily pushing to the voters with just one truth."

"Is that right? And what truth might that be?"

Gabrielle stood and looked into Lawrence's eyes. "That you're the father of an eight-year-old little girl who is going to die if she doesn't get a bone marrow transplant soon."

Lawrence laughed. "And that's supposed to prove I'm not who I say I am? Something from the word of a woman who most would consider one step above being a hooker?"

Zachary balled his hand into a fist. Gabrielle grabbed his hand and held it in hers. "Let him say whatever he wants," Gabrielle said. "I know the truth, and deep down, so does he. He knows this child is his."

"I know no such thing." Lawrence picked up the red folder. "According to this, it appears you and my son-in-law knew each other around that same time. That's just one person my people have located." Lawrence looked at Zachary, who was apparently not aware of that piece of information. "Oh, she didn't tell you the other day when she and Andrew ran into each other at the hospital cafeteria that the two of them already knew each other?" Lawrence smiled.

Zachary tried to hold it together. Gabrielle had indeed not told him that.

"So what are you doing? Having my entire life investigated?" Gabrielle said, looking from Lawrence to Zachary. "Is it so important to you not to help this child that you'll do anything?"

"I told you. I don't have anything against that child. But she's not mine."

"Be tested and see," Gabrielle said, her voice escalating. "I'm not asking you to acknowledge her as yours. All I'm asking is for you to have the initial test done to see if there's a possibility you could be a match. If you're so sure that you didn't father her, what harm would it do for you to go and let them put a cotton swab in your mouth to get what they need to see if it's possible you might be a match at all."

"And I can tell you as a doctor, you could still be the child's birth parent and not be a good match."

"Yeah. Gabrielle told me that the first time we talked." Lawrence sat down.

Gabrielle eased down in her chair and leaned in toward him. She was wiping away a few tears now. "I told you. I'm not trying to hurt you or your family *or* your career, for that matter. Truthfully, I'd prefer no one find out about *any* of this. But I saw her the other day, Lawrence. I got to meet her for the first time since I gave her up. And she is so beautiful. She's smart. And she has your eyes and your high cheekbones. But in truth, she also looks like my mother."

Gabrielle looked in her purse and pulled out an old photo of her mother and handed it to him. He refused to take the photo and look at it. She put it back. "I can't sit back and just let this child die. I can't. You might not have wanted her and I was in no position to take care of her. All I could do for her was to give her up for adoption. But she's here, Lawrence. And she's a child you and I made together."

Zachary sat down, obviously a bit more composed now. "If this was any of your other three children—"

"Not other." Lawrence interrupted him. "Nothing has been established that proves this child is mine."

"Fine," Zachary said. "If this was any of your three children, what would you do? Wouldn't you do everything possible to save their lives if it was within your powers to do so? Wouldn't you? Wouldn't you move heaven and earth to find someone to help one of them if you felt someone out there might be a match and they could possibly save your child?"

Lawrence sat up more stoically. "I empathize about this situation. I truly do. But there are lots of problems out there; I can't help affect them all." Lawrence looked at Zachary. "Now let me ask *you* something."

"Go ahead."

"Would you risk your career for this situation?" Lawrence said.

"I'm sorry. I'm not quite following you," Zachary said.

Lawrence looked at Gabrielle as he spoke. "When Gabrielle and I spoke that other time, she indicated, or one might say *threatened*, to use the information about me and her to get me to do what she wanted."

"I didn't actually threaten you," Gabrielle said. "I was just letting you know that this was important and that I'd do whatever was needed to help save her life."

"You say toma-toe; I say to-mato," Lawrence said. "I don't like being threatened or *made* to do what others say I have to. If you're the child's birth mother and you don't match, what makes you think I would be a match, even if I was the birth father? What I'm afraid of is that you'll try and pull my children into this—"

"With all due respect," Zachary said. "Siblings are much better at being a match than even a parent is most of the time."

"That may very well be," Lawrence said. "And if this was one of the three children my wife and I had produced, there might be more of a case for that being true. But let's just hypothetically say that this child is mine, hypothetically now. My other children have the DNA of me and my wife. We would all actually be going through a bunch of trouble for nothing because the likelihood of any of them matching with a child I supposedly had with this woman here"—he used his head to point to Gabrielle—"would be no better than another set of strangers possibly matching. You would be tearing up my family for nothing."

"May I make a suggestion," Gabrielle said. "The only people who know anything about this at this point are me, you, and Zachary."

"And William," Lawrence said. "William knows."

"Okay, then," Gabrielle said. "Me, you, Zachary, and William. Why don't you use this issue as part of your reelection campaign platform?"

Lawrence leaned in closer. "I'm not following. What do you mean?"

"I mean you say that you're pro-life. Why does pro-life only seem to mean protecting the unborn child? Why is pro-life not about life *after* a child is born? Think of the good you'd do if your platform somehow brought awareness to those in need of donor-type help . . ." Gabrielle stopped to compose herself. "Black people aren't so great when it comes to being donors. If you were to take the initiative on something like bone marrow transplant, you could help bring more awareness to the forefront. At the same time of leading in this, you could show how lives can be saved, if it turns out you or one of your children is a match and becomes a donor."

"I just don't know about my children being involved. And let's just say one of them turns out to be a match. I would never force them to do something like this, not if they didn't want to do it on their own."

"If one of them turned out to be a match," Zachary said, "at worst, their part would only require them to have a special needle draw marrow from their hip bone. Here lately, they've developed a way to do it like taking blood, separating the cells needed and pumping the blood back into the donor. And since the donor's part is an outpatient procedure, there's no real recovery time required. The body replenishes the extracted morrow cells very quickly."

"Still, what you're proposing," Lawrence said to both Gabrielle and Zachary, "might be something to consider as a possible win for all. But I'd have to think about it a bit longer. I'm not quite sold on the part that if I'm not a match, I'd need to involve my children. That's the part causing me pause and concern. Also feeling as though I'm being blackmailed into doing this doesn't sit well with me either."

"I'm not blackmailing you," Gabrielle said. "I'm merely fighting for a child who didn't ask to come here and who appears to have been dealt a bad hand. I'm praying for her healing but doing what I can to help. I don't match, so I'm on step two of the process of what comes after that. And that just happens to involve you."

"Well, if God were to heal her, it would certainly save all of us a lot of heartache and trouble," Lawrence said. "I wouldn't have to be weighing my options right now. And you, Dr. Morgan, wouldn't have to be wondering what tangled webs you may have gotten yourself into."

Zachary stood, reached down, and took Gabrielle by the hand, helping her to her feet. Gazing lovingly into Gabrielle's eyes, he said, "I don't have to ever worry about what I've gotten myself into. I'm just thankful to God that I'm here. And I can assure you: I'm going to do all that I can, in any way that I can." He turned back to Lawrence. "I'm confident God will take care of this little girl, He'll take care of Gabrielle, and He'll take care of me as we go through whatever we may find ourselves facing."

Lawrence stood to his feet. "Well, I will pray about my next move."

Gabrielle picked up her purse and took out a card. "Here's the info you need to schedule the test to see if you're even a possible candidate to be a match. If you'll provide them with that access code, it will let them know you desire to be tested for that particular recipient and *only* that one."

Lawrence took the card and gazed down at it before looking at Gabrielle. "This is good, because I'm *seriously* not trying to be a donor for anybody else I might end up being a possible match to." He laid the card down on his desk.

"Oh, and since I have such a hard time getting past Ms. Stevens when I call to talk to you, will you—"

"I will inform Mattie to put you through if I'm available. And if I'm not, I promise to call you back as soon as it's convenient. But I'd like to put this to rest, once and for all, to take this completely off the table. So I'm going to go get tested. And should the results return stating that I'm not even *remotely* close to being a possible match, then let's all agree to leave this and be done with it. Agreed?" Lawrence presented his hand to Gabrielle to shake in agreement.

Gabrielle looked at his open hand, then shook it. "Agreed," she said.

He held out his hand to Zachary next. As Zachary shook it, Lawrence grabbed him by the elbow with his other hand, giving it a nice strong pump. *A power move,* Zachary thought as he smiled. *Okay, so . . . he's trying to prove he's the more powerful between me and him.* Zachary nodded.

Chapter 23

I did know thee in the wilderness, in the land of great drought.

—Hosea 13:5

William was in Lawrence's office before his two visitors were out good. He practically slammed the door. "What was *that* all about?"

Lawrence had his chair turned as he stared out of the window. He turned around slowly.

"And why did you send me out of here? You know I would have gotten the two of them out of here quickly and with minimal damage," William said, sitting down.

Lawrence rocked his chair back and forth.

"Will you say something?" William said.

"It's okay. I think I handled things all right. You know I'm quite capable of watching my own back. I was doing it long before we met."

"Yeah. Back when neither of us had a pot nor a window to throw anything out of."

"Must you always go there?" Lawrence said.

"Well, at least I cleaned the quote up. But you know I'm speaking the truth. You and I were out there wandering in the wilderness. Times were tough. We were eating dust from drought," William said. "You'd met Deidra and she was more accustomed to the finer things in life."

"Yeah," Lawrence said. "And still, I won her over."

"You with your good little church boy act. Quoting scriptures and having folks saying that you had a calling on your life. You have a certain charm, that's for sure. And your charm is definitely an asset in politics. But some of the messes, which come as a result of fallout, can be hard to mop up."

Lawrence opened the red folder. "I'm more interested right now in this tidbit of information you just dug up about my son-in-law. So it appears Paris was right. Andrew *did* know Gabrielle prior to the other day."

"It looks that way. Not that there's anything listed saying that they dated or anything. But there was definitely something that went on."

Lawrence closed the folder. "Well, all of this is starting to get out of hand. I was just with Andrew and he pretty much lied to my face."

William laughed. "That's funny coming from you."

"I don't lie. What I do is called massaging the truth."

"Yeah. Some form of truth is generally in there somewhere. It's just a matter of finding where and getting your hands on it. But on another note: Your little girlie friend that just left appears to be a problem we really don't need. Mattie told me that was Dr. Morgan with her. So I suppose our plan to expose her past to him in order to get her to back down is out of the window now?"

Lawrence nodded. "He knows everything. Except that one bit of news I sprung on him about her knowing Andrew. Apparently Gabrielle totally forgot to mention that to him even after running into Andrew the other day. Maybe the two of them are not as tight as they'd like me to believe. I have to give it to him though; he's standing with her on this. I don't know if she's *that* good or if he just really cares about that child in need of that transplant."

"Speaking of which," William said. "As I'm sure you saw in the folder, there really *is* a child, and she really *is* in need of a bone marrow transplant. Whether the child was fathered by you or not, without a blood test or DNA to confirm it, I honestly can't say." William reared back on his chair's hind legs and smiled as he looked at Lawrence.

"If your question is: Was I there at one point in time and is there any possibility, then the answer is yes. But that admission is strictly to remain between me and you."

"Man, you know I'm not going to say anything. I've kept all your *other* secrets all of these years."

"As I have yours, in case you'd like to believe you're some saint without sin and can freely cast the first stone." Lawrence's face was stern.

"Hey, that's what blood brothers do. That's what being a blood brother is all about. And you and I are brothers to the end. We've come too far to mess up now. So"—William clapped his hand—"what are our plans for the present mess we find ourselves in? In addition to, of course, that Rev. Walker fiasco that I believe we may be able to get out of easier than even *we* first thought. Greed is such an ugly animal. Someone should have informed Marshall Walker of that, a long time ago. So, I think we can cross Rev. Walker off the *done* list. And now that we've run into this information on Andrew, he just *might* help us more than he was originally willing to do if we need it." William beamed with pride. "Conflict of interest, my foot!"

"Andrew is *still* family now. Whatever negatively affects Andrew, affects my daughter. And whatever affects Paris—"

"Affects the whole entire world," William said. "Especially since Paris thinks the whole world revolves around her."

"Precisely. If Paris is affected, then her mother will most certainly get involved. Then I'll be left to have to act like I care and that I'm doing all I can to fix it. I don't want to even start down that road. Not with everything else that's going on and most likely will be still going on if this bone marrow donor situation breaks the wrong way. Leave my son-in-law to me. You just remain focused on getting me reelected or we'll *both* find ourselves looking for a job."

"Right," William said. "And what about Miss Goodness and Mercy . . . Gabrielle Mercedes?"

"William, I know you'd love nothing more than to put her in her place. But I must say: She offered a pretty compelling solution to this whole mess should we need to go there. I didn't dare let on too much to either of them today, but I believe her idea could be just what this campaign needs to give me that air of caring boost that those focus groups you paid all that money to claimed I lacked and needed to strengthen my reelection bid."

"Okay," William said. "I'm all ears."

Lawrence recapped what Gabrielle had said about a bone marrow donor awareness campaign where he and his family would appear to be leading the charge.

"So let me see if I've gotten this straight," William said. "You want us to pretend we're taking this on, highlighting awareness for folks to consider becoming donors in some form or another, highlighting the plight of those especially in need of bone marrow transplants. You'll parade your family out to the public to prove just how serious and how much you truly are behind this rhetoric."

William made several approving facial expressions. "Admirable. But what happens if, let's say, you or one of your children turn out to be a match? Then what? Can you seriously convince your family to go along with something like this? Being a donor for most folks is no joke. Black folks don't even want to hear about it, let alone possibly offer themselves up. And I don't mean to beat a dead horse to death, but I'm sure Paris will be the first to give you attitude about doing anything like this."

"I've thought about that. But we're basically planning to highlight only one person to bring home the point. We're not putting ourselves out there to be a donor for just anybody in need. Think of all the publicity we'll generate doing something like this. We make a big show about the initial test required, complete with the cotton swab inside the cheeks. Again, using this one person as the one we're trying to help. When it comes back that none of us are even *possible* candidates for any further matching testing, then it's done . . . it's over. My candidacy profile is raised considerably. Me and my family appear to truly care about others. And this child's plight has gained exposure she otherwise wouldn't have received, possibly finding her a *real* donor."

"Okay. I get that part. But *if* there's another person that one of you matches and you refuse to help, how will it look if you balk at going further for *that* person?"

"That's why I'm expecting you to have this all crafted to protect us from anything remotely like that happening. Again, we'll emphasize our main goal is to shine the light on help for this young child, which will absolutely be true. And just imagine the residual publicity that will occur if a match is found from someone who was encouraged to be tested through our campaign drive."

William nodded. "Yeah. This could really give you a boost in the polls. It will definitely get you tons of publicity that we *absolutely* can use to get more of the word out about your political agenda. I have to admit, Lawrence: This really could turn out to be a win-win for everybody."

Lawrence leaned back in his chair as he gazed up at the ceiling. "It would definitely be a win-win for *all* concerned."

"The real win will be you getting your family on board with this."

Lawrence sat back straight and faced William. "You handle your part and leave my family to me."

William stood up to leave. "I'll get right on it."

"Oh, and William?"

William stopped. "Yeah?"

"Do your magic or whatever it is you do, and get Mattie to start putting Gabrielle's calls through to me if she calls in the future. I don't need Gabrielle riled at this point. If we play this right, she won't be bothering us too much longer, especially after this is all over."

William chuckled. "Man, you know you have more influence over Mattie than I do."

"Yeah, but when something like this comes from you, she knows we're not playing and there's no room for her creative implementation of the order."

"I suppose what you're *really* doing, in your slick way, is letting *me* know that I need to cooperate better with Gabrielle as well. That's what you're really doing right now." William nodded. "I don't know why you're trying to play me."

"I just don't need any more trouble coming from Gabrielle. If we play our cards right, I'll do this little swab test, get the word out about the plight of this child, who I'm sure is a sweet child regardless of *who* her father really is, and in just a few weeks . . . tops, all of this goes away. Poof! A mere distant memory of what was."

"Yeah. A blip on the radar, then we're on to our *next* exciting opportunity that awaits us with open arms."

"Oh, and William? One more thing."

"Yeah?"

"I want you to participate in the swab test phase along with us. And get as many on our staff and working on my campaign as possible to sign up as well."

"Me? You want *me* to do it? How did I get involved in this?" William said. "I didn't sleep with her."

"We're a team, remember? And we want people, including my family, to believe this is a team effort. If we're going to do this and not draw attention or scrutiny, then we all need to put some skin in the game. Or as will be in this case: a little saliva on a piece of cotton."

"And I suppose it goes without saying that we're on a short timetable for all of this to take place?"

"Yeah. I'm going to go get tested tomorrow so I can see where I stand," Lawrence said. "I'm going to do it through their anonymous system first."

"You know, if it turns out that you're a good candidate for a match, then maybe none of us will need to do it at all. What say before I begin to move on this, we wait on your results to come back first? If you end up being a match, then I'd recommend we adjust this strategy completely."

Lawrence looked up at the ceiling again. "You know . . . that's probably the best plan. Because if I *am* a match, we'd really need to keep this as hushed as possible," Lawrence said.

"Yeah. And if you're a match and end up qualifying as a donor for her, we could easily manufacture a business trip for you while you have the procedure done and the time you need to recuperate."

Lawrence nodded. "Good looking out. But if they say I'm not

even a potential candidate to proceed any further and we need to involve my children to satisfy Gabrielle and keep her quiet with what she knows, then we'll enact Operation Become a Possible Donor."

"Hey, I like that: Operation Become a Possible Donor." William walked to the door and opened it. "I like that." He closed the door as he left.

Lawrence retrieved the card Gabrielle had given him with the special number connected to the child in need of the bone marrow transplant, picked up the phone, and made an appointment. He then called Andrew and told him he needed to see him again, sooner rather than later.

It was on now.

Chapter 24

Gather yourselves together, yea, gather together, O nation not desired.

—Zephaniah 2:1

"Thank you," Gabrielle said after she and Zachary stepped into the foyer of her house.

"No problem," Zachary said.

Gabrielle turned to him. "I know you want to know."

Zachary smiled slightly. "Know what?"

"Look, Zachary, I saw how you reacted when you heard that I knew Andrew."

Zachary took Gabrielle by her hand and led her into the den. He sat down, pulling her down alongside him. "All right. Let's get this out of the way once and for all."

Gabrielle looked toward the ceiling.

Zachary touched her chin. "It's not like that."

She lowered her head and looked at him. "You're telling me that you're not upset? Seriously? After all that tall talking you did making Lawrence believe we harbored no secrets between us, and then you get blindsided with that information."

"Listen, Gabrielle, you and I are just getting to know each other. We don't know everything about each other yet. In fact, even if we were married, I'm sure there would be things we still wouldn't know," Zachary said.

"But the thing is, Zachary, this was something that just took place. I should have told you that I knew Andrew right after it happened."

Zachary took her hand and placed his fingers in between hers. "And when might you have done that? Come on, think about it. Your friend Paris—"

"Paris is not my friend."

Zachary nodded. "Okay. Paris and her husband came over to us, and her husband never let on that he knew you."

"If you knew Paris the way I do, you'd understand why."

"Then help me understand. What kind of a person is she?"

"She's selfish and quite possessive." Gabrielle turned her body squarely toward Zachary. "It's like this: Paris had a boyfriend. When I stayed at her place for that short time, he came over a few times. She thought her boyfriend and I were trying to hook up behind her back."

"Is that why she put you out?"

"I don't know why she put me out. That could have been why. I wasn't quite sure what set her off. I'd gone to pick up a few things from the grocery store and when I returned, she was blowing a gasket, yelling and screaming that I had to get out. I asked her what had happened to get her so upset. She never really told me. Just kept saying that I knew what I'd done. To be honest, I thought she'd found out about me and her father. He'd just learned that I was pregnant a few days earlier, and he definitely hadn't been happy about the revelation. He was telling me I had to get rid of it and I had to do it right then. He gave me money to have the abortion. Said he would help me in whatever way I would need to get on my feet after I got rid of the baby. Then a few days later, here comes his daughter giving me a few hours to get all of my stuff and leave. What was I to do? I had nowhere to go. But I got my stuff and started walking."

"Wow," Zachary said. "It breaks my heart to hear this. I can only *imagine* what it must have been like for you."

Gabrielle stood up while hugging herself. She began to walk toward the window.

Zachary stood and went to her. He grabbed her by the arms that were still hugging her. "I'm not upset about anything, do you hear me? I just want to do whatever I can to help you now."

"Yeah, but you were standing up for me. And you got hit with something that I could have told you myself . . . I should have told you myself."

"Okay, so would you like to tell me *now* about you and this guy Andrew . . . Drew, whatever his name is?"

"It's Andrew Holyfield. And, yes, we did know each other. He was Paris's boyfriend's friend at the time."

Zachary laughed. "That's a mouthful."

"Yeah."

"Okay. But if her boyfriend and Andrew were friends, why would she not know that you two had met prior to her introducing you the other day?"

Gabrielle walked back over to the couch and sat down. Zachary followed and did the same. "She didn't know I had met him. It was before the two of them even met, most likely. You see there was this time that Cedric, that was Paris's boyfriend, brought Andrew over to the apartment with him while I was there. Paris had already left for the club she liked going to. I'm not sure about the details; I don't know if the real deal was that Cedric didn't own a car or that his car only ran half the time, because Paris seemed to be the one having to always pick him up. I'm not sure what happened this time around; she didn't exactly ever confide in me. She must have been mad with him, so he got Andrew to bring him over. When he saw me, he must have thought it would be a neat idea if the four of us hung out or something. Who knows?"

Gabrielle crossed her legs at the ankles. "I later learned from Drew that Cedric hadn't presented that idea to Paris before deciding to do it. Paris called him on his cell phone while we were on our way to the club. When he mentioned the idea of me and his friend, the four of us, hooking up at the club, she reportedly had a fit. Apparently, Paris hadn't made it clear to Cedric that I wasn't a friend or much of anything in her eyes. All I did was kept the place clean and cooked in exchange for somewhere to stay. That was it. I was not someone she cared to be seen out in public with—ever."

Zachary pulled Gabrielle into his arms. "Wow. Paris sounds like she was a real piece of work back then."

"Oh, it was fine. I knew she and I weren't really friends or anything like that. But when you have nowhere else to go, you do what you have to do to survive. I was just thankful she was kind enough to let me stay with her. But what she told Cedric about me was misleading. I gave her money for half the rent. The rest that I did was pretty much what I'd been doing pretty much all of my teenage life: cooking and cleaning up after other folks who sat around like they were kings and queens." Gabrielle flicked a tear from the left side of her face.

"So Paris didn't know you'd met Andrew?"

Gabrielle shook her head. "No. Cedric wasn't going to tell her then that he'd just been to the apartment and convinced me to come with them. Not after Paris let him know that I was neither welcomed nor worthy to be in her presence outside of the apartment. So Drew dropped Cedric off at the nightclub and brought me back to the apartment. Drew and I talked for a little while. He's really a very caring guy. I suppose he thought I'd been treated badly and he was trying to make it up to me. About a month later, everything pretty much went south for me, and then crossed the border."

Zachary squeezed Gabrielle tight. "You know I have a lot of questions swirling around in my head after hearing all of this."

"Yeah." Gabrielle broke from his embrace. "So here I was being thrown out on the streets for the second time in three months with nowhere to live. I had money in my purse for an abortion, from the father of my baby, with strict instructions to get rid of the baby, and the knowledge that he wanted nothing to do with any child of mine. So I'm walking down the street pulling two large suitcases behind me, trying to decide where to go while I figure out where to go, when this car pulls up alongside me." Gabrielle looked toward the ceiling and smiled before looking at Zachary. "It was Andrew Holyfield."

"Great timing."

Gabrielle let out a short laugh. "Yeah. That's what I thought when he rolled down the passenger-side window and asked if I needed a ride somewhere. But since I'd met him only that one time, I really didn't know him well enough to be sure I could trust him. I wrestled with whether I should get in the car with him or not."

"That was smart. At least you stopped to consider the possibilities of what could happen."

"Yeah, but I was pregnant, walking down the street, with nowhere to go, and no way to get there." Gabrielle looked at Zachary so she could better gauge his reactions to everything she was saying. "I did decide to get in, which really could have turned out badly, but thank God, it didn't. Andrew asked me where to. And that's when I lost it and broke down completely, right there in his old Chevy."

Zachary gathered her back into his arms.

Gabrielle pulled away again. She didn't want him holding her while she told him the rest of the story. "He didn't know what to do; he wasn't that kind of guy."

"But still he took you to his place," Zachary said resigned.

Gabrielle smiled. "Oh, yeah. He took me home to his place." She let out a short laugh.

Zachary nodded. "It's okay. I understand."

Gabrielle touched Zachary's arm softly with her hand. "No . . . you *don't* understand. Andrew lived at home with his mother. He was working and attending college, studying to be a lawyer. His mother was such a sweet woman. And she was a Christian who didn't play that 'playing house' stuff. But she welcomed me into her home with open arms after Drew told her exactly what was going on."

"Did he know you were pregnant? Did you tell him about the baby?"

Gabrielle shook her head. "No. That was something I've pretty much kept from everybody all of these years . . . everybody, that is, except for you. Oh, and Johnnie Mae Landris. Andrew only knew that I had nowhere to live. He knew about my aunt and how she'd shown me the door the day after I graduated from high school. And he knew Paris had just put me out."

Gabrielle stood again and cupped her neck with both hands before sitting back down. "I didn't know what to do next. I knew I couldn't stay with them for long. I would be showing soon. I had no job anymore, no home, and a baby I was determined I wasn't going to abort. I had no one to turn to for answers. So for the first time in my life, I looked toward the sky, and I said, 'God, please help me. I don't know what to do.' I didn't know it then, but God absolutely heard me and He answered my prayer."

Zachary smiled at Gabrielle, then nodded.

"By some divine intervention, I saw a promo on television about a home for unwed mothers who didn't want to get an abortion. It was advertised as a caring place. So I took down the number and called. I visited them and decided to go there."

"And you told no one."

"Who did I have to tell? I was there with Drew and his mother for ten days, not enough time for them to figure out I was pregnant. I told her I had found somewhere to stay. She asked me to let her know once I was settled."

"So did you?"

"I called when I arrived at the home to let her know I was okay. After giving birth to the baby, I called once more just to say hello. That was the last time I spoke with either her *or* Andrew."

"So there's no way Jasmine might be Drew's? I mean, if there's even a *remote* possibility, then you should let him know so he can be tested to see if *he's* a potential match."

"Paris would have a fit if she even *thought* that Drew and I hooked up, especially now that they're married." Gabrielle laughed. "She never knew he'd come to her apartment. I certainly never told her, and I'm pretty sure Cedric never said a word."

"Wait a minute. You *did* say that Drew was her boyfriend's friend. I wonder how the two of them hooked up and ended up married."

Gabrielle shrugged. "Beats me. But if I know Paris, when she met Andrew, she decided that Andrew was a better catch than Cedric and merely dumped him like two-week-old spoiled milk. Andrew had goals; Cedric seemed content in merely hanging out and having fun off of other people's money. Whatever happened that brought them together as a couple, I guess Andrew never mentioned anything about having known me to Paris, which is fine by me."

Zachary's pager went off. He pulled it out and looked at it. "I have to go. There's a badly burned patient en route to the hospital." He stood up.

Gabrielle hated when Zachary's pager went off like that because usually he had to leave quickly. She also knew this was a part of his world, thus a part of hers now. She'd once asked Zachary why they all continued to use pagers in a world of high-tech phones and gadgets. He'd said that pagers were still more reliable than cell phones. In certain places, like even the basement of a hospital, you might not be able to receive a signal from a cell phone, but pagers still worked. As a burn specialist, every second counted.

Because Zachary had to leave so quickly, she didn't get to answer whether or not she'd ever slept with Drew. Whether it was the night he'd been so caring and brought her back home after she'd been dismissed by Paris (which would make it possible that Jasmine could be his child) or during those few days she'd stayed at his home.

She'd made a promise to herself to be totally honest with Zachary about everything, no matter how difficult the truth might be. She refused to harbor secrets between them.

So the next time they talked, she would need to give him an answer. She never again wanted him to be blindsided like he'd been today.

Not if she could help it.

Chapter 25

And, behold, a woman of Canaan came out of the same coasts, and cried unto him, saying, Have mercy on me, O Lord, thou son of David; my daughter is grievously vexed with a devil.

—Matthew 15:22

Gabrielle walked into her office at the church. She'd missed some normally scheduled time at work from those times she'd tried catching up with Lawrence. This last time of lost time, she and Zachary had gone together. She finally felt she may have made some headway in getting Lawrence to at least *see* if he could be a possible match for Jasmine's bone marrow transplant. She fully planned to make up for the lost time. So she was more than concerned when she read the note, front and center on her desk, from Pastor Landris requesting to see her in his office as soon as she received the message.

Nervous now, she didn't even put her purse away as she quickly made her way to his office. Someone was already in there, but his secretary said he wouldn't be *too* much longer and told Gabrielle to have a seat. Apparently, he'd given instructions for Gabrielle to wait, should he be busy when she came to his office. This sober realization caused Gabrielle's stomach to *really* turn somersaults. She certainly didn't want to lose her job, not here . . . and especially not *this* one. Sitting there, she began to replay in her mind what she'd done and how she'd done it to be sure she'd kept in line with the terms of her employment as the director of the dance ministry.

The person in Pastor Landris's office came out twenty minutes later. Pastor Landris's secretary must have electronically sent him a message telling him Gabrielle was out there since Pastor Landris also appeared in the doorway and said, "Gabrielle, please come in."

Gabrielle's hands were clammy now. Her heart was beating fast. She forced a smile as she stood up and walked into his office.

"Please, have a seat," Pastor Landris said in his usual welcoming voice. The man she'd been surprised to learn once sported dreadlocks, even as a pastor, now wore his hair cropped low to his head. His moustache was always perfectly trimmed.

Gabrielle sat down. She didn't know what to say since he'd been the one to request this meeting, and she wasn't exactly sure why. She waited for him and, even though it was only seconds, it felt like it was taking him an eternity to say anything.

"So, Gabrielle, how are you?"

Gabrielle knew he hadn't called her into his office merely to find out how she was doing. Pastor Landris was too busy of a man for that. Everybody pretty much wanted him to counsel them when they had a problem, even though it was continuously emphasized that others were on staff capable of doing it just as well as he. As director over the dance ministry, she was experiencing only a *taste* of what he had to be dealing with, and she couldn't even *begin* to imagine how he did it all.

"I'm okay, Pastor Landris. How are you and the family... Johnnie Mae and the children?" Gabrielle hadn't done more than to wave at Johnnie Mae, Pastor Landris's wife, in passing in the past weeks. The last time she'd been close enough to have a conversation with Johnnie Mae was at the one hundredth birthday celebration of Ransom Purdue, her friend Clarence Walker's grandfather, when Clarence asked her to dance to a song he sang.

Johnnie Mae had come to her after she finished dancing and hugged her, telling her how powerful and anointed that dance had been. Gabrielle broke down in Johnnie Mae's arms, wanting so much to just stay there until all of her hurt had melted away. No one had a clue she'd just learned she wasn't a match as a donor for Jasmine. And that what she would have to do next was *not* going to be easy.

"I'm fine and Johnnie Mae is doing well, as are Princess Rose and Isaiah. I'll tell her you asked about her," Pastor Landris said right before locking his fingers together and leaning forward. "I suppose you're wondering why I asked you here."

Gabrielle swallowed hard, then tried to smile. "The question *has* presented itself a few times in the last twenty-five minutes."

Pastor Landris freed his fingers and sat back in his high-backed chair. "You've come up in my spirit quite a few times, in the past week in particular. I wanted to ask you what's going on. I've been praying for you, but God prompted me that I needed to talk to you face-to-face. So, tell me, Gabrielle, what's going on?"

Gabrielle began to cry. She was crying because she hadn't said anything to anyone about this, other than to Zachary. And here was God Almighty, her Heavenly Father, in His supernatural and loving way, relaying to her spiritual father here on earth that she was having problems. *What a mighty and loving God!*

Pastor Landris yanked tissues from the box on his desk and, leaning forward, handed them to her. She took them and dabbed her eyes as she tried to pull herself together. What she loved about Pastor Landris was how, at this moment, he wasn't pressing her while she cried. He allowed her to pull herself together at her own pace.

"I'm sorry, Pastor Landris," Gabrielle said, dabbing her eyes with a now soggy ball of tissue.

Pastor Landris pulled out more tissues and handed them to her. "It's quite all right. When you're ready, if you want, you can tell me what's going on with you."

"I know I've missed some of the time I had scheduled to be here working in the office."

"Oh, I wouldn't know anything about that. However you set your office hours and schedule is on you, just as long as you're not cheating the church out of the time you agreed to. So that's not why I asked you here at all. I just felt there was something going on, and whatever it is, I want you to know that I'm here to listen *and* to help, if possible."

Gabrielle groaned slightly. "I'm not sure how much you'd be able to help with this. But there is *definitely* something going on. I don't know if what I'm doing is the right thing to be doing or not." Gabrielle reached over and pulled several tissues from the box he'd pushed toward her, and wiped her tears before patting her face dry.

Pastor Landris smiled. "Do you need any water or something to drink?"

"Water would be good."

Pastor Landris got up and went to a small refrigerator in his office. Returning with a bottle of water, he handed it to her and sat back down.

Gabrielle twisted the cap off the bottle of water and took a few sips before replacing the cap. "I know whatever I say to you will remain between us." Gabrielle said it as a statement. But the way it came out, it could very well have been a question.

"Whatever you say here won't go any further than us," Pastor Landris said. "I won't share or divulge anything you don't give me permission to share. You have my word."

Gabrielle nodded. "There's a little girl. She's eight years old, nine on March thirtieth, in need of a bone marrow transplant. And if she doesn't get a match soon, and I'm talking about possibly weeks now, she'll likely die." Gabrielle began to cry again.

"It's all right. Take your time; I'm in no huge hurry," Pastor Landris said.

"I was tested to see if I was a possible match, but I'm not. She can't die, Pastor Landris. She just can't."

"I'm sure they're going to find a match for her. But this sounds rather personal. So what are you *not* telling me?"

"It *is* personal." Gabrielle swallowed hard. If she was going to do this, she needed to go on and tell him everything. There was no reason to have God care enough to lay on Pastor Landris's heart to talk to her, and she hold back. "Pastor Landris, the reason this is *so* personal for me . . . the reason I'm so emotional right now, is that eight-year-old little girl . . . the little girl in need of a bone marrow transplant . . . she's my biological daughter."

Pastor Landris didn't act like hearing that was a shock to him, although Gabrielle was sure it had to have taken him by surprise. Had to. Unless, of course, God had *already* revealed *everything* to him. "She's your biological daughter?"

Gabrielle nodded. "Yes. I know you must be trying to figure this out since you didn't know I had a daughter. Daughter may not be the best way to describe this. But you see: I gave up a child for adoption over eight years ago. Honestly, I wasn't expecting to even be having this conversation with *anyone* at this point in my life. I figured she may come looking for me after she turned eighteen, but not now . . . and especially not like this."

Pastor Landris stood up and walked around to where Gabrielle sat and sat in the chair next to her.

Gabrielle looked over at Pastor Landris. "She's sick, Pastor Landris. Really sick. Her adoptive mother sought me out, hoping I'd be a match. But I wasn't." Gabrielle wiped her eyes with her hands. "For the past few weeks, I've been trying to get in touch with the man who fathered her." She looked up and smiled. "Her name is Jasmine . . . the little girl's name . . . it's Jasmine." Gabrielle was calming down now.

Pastor Landris reached over and pulled out more tissues and handed them to her. "So have you met the child . . . have you gotten to meet Jasmine?"

Gabrielle shook her head, not actually saying no, but conveying her disbelief of everything that had taken place in the past few weeks. "In the beginning, I didn't. But we met her last week."

"We?"

"Yeah. Zachary and I. Zachary went with me to the hospital."

"So does Jasmine know everything? Does she know you're her birth mother?"

Gabrielle shook her head again. "No. She thinks I'm a friend of her mother's."

"So, have you been able to locate the birth father yet?"

Gabrielle nodded. "I did. And he denied the child could even possibly be his." She made a side to side motion with her head. "He thinks I'm trying to run a scam on him or something. At first he didn't even believe there really *was* a child."

"After close to nine years?" Pastor Landris shook his head in disbelief.

"I admit that some of his doubts are my fault, and founded,"

Gabrielle said. "He never knew I gave birth to her. He thought I aborted her. Unlike me, he had no reason to ever expect a child to possibly someday come in search of him. He didn't know I'd had the baby and given her up for adoption."

"Well, if you ask me, I'd say he needs *real* prayer. He got you pregnant and, in all those months of you being pregnant, he never checked on you? If he had, he would have known you didn't have the abortion."

"That part is a long story, but suffice it to say that after he learned I was pregnant and gave me money to get rid of the baby, as far as he was concerned, that's what had taken place. Also, he was married with a family of three children."

Pastor Landris nodded. "I see."

"But things are different now. Now, it's a matter of life and death. Jasmine is barely holding on. She doesn't have time for us to waste or to play games. And I'm not sure, in spite of all I've said to him, if he really will go see whether he's a possible match or not."

"Well, I'll tell you what we can do here at the church. We can let the congregation know a child is in need of a . . . bone marrow donor, is it?"

Gabrielle nodded as tears flowed. She picked up a used tissue from her lap and dabbed her eyes again.

"We can let the people here know that a little girl is in need of a bone marrow donor and encourage folks to see if someone might be a match." He tilted his head.

Gabrielle wasn't expecting this. "You would really do that?"

"Of course. No one needs to be privy to the particulars behind *why* we're doing it. It can just be something our church takes on to do what we can to help."

Gabrielle began to really cry. Pastor Landris allowed her to put her head on his shoulder. When she'd gotten her tears under control, she looked at him. "Thank you *so* much for this. I don't know what to say."

"You just get me the information needed to put this into play, and we'll get right on it. You said there's not much time, so the sooner—"

"Absolutely!" Gabrielle nodded excitedly. "I have all the info needed in my purse here." She gathered the used tissues from her lap, stuck them in her purse, retrieved the information, and handed it to him. "Folks can even do this anonymously, if they want. There's a special code assigned exclusively for Jasmine, so people don't even need her name." Gabrielle covered her mouth with her hand, then took it down. "God is so awesome! Oh, my goodness! I'm just in awe of His goodness and mercy!"

Pastor Landris stood up and walked back to his side of his desk, laying down the information she'd just given him. "We haven't found a match just yet, but we'll definitely be praying that God moves mightily in this situation. I'll be praying, as well, that the birth father will step up and do the right thing. Is he still married?"

"Yes . . . to the same woman. They have three children, and the doctors say that a sibling has a higher chance of being a match than even the parents," Gabrielle said. "So while we're praying, can we also pray that if he ends up having to, that he figures out how to bring his children in to be tested. Pastor Landris, I'm not trying to hurt Jasmine's birth father *or* his family, nor am I trying to take him down in any way. I'm not. I'm not trying to mess up his career or his standing in the community. That's not my intentions at all."

Pastor Landris smiled. "He sounds to be a powerful figure . . . someone of prominence and importance."

"He is."

"Well, let the Holy Spirit lead you on how to handle him. Men of power and influence can be ruthless if they feel threatened in the least. Trust me on this from personal experience. And according to how powerful and influential this man is—"

"He is quite both." Gabrielle was debating whether she should tell Pastor Landris everything, including Lawrence's name. "Pastor Landris?"

"Yes?"

"What should I do if this man refuses to do whatever he can to help?"

"Is the man *that* cold and evil?"

"Evil is a pretty strong word. But I believe he can be ruthless if he has to be. And I don't think he would hesitate for a minute to destroy anyone who might get in the way of his ambitions, including me and a little girl who desperately needs him right now." Gabrielle dabbed her eyes. "So as not to speak *totally* ill of him, let's just say that he's on the *other* side of goodness, and we'll leave it at that."

"Would you care to tell me who this man is?" Pastor Landris scrunched his face into a frown. "You don't have to now, but if you want to or even *need* to . . ."

"I *want* to tell you. But for now, I think it best that I keep his name to myself."

Pastor Landris nodded. "Okay. But if you should change your mind, know that I'm here for you. Let me ask you this though: Does anyone else besides you know who he is?"

Gabrielle twisted her face. "Are you concerned that he might actually do something to physically harm me?"

Pastor Landris shrugged. "Who can ever say what another will do to protect what one thinks is important to him or her. I'm not saying that he will or won't. But you never know for sure about folks these days. And a man with power and influence is one I wouldn't turn my back on when I walk away from him. Don't misunderstand me. I'm not saying that God won't protect us no matter who might try to harm us. But God also gives us common sense He expects us to use." Pastor Landris sat down.

Gabrielle considered his words. "To answer your question about anyone else knowing his name besides me, Zachary does. He knows pretty much everything."

Pastor Landris smiled. "Brother Zachary. I see you and he are yet going strong."

Gabrielle blushed. "He is *so* wonderful."

"Do you love him?"

"Pastor!"

Pastor Landris laughed a deep, jolly, baritone laugh that made one think of Santa Claus. "Now you *know* I don't play around here. So, are you two in love?"

"Yes. I'd say we are."

"And you're both keeping yourselves holy?"

Gabrielle became totally serious. "Oh, yes, sir. Absolutely!"

"All right, then." Pastor Landris grinned. "You two can let me know when we need to start premarital counseling. You know Johnnie Mae will insist that she and I handle the two of you ourselves. My wife is crazy about you."

Gabrielle couldn't help but to smile. Johnnie Mae had been like a mother to her since she'd become a member of the church and started dancing there. "I love her as well. You both have been there for me in ways I only wish other folks could know. Not many have a pastor and wife in their lives like the both of you. You're not on some power trip. It's not about money and prestige. You *really* care about God, and you *really* care about us—Jesus's lambs and sheep."

"That's because I know who all of you *ultimately* belong to, and that is Jesus—the Good Shepherd. I'm merely an undershepherd. Jesus told Peter if he loved Him to feed His lamb . . . feed His sheep. I love God, and I'm going to be sure I take care of, as well as feed, His sheep." Pastor Landris glanced down at his watch. "I suppose my next appointment has been waiting long enough."

Gabrielle stood up. "I'm so thankful God laid my name on your heart. I have wanted to talk to you so badly, but I just know how busy you are." She threw the balled-up, spent tissues left into the trash can on the side of his desk.

"Well, no matter what the secretaries around here do to keep me on a tightly held schedule, God will definitely rearrange things to fit in what He desires. That's exactly what God did today. If you need to talk some more, you just let me know."

"Thank you. And I promise I'll try not to bother you if I can at all help it."

"Gabrielle, you're a daughter here. And children *always* have privileges that others don't. You're not a bother; you're part of this family . . . a part of the body of Christ . . . a supplying joint. And believe me: You're nothing like some folks who try to take up all my time, for taking-up sake."

"I assure you: If I need to talk with you about anything more dealing with this, I'll be judicious with your time. Pastor Landris, I appreciate you so much." Gabrielle headed for the door. "Now back to work. I have a lot of catching up to do."

Gabrielle closed the door behind her and breathed a sigh of relief. *God, You are so awesome! Thank You.* She did a skip and a hop, smiling as she went along.

On that night, Gabrielle finished up the conversation with Zachary concerning Andrew.

No, there was *no* chance that Andrew Holyfield was Jasmine's father. No way at all.

Chapter 26

But he answered and said, It is not meet to take the children's bread, and to cast it to dogs.

—Matthew 15:26

Lawrence met with Andrew. He confronted him with the information he'd learned about him indeed having known Gabrielle Booker, now Gabrielle Mercedes, prior to his daughter introducing them, just as Paris had accused. Lawrence asked him point-blank whether or not he and Gabrielle had ever slept together. Andrew told him that whatever he and Gabrielle may or may not have done, and when they may or may not have done it, was neither his business nor his concern. Lawrence made it clear that whatever affected his daughter, indeed, was both his business *and* his concern.

Lawrence's battle plan was to get tested, and when he learned he was not even remotely a possible candidate for the next step, he'd confront Andrew for him to be tested. That would most likely cause Andrew to tell the truth about his relationship with Gabrielle. Lawrence *was* tested and told he was indeed a "remarkably great candidate" to be a possible match as a bone marrow donor for the coded number he was applying to be tested for. Whether he would be a good match with his bone marrow matching the recipient was another matter completely. The woman he spoke with had used those words. But he'd heard the real meaning between what she may or may not have realized she was confirming: that he *was* the father of this child.

His emotions were all over the place now. He wasn't sure

how he felt about the revelation. He had another child out there. A child he'd never seen before. A little girl. A little girl that would die if she didn't get the donor she needed. He hadn't realized just how much this meant to him until he found himself silently praying that he would be a donor match.

Of course, William would say he was only praying for this outcome because he was aware of the potential fallout and damage control that would need to be mounted on his behalf if his other children became involved. But for reasons he couldn't quite grasp with total clarity, there was more to this than self-preservation. There was a little girl out there, carrying parts of his DNA, and he didn't know her at all. And if they were unable to find a match for her, she very well might die.

But surely they'd find a match. If not now, then definitely soon . . . before she died. Wasn't that how it always worked?

Lawrence felt there had to be a way for him to be able to help this child and still keep everything else he cherished dearly and had worked hard to obtain in life. He and William had concocted a good backup plan in case he turned out to be a donor match. They would just have to implement that plan. He would reportedly "be out of town" for a few days, give the necessary bone marrow, recuperate, and get back to his normal life soon after. But if it turned out that he wasn't a donor match, they would then need to implement the other plan. He would have to. He couldn't take a chance that Gabrielle might go public. And he truly had no reason to believe she wouldn't.

William didn't believe she'd actually do it. He felt they could intimidate her with the fear of her possibly being charged with extortion of a government official. William believed he could convince her just how brutal messing with them might be for her. William's team was known for digging up embarrassing photos (framing whoever their target was at the time in a horrible light). Whether the photos were real or staged, only William and the people he hired to produce them knew the truth.

But Lawrence didn't want to take a chance with this one. Gabrielle had more going for her than the others they had threatened in the past to decimate. Gabrielle had shared an apartment with his daughter Paris. Sure, he could use as a defense that he'd been set up. But it definitely didn't bode well that Gabrielle was eighteen at the time this alleged setup would have occurred. In fact, he could end up looking like a child molester to some, and at best, a dirty older man who'd taken advantage of a teenage girl, to others.

No, the best route—he and William had come to agree upon if he wasn't a match—was to begin their much-discussed Operation Become a Possible Donor campaign.

And that's where they all were right now—in the midst of this possible bone marrow donor campaign. Of course, as predicted, Paris was giving him a fit about doing it, voicing what a ridiculous idea she thought it was.

"Why do I care about somebody in need of some bone marrow transplant?" Paris said at the family gathering Lawrence had called to discuss his latest endeavor.

Malachi laughed. "Leave it to Miss Compassionate over there to put voice to what she really thinks."

Paris rolled her eyes at her twenty-six-year-old chiseled brother. "It was not Miss *Compassionate*," she said, believing he was talking about her win in the last pageant she was ever in. "It was Miss *Congeniality*, Malachi Everett."

"Yeah," Malachi said with another round of laughter. "Right . . . right. How could I ever get those two things mixed up?" he teased.

"Because maybe you're not as smart as you want everybody to believe that you are, Mister Business Admin Grad Banker Exec," Paris said.

"That's enough, you two," Deidra said, looking at Paris first, then Malachi. "Paris, I think what your brother is trying to say is that what you just said is not a very compassionate thing to say."

"I'm merely saying what all of you are thinking, but too scared to say," Paris said. "I don't want to donate anything to anybody . . . ever. Least of all, donate anything from my body. I figure if God intended for us to have them, He would have given us spare parts when we were born."

"Oh, you mean like the two eyes, two ears, two arms, two legs we have? So we would have a spare if we needed it?" Malachi teased again. He stopped grinning when his mother shot him another look.

"Well, to be honest: I'm just wondering whose bright campaign idea this was." Deidra looked to her husband first, then over to William.

"Probably William's," Paris said. "It sounds like something he would come up with. He's always trying to devise some wild scheme to get Dad votes. He's the genius behind Daddy switching to the Republican Party. I suppose that's going over so horribly that they're scrambling to find a way to take the focus off of *that* stupid move. Because if he tried to switch back, he'd be branded a real flip-flopper."

Deidra looked at William, who was neither confirming nor denying anything. She turned to her husband. "This really *did* just seem to come out of nowhere. I mean, I've known you all these years, and you've never shown even the *least* bit of interest in anything *remotely* like this. You won't even donate blood. And now you want this entire family to subject ourselves to this in support of a bone marrow transplant? Is this someone that you or William happen to know? What? Help us all out here."

"Listen, we just wanted to bring attention to something that gets little attention, especially in the African American community." William drew all eyes his way. "I personally think it's a wonderful way to show compassion for our fellow man while serving the community and educating them on something few know about."

"In other words, we just found the mastermind behind this great idea," Paris said, folding her arms and sitting back hard against the couch where she sat next to her husband. "Well, I for one am not doing it! I'm not. So you can count me out of this family function this time around."

"Surprise, surprise!" Malachi said. "Paris doesn't want to do it."

"I wish you'd mind your own business, Malachi," Paris said. "Oh, wait! That's right; you don't have much business to mind these days since your *girlfriend* found out you had two other women on the side and dumped you."

"Paris, stop it!" Deidra said.

"Well, he started it," Paris said. "All I said is that I don't care to participate in Daddy's or William's or whomever the genius was that came up with this . . . lame plan. I have that right to decline, and I'm *fully* exercising my right! And anybody who doesn't like it can—"

"Paris!" Deidra gave her the look that said she was serious about her stopping, and she meant now.

Paris shrugged. "Fine. So Malachi's in. Who else?"

"Hold up," Malachi said. "Now I haven't said I was in."

Paris grinned and danced her head around a few times. Deidra looked at her sternly again and Paris stopped and sat still.

Lawrence covered his face with both hands. "Argh!" he yelled from between his fingers before taking his hands down. "Listen. I'm not asking anybody to be a donor. I'm merely asking us, as a family, to unite and show how truly caring we are when it comes to the plight of others."

"Yeah, but what happens if one of us turns out to be a match or something?" Malachi said. "Has anyone thought that far ahead?"

"Can I be honest with you?" William said. "The likelihood of any of you being the level of match needed for the person we've chosen to highlight for this campaign is probably not all that high. It takes a lot even to be a *good* match. But just think: We could inspire someone who hadn't considered this or didn't even know there were folks in need like this, to come forward. And from our actions, someone out there *may* end up being a match. Wouldn't that be a marvelous thing?"

"But it's like you're asking us to put what's ours out there to help someone who's not even in our family," Paris said.

Imani laughed.

Paris leaned forward and looked at Imani. "What's so funny?"

"I was just thinking about this scripture I just read the other day in the Bible," Imani said.

Paris chuckled. "Yeah, like you actually read the Bible just because. Imani, you really don't have to try and impress anyone here. It's just the family . . . and, of course, William. We're not on the campaign trail trying to make Dad's constituents think we're the perfect little wholesome family who reads our Bibles daily." She waved off Imani.

"But I do read the Bible. And I happen to enjoy reading it," Imani said.

"She really does," Deidra said. "Go on, Imani. What were you about to tell us?"

Imani looked at Paris, then her brother, before letting her eyes rest on her mother. "It was the scripture about the Canaanite woman. The story in Matthew fifteen where this woman comes to Jesus about her daughter that was demon possessed and she was trying to get her daughter some help."

"For sure you can't get any better help than coming to Jesus," Lawrence said. "Go on, Imani."

"Well, the woman was a Gentile and, of course, Jesus was a Jew. When she asked Jesus to have mercy on her and to help her daughter, Jesus's disciples started telling Jesus to send her away because the woman was bothering them," Imani said.

"That sounds familiar," Paris said under her breath, but loud enough for her mother to give her a sideways look this time. Paris pantomimed the zipping of her lips and nodded.

"Go on, baby," Deidra said as though she didn't know the story and was interested in hearing what happened.

"Jesus told the woman that He wasn't sent to folks like her, but to the lost sheep of the house of Israel. As I stated, the woman was a Gentile, as was her daughter, so Jesus was telling her that He wasn't sent for them. But then the woman did something awesome. She came to Jesus and worshipped Him. She said, 'Lord, help me.' That was it. She didn't say anything to insult Him or get back at him—nothing like that. She was merely trying to get help for her child." Imani scooted more to the edge of the chair where she sat. "Do you know what Jesus's answer was to her plea?"

"He's Jesus," Paris said. "Of course we know. He either went and healed the woman's daughter or He spoke a Word and her daughter was healed *that* way."

Imani smiled. "Nope. Jesus said, 'It is not meet to take the children's bread, and to cast it to dogs.' That's what Jesus said to her."

Paris jerked back. "What? Jesus said *that*? He called the woman and her daughter dogs?" Paris turned to her father. "See, Dad; there you go! There's your answer, coming from the mouth of one who *apparently* studies the Bible way more than any of the rest of us do. Jesus called the woman and her daughter dogs. That means not everybody should be helped, which means that we as a family don't have to care about this child we don't even know or anybody else, for that matter." Paris stood up. "So I suppose this means we can go home now. Come on, Andrew—"

"Where again is that in the Bible?" Malachi asked, his cell phone out. "What scripture is that again?"

"I'm not finished yet," Imani said, more to Paris.

"Well, you've said enough for me." Paris put her hand on her hip. "Jesus called them dogs. It doesn't get any worse than *that.* Dogs? He called them dogs?"

"Sit down, Paris, and let your sister finish." Deidra turned and smiled at Imani. "Go on and finish, Imani."

"Yes, *please* hurry up and finish, Imani, so those of us who *don't* live here can go home." Paris was still standing.

"Malachi, it's in Matthew 15:21–28," Imani said. "I remember because I'm fifteen and Paris is almost twenty-eight."

Paris laughed, then quickly looked at her mother and stopped.

"After Jesus said that, the woman said, 'Truth, Lord; yet the dogs eat of the crumbs which fall from their masters' table.' " Imani smiled. "Wasn't that awesome?"

Paris couldn't hold it in any longer. She burst into an unrestrained laugh. "Oh, *really* awesome! 'Yet the dogs eat of the crumbs that fall from their master's table!' "

"Paris, don't you get it?" Imani beamed.

"The way you're grinning, I guess I don't," Paris said.

"When Jesus used the term dogs, he wasn't being mean. A dog in those days meant housedog. If you were a housedog, you had a master and were allowed to sit at the feet of your master. True, the children may have been well taken care of and got to sit *at* the table. But even the dogs, as the woman correctly pointed out, were allowed to eat the crumbs from their masters' table. Have you ever seen children eat? The woman knew that even though she might not be considered family, she was still in the house. She still had access to the crumbs that fell from the Master's table."

Malachi smiled. "And crumbs from the *Master's* table are powerful." He went over to Imani and hugged her. "And *that*, dear Imani, was powerful!" Malachi looked down at his cell phone. "In verse twenty-eight, Jesus confirmed what Imani just told us. It says, 'Then Jesus answered and said unto her, O woman, great is thy faith: be it unto thee even as thou wilt. And her daughter was made whole from that very hour.' " Malachi hugged Imani again. "Powerful, little sister. 'Be it unto thee even as thou wilt.' " Malachi released Imani. "Dad, you can count me in. The least we can do is to help in however way that we can. If this brings attention and will help, I'm in."

Lawrence nodded. "Thanks, Son. I appreciate that." He hugged Malachi.

"I'm in," Imani said with a grin. Her father went and hugged her.

"Okay, I don't suppose I can't let my children jump in and I sit out," Deidra said. "Count me in." Lawrence smiled at her, winked, then nodded.

"Well, you can count me in, too," Andrew said.

Paris jerked around and stared down at Andrew.

"You already know that I'm in," William said.

Paris looked at her father. "I thought this was just to our family?"

"I want it to begin with our family. But our goal is to bring in as many people as we can," Lawrence said. "So, Paris. Can we count on you, as a family?"

"Sure. You can count on me, as a family." Paris walked over to her father. "But I'm not participating in any bone marrow transplant campaign. It would just be *my* luck I end up being a perfect match. So I'm not going to even put myself in the position of finding out that I match, and then having to say no I'm not going through all of that." She kissed her father on his cheek. "Sorry, Daddy. And *that's* my final answer. Andrew, are you ready to go?"

Andrew stood up. "I'll be in touch to find out what I need to do next."

Deidra stood and hugged Andrew first, then Paris, escorting them to the door.

Chapter 27

But she that liveth in pleasure is dead while she liveth.

—1 Timothy 5:6

"I don't believe how you acted at your folks' today," Andrew said as he walked behind Paris up the stairs to their bedroom. "That was *absolutely* something. That's the nicest way I can describe how you were. I mean, I couldn't say *anything*."

"Oh, you said plenty." Paris tossed her purse onto the bed as soon as she entered the bedroom. She flopped down next to her purse and started unlatching the strap of her blue left shoe.

Andrew came and stood over her. "I can understand you not wanting to participate, that I got. That's classic Paris."

Paris slipped that shoe off, let it drop, and began undoing the other one. "Say whatever you want, Andrew, because I don't care. Everybody wants something from me, but nobody ever seems to care what I might want."

"What are you talking about? It seems that's all everybody does: cater to what *you* want. You don't want to cook so we pretty much eat out every single night of the week. But you love boiled eggs, so we have plenty of eggs in the refrigerator."

"We don't eat out every single night. You go over to your mother's and we go to mine's sometimes. And we order in." Paris let the other shoe drop.

Andrew threw his hands up. "Exactly! That's exactly what I mean. Has it occurred to you that maybe, just maybe, I'd like to eat a home-cooked meal at *home* that my own wife *cooked* with her *own* hands?"

Paris laughed. "See. That proves *just* how much I think of you. I can't cook, Andrew; you knew that when you married me. So I actually do you a favor, sparing you the trouble of pretending what I've cooked is good by us eating elsewhere."

"If you were to ever practice, you'd see that you would get better at it."

Paris jumped up and strutted across the room in her bare feet. "That's the thing, Andrew," she yelled back as she walked toward the master bathroom. "I don't *want* to get better at it! I don't want to cook!" She went into the bathroom and came out a few minutes later wearing a flowing, silk, tan paisley caftan. "Why would I want to get better at something I don't even like to do? Huh?"

"Personally, I think the things you said at your folks' house a while ago were kind of sad. It's no wonder God hasn't blessed us with a baby yet."

Paris stopped and walked over to the bed where Andrew was sitting. "Excuse me? So are you saying the reason I can't get pregnant is because of the way I act? Is that what you're saying, Andrew? That because I'm honest enough to say what I think, as opposed to y'all who say what's politically correct, you're asserting that *that's* why God won't allow me to get pregnant?"

Andrew stood up; Paris pushed him back onto the bed. "Don't be getting up," Paris said. "You can answer the question from down there."

"Paris, I'd like to have a baby."

"As would I."

"But look at what you said. Do you really believe God thought highly of how uncaring you were today?"

"I don't want to be a donor of any kind. That's me being honest. What's so hard about *that*? I'm not going to pretend I'm going along with something that I *know* is pretty much a complete sham. I'm not. I'm not going to stand up there with Daddy at some press conference that William puts together, and lie about something I *know* I'm not going to do." Paris moved her face in a bit closer to Andrew's. "So if you want to say that God is punishing me in not allowing me to get pregnant, then you need to ask yourself why *you're* being punished, too."

Andrew stood up. Paris put her hand on his chest again, fully intending to push him back down. He grabbed her by the wrist and pushed her hand away from his chest, then started out of the room.

"Where are you going?" Paris rushed after him. He kept walking. "Andrew! Where are you going?"

She ran and caught up with him downstairs.

Andrew turned to her. "I don't get you, Paris," Andrew said. "My mother tried to warn me about you."

"Oh, your mother has *never* liked me."

"My mother has tried her hardest to get along with you. But it's things like this that make it difficult for anyone to . . ." He stopped. "You know what . . . just forget it." He headed to the kitchen.

Paris followed. "Oh, don't stop on my account! Why don't we get all of this out into the open, right here . . . right now? Come on. Bring it!"

Andrew opened the refrigerator and took out the carton of eggs and a stick of butter and set them on the counter. He went to the sink and washed his hands, then took down a small glass bowl. He looked under the cabinet next to the oven and pulled out a medium-size, nonstick frying pan.

"What are you doing?" Paris had her hand on her hip as she twisted her mouth from one side to the other.

Andrew cracked four eggs as he heated a tablespoon of butter in the pan. "What does it look like I'm doing?"

"It looks like you're cooking."

"Okay, then."

"Why are you cooking, and *why* are you cooking breakfast food for dinner?"

Andrew whipped the eggs with a fork. "I don't know. Maybe because I'm . . . hungry?"

"Oh, you're just being funny now! I see *exactly* what you're up to; you're trying to make a point. All right, Andrew. I get it. I get it."

He turned the heat down to low, then poured the mixture into the pan, using a silicone spatula to push the mixture to the center, tilting the pan to allow the runny part to be touched by the heat from the stove.

"You can stop now." Paris went to the drawer with the menus in it. "I'm ordering us something for dinner. See," she said, holding up a menu.

Andrew continued until the eggs were 99 percent done. Only after he turned the heat off did he sprinkle salt and pepper on it. "Waiting until it's done to put the salt in keeps your eggs from being tough," he said.

Paris picked up the phone. Andrew poured the cooked eggs into a bowl. He went and took down two plates, raking half of the cooked eggs onto each. Handing Paris one of the plates, he pulled two forks out of the drawer, put one on the plate Paris held and the other on his, sat down at the table in the kitchen, said a quick prayer, and began to eat.

"You have *got* to be kidding me!" Paris said, standing there holding her plate.

"You'd better eat it before it gets cold."

"I'm not eating eggs for dinner!" Paris set the plate down.

"Suit yourself. But it's good, if I say so myself."

Paris stood over him with her fists thrust into her sides. "What is your problem?"

Andrew looked up at her. "I'm not like you. I'm good. You live in pleasure, but it's like you're dead inside or something. I don't understand why you can't see that. God has blessed you so much, Paris. But for some reason, it looks like it's never enough for you."

"This is about the baby you want, isn't it? Isn't it, Andrew?"

Andrew shook his head. "You made it clear, early on, that you really didn't want a baby. You say you want one now. But honestly, Paris, I don't know what to believe anymore when it comes to you." He put the last of his eggs in his mouth and stood up. "Cedric warned me about you. He said everything was all about you and what you wanted. Maybe I should have listened to him." He took his empty dish and fork to the sink, washed them, then laid them on a paper towel to dry.

"So you want to bring up Cedric, huh? You want to bring up my ex? Well, I'll have you know that he was a real loser. He didn't *have* anything, and he wasn't trying to *be* anything, other than a scrub."

Andrew turned to look in her face. "Is that the real reason you came after me? Because you thought I *had* something? Well, surprise! I didn't have anything to offer you much, either, Paris. I grew up poor, and I've had to work hard for everything I've ever gotten. So I didn't have anything substantial to offer you when you came after me."

"Except your heart," Paris said.

He looked at her and his heart couldn't help but to soften now.

Paris was starting to cry. "You *have* had to work hard for everything you've ever gotten. I, on the other hand, grew up somewhat privileged." She stepped closer to Andrew. "Still, through all of my pretending, you saw past my façade . . . you saw the real me. The girl that everybody always said was pretty, but no one ever saw I was also pretty smart." She touched Andrew's arm. "You, Andrew Holyfield, saw that, underneath my layers of nastiness and pettiness, that I have a heart."

"Of course, you have a heart, Paris." He touched her face. "You just get caught up in what's going on around you and forget that what you say and do can sometimes hurt others, even though you might not think that it does."

"I know. And you're right; I want to be a better person. But I need you, Andrew. I need someone in my life that can show me how to be better and to love me unconditionally. And you've always done that. Whether I cook or not, whether I clean or not, whether I'm nice or not . . . you seem to still love me."

"I do love you, Paris. I do."

"And I love you. I'm sorry for the way I've acted lately. So will you forgive me?"

Andrew smiled. "Of course."

"Hold up a second." Paris went over to the kitchen counter and came back holding her plate of eggs out to him.

He looked at the plate. "Why are you bringing this to me? If you don't want to eat it, just scrape it into the garbage disposal."

She grinned and began flipping her hair back. "I was hoping I might be able to entice you to serve me breakfast in bed."

He laughed. "Yeah, okay."

"I'm serious," she said. "I was thinking we could get an early start on that baby project we're working on, *if* you know what I mean."

He grinned. "Serious? Well, now, you know . . . I think I can accommodate that request. I mean: A man's gotta do, what a man's gotta do." He took the plate, set it down on the table, and scooped her up into his arms.

Paris let out a loud yelp. "What are you doing?"

"Isn't it obvious? I'm sweeping my baby's mama off her feet. If we're going to get this started, then I want to start it off right. You say I'm slightly a perfectionist. Well, practice makes perfect."

Paris giggled like a teenager as he carried her up the stairs to their bedroom.

Chapter 28

My little children, let us not love in word, neither in tongue; but in deed and in truth.

—1 John 3:18

It was early when the phone rang, awakening Paris. Paris quickly looked at the caller ID; it was her parent's home number. Andrew rolled over. She slid her feet into her light blue silk slippers, slipped on her silk robe, and dashed out of the bedroom into the hallway so not to wake Andrew completely.

Paris pressed the TALK button. "Hello," she whispered.

"Did you happen to see the news this morning?" Deidra asked before saying hello back or asking Paris how she was.

"No. We happen to still be asleep."

"Still asleep? At nine o'clock in the morning?"

"It's Saturday, Mother. People tend to sleep late on the weekends, especially when they don't have to get up and go to work," Paris said.

"But you don't work," Deidra said.

"Yeah, but Andrew does. And he's off today." Paris sat down on the top step, wrapping her robe around her better to ward off the chill. "So what were you saying about the news? What happened?"

"Your father . . . he's all up in arms. He just learned that someone stole his bone marrow donor campaign idea," Deidra said.

"Stole his idea? How does someone steal an idea about becoming a donor?"

"Apparently this pastor on our local NBC morning news is talking about his church spearheading a drive to bring awareness of a little girl in need of a bone marrow transplant," Deidra said. "I believe it's the same little girl your father was planning to highlight. So, of course, your father is livid. He claims this will undercut the impact of his plan before he can even get it out there."

"Why does Daddy care who spearheads this if the whole point was to bring awareness and possibly find a donor for her? You'd think Daddy would be happy."

"Because your father wants to tie this effort in with his reelection campaign. If someone else is doing it, it takes away from him appearing to be leading the charge."

"Well, he'll make it work to his advantage," Paris said. "He always does. And honestly, this *absolutely* works for me. Now I won't have to feel bad about not standing with all of you had Daddy done this the way he was planning to."

"Oh, he's still planning on doing it his way now. He just has to step up the timetable so he can take this narrative back from that church before it looks like it's really their idea. He's been on the phone with William and their PR person all morning setting things up. They're trying to schedule a news event right now so he can make it on the evening news. He's hoping the newsfeed will get him picked up on a larger scale after it airs here. You know how these things work."

"Great," she said. "Well, I hope everything works out for him."

"He still wants to make a good showing at the news conference. He wants all of us standing together as a family, like what he was saying yesterday," Deidra said.

"Okay. Well, I'll let Andrew know when he wakes up."

"Paris, I know what you said yesterday about not wanting to take part. But I really think you should come and stand with us. If not for your father, do it for me."

"Mother, I hear you. I heard Dad. But I'm honestly not interested."

"Hold on a second, Paris. Your daddy wants to talk to you for a minute."

Paris didn't want to talk to her father. Not after the wonderful time she and Andrew had together last night. She looked up at the ceiling and shook her head.

"Paris, this is your father."

"I know, Daddy," she said, standing up now. She went down the stairs to the den. Even though Andrew was likely still asleep, she didn't want him hearing any of what she might say in response to her father and start the friction between them all over again. Not after last night.

"I need you at the news conference so we can stand united as a family."

"Daddy, I already gave you my answer."

"I heard you," Lawrence said. "And I was fully willing to allow you that. But things have changed overnight. Pastor Landris was on television this morning talking about doing the very thing I said we were going to do. Speciously, there's a spy in my midst. How else would that preacher end up coming up with the very thing we'd discussed doing? This is definitely no coincidence, I'll tell you."

"I don't think this is anything that merits stealing. Just like you and William decided on it, I'm sure the way William found out about this child's dilemma, so may have Pastor Landris. I personally think it's great that this is being done for this little girl and her family and I don't have to be involved."

"Where's Andrew?"

"Still asleep."

"Asleep? Then wake him up."

"Daddy, I'm not going to wake Andrew up. I'll just have him call you when he wakes up."

"Listen, Paris Elizabeth, I don't have time to play. I need all hands on deck. Andrew said he would stand with us on this, so I need him to know the plan."

"Then tell me and I'll tell him."

"Why would I tell you? You've made it abundantly clear that

you want nothing to do with *any* of this," Lawrence said. "So wake up your husband and give him the phone. We need to be sure we come off as sincere and creditable in this as possible. We have to take hold of this before Pastor Landris and his church completely upstage us and get all the credit. We can't just talk; we're going to have to prove that we mean what we say. So put my son-in-law on the phone and hurry up about it! We're wasting time, all right?"

Paris pressed her mouth tight before forcing a smile. "Sure, Daddy. Just a minute."

She walked back upstairs to her bedroom. Andrew was just coming out of the bathroom. "Daddy wants to speak to you." Defeated, she handed her husband the phone.

Chapter 29

These are murmurers, complainers, walking after their own lusts; and their mouth speaketh great swelling words, having men's persons in admiration because of advantage.

—Jude 16

Lawrence had called Gabrielle as soon as he saw the news, even before he phoned William. He wanted to find out from her what was going on. Had she decided not to pressure him to do all he could, now that he'd told her he'd been tested and learned he was a blood match but wasn't a bone marrow match?

Gabrielle had calmly explained to Lawrence that her pastor had been made aware of the little girl and wanted to do something to help. Pastor Landris announced it to the congregation. It just happens that lots of prominent people attend Followers of Jesus Faith Worship Center, many with connections to the media. One such person thought what they were doing as a local body, bringing awareness to this type of problem and volunteering to be tested, deserved a larger audience than merely their members. So that's what was apparently happening now.

"Then it sounds like I can scrap plans for my family to be tested," Lawrence had said with relief.

"Lawrence, your children still need to see if any of them may be a match," Gabrielle said. "Finding a perfect match is difficult; finding a good match is not that easy, either. It's not like donating blood that would likely find matches needed in a number of folks. Your children still need to be tested to see if any of them match."

Lawrence had been disappointed by her answer. He was hoping this new development with the church stepping up would allow him to remove his children from the equation completely.

Paris had already stated she wasn't going to cooperate, not even with the staging of him revealing what he was planning to do. It would be difficult, if not impossible, to get her to change her mind. This church doing this now could have been a great out for sure, but Gabrielle wasn't letting them off the hook. She was going all out to save this child and, in Lawrence's opinion, she could care less about any possible debris left along the way.

So Lawrence had to alter his plans since someone else had now preempted his planned announcement. William was the one who felt they had to hold a larger news conference in order to wrestle away any thunder Pastor Landris may have taken from them. William suggested one other thing they hadn't planned to do originally.

"I think we should get with the mother of this child and see if we can make the announcement from the actual hospital," William said.

"Do what?" Lawrence was totally not expecting this. "Are you out of your mind? You want me to tie myself to those people in that way?"

"Follow me on this," William said. "You get me the information on the mother. I'll speak with her, let her know we heard about her little girl, and that we want to use your office to do what we can to help. Didn't you say that Gabrielle hasn't revealed who you are to this little girl to anyone other than her boyfriend?"

"That's what she told me. But who's to say she's telling the truth, and who's to say her boyfriend hasn't leaked anything?"

"Well, from our side of things, nothing appears to have been revealed concerning you. Believe me: We'd be hearing some kind of rumbling if there had been. So I'm thinking you could call Gabrielle and ask her for the mother's contact information. I could then contact the mother, tell her what we'd like to do for her daughter by way of a televised news conference that will certainly cover a greater area than ever before, and voila!"

"So you want us to go to the hospital, if we get the clearance, and make the announcement of our intentions to be tested as a family from there?" Lawrence said.

"Exactly! Picture the optics. And honestly, I believe this is a better way to sell it to everyone, including *your* family. It would appear really sincere, and if we get the mother on board, we would no longer be speaking generically, and it would be more than an abstract thought. We'd have a real live person who's being affected by this need, placed before the people," William said. "The media loves a feel-good story."

"All right. Let me see what I can do from my end. I'll get back with you as soon as I hear back from Gabrielle and she hears back from the child's mother, if we get that far." Lawrence hung up.

He called Gabrielle again and explained the plan. She told him she would get in touch with the mother and call him back. Lawrence stressed to Gabrielle the importance of the child's mother believing he, as an Alabama representative, had heard of their plight and wanted to help. Gabrielle called him back within five minutes.

"Okay. I spoke with the mother. Her name is Jessica Noble. She totally broke down and cried when I told her you were interested in bringing more attention to the search for a bone marrow donor," Gabrielle said. "She said it would be fine for your people to contact her. She'll be looking for the call. But now she did ask how I happened to have spoken to you about this. She wanted to know how you knew to call me in the first place."

Lawrence's breath caught in his throat. He hadn't even thought about that. "What did you tell her?"

"I told her I had made great efforts in contacting your office, which is true. And that I was asking for whatever help *anyone* could give toward assistance. She already knew what my pastor and the church were doing. So this fell right in line."

"Wonderful," Lawrence said with a smile. "Then if you'll give me Jessica Noble's phone number, I'll get this ball rolling."

"What about your family? Is everyone on board?"

"I spoke with everyone yesterday. *Almost* everyone is on board to be tested to see if they might be a candidate for further testing as a match."

"*Almost* everybody?" Gabrielle said.

"Yeah. Paris doesn't want to participate."

"But what if—"

"Listen, I need to get off the phone," Lawrence said, deliberately interrupting her. "I need to let William and his team know that this is a go. We don't have a lot of time to waste. I'll talk with you should I need anything more, which I don't think I will."

"Sure," Gabrielle said, then gave him Jessica's cell phone number. "Thanks, Lawrence. I really appreciate this."

"No problem," Lawrence said. "Besides, what other option have you given me?" He hung up, then thought about whether that last sentence had truly been necessary. After all, she was only trying to save the life of a child she'd already saved once. Lawrence, on the other hand, was looking to save only what mattered most to him—his wife, family, and his political career.

William pulled everything together. The optics of being at the hospital to make the announcement were perfect. Doctors explained the medical what and how. Lawrence's family stood together, surprisingly including Paris. Lawrence wasn't sure how Andrew had managed to pull that one off, but it appeared he'd been the one to convince her to be there with the family.

When the cameras rolled, Deidra spoke from a mother's point of view. It was very touching. But the star of the news conference turned out to be Imani. She brought home the point, emphasizing that they were talking about an eight-year-old little girl with her whole life ahead of her. And all she needed was a little marrow.

"I'm going to be tested," Imani said. "And I *pray* I'm a match. Can you imagine being able to help someone in that way? Hey! It won't kill you to do this."

Some in the audience laughed after she said that. She was right; to be tested and, if a match, to give the bone marrow, without a doubt, wouldn't kill anyone.

After the news conference, Jessica Noble came up to him. "Representative Simmons," she said. "Thank you so much." Tears rolled down her worn face.

Lawrence nodded. "I'm happy to be able to do something that we pray will help."

Jessica shook her head slowly. "I just don't know what to say. In this past month, when I've been at my lowest, God has sent me angels, disguised as people, right here on earth. When I received that call this morning from Gabrielle that you wanted to put a call out there in a big way, I couldn't believe it."

"Well, when my office heard about this, we wanted to do what we could."

"Yeah, but having your whole family want to come in and be tested . . . to lead the way like this, this is huge," Jessica said. "Gabrielle has truly been a blessing through all of this. She has tirelessly been out there trying to help us find a match."

"I will say, according to my secretary, that Gabrielle Mercedes has been *relentless* in attempting to get us involved in this effort. When I heard about it, something touched my heart about it. I asked myself, what would Jesus do, if He was here, and how would He do it? It came to me what and how, as a Christian who *truly* values life, I had to do. God is good. His mercy endures forever."

"I would love for you to meet my daughter. I know she would absolutely get a kick out of meeting someone like you," Jessica said.

Lawrence's smile tempered temporarily. "Oh, it's fine. I'm sure it's not good having too many strangers around her during this time. I'm aware that her immune system is severely compromised at this stage. My intent is to help her in getting well. I certainly wouldn't want to be the cause of anything bad happening because of anything I might do. She and I will meet after she gets well. I'm not going anywhere, not anytime soon. I plan on retaining my political office, so we have plenty of time."

"Of course," Jessica said. "I know you're very busy. Whenever you're ready."

"Always something vying for my attention, that's for sure," Lawrence said.

William stepped in on cue. "Representative Simmons, we need to go. You're going to be late for your next appointment."

Lawrence turned back to Jessica. "It was a pleasure meeting you. And if you happen to be a member of the district I represent, I certainly hope you'll consider voting for me." He chuckled like it was a joke, but he was serious. "And if you have friends or know people in my district, be sure and tell them to vote for me as well."

"Absolutely," Jessica said. "You didn't even have to ask."

Lawrence and William walked off.

"Great news conference," William said. "My phone has been ringing off the hook since you and your family took the stage. I think you've risen ten points in the polls with this. And I'd give Imani something extra in her allowance. That girl is a natural, and she doesn't even know it. She *completely* sold this today. Heck, after she finished, I would have stepped up to be tested if I hadn't already committed to do it."

Lawrence nodded as they walked. "Imani was good. That girl has a heart of *pure* gold. She meant every word she said. This isn't a game for her. She's for real."

"Yeah, she takes after her mother." William laughed. "Because anybody who *really* knows you, know they're dealing with fool's gold." William kept walking as Lawrence stood there pretending to be offended. William turned around and walked backward as he spoke. "Oh, and, Representative Simmons! Happy Hanukkah!"

Chapter 30

Be watchful, and strengthen the things which remain, that are ready to die: for I have not found thy works perfect before God.

—Revelation 3:2

The news conference had been two weeks ago. In that time, a special unit had been set up to receive all of those who were signing up to be tested as a possible bone marrow donor for the little girl everybody was now calling Jazz, short for Jasmine. That had come from Jasmine herself.

After the news aired, people wanted to see, if nothing more, a glimpse of the little girl whose story was touching their hearts and garnering conversations from the water cooler to social networks. So one of the news folks convinced Jessica that it would be great if they could get just a few minutes of footage of her daughter to humanize the story even more.

In conjunction with the doctors, who thought a few minutes would be okay, Jessica had agreed. Jasmine had been on for only five minutes and she'd captured hearts. She told them her name was Jasmine, but that she liked being called Jazz.

"Miss Jazz is what my *special* friend calls me," Jasmine said, not revealing the name of her special friend. "He's a doctor who knows how to play a game called Alabama Hit the Hammer. Do you know how to play that game?"

Everybody in the room laughed as a few heads nodded.

"The first time he came, he played that game. He had a piece of hard candy in his hand instead of a rock, which is the way most folks play it. Now when he plays it, he has an encouraging message in whichever hand I pick," Jasmine said. "My favorite message is this one"—she held up a small slip of paper—"that says, 'By His stripes, I am healed.' I keep this one on my night table. My friend explained how Jesus came all the way from Heaven to earth just to save us. Jesus was whipped for nothing that He'd done. But by Jesus's stripes, I am healed. So whenever I get a little down about my condition, I just read this one. I am healed. God is going to heal me."

Everybody in Lawrence's family, except Paris, went to find out if they were a possible candidate to match. Nothing anyone said could make Paris change her mind. She'd made it clear that this was all just for show, since the chances of any of them matching were nil and not worth wasting her time. Besides, it wasn't like her not doing it was really going to hurt her father's image. If nothing more, she'd be the one now who appeared the most self-regarding instead of him. And that was fine with her.

It was three days before Christmas when the phone rang. The woman on the other end stated who she was and proceeded to explain why she was calling.

"You're not going to believe this," the woman said with joy exuding from her voice. "But the bone marrow transplant recipient you were tested for? Well, you're a match, an almost perfect match! We need to proceed to the next step in the process now, if you're willing to do that. Honestly, I can't even express how thrilled we are. We're rejoicing here! If you agree and it works, you'll be saving this little girl's life!"

Chapter 31

Holding forth the word of life; that I may rejoice in the day of Christ, that I have not run in vain, neither labored in vain.

—Philippians 2:16

Jessica called Gabrielle. She could barely contain herself. "They found a donor!"

"They did! Thank You, Jesus!" Gabrielle yelled back into the phone. "I'm sorry. I didn't mean to holler like that."

"Oh, it's okay. When I got the call, I had to leave out of the hospital and go to the parking area because I was afraid I'd start screaming for joy and they would have to put me out for disturbing the patients." Jessica laughed.

"Wow. Wow," Gabrielle said, her hand loosely covering her mouth. "They found a donor. They actually found a match. God is so good! He answered our prayer."

"Yes. And it appears that everything is a go now."

"Are you sure?" Gabrielle asked. "I mean are they sure?"

"I just got off the phone with the people handling this. They told me they had a match, they had called to let that person know, and everything was a go now," Jessica said. "They found a match! I can't believe it, but they finally found a match!"

"Did they happen to tell you who the match was?" Gabrielle asked.

"No. And honestly, I don't care who it is as long as whoever it is has agreed to go through with the procedure needed to get my child what she has to have. We know they allow anonymous donors. So it's very possible this person might not ever want their identity revealed," Jessica said. "But I thank God for them, whoever it is."

Gabrielle smiled. She rarely heard Jessica say much about God, not since they'd connected. Maybe Gabrielle's being there, sharing the love of God with Jessica through all of this, was having an effect. "Well, you know I'm thanking and praising God with you. Now Jasmine can get the transplant she needs, and she'll be on her way to a full recovery soon, in Jesus's name. In fact, she'll be even better than before."

"Amen," Jessica said. "I agree with you on that prayer. Gabrielle, I also want to thank you for all that you've done these past months. You have run this race with me, especially on this last leg when I was feeling tired and defeated and, truthfully, I was almost ready to give up. But you've been there with me. You've labored to do all you can to get folks to step up and be tested. You were able to first get your pastor, and then Representative Simmons and his office. Oh, my goodness! It certainly looks like your labor has not been in vain."

Gabrielle didn't care about being thanked for what she'd done. She did what she needed to do . . . what she was supposed to do. "Have they given you a date when they're planning on doing the transplant?"

"They're going to get back with me on all of that. They have to get the person ready to extract the marrow, which will take a few days with them using the less invasive procedure they say they'll most likely use. The doctor told me that instead of putting the donor under general anesthesia and extracting the cells from the hip bone, they're going to give the donor injections of medication for a few days. That will cause the stem cells to move out of the bone into the bloodstream where blood will be taken from the donor's vein, filtered by a machine that will collect the stem cells, and the blood will immediately be returned back to the donor. Jasmine's part will be more complicated though. In order to kill Jasmine's remaining bad stem cells, she'll receive high doses of chemo, possibly radiation, to make room for the incoming new good stem cells. They'll give her the new stem cells intravenously, just like a blood transfusion."

"I thought those cells needed to be in the bone—you know, bone marrow."

"They do. And when they do this procedure, the stem cells will make their way to her bone and begin to grow and create more cells. Sounds easy enough, doesn't it? To ensure that her body will receive the transplanted cells and not reject them, they will also be giving Jasmine other medications. So I'd say it will be another few days *at least*, possibly a week, for everything needed to take place."

"Will you let me know when they do it? That way I can be praying on that day along with you?" Gabrielle didn't want to impose during that time by asking if she could be there, even though she wanted nothing more than to be there.

"You're welcome to come and be here with us, that's if you can, and if you'd like to. You don't have to feel obligated or anything."

Gabrielle felt the tears as they began to well up. "I would really like that. I would. That's if you don't feel I'd be imposing."

"Gabrielle, you and I are in this together now. I'm not going to cut you loose, not at this point. Not when we're nearing the finish line. For now, we'll just take things one day at a time. You're like a friend now, both you *and* Dr. Morgan. You two are a part of Jasmine's life. I told you sometime back: She needs all the love she can get. We can sort things out later as to how we'll proceed. But for now, she and I both need you here with us."

The tears streamed down Gabrielle's face. "Thank you, Jessica. Thank you. Oh, and, Jessica?"

"Yes?"

"Merry Christmas! Jesus is worthy to be praised!"

"Yes, He is. And this is going to be a merry Christmas indeed."

Jessica got off the phone. And Gabrielle began to dance around the room and, before she knew anything, she had knelt down on the floor and was crying and thanking God with all that was within her.

Chapter 32

And what is the exceeding greatness of his power to us-ward who believe, according to the working of his mighty power.

—Ephesians 1:19

It was three days after Christmas, two days before New Year's Eve, the day of Ujima in the Kwanzaa celebration (with the principle being collective work and responsibility, building and maintaining the community together, and making our brothers' and sisters' problems *our* problems to solve together). Zachary and Gabrielle were at the hospital for Jasmine's bone marrow transplant procedure. They'd sat in the waiting room while Jessica stayed with Jasmine. It had been a tremendous success and Jasmine was on her way to being well again.

But it appeared all of this had taken a toll on Jessica. Gabrielle understood how it would. Jessica had rarely left Jasmine's side throughout the entire ordeal. Gabrielle and Zachary insisted she go home and get some real bed rest, promising to sit with Jasmine for as long as she needed them to do.

"That's only if you don't mind us being here for that long," Gabrielle respectfully said to her.

"Oh, I don't mind *that*. I just don't want to leave her. You understand," Jessica said.

"Well, will you at least go home for a bit?" Zachary said. "If not for you, then for Jasmine's sake. She's going to be sleeping for a while anyway. We'll stay with her until you get back. I promise. We're off for the holidays. I'm sure, besides needing some well-deserved rest, you'd like to get some things done for when she comes home. Because you know it won't be *too* much longer now. Another few months."

A huge smile spread over Jessica's face. "God is *so* good! I'm still in awe of Him. Mere days before they found a donor, the doctor was preparing me . . . telling me it wouldn't be too much longer before she might not be with us. Now here we are, talking about it not being too much longer before she'll be going home. A few more months. I'm truly . . . truly . . . I just don't know what to say *except* that God is good."

Gabrielle hugged Jessica. "There's nothing more *to* say. God is surely good. This is the exceeding greatness of God's power. Just when the devil thinks he's made a knockout, God shows Him the blood of Jesus shed for us and reminds him that he's already been defeated."

Jessica laughed. "I like that. And when Jasmine gets out of this place and gets to go home in another few months, I'm going to be sure the two of us find a good church home and start going to church on a regular basis."

"Just make sure wherever you choose that you're being fed the unadulterated Word of God. Don't do like some and go just so you can say that you went to church," Gabrielle said. "Find a place with some meat and some real substance to sustain you. And believe me: There *is* a difference. Being in the right place can make all of the difference in the world. It can be the difference between life and death."

Zachary put his arm around Gabrielle. "Where we fellowship has definitely made a difference in both of our lives."

Jessica nodded. "Over with Pastor Landris. I definitely plan on visiting there. Pastor Landris has been nice enough to come by a *couple* of times. He prayed a powerful prayer for both me and Jasmine. In fact, he'd just prayed and later that day, they called and said they'd found a donor."

"Well, I can tell you now: We all would love having you," Gabrielle said, hoping Jessica didn't think it was because she only wanted to be able to see Jasmine after all of this was over. "Maybe if you decide to become members, Jasmine will join the dance ministry. I'd sure love having her on the young people's dance team. She looks like she would be a magnificent dancer."

"Oh, now, she does like to dance," Jessica said. "I used to wonder where she got that from, because I'll tell you: I am *not* a dancer. Oh, no. You definitely don't want to see me twirling around a room. And if I do, you'd better move everything out of the way." Jessica laughed.

Jessica went over and got her purse. "If you're both sure about staying for a little while, I believe I will take you up on your offer. I need to take care of some things. I know Jasmine will be over the moon to see you both. And for sure, I know she'll be in good hands while I'm gone."

Gabrielle swallowed hard. She received the message Jessica was saying, without her saying it: Jessica trusted them. She trusted them enough to leave her most precious possession . . . the love of her life, in their hands. Even *if* it was for only a few hours.

Chapter 33

Having predestinated us unto the adoption of children by Jesus Christ to himself, according to the good pleasure of his will.

—Ephesians 1:5

Jessica returned to the hospital a little over eight hours later. "I'm so sorry," she said, apologizing to Gabrielle, who was half asleep in a chair near the bottom of the bed. She kissed Jasmine's forehead. "I left here, went and handled some necessary business, drove home, took a nice hot shower, lay down on my bed, and the next thing I knew, I was opening my eyes to a pitch-black bedroom."

"It's okay," Gabrielle said, sitting up straight now. "It really wasn't a problem. I told you I would stay while you got some rest. I was fully prepared to stay the night. I don't have anywhere I have to be. The business side of the church where I work is closed until after New Year's. So I am free as a bird to be here."

Jessica sat down in the chair on the other side of Gabrielle closest to the head of the bed. "Are you sure? I know you and Dr. Morgan must have plans."

Gabrielle reached over and gently touched Jessica's hand. "I'm positive. And Zachary is in full agreement that I should be right here helping the two of you. He was here up until he got an emergency call about three hours ago and had to leave."

Jessica looked lovingly at a peaceful, sleeping Jasmine. "How's she doing?"

Gabrielle also looked at Jasmine. "Just sleeping a lot. She's barely been awake the entire time you were gone. She'll likely sleep most of the night, except when the nurses come in and wake her for various reasons."

"Yeah. I was saying the other day that if you want to get some rest, a hospital is definitely not the best place to do it. Someone always needs something from you. Take blood, check on your temperature, check your blood pressure, see how you're feeling or if you need anything. It's always something. But I'm so thankful for the love and care they've given her here. I truly am." Jessica smiled as she leaned closer to her daughter. "And Jasmine has just been a little trouper through all of this, for all of these months. She's a special blessing from the Lord indeed."

Jasmine suddenly started moving before a smile spread across her face and she opened her eyes completely. "Mama," she said.

Jessica stood and went to her, touching her hand. "Hi, baby."

"Mama, I'm so tired. I just can't seem to wake up."

Jessica gently touched her little face. "That's because you need rest while your body is repairing and healing. You'll be up and at 'em before we know it."

"I dreamed Dr. Z and Miss Gabrielle were here."

Jessica smiled. "You weren't dreaming. Dr. Z was here earlier. He had to leave." Jessica looked over at Gabrielle. "But Miss Gabrielle is still here."

Jasmine seemed to be trying to sit up to see. Gabrielle stood up and came closer so Jasmine could see her without having to strain. "Hi there, Miss Jazz."

Jasmine smiled. "Hi there, Miss G."

"Miss G?" Jessica said with a chuckle. "Where did *that* come from?"

"Well, I was thinking. Since I call Dr. Zachary, Dr. Z, I should call Miss Gabrielle, Miss G. It sounds right, don't you think?"

Jessica swapped places with Gabrielle so Jasmine and Gabrielle would be able to talk easier.

"I love it," Gabrielle said with a grin. "I hear you're doing great, Miss Jazz."

"Then everything went okay?" Jasmine asked.

Gabrielle didn't want to overstep her boundary. She looked over at Jessica for her to answer.

"Everything went wonderfully," Jessica said. "Absolutely perfect. I spoke with the doctor, and she's pleased with how things are progressing. Your new cells just need to get to work and start doing their jobs producing more cells. The doctor says she wants those new cells to be fruitful and to multiply, and you'll be home before you know it."

There was a quick sharp knock on the door. "Come on," Jessica said.

Zachary peeked his head inside. "It's okay if I come in?"

"Oh, quit! You know it is," Jessica said with a smile in her voice.

Zachary walked in, stopping at the foot of the bed. "How are you feeling, Miss Jazz."

"Much better, thank you very much," Jasmine said softly. "I can feel my new cells *working* already."

He chuckled. "That's wonderful to hear. Your color is starting to come back. That's a really good sign." Zachary smiled.

Jessica looked Zachary's way. "Dr. Morgan, would you mind staying with Jasmine for a few minutes while Gabrielle and I go get something from the cafeteria?"

"I would love nothing better," Zachary said with a bow toward Jasmine, whose smile morphed into a huge grin. Both women stepped away from the bed. Zachary went and sat in the chair nearest Jasmine.

Gabrielle and Jessica went to the cafeteria. "Do you want anything?" Jessica asked Gabrielle when they entered.

"No. I'm fine."

"Well, I wanted to talk to you . . . away from Jasmine's hearing."

"I thought that might be what you were doing," Gabrielle said.

"Jasmine doesn't have anyone left to take care of her other than me. I want you to know how much I appreciate you and Dr. Morgan. Since you found out what was going on, you've been with us every step of the way. And I thank you so much for that."

Gabrielle touched Jessica's trembling hand. "No thanks are necessary. It hasn't been a problem, and that's the truth. Zachary and I wouldn't have wanted it any other way."

"Still, if these past months have taught me anything, it's the fact that, in this life, we never know what's around the next corner. We may *want* to think that we're invincible and that we'll live, maybe not forever. But we don't always think about how precious and how quickly life can slip from our grasp."

"Like a vapor," Gabrielle said, recalling a scripture she'd read that spoke of how life was like a vapor.

Jessica slowly nodded her agreement. "Yes." Jessica cast her eyes down, then back up at Gabrielle. "I know you and I agreed that once this ordeal was over and Jasmine was well again, that we'd all go back to our normal lives."

Gabrielle nodded as she wondered where Jessica was going with this.

"Gabrielle, I need to ask something of you. And if you don't want to do it or don't care to do it, please don't feel bad in telling me so. I need for us to be straight and honest with each other, especially at this point."

"All right. What do you need to ask?"

Jessica took in a deep breath and released it slowly. "If something was to happen to me, will you take Jasmine and raise her for me?"

Gabrielle tried not to show the shock she was experiencing. This *absolutely* came out of the blue. "Oh, I'm sure you're going to be around for a very long time."

"No . . . I'm not." Jessica wiped at tears that were now rolling down her cheeks. "I would like to believe that I'm going to be around, but that would be both irresponsible and unfair to Jasmine."

"Is there something you know? Something you aren't telling me?"

Jessica wiped her face with both hands and looked upward, then releasing a slight groan, she looked back at Gabrielle. "I have breast cancer."

Gabrielle put her hand up to her mouth. She hadn't meant

to react in that way, but this revelation had come completely without prior warning. "Are you sure? Have you seen a doctor?"

Jessica nodded. "Oh, I'm sure. I'm definitely sure."

"Well, things have advanced so much in just the past few years. Folks are beating breast cancer. They have advanced in treatments. People are surviving."

"Unfortunately, I'm not going to likely be one of those survivors."

"You need to stop saying negative things. That's just the devil trying to use the power of your tongue to speak death over your life. You need to stop doing that and start believing God will heal you just like He's doing for Jasmine." Gabrielle was speaking so fast now, almost as fast as her heart was beating.

"Gabrielle, I thank God for what He's done for Jasmine, I really do." Jessica wiped her eyes with her hands again before getting up and picking up napkins left on a table next to theirs. Sitting back down, she wiped her eyes, pressing the white paper napkin to her whole face at one point.

"Well, I think you're just in shock in learning about this right now, so you're not thinking clearly." Gabrielle flicked away a few of her own tears. "I'm sure when folks hear the word 'cancer,' their minds race to the worst possible conclusion."

"I've known about this since Jasmine first became sick. My doctor told me I needed to take care of it back then. But it would have required me to have surgery, extensive chemo, and radiation. If I had agreed to do what he was saying I needed to do at that time, I wouldn't have been able to take care of Jasmine. It was either Jasmine or me . . ."

Gabrielle was crying now. "And you chose her."

Jessica nodded as she bit down on her bottom lip. "I didn't know what else to do. Jasmine is just beginning to live; she has her whole life in front of her."

"But she also needs her mother," Gabrielle said, touching Jessica's hand that now rested on the table. "So you have to fight and not give up. You can beat this. I know you can."

"I *have* been fighting." Jessica looked up. "I've been fighting for my child. And now we've won; she's going to be okay." Jessica nodded as she smiled, her mouth trembling. "Jasmine's going to live and not die. God answered my prayer. I was thinking He wasn't listening or that He didn't care. But in the end, He was right on time. Jasmine's going to be all right!" She nodded again as she looked at her hand.

"But now you have to fight for your life so you can be here to see her grow up, graduate high school and college. Your little girl needs you. You can't give up."

"I'm not giving up. I'm just being a realist. Yes, I'm going to fight. But I need your help. I need you to promise me that should I lose this battle, you'll be there for Jasmine."

Gabrielle shook her head slowly as she frowned. "You don't even have to ask that. I'm here now. If you need my help in the future, I'll be there. I will. But I'm also here for you. Whatever you need; I'm here."

Jessica smiled. "Thank you." She released a short laugh between her flowing tears and cries. "Thank you." She nodded. "Thank you."

Gabrielle forced a smile. Jessica had to fight. She had to! She needed to be there for Jasmine herself. That little girl has already been through more than any person, let alone a child, should have to endure. Jasmine couldn't lose her mother. Not now. Not now. *Jessica, you have to fight this! You have to!*

Chapter 34

Thou wilt say then, The branches were broken off, that I might be grafted in.

—Romans 11:19

Gabrielle and Zachary visited Jasmine every day of the twenty days she was in the sterile area of the hospital recovering from the transplant. Only Gabrielle, Zachary, and Jessica were authorized to visit her at this point, outside of the medical professionals.

Gabrielle saw how tired Jessica was becoming and insisted (privately) that she do whatever she needed to get well. Jessica promised she would, but only after she was certain Jasmine was completely out of the woods and truly on her way to a full recovery.

Thirty days after the transplant process first began, Jasmine was moved to the facility where she would technically not be considered hospitalized, but more like an outpatient. While there (for the next sixty to seventy days), she would continue to be checked daily for possible infection or other immune-related complications.

Jessica's health continued to decline. Gabrielle told her she would take care of Jasmine, provided Jessica didn't object to her being around so much, while she began her own (what would now be) aggressive chemotherapy treatments. Gabrielle was deeply concerned about Jessica now, and she made her concerns known.

Too tired to fight Gabrielle any longer about it, Jessica was grateful to have someone who genuinely cared. With stage-three cancer and having been told that she *really* needed surgery, Jessica's doctor informed her that she could no longer put off, at a minimum, chemo and radiation, if she wanted even a *fighting* chance of being around just a *little* longer for her daughter. Her doctor had been emphatically blunt, telling her she'd likely be dead in a month if she didn't begin right then. Jessica told Gabrielle she would agree to take the prescribed treatment on one condition.

"And what's that?" Gabrielle asked.

"If you'll come work for me. Allow me to pay you to take care of my child."

"What?" Gabrielle was more shocked than insulted.

Jessica was so weak now she could barely get her words out. Even if she hadn't told Gabrielle, it was obvious from her frail body that something was wrong other than the toll Jasmine's sickness had taken on her. She'd totally ruled out surgery because she knew it would take her out of commission. Right now Jessica was using every ounce of strength she could muster just to keep Jasmine from knowing how truly sick she was.

"Hear me out completely," Jessica said, swallowing hard enough that Gabrielle could see her do it. "I can't do what's needed anymore. And frankly, you can't continue trying to keep up with your full-time job at the church and be here for me and Jasmine when we need you. Not the way we'll really need you at this point."

"Oh, you don't have to be concerned about me. I'll be okay. So far it hasn't posed a problem. And it won't be a problem now." Gabrielle leaned in on the table in the room where they sat alone. "Besides, Jasmine will be going home soon."

"And then what?" Jessica sat back against her chair, looking like she would tip over if someone merely walked by and caused a slight breeze. She stared at Gabrielle. "When Jasmine comes home, then what? Huh? She's still going to need someone who can do what needs to be done. And honestly, there will be days when I know she'll be a little down and need me, and maybe that will be the day when I can barely get out of bed, if I can get out at all. What then, Gabrielle? What?"

"If you're telling me you'd like me to continue to do what I can just as I've already been doing here and at the hospital before here, then I'm telling you it's not a problem. I can do that. I've tried to be respectful of you and Jasmine, being aware of the boundaries that must be maintained. But if you're asking me to come to your house after Jasmine is released to go home and help you out"—Gabrielle smiled—"then I'll be more than happy to do that. You don't have to offer to pay me to do that."

Jessica leaned on the table, resting her upper body on her folded arms. Her face was tired. She looked like a person too tired to go on. "We need you," Jessica said. "I need you to help me make sure Jasmine is all right. And let's be honest: It's not fair to ask you to work a full-time job somewhere and then come and help us pretty much full-time. It's just not right. So I'm asking you, if you would, please consider working full-time for me and allow me to pay you for your services."

"Jessica, I'm sure you can hire plenty of folks who are more qualified than me."

"Yes, I could hire a nurse or someone else to do this. But Jasmine needs stability in her life. She needs love. And I need someone around who I know, without any doubt, loves my little girl as much as I do and would do anything to ensure that she's okay. At this point, I don't know anybody else who fits that description other than you. So please"—she sat up and grabbed Gabrielle's hand, almost in a death grip—"I'm asking you . . . begging you: Please do this for us. And if not for me, then do it for Jasmine. At least consider it."

Gabrielle sucked in a deep breath and fell back hard against the chair. "All right. I'll consider it. But I'd like to talk this over with Pastor Landris and Johnnie Mae. Both of them have been so wonderful to me. They're like my parents."

Jessica released Gabrielle's hand. "That's fine. Talk it over with whoever you feel you need to. All I'm asking is for you to think about it and let me know. And if your answer is no, then I'll respect that and work this out somehow another way. But almost nine years ago, you made me a part of this wonderful little girl's life when you opted to give her life, then she was given to me. Now it's like you've been grafted into our lives . . . into our little family. Somehow, we've managed to bring our two worlds together and make this work. Just like that wonderful person's donated cells were grafted into Jasmine and have now become a part of her."

Gabrielle called Johnnie Mae and left a message for her to call her as soon as she got a chance. Gabrielle truly didn't want to quit her job. Becoming the director over this dance ministry had been the best thing that could have ever happened for her. It was a dream come true. To be able to do what she loved, and get paid to do it. And on top of that, the work she happened to be doing was ministry—no, it didn't get any better than *that*!

And yet, she was being asked to sacrifice one special love for another.

She looked up at the ceiling. "God, what do I do? What do I do?"

Chapter 35

And they also, if they abide not still in unbelief, shall be grafted in: for God is able to graft them in again.
—Romans 11:23

Johnnie Mae called back fifteen minutes after Gabrielle left her message. Said she was driving when the call came. And anybody who knew Johnnie Mae knew the pastor's wife neither talked or texted while driving. She'd waited until she'd reached home, having just left visiting her mother at the nursing facility, to return the call.

Gabrielle wasn't sure how to say it. For that matter, she wasn't even sure *what* she wanted to say. So she opted to merely tell Johnnie Mae what was going on, holding back nothing. After all, Johnnie Mae knew all there was to know about many of her secrets that no one, other than Zachary, knew. She knew about the baby she'd given up for adoption, and recently how the eight-year-old child had been in need of a bone marrow transplant (she'd told her all of these things herself). Johnnie Mae also knew, just as everyone else now, that someone had *indeed* been a match (although to date, no one, including Jessica, knew who that mystery someone was).

Gabrielle communicated to Johnnie Mae the latest development. That Jessica Noble, the adoptive mother and the only family Jasmine has left, had been diagnosed with breast cancer, reportedly stage three. "Jessica really needs me now," Gabrielle said.

"So she's asking for your help?" Johnnie Mae said. "But you're helping her already, aren't you?"

"Helping, yes. But Jessica feels she may be taking advantage of me with me working a full-time job at the church, then going there to help them," Gabrielle said.

"Okay. Apparently I'm not following you. What are you trying to tell me here?"

"Jessica wants to hire me full-time to work for her."

"So are you calling to resign your position at the church?" Johnnie Mae asked. "Is that what you're trying to convey?"

Gabrielle sighed. "I really love what I'm doing at the church. But Jessica doesn't have anyone to help her. And she and Jasmine need someone. I don't know what I'm trying to say. I did tell her it wouldn't be a problem for me to still do both."

"Gabrielle, tell me what's going through your head right now. Just say what's on your mind. I'm here for you. I've always been here when you've needed me. So tell me flat out," Johnnie Mae said. "What do you want to do?"

"Well, I don't want to quit my job at the church. I love what I'm doing."

"And you're good at it," Johnnie Mae said.

"Thank you," Gabrielle said. "But how can I, in good conscience, not help someone when they need me the most?"

"So, do you feel you owe it to them to go it this way?" Johnnie Mae asked.

"No. I'm not doing it, or even *thinking* about doing it, because I feel obligated. It's just . . . I know what it feels like to need somebody to help you and not have anyone there to do it. I know what it's like to feel all alone with nowhere and no one to turn to for help. I know. And I also know what it's like to have someone to step in and give you a hand up until you get back on your feet," Gabrielle said. "The way you and Pastor Landris stepped in and gave me a hand up when I was down. The way my dance mentor, Miss Crowe, helped me when I desperately needed someone."

"Well, I want to go on record that Pastor Landris and I didn't *give* you anything; you *absolutely* worked for it. You earned it, and you deserved it."

Gabrielle wanted to cry after hearing that. "Thank you. I appreciate you so much for saying that. You just don't know."

"Okay, so tell me, Gabrielle: What do you want to do? What do you want?"

"I want to be able to help Jessica and Jasmine get through this, but I don't want to lose my job with the dance ministry in the process. Honestly, I'd like to be able to do both: help them but not lose my job at the church."

"All right, then. Let me offer a possible solution. Why don't you just take a leave of absence from the church for a few months?"

"I can't do that. I haven't been here long enough. Besides, that wouldn't be fair to the church. I can't do that."

"Yes, you can." Johnnie Mae paused for a second, then continued. "Gabrielle, why do you think we exist as a ministry?"

"I'm sorry. I don't understand your question," Gabrielle said.

"As a ministry; why do you think we exist? What are we here for?"

"To do the work of the Lord, to serve God, and to serve people."

"Right. And what you're wrestling with right now is not a bad thing or a selfish thing. What you're over there trying to figure out is how to be a blessing to a widow, the fatherless, and the sick," Johnnie Mae said. "It doesn't matter that they're not members of our congregation. We always need to show the love of God. So you know what I want you to do?"

Gabrielle was sobbing now. She managed to speak. "What?"

"I want you to put in paperwork for a leave of absence for however long you think you'll need. I want you to go on and help them. And I don't want you to worry at all about your job at the church. It'll be waiting for you when you're finished."

"Thank you." Gabrielle wiped her eyes as she tried to pull herself together. "Thank you. Forgive me. My eyes are like fountains. I seem to be crying a lot lately."

"It's okay. You've had a lot to deal with. But you have such a kind heart and a wonderful spirit. Personally, I wish there were more people in the world like you. People look at Christians these days and they're not seeing us exemplifying the love of Christ like we should be doing. They see all of these colossal edifices, but they don't see colossal expressions of Jesus in our lives the way we should be showing of Him. Jesus said that whatever we did to the least of these, we're doing it unto Him. Well, I happen to know for a fact that God keeps good records."

"Thank you, Johnnie Mae. I don't know what to say. I've been so blessed to have people like you and Pastor Landris in my life. I have . . . I have."

"To God be the glory," Johnnie Mae said. "So put in the paperwork for a leave of absence and do what you can to help those in need of your help right now."

"I will. But I'll still do what I can for the dance ministry when I can. Again, I thank you so much for this." Gabrielle hung up and closed her eyes, lifted her face toward Heaven, and as the tears rolled down her face, she whispered, "Thank You."

Chapter 36

For which cause also I have been much hindered from coming to you.

—Romans 15:22

Deidra was waiting at the door when Lawrence entered the house.

"Where is she?" Lawrence asked his wife of his youngest daughter.

"In her room," Deidra said.

Lawrence went up to Imani's room. She was lying facedown on her bed. He went over, sat down, and placed his hand on her back. "Honey, what's wrong?"

"Nothing," Imani said, not bothering to turn toward him.

"Well, we know something is going on. Your mother called me a bit frantic. She's worried about you. Are you feeling okay? Is something hurting? Do we need to take you to the doctor? Come on, talk to me." Lawrence tried to pull her to an upright position, but she resisted.

"I'm fine. Mom shouldn't have bothered you. You can go on back and do whatever you were doing before she called."

"Listen, Courtney—"

Imani popped up and looked hard at her father. "It's Imani! My name is Imani! And I wish you'd stop calling me *Courtney* and call me by my *name.*"

Lawrence rested his hand on her shoulder. "I *am* calling you by your name."

"No. You're calling me by what you and your stupid campaign folks have decided you'll call me." Imani tucked strands of her hair that dangled in her face securely behind her ear.

"Courtney"—Lawrence caught himself—"Imani, we've talked about this. I told you that I'm in a really difficult reelection this time around. I'm being forced to do some things differently to ensure that I retain my seat. The entire family has had to make sacrifices, me included. Do you *really* think that I want to be a Republican? All we're doing, when it comes to you, is using your first name—the name you were given at birth and that's on your birth certificate: Courtney." Lawrence tilted his head.

"Whatever, Dad. In the end, you always get everything your way. It doesn't matter what any of the rest of us want. We don't matter. It *has* to be your way. Fine."

Lawrence gently placed his hand on her arm. "I know it might feel that way sometimes, but that's not actually true. I love you, Imani. And I want you to have things I never did. Things like this house we live in, the cars we drive. I mean look at your room." He made a show of scanning her bedroom. "You have practically anything anybody could ever want or imagine, just here in your room alone. There's a top-of-the-line computer, a forty-inch high-definition television on the wall, iPhone, iPod, iPad, stereo system, the bedroom suite that *you* picked out. And this year, when you turn sixteen, we're buying you a brand-new car. Not used, new. Imani, there are *so* many children who wish they were you . . . wish they could trade places with you."

"It's just stuff, Dad. Stuff breaks. Stuff stops working. Stuff tears up. Stuff gets old and outdated. I don't care that much about *stuff.*" Imani looked hard into her father's eyes. "Tell me: Why can't I go and see her? Huh? I want to know. I just want to see her. I want to see for myself that she's doing okay."

Lawrence nodded. They were back to this again. "Imani, I know this has been hard on you these past few months. I understand; I promise you that I do."

"You paraded us out there before everybody, talking about how important it was for us to be an example and do what we could to help. You were acting like you really cared about her and what might happen to her."

"I *did* care. And I'm honestly thankful a match was found.

But her part of the process involved a lot more than the donor, not that I'm diminishing the donor's part in the least. Your contribution as a donor was major. I dare say that you're the reason she's still alive. But that little girl, most likely, is not supposed to have a lot of visitors. And specifically not strangers traipsing in and out, carrying all kinds of germs, as she builds back her system. We don't want to do anything to harm her now, do we?"

"But I want to see her, Dad. I want to meet her. I want to ask her myself how she's doing," Imani emphasized again.

"And one day, you will. I'll see if I can arrange it. But for now, we don't need to add to her mother's worry." Lawrence took his hand and gently lifted Imani's chin. "Please say you understand. I hate it when you're sad like this."

Imani moved her chin out of his hand. "I understand that all of this was likely exactly what Paris said it was: a political stunt to get you publicity. Well, it worked, Dad. It . . . worked. People think you're absolutely wonderful for having led the charge in heightening the awareness of something most folks knew nothing about. You came off as someone who cared. Congratulations! Mission accomplished!" Imani stood up.

"But you don't care anything about her." Imani went to her desk and sat in her chair. "The only thing you care about is getting reelected. You could care less that I don't want to be referred to as Courtney in your political mailings or when we're out with you as though Imani doesn't exist. Do you have any idea what it's like for me to be teased by the kids at school because my father appears to have disowned me?"

Lawrence stood, went over, and hugged her. "Honey, you know that's not the case at all. I've explained this."

Imani turned on her computer. "Yeah. You explained it. The name *Imani* is 'too *ethnic* sounding' for some of the people you're trying to reach. Courtney is much more 'mainstream.' Well, Dad, I think you should get your folks to do a poll since they love polling, and you'll find out just how many black girls, and guys for that matter, are named Courtney."

"I don't need a poll. I happen to know that lots of black folks are named Courtney." Lawrence started to chuckle, hoping to break up some of the tension. "I happen to love the name, that's why I wanted you to be named that."

"Yeah. And Mom wanted to name me Imani. But because you wanted to name me Courtney, once again, your desire won out. I guess I need to just get used to it and stop trying to fight it. Things will always be *what* you want and how."

Lawrence grabbed her chair and turned her to face him. "I promise, Imani. If by the end of the year you still want to see her, we'll see what we can do to make it happen."

"Yeah. You mean after the November election so it won't get in your way."

Lawrence smiled. "I'm not trying to time it for after any election."

"Sure, Dad. Okay." Imani got up out of her chair, went back over to her bed, flopped down on it, and crossed her arms. "Fine. You say I can't see her until you say so, then fine. I just wonder what you're afraid of. Why are we going to such great lengths now to keep everything a secret when you didn't have any problems with going public about us all participating in the bone marrow drive? Why is that?"

Lawrence sat down beside Imani. "Imani, the rules of volunteering to be a possible donor normally only allow those between the ages of eighteen and sixty to even test. You were fifteen, well below the minimum age. That's why I had to sign to allow you to be able to do it."

"So you're saying you don't want anybody to know that we broke some rule? Is that what you're trying to say now?" Imani stared at him as she awaited his answer.

"I'm *saying* that I don't want people bothering you." He touched her arm.

She uncrossed her arms. "Yeah, that's right. You don't have a problem parading us in front of the cameras to get you publicity for possibly doing a noble thing. But when your youngest daughter ends up being a perfect match for the person we were obviously pretending to be helping, you don't want anybody to know it." She crossed her arms again. "Makes a lot of sense to me. Well, I'd like to meet the girl my stem cells happened to save. I want to see for myself that she's getting better."

Lawrence smiled. "Okay. Okay, I hear you loud and clear. So let me see what I can do. We'll put in a call to her mother to see if we can't arrange something soon. But if her mother says no or not right now, will you let it go until she says otherwise?"

"If you come back and tell me that her mother said no, it will make me wonder why she said no or if she really said no. Because I can't imagine a mother whose child was dying and is reportedly doing better, now that she's received the transplant she needed, would say she doesn't want to meet the person who donated her marrow if that person wanted to meet them." Imani uncrossed her arms and looked squarely at her father. "So, Dad, if you come back and tell me that she doesn't want to meet me, then I'll just figure it's you coming up with an excuse to keep us apart. For what reason, I don't know."

Lawrence swallowed hard, then nodded as he turned up his mouth a bit. "I love you, Imani. I really do." He stood up, leaned down, and kissed her on the top of her head. He then put his hand on her head softly. "I really do."

Chapter 37

Lest Satan should get an advantage of us: for we are not ignorant of his devices.

—2 Corinthians 2:11

Paris picked up her glass of water and took a sip. "Thank you, Daddy, for agreeing to meet me for lunch."

"No problem. I was both surprised and pleased when you called and suggested we do it," Lawrence said.

"You and I haven't spoken much these past months. It's March and spring has sprung. I just wanted us to reconnect." Paris took another sip of water.

"The disconnection wasn't my doing."

Paris sat against the cushioned red booth seat and smiled. "I know I can be a spoiled brat at times. But I always come to my senses when it comes to you, Daddy."

He nodded. "That you do."

"I don't know whether you know, but I've been under a lot of stress. I don't know if Mom mentioned it, but Andrew and I aren't in the best place lately."

Lawrence picked up his menu and peered over it at Paris. "She may have mentioned something to me to that effect."

Paris released a loud, deliberate sigh. "Andrew really wants a child."

"And . . ."

"And, I can't seem to produce one for him."

"All I can tell you is not to stress out about it, and eventually, it'll happen." Lawrence closed his menu and looked for someone to come take their order.

"It's not that easy. We've been trying for over a year now. Andrew is beginning to act different toward me. Do you think he might divorce me?"

Lawrence laughed. "Because you haven't gotten pregnant yet? I don't really think Andrew will divorce you for something like *that.* Not *that* anyway."

"You laugh like it's unheard of or something. Tamika and her husband are getting divorced."

"Are you talking about Tamika with the three kids?"

"Yes. And she has four."

"I don't think she's getting a divorce because she can't have children." Lawrence waved at a server to get his attention. "I don't know why you picked this particular restaurant. Service so far has been horrible."

Paris looked around as though she, too, was searching for someone. "I happen to like their food. And, no, Tamika isn't getting divorced because she can't have children. But it's sort of due to their children. It seems a lot of folks get divorced, often something to do with their children. Either they can't agree on how to raise them or money is tight because children are costly, what with daycare and things like that. That was why I wanted to wait a while before Andrew and I started a family."

"I'm sorry, sir," the waiter said. "We're a bit short staffed today. My sincere apologies to you. What can I get you both today?"

"I'll have the small watermelon and feta cheese salad, chicken scaloppine with fettuccine pasta, and for dessert, the red wine poached pear with ice cream," Paris said, holding up her menu when she finished.

The waiter took Paris's menu and turned to Lawrence. "And I'll have the house salad and steak au poivre with spicy black peppercorn sauce."

"What type of dressing for your salad?"

"The house dressing is fine," Lawrence said.

"And dessert?" the waiter asked. "Or would you like to wait to order it?"

Lawrence closed his glossy menu. "That chef's layer cake sounds good."

"Daddy, you really should try the red wine poached pear. Live a little, why don't you?"

"Oh, you think, huh?" Lawrence handed his menu to the waiter. "Okay, I'll try the poached pear with ice cream."

They both ordered sweet tea to drink. The waiter left.

"Okay, now where were we?" Paris said. "Oh, yes. I was talking about children. I think if Andrew and I don't have a baby soon, he's going to leave me."

"Paris, Andrew is not going to leave you just because you haven't gotten pregnant. He's not that kind of a person."

"That's the old Andrew. The new Andrew is different. Andrew has changed a lot in the past four months." Paris picked up her crisp, white cloth napkin and opened it, laying it on her lap. "And it all appears to have started right after we ran into Gabrielle Booker; oh, I'm sorry, it's Gabrielle Mercedes now. That's when he really started changing . . . started getting bolder . . . something . . . I don't know."

"What you mean is that he finally stopped letting you yank his chain." Lawrence sat back against his seat. "A man can only take so much."

"Of course. As usual, turn it all on me."

"Excuse me," a man said having approached their table. "Paris, is that you?"

Paris looked up. "Oh, my goodness! Hi," she said, standing and hugging the man three inches taller than her even with her heels.

"I wasn't sure, but I thought that looked like you." He reared back a tad and slowly began to scan her, starting at her head. "You look *good.*"

"Thank you." Paris turned to her father. "Daddy, this is Darius Connors. Darius, this is—"

"The Honorable Representative Lawrence Simmons." Darius extended his hand. "It's nice to meet you."

Lawrence looked at his hand, but didn't shake it. Lawrence didn't shake hands when he was eating. "Nice to meet you. Forgive me for not shaking your hand." He held his fork in the air.

Darius let his hand drop to his side. "My bad. It's no problem." Darius turned back toward Paris. "It is *so* good to see you. How long has it been?"

"Too long," Paris said. "Are you meeting someone here?"

"I was supposed to be, but he called just as I came in here and said something came up," Darius said. "I guess we can say I got stood up."

"Then sit with us," Paris said, sitting back down and scooting over to make room for him. "You don't mind, do you, Dad?"

Darius sat down before Lawrence had a chance to answer. "So how have things been? How many children do you have? You look *so* good. Wow . . ."

"*Me?* Look at you." Paris grinned. "I don't have any children yet."

The waiter came back with their salads. "Can I get something for you, sir?" the waiter asked Darius as he matched each salad with its owner.

"No. I don't want to impose," Darius said, directing his attention at Paris.

"Oh, please stay and eat," Paris said. "You were coming to eat already."

Lawrence sat back against his seat. He couldn't believe Paris had invited him to lunch, and now she was inviting someone else to infringe on their time together.

"If you're sure it's okay," Darius said as though it was settled.

"I'll get you a menu," the waiter said.

"It's okay. I'll just have whatever she ordered." Darius pointed his head at Paris.

Paris laughed. "You don't even know what I ordered."

Darius looked at Paris and smiled. "Oh, I trust you." He looked back to the waiter. "What she ordered is fine."

"And what to drink?" the waiter asked him.

"A glass of red wine," Darius said to the waiter. He then turned to Lawrence. "I'm not on the clock, so it's okay for me to have a glass of wine."

Lawrence shrugged to let him know he really didn't care what he did.

"So tell me," Paris said. "What's been going on with you? Darius Connors . . ." She ran her fingers through her hair, tossing her curls a few times.

"Let's see . . . what's going on with me? Bills, bills, and oh, yes, more bills. You know how it is these days," Darius said. "On second thought, you come from money. So you likely don't know how it is. But let me assure you that it's rough out there for the rest of us squirrels just trying to get a nut or two. Of course, I'm married—"

"To someone named Tiffany, right?" Paris said. "I heard that somewhere."

"Yes," Darius said, clasping his hands together and leaning forward. "And we have three crumb-snatchers: two girls and a boy. My oldest is a girl and she's almost nine. In fact, she's about the same age as that little girl that needed the bone marrow transplant some months back. It was all over the news at one time. You know about her, don't you?" Darius directed that last question to Lawrence.

Lawrence stared hard back at him. "Yes."

"Yeah. Look at me. What am I saying? Of course, you know. I heard that all of y'all were on television trying to get people to be tested to be possible donors." Darius nodded. "My pastor was also promoting and pushing us to do that as well."

"Who's your pastor?" Paris asked.

"Pastor George Landris. Yeah, he's all right. Better than a lot of preachers out there, that's for sure. He's a straight-up Bible guy. At least he's not caught up in mess like that Rev. Walker got himself tangled all up in. They picked him up on IRS-related violations and some other pretty shady activities. I heard he's taking a plea deal. Likely going to get four years, which generally means he'll likely only serve about eighteen months. Did you hear who happened to be one of the people that helped bring his little empire down? Reputation wise, anyway."

"No," Paris said with a grin as she giddily looked over at him. "Who?"

Lawrence looked at Paris and turned the corners of his mouth down, showing disapproval of the conversation, although in truth, he was rather enjoying hearing this bit of underground gossip. Lawrence was *more than* familiar with both George Landris and Marshall Walker. In fact, he'd almost gotten caught up in this Rev. Walker mess. William just happened to be really good at covering his tracks. In fact, now that he was thinking about it, he needed to give William a raise soon.

"Well, I don't know how true it all is," Darius said. "But I heard one of the people was Knowledge Walker, Rev. Walker's oldest son. They say Knowledge was a little ticked because his younger brother, named Clarence, who incidentally is a member of my church, had been out there doing everything in the world while the older brother stayed there alongside his father, holding things down. But then the youngest son got his life together and came back home to the church, giving his life to the Lord, which the father equated as his son finally coming home—"

"This sounds just like the parable of the prodigal son," Paris said.

"Exactly like it, now that you mention it," Darius said. "Anyway, when the youngest son came to his senses and returned home, his father welcomed him with open arms just like the prodigal son. It appears the oldest got upset about that."

"Again, just like in the parable," Paris said.

"Yeah," Darius said. "Well, from what I hear, Rev. Walker couldn't stand Pastor Landris. And it didn't help matters that Clarence didn't go back to his father's church, but like I said, he hooked up at ours with Pastor Landris. So Rev. Walker was planning to take Pastor Landris down in a *big* way."

"Wow," Paris said. "And these are *preachers* you're talking about."

"Yeah. They say Pastor Landris had some information on Rev. Walker that was never supposed to see the light of day. Some older preacher had it and had given it to Pastor Landris some years back, right before he died, to help keep Rev. Walker in check if he ever came after Pastor Landris. It was information Pastor Landris *could* have used, and at any time, to take Rev. Walker down. According to Rev. Walker's secretary, who Rev. Walker initially accused of being the one to leak what had been legally sealed information to the public, Pastor Landris had walked all bold-like up into Rev. Walker's office and handed the entire package over to him. Honestly, I don't get that. Because everybody knows Rev. Walker was trying to take Pastor Landris down right about then. My motto is: Get them before they get you."

"Scandalous," Paris said cheerily, then looked at her father as he showed his displeasure of all of this. "It's scandalous that men of God, who are supposed to be examples for the rest of us, would actually act in such a way."

"Well, I got to stick up for my pastor," Darius said. "They say Pastor Landris could have used that information to do Rev. Walker in a long time ago, but he chose not to. And when Rev. Walker was trying to set Pastor Landris up—"

"Set him up?" Paris chimed in.

"Yeah. Rev. Walker was trying to force Pastor Landris into some deal with some politician. I don't know all to that part." Darius looked at Lawrence and grinned as though he knew the politician was actually him. "Anyway, Rev. Walker was in it up to his receding hairline, and he was trying to force Pastor Landris to get involved. Somehow, Pastor Landris was being set up to take a fall or to be blackmailed into what Rev. Walker and this politician wanted him to do. But Pastor Landris didn't fall for it. And instead of Pastor Landris using the information he had against Rev. Walker to put him in check, he gave the whole package to Rev. Walker and essentially told him he was leaving it all in God's hand."

"Well, maybe Pastor Landris made a copy and used the copy to mess him up so he would appear all righteous when the information came out," Paris said.

"No," Darius said. "They say Rev. Walker had the package on his desk. His son came into his office at some point that day, found the package on his desk, and looked inside. For some reason, for which we may never know, the son decided to leak it to the newspaper people. When it came out, Rev. Walker thought his secretary had done it. Especially after he realized the package was gone. She was the one that pointed the finger at the son Knowledge, who admitted he was the one who gave it to the news folks."

The waiter brought their entrees and Darius's salad and entrée.

Darius began to eat.

Lawrence sat watching him as he shoved food into his mouth while he talked. There was something about Darius that he didn't care for, something about him that just didn't sit well with him.

"On another subject," Darius said right before putting more food in his mouth. "That little girl that needed the transplant . . . well they ended up finding someone who matched her. I was sure they weren't going to find a match. I mean: What are the odds?" Darius nodded quickly. "Yeah. There's something up with that, if you ask me. At least, that's what everybody is saying. Yep." He nodded as he chewed hard with his mouth open.

"Well, frankly," Lawrence said. "I think people who do the most talking really don't know what they're talking about most of the time. It's always 'they' said. Who is this 'they' that supposedly knows everything but in the end generally knows nothing?"

Darius nodded quickly as he shoved more food in his mouth. "True that. Because, with all due respect to you, Representative Simmons, they say the way you were acting that you must be that little girl's father." Darius stopped chewing and grinned.

Lawrence sat back and looked at him with a cynical face. "Is that right?"

Darius nodded, then put another bite in his mouth as he looked on at Lawrence. "Yep. That's the latest talk around town. They say that's why you took that project on as vigorously as you did. Of course, we never *did* learn who the matching person turned out to be. They say you're the one making sure that information remains under wraps so folks won't know the real truth."

"Oh," Paris chimed in with a dismissive wave. "Folks are always saying things when it comes to my daddy. He's been called everything but a child of God."

"Well, personally, I don't get into other folk's business too much myself. I have enough of my own to tend to and keep me busy," Darius said.

Paris then changed the subject and they talked about other things.

After about fifteen more minutes, Lawrence got the attention of the waiter to pay the check. "Well, I need to get back to the office," Lawrence said.

"Daddy, thank you so much for coming. I really enjoyed this," Paris said.

"Sure," Lawrence said. "So, Paris . . . are you ready to go?"

Paris pointed with her fork at her plate. "I'm still eating."

"You *could* get the rest to go," Lawrence said, standing next to the side of the table.

"Oh, I'll be fine. You go on," Paris said. "Thank you, Daddy. I love you."

Darius got up and moved over to the now vacated side, directly facing Paris. "Thanks, Representative Simmons, for the meal. I really appreciate it." Darius nodded.

"Sure," Lawrence said to Darius. "Paris, are you sure you're going to be all right? I can wait."

"Yes, Daddy. I'm a big girl. I'll be all right. You can go. I'm fine."

"I know you're a big girl," Lawrence said. "Okay, but call me when you get home."

"Will do." Paris jumped up and gave her father a big hug. "We really have to do this again soon. I had fun!" She sat back down and started back eating.

Lawrence nodded. "Yeah." And without another word, he left.

Paris watched her father walk out of view, then let her fork drop to her plate, making a loud clink. "You were *so* good," she said, leaning in toward Darius.

He picked up his glass of wine and teetered his glass a few times. "Of course. Were you expecting anything less?"

"Did you see the look on my father's face when you said that about your daughter being the same age as the little girl who needed the bone marrow transplant?" Paris grinned, flicking her hair again. "Oh . . . my . . . goodness!"

"Now that was priceless. You can't buy a look like that," Darius said, taking a sip of wine. He smacked a few times before leaning forward and gazing into Paris's eyes. "And to think: I not only got to spend a little quality time with a beautiful woman of your caliber, but I ended up getting a nice meal *with* fine wine to boot. It doesn't get any better than this." He set his glass down and leaned back and slightly to the side. "So what's next, Madame Butterfly?"

Paris smiled. "Oh . . . I can take it from here."

Darius grinned. "I just hope you allow me to tag along for the flight. I really like the view from where I'm perched now." He started a slow scan of her body.

Paris narrowed her eyes at him, picked up her glass of tea, and tipped it his way. "Cheers," she said.

He raised his glass to her. "Cheers." He smiled.

Chapter 38

Forget not the voice of thine enemies: the tumult of those that rise up against thee increaseth continually.
—Psalm 74:23

Lawrence went back to his office madder than he'd recalled being in a long while. He paced from the window to his desk. *How dare Paris do what she just did? What kind of a fool does she take me for?*

His daughter had called and asked to take him to lunch. He was fully aware that her offering would mean he would end up footing the bill as always, but that was Paris. He hadn't minded that. He and Paris hadn't spoken much of late. Not since that whole thing with the bone marrow transplant campaign he'd told his family he wanted them to get behind and support wholeheartedly.

To Paris's credit, she did participate in the news conference. But that was it. She refused to be swabbed to see if she was a possible match. Turns out, it was just as well. Everything had worked out even *better* than planned. Although at first, he wasn't sure how he felt when he learned that his youngest daughter was identified as a possible match, then a nearly perfect donor match for the little girl.

He wasn't going to allow Imani to be a donor. She was only fifteen. And by law, no one would actually know she'd been a match. But Imani had argued that she was old enough to decide herself and she had wanted to do this . . . had to do this. When Deidra and he talked privately about it, he'd confessed to her that the whole thing wasn't supposed to be anything more than a campaign gambit. He admitted to Deidra how it hadn't initially been his idea and that he had to be convinced to move forward with it.

That part had been true. He hadn't *wanted* to do it. Gabrielle had been the one to first bring it up. She'd thrown down a pretty heavy-duty gauntlet. He didn't have much of a choice but to at least *look* like he was trying to do what he could. And had he been a match, none of this would have had to come out at all. But he, like Gabrielle, had not been. Gabrielle said that a sibling had a greater chance of being a match and she was fully expecting him to have his children tested, if it would possibly save the child's life.

He still couldn't quite wrap his brain around the idea that he had another daughter out there. And as much as he had wrestled with the idea, he hadn't gone to see her. He could have gone, if nothing more than as the representative of the House who orchestrated the donor campaign. But he was afraid to see her. *No one can ever say with certainty how they'll react to something until they're faced with it.* If he was to visit with this child (which the mother had long before indicated she would have welcomed, especially after what he'd done to bring attention to her daughter's plight), he couldn't be sure what he would feel . . . what he would do. So he was choosing to play it safe and stay away.

And everything had somehow worked out. His wife and children were none the wiser about what was really going on. Deidra, in fact, was the one who pressured him into allowing Imani to be the donor. But Deidra and Imani had a close bond. And Imani always seemed to get her way when it came to her mother. At least, that's what Lawrence concluded.

"Our daughter is an amazing young lady," Deidra had said. "She's smart. She's caring. But most of all she really, honest and truly loves the Lord. Imani feels right now that her being a match is a God thing and something God would want her to do. If we don't let her do this, it could affect her for the rest of her life. And if that child dies because she didn't get a match, learning something like that could destroy Imani. Lawrence, we need to let her if this is what she wants to do. And she does."

Lawrence shook his head slowly as he thought about what his wife was saying. "I don't know, Dee. I don't want our baby having to go through whatever she'll have to go through to be a donor to . . . a stranger essentially." Lawrence had hesitated when he came to the word to call this little girl he knew now was his own daughter. In truth, she *was* a stranger, because they didn't actually *know* her. But by DNA she was also family; she was his child. And if Imani became her donor, she would principally be donating to her own half sister.

"Well, you know *exactly* what Imani would say to that," Deidra said. "She would pull out some reference in the Bible about when Jesus was in need and He presented Himself in the form of a stranger, that in turning away that stranger, we may have been unknowingly turning Him away." Deidra placed her hand on Lawrence's chest. "From what those people told me as to what would be required if Imani were to do this, it will be much like donating blood. She'll be given a few injections—"

"See what I mean," Lawrence said. "They'll be sticking our child with a needle. And what if whatever they're injecting into her body causes her to get sick?" Lawrence shook his head. "No. No. I don't want my child going through that."

"She's our child," Deidra said. "And she's gotten stuck with needles plenty of times before. It would only sting for a little bit, you big baby." Deidra laughed. "She would receive a few injections, go to the place where they'll hook her up to a machine, take her blood where they'll extract the needed cells, then recirculate her blood back into her body. That's it."

"That's it? Are you sure? You're *sure* she's not going to end up losing something that her own body might need?"

Deidra laughed. "You know, you are *such* a great father. You truly care about your children. But to answer your question, they'll only be taking some of her marrow cells . . . stem cells. In fact, she'll be able to come home right after she's done. And school is out for the holidays, so she won't even miss any days of school."

"Well, if we decide to say yes, I don't want anyone knowing that she was the match or even that she was the donor," Lawrence said. "Okay?"

Deidra had a puzzled look on her face. "Why not? I would think you'd want *everyone* to know how well your efforts paid off. Then folks will see this really wasn't a gimmick."

"*This* is not about my campaign right now. This is about *our* little girl. And I don't want this being exploited for any reason—political or otherwise."

Deidra smiled. "And to think: Everybody thinks you don't really care. You are such a softie, Representative Simmons. And I am so glad that I married you."

He looked at his wife. She was truly a remarkable woman. She'd been there by his side every step of the way. So in the end, he was glad he'd chosen this route. He wouldn't want word of his past transgression to get out; it would destroy Deidra and destroy their marriage. And he wasn't going to let that happen. Not if he could do anything to keep it from happening. Consenting to Imani being the bone marrow donor had closed a lot of open doors. And everything in their lives seemed to be getting back to normal, whatever normal was.

But now here was Paris and her little friend who just "happened" to show up trying to stir things up. Darius Connors's appearance was a bit *too* convenient for Lawrence.

Here he'd just gotten Imani calmed down about wanting to visit the little girl, at least until after his election. *Now here comes Paris snooping around.* But just how much did Paris really know? Too many things were starting to overlap for Lawrence's comfort.

There was Gabrielle Mercedes, who truly looked like she wasn't out to get anything from him, other than to save that child's life. Now that *that* was done, he hadn't heard anything more from her. Still, Gabrielle and Paris lived together for that brief time, and they didn't exactly part on great terms. He had yet to get the full story on what happened. But he also knew that whatever it was, it was likely his daughter's doing. Then Paris happened to run into Gabrielle at the hospital cafeteria. That wouldn't have been about anything had it not been for Paris's suspicions that her husband and Gabrielle possibly knew each other and that Andrew wasn't being totally straight with her.

Of course, it would turn out that Paris was right in her suspicions, although she has no idea just how right. It hadn't been easy, but William's people had done some digging around and discovered that Andrew and Gabrielle *did* know each other. Fortunately, their encounter was during an innocent time period—Gabrielle's pre–Goodness and Mercy days of being an exotic dancer and post her having gotten pregnant. If it had turned out that Andrew had been in Gabrielle's life other than when he seemed to have been and Paris found out, Lawrence knew his daughter. She would blow up everything around her.

So his lunch date with Paris had his mind going ninety miles an hour now. Had Paris somehow found out about him and Gabrielle? Did she know he'd fathered a child out of wedlock that had been given up for adoption (unbeknownst to him at the time), and now the truth was in someone's possession other than the few he'd been told? And who was this Darius Connors character? What role was he playing?

Lawrence called William into his office.

"What's up?" William said, sitting down. "How was your lunch with Paris?"

Lawrence slowly spun around from gazing out of the window. "I'm not sure you can call what we just had 'lunch' together. Listen, I need you to check somebody out for me. See what you can find out about him and get back to me as soon as possible."

"Okay. Who's the unlucky person this time around?"

"Darius Connors. And put a rush on it, will you."

William stood up and headed for the door. "Consider it as good as done!"

Chapter 39

But I have understanding as well as you; I am not inferior to you: yea, who knoweth not such things as these?

—Job 12:3

Paris was on the computer when Andrew came home from work.

"What are you doing?" Andrew said as he kissed her.

She normally would be watching television or something around this time of day, but she was gazing intensely at the computer screen. "Just checking on some things." She turned and looked at Andrew. "Dinner is ready when you are."

"You cooked?"

She tilted her head. "No, I didn't *cook*. I got carryout from my favorite restaurant when I was out today."

"Oh, so you went out today." He rolled his eyes ever so slightly.

Paris stood up and stepped away from her computer. "Yes, I went out today. I had lunch with my daddy." She was almost giddy about it.

"Wow, so you and Daddy had a date today? That's great. How did it go? That's if it's safe to ask. Did you two make up . . . bury the hatchet?"

"It went wonderfully, if I must say so. He and I had a really nice talk."

"So that means everything is cool with you two again? It's been over three months now."

"Let's just say: I think we're on the right path. We're getting there."

"Well, that's the best news I've heard all day. I hope you two continue on this right path. I'm going to check out dinner." Andrew left the room, headed for the kitchen.

Paris went back to the computer. She was checking out everything she could find on bone marrow transplants, specifically about those who normally matched.

From the start she'd been suspicious of this whole thing. As far back as she could remember, her father rarely did anything for anyone (outside of his family and, of course, William) unless there was a good reason or a payoff behind it. She was first thinking that his push for the whole family to show them as caring about someone in need of a bone marrow transplant was merely a campaign maneuver. But the more she was putting two and two together, the more things were arriving at another mathematical conclusion other than four, like some kind of quadratic equation.

Her mother didn't think the way she did. Deidra took people and things at face value *until* she was proven wrong. Paris, on the other hand, was forever suspicious of people and the true likely motive behind whatever they might be doing. Sometimes she was wrong, but most times, she was right or, at least, on the right track. Such was the case with her father and this bone marrow issue.

Her father had pushed too hard on this; he'd been more aggressive than usual, even for him. And when she'd balked about what he was asking of them, she saw his veins pop up in his neck. If there wasn't more to this, then why had he reacted in such a way? She just didn't know *what* wasn't matching up. *Yet.* But Darius had helped her tremendously in getting closer to an answer.

She'd run into Darius when she'd gone into her favorite jewelry store. He'd reared back on his heels, staring at her in a classic player way. She first thought he was just another guy trying to hit on her like she got more times than she cared to count. And even though he was definitely a fine specimen of a man, she wasn't planning on giving him any play. He'd strolled over to her with a certain swagger to his walk. She'd quickly let him know how unimpressed with him she was by moving to another counter just as he was about to approach her. Most guys got the message that, should they persist, her next move would likely be to embarrass them and it was in their best interest to keep it moving and not force her hand.

Apparently Darius didn't get the message and continued to follow her. He slinked up to her. "I know you're not going to act like you don't know me."

She turned and stared hard at him, her mouth already fixed to shatter his tired old line, when she suddenly realized who he was. "Darius? Darius Connors?"

"The one and only," Darius said. "Like Jay-Z and Beyoncé, I'm pretty much known by a single name."

"I see you're still full of yourself."

He flicked the bottom of his chin as though he were brushing something off it, and smiled. "How you doing, girl?" He leaned down and hugged her. "You certainly are looking good. No, I take that back; you look *better* than good." He kissed her fingers and smiled even more. "Good enough to eat."

Paris wasn't impressed by his assessment; whenever she stepped out of her house door, she always looked good. Still she'd been taught to be polite. "Thank you," she said.

"Yeah, I see aging hasn't affected you at all."

Paris pulled her body back. "Aging? Who's aging? I know you're not talking about me! Number-wise, I'm only twenty-seven, soon to be twenty-eight in a few months, and I'm still finer than a lot of teenagers I've seen these days."

"I heard that!" Darius said. "So, how's Daddy dearest?"

"My father is fine, thank you very much."

"Really? Well, that's not the word on the street." Darius nodded. There was a certain twinkle to his eyes.

That's what got Paris's attention—the way his eyes appeared to sparkle. Like he knew something and it was hard for him to hold it in, so his eyes sent out a signal to say what the mouth hadn't. "Oh, really now? You mean to tell me that a smart guy like yourself is foolish enough to believe what you hear on the streets?"

"Would you like to go get some coffee or something and

compare notes? You and I were always great when it came to copying off each other's papers. Remember, Paris?" He smirked.

Yes, Paris remembered. He'd taken one college course, Psychology 101, with her while he was there. They'd been friendly, though not really friends. She'd even danced with him once at a party. So when he realized one day that she was struggling with a particular test that honestly, she hadn't studied for because she'd been out partying the night before, he creatively found a way to give her the answers she so desperately needed. She in turn paid him back by sharing answers to the next test a friend had somehow gotten his hands on. Darius dropped out of college after that semester. Although someone told her he'd married Tiffany, that homely girl he'd brought with him to a party once, she personally hadn't seen or heard from him since.

Until now. And once again, he was helping her with a test of sorts, filling in some of the missing blanks. But Paris didn't fully trust him, at least not enough to let him in on her total plans. She and he had devised that lunch date rendezvous that included her father. She had to admit: It really was good hanging out with her father again. For once, he hadn't made her feel inferior like he had a tendency to do. She almost hated that she'd ruined such a nice time by having Darius show up like that.

But what was done was done. Maybe she'd ask her father out again, only the next time it would be for real, and not a setup.

Still, she and Darius had plans to meet up again. She was aware that he was interested in more than being her sidekick. But she also knew how to handle men like Darius. There wouldn't be anything happening between the two of them. Her only interest with Darius was her discovery of the truth project.

She and Andrew were working on making a baby. Unfortunately, *that* little project wasn't faring so well. And it didn't help that Andrew seemed to be changing so much. He wasn't as attentive to her needs as he'd been in the past. Her whining didn't seem to move him in the way that it used to. She wasn't sure what was going on, but she knew she had to step up her game if she didn't want to lose him.

And she didn't want to lose him.

Chapter 40

Let love be without dissimulation. Abhor that which is evil; cleave to that which is good.

—Romans 12:9

Jessica had to have chemo treatment three times a week and wasn't able to see Jasmine much at all. Gabrielle was glad she'd agreed to take a leave of absence from her job at the church to take care of Jasmine and her mother full-time. She didn't get to see Zachary as much, but he was *so* understanding. He would come see Jasmine every day, even if he could only stay for a few minutes. His visits totally made Jasmine's day. Gabrielle was also taking Jessica back and forth for her chemo treatments and staying with her until she was settled in after taking her back home. She would then go back to the facility and sit with Jasmine.

Jasmine had been a real trouper about everything, not just about her situation, but about not getting to see her mother much. At the start of Jessica's chemo, her hair immediately started to fall out. Jessica decided to shave her head and wear beautiful scarves. In the beginning, she didn't tell Jasmine that she was sick. Instead, she told her she didn't want her to be the only one with short hair so she had hers shaved to show her true solidarity. When Jasmine asked Gabrielle why she wasn't showing her solidarity with them by shaving her head, Zachary valiantly stepped in and saved the day.

"Blame it on me, Miss Jazz. I'm her boyfriend and I like to pull her hair," Zachary said. "Not that I don't like your and your mother's hairstyle. I think you both are too cute. It's just . . . well, just call it a Dr. Z thing. But I like to walk up and pull Gabrielle's hair." He gently pulled a curl and let it spring back. "See?"

Jasmine giggled. "Like Ellis, this boy that was in my class. He would pull my hair like that back when I *had* longer hair before it came out. Mama said he pulled it because he really liked me. So are you and Miss G going to get married?"

Gabrielle was about to tell Jasmine that it wasn't nice to put a guy on the spot like that, when Zachary preempted her. "As soon as you get out of this place and are well enough to be our flower girl, we most certainly are."

"For real!" Jasmine said. "For real? I would so love that. Can I, Mom? Can I be their flower girl at their wedding?"

"Of course you can, sweetheart. If you want to be a flower girl and they want you to be, I'll be right there beaming and cheering you on as you walk down that aisle, casting flower petals onto the floor, making me *so* proud." Jessica hugged her.

"I love you, Mom."

"I love you more," Jessica said. "I love you . . . more."

It was a Tuesday, exactly eighty-six days since Jasmine's bone marrow transplant. She'd done remarkably well. Her white cell count was great. Her immune system was operating just as the doctors wanted. Her hair was growing back so pretty, like baby fine hair. To Gabrielle, it was like having a baby and watching that baby grow and get stronger every day.

Jessica was home, resting from her last round of chemo. She was so weak. She'd wanted to be there on this day more than anything in the world, and she'd tried her best. But she was throwing up and she couldn't get out of bed, no matter how hard she tried. Gabrielle told her to just rest and she'd take care of everything for her. She and Jessica were on the same page; everything they did was for Jasmine's sake.

Zachary had gone with Gabrielle to the facility where Jasmine was. He'd walked in with a huge grin on his face and two balled-up fists crossed at the wrist.

Jasmine giggled. It had been a while since he'd done that.

Zachary held his crossed fists out to Jasmine as she sat in the chair next to the window. "Alabama hit the hammer, high or low. If you pick the right one, you may go."

Jasmine tapped the right fist. He opened it and held his hand out.

Jasmine picked up the piece of paper, unfolded it, and began to read it. It said, *You may go. You're going home today.* Jasmine looked at Zachary, then Gabrielle.

Gabrielle nodded, almost in tears at this point.

"For real? Are you serious? I'm going home today?"

Gabrielle hugged Jasmine as she sprang to her feet. The two of them, locked in an embrace, started jumping up and down. "Yes. You're going home today. For real!"

Jasmine stopped and stood still. "Where's my mother? Is she signing the papers for me to leave?"

"No, honey," Gabrielle said. "She's not here. She's not feeling so hot today, so she asked me and Dr. Z to come and get you and bring you home." Gabrielle gazed down into Jasmine's little face. "Your mother can't wait to see you." She gave Jasmine a quick wink.

Jasmine was no longer smiling now. "Is my mother going to die?" Jasmine asked, tears in her eyes, then falling.

Gabrielle put on a brave face. "Let's not have any of that kind of talk on a day like this. You're going home, Jasmine! You're going home!"

Jasmine bolted into Zachary's arms. "I don't want my mother to die! Please Dr. Z! I know you can help her! Please don't let my mother die!" she cried.

Zachary held her tight. Gabrielle came and hugged the two of them in a group hug. Gabrielle couldn't tell Jasmine the truth: Her mother was very sick. The more Gabrielle thought about it, the more she was thinking that maybe Jessica had been right when she'd asked her not to bring her to her house today, but to take her to Gabrielle's home until she'd gotten a little more of her strength back in a day or two.

"I don't want Jasmine to see me like this," Jessica had said before Gabrielle left to go pick up her daughter. "Not the first time she gets out of that place. I don't want me, looking like this, to be the first thing she comes home to. I don't."

Gabrielle had argued that Jasmine could care less *what* Jessica looked like. She just wanted to see her and to be with her. But now Gabrielle was reevaluating that decision. Maybe she *should* have agreed to take Jasmine home with her.

At least for this joyous first day of Jasmine finally getting to leave this place, she deserved one day of no worries.

Maybe she should have . . .

Chapter 41

If it be possible, as much as lieth in you, live peaceably with all men.

—Romans 12:18

Before Gabrielle and Zachary could get out the door with Jasmine, there was a knock at her door.

"Hello." A singsong voice came as a head slightly peeked in.

"Hi," Gabrielle said, walking toward the door to see who was there. "Come on."

The person came in as did a teenage girl along with her. Gabrielle stopped in her tracks. She couldn't believe her eyes. It was Paris Simmons-Holyfield ("with a hyphen"). "Hi there," Paris said, not seeming to notice Gabrielle as she looked past her to Zachary. "I'm sorry. I was looking for—" She looked at Jasmine sitting in a chair. "Would you happen to be Jasmine?"

"Yes, ma'am," Jasmine said.

"Okay. Then I guess I *am* in the right place." Paris looked from Jasmine back to Zachary. "You're so pretty. You're absolutely beautiful." It was then that she must have noticed Gabrielle, since her body literally stiffened as she yanked back.

Jasmine was blushing. "Thank you," she said to Paris.

The teenager with Paris stepped forward. "Hi." Her smile was huge, her full attention directed totally toward Jasmine.

"Hi," Jasmine said, her big brown eyes looking upward as she smiled.

"Oh! Where are my manners?" Paris said to Gabrielle, who

stared hard at her now. "This is my little sister, Imani Simmons."

"Hi, Imani," everyone said almost in unison.

"Hi, all," Imani said. "But if you've seen any of my father's political materials, you probably recognize me as Courtney. But I prefer my middle name Imani."

Zachary went over to Imani and shook her hand. "Well, it's really nice to meet you, Imani."

Gabrielle went and stood over Jasmine like an eagle protecting her nest as she tried to figure out what was *really* going on here.

"I've wanted to meet you for months now," Imani said to Jasmine. "But my daddy wouldn't let me. He said your immune system could be compromised, so of course, we didn't want to do anything to set you back in your getting well."

"Thanks," Jasmine said. "But I'm doing great now. In fact, I'm going home today!"

"You are?" Paris said it like she was the nicest person around. "Wow. Well, I'm glad we came by today, then. Otherwise, we would have missed you completely."

"I'm sorry," Gabrielle said to Paris, deciding she was going to find out what all of this was about. "Do you *know* Jasmine? I mean, other than from the news."

Paris smirked. "Well, this is our first time meeting her in person. But I suppose you could sort of say we know her . . . we've sort of met. Maybe not as much me as my sister here." Paris placed both her hands onto Imani's shoulders.

"What my sister here is *trying* to say, Jasmine, is that our cells have met," Imani said. "I'm your bone marrow donor."

Jasmine grinned really big then. "You are? For real? You are!"

"Yes," Imani said, matching Jasmine's grin. "Yes. For real." Imani went over to Jasmine and the two hugged. "We sort of favor a little. That's something, huh?"

"Our cells match and we sort of match." Jasmine giggled. "I look like my mother. I have her eyes. That's what everybody tells me."

Imani laughed. "I look like my daddy. I have my daddy's eyes. That's what everybody tells *me.*"

Paris looked at Gabrielle like she'd just eaten a green persimmon before primping her mouth, then forcing the corners of her mouth into a smile. Paris took out her cell phone. "Hey, you two," she said. "Let me get a picture of the two of you together." The two girls put their faces side by side and struck a pose. Paris snapped several times with the camera feature of her iPhone. "Beautiful!" she said when she was finished. "Just beautiful."

"Thank you, Paris," Imani said, then squeezed Jasmine again. The two of them held each other before releasing and hugging two more times.

"So," Paris said to Jasmine after Imani and Jasmine stopped their hugging marathon. "You're going home today. That is so great! Where is your mother? Imani and I were looking forward to meeting her."

"She's not here. Miss G and Dr. Z are taking me home."

"Is that right?" Paris smiled, her cheesy phoniness starting to sicken Gabrielle at this point. "Gabrielle, or Miss G as you call her, and I were once friends. In fact, for a few months, we were even roommates. So how exactly do you know Miss G?"

"Miss G and Dr. Z have been with me pretty much through this whole—"

"Jasmine, are you sure you've gotten everything?" Gabrielle said, purposely interrupting her. "We don't want to end up forgetting anything, you know."

"I'm pretty sure," Jasmine said. "I even got all of my messages Dr. Z brought me. But I'll check one more time and be sure."

"That's okay. I'll check for you," Gabrielle said. She then turned to Paris. "I know she's eager to get home. So we're going to get out of here now. But it was so good of you to come by." Gabrielle walked over to Imani. Tears began to well up in her eyes as she looked at this young girl who stood tall before her and essentially had saved Jasmine's life. "It was *truly* great to meet you, Imani. Your name means faith."

"Yes, it does."

Gabrielle nodded and smiled. "Imani: a blessed name of a

blessing of a person. On behalf of Jasmine's mother, I want to thank you for what you did for Jasmine. That was a great and noble thing that you did, it really was. And God is going to reward you greatly for it. I believe that. My pastor's wife always says that God keeps great records. And He does. He really does."

Imani smiled. "Thank you for that." She hugged Gabrielle as Gabrielle tried inconspicuously to wipe away her emergent tears, hoping no one would see that she was crying, particularly not Paris.

"Thanks for coming by," Zachary said, stepping up and taking Paris by her elbow as he led her toward the door, essentially blocking her line of view to Gabrielle.

"Bye," Imani said to Jasmine before going over again and giving her one more hug. "Now I want you to take good care of my cells for me. All right? Is that a deal?"

Jasmine laughed. "All right. I will. That's a deal. You're really funny."

"I've been told that," Imani said. "But seriously: I'm so glad you're okay."

"Me, too," Jasmine said.

Imani left with a wave. Paris pulled up the rear, exiting right behind her.

Zachary took Gabrielle in his arms and hugged her tight. "Are you okay?" he whispered directly in her ear so only she would hear.

"Yeah," Gabrielle whispered back. "I don't know why, but I have a bad feeling about Paris and what just happened here."

"You and me both," he said still whispering. "Her sister seems really nice though."

"Yeah."

"Hey, you two!" Jasmine said, almost yelling at them. "Are you going to hug and make goo-goo eyes all day, or are we going to finally break out of this joint?"

Gabrielle wiped her eyes once more, turned to Jasmine, laughed, and said, "Let's make like a banana and *split*!"

Jasmine laughed as she took a leap into the air. "Yes!"

Chapter 42

If thine enemy be hungry, give him bread to eat; and if he be thirsty, give him water to drink.

—Proverbs 25:21

Lawrence pressed his back hard against his seat as soon as he saw him approaching his table. Lawrence had arrived earlier than the five P.M. requested time because he preferred being on the passing end, rather than the receiving, specifically for this particular meeting.

Darius sat down in the booth seat across from Lawrence without being asked or a proper greeting on his part. "Thank you for agreeing to see me on such short notice." He leaned in as though he thought he was really someone important.

"Well, you did say that it was in my best interest that I meet with you today. So let's hear it," Lawrence said.

Darius smiled and sat back against his seat. "I see you don't waste any time."

"You've heard the old saying: Time is money. So let's hear what you have." Lawrence held a rigidness to his face that conveyed he wasn't one to be played with.

"What say we order something to eat before we get started?"

Lawrence tilted his head. "Suit yourself."

Darius looked around the area where they sat. The waiter must have seen him and came over immediately. "What we got on the special today?" Darius asked him.

The waiter rattled off the special for the day and his recommendations when Darius asked what he thought was good. Darius ordered, then turned to Lawrence.

Lawrence shook his head and waved the waiter away.

"So, you're not going to eat anything?" Darius asked.

"I don't intend to be here that long." Lawrence picked up his glass of water and tipped the glass toward Darius.

"That's fine," Darius said. "As long as you still pick up the bill, you don't have to eat a thing."

"You ask me here and you're also expecting me to pay?" Lawrence took a sip from his glass as though he were drinking something stronger than mere water.

Darius smiled. "If we're getting straight to it, I suppose you *can* say that I asked you here and, yes, I expect you to pay. Maybe you can write it off as a campaign expense."

"Did my daughter send you to try another ruse on me?"

Darius fell back against his seat and grinned. "You talking about Paris? Paris doesn't even know I'm here. She's a sweet girl though. A bit too trusting maybe. I said *maybe* now. You see, she was the one that helped me put this all together."

Lawrence leaned in. "All of *what* together?"

Darius leaned in as well. "All of the pieces. About how dedicated you were to finding a donor for that child. Then there was your reaction when I brought up what I'd heard about that child possibly being yours, when we all were eating lunch the other day."

Lawrence began a phony chuckle. "Listen here. Do you have any idea how many things I've been accused of doing that have no merit?"

"Probably just a few shy of what I've been accused of. The only thing is: I know which things that are said about me that happen to be true, as I'm sure you do as well." He glanced in the direction where the waiter had disappeared to. "I wonder what's taking so long for my salad and some rolls to get here. They have the best yeast rolls. Have you tried them before? If you're not careful, you can get full just eating the rolls."

"I'd appreciate it if you'd just get to the point of why you're sitting in my face right now. If all you came to do is rehash gossip that's easily purchased from any filthy rag on a newsstand, then I would say our business here is concluded."

"How about this: I know you're the father of that child, and I can prove it."

Lawrence started to laugh. "Once again speculation, rumors, and lies."

"Your baby girl, Imani, or as you prefer to call her, Courtney, was a match for the little girl. Now what are the chances of *that* also happening? I mean really. And, yes, I believe in God and the power of prayer as much as the next person. In fact, I happen to attend church regularly, although I've not quite latched on to the entire concept the way my wife has."

Lawrence smiled. "Your wife's name is Tiffany, isn't it?"

Darius stopped and frowned. "How do you know that?" He grinned. "Oh, that's right. Paris mentioned that the other day at lunch." He began nodding like a bobble-head doll.

"And you have three children: two girls and a little boy you call Junior. Jade is your oldest; she's eight. Dana is six, and Darius Jr. just turned three last November." Lawrence steepled his fingers together. "How am I doing so far?"

The waiter brought Darius's food, made sure he didn't need anything else, then left.

Darius stared at Lawrence almost the whole time the waiter was there.

"Don't let me stop you," Lawrence said, making a sweeping motion with his hand. "Eat up. Drink a little of your water. All of a sudden you're not looking so hot."

Darius continued to stare at Lawrence as he picked up his fork and speared a grape tomato on his salad plate.

"You're not going to say grace? One shouldn't eat before praying and thanking God for the food provided. Who knows: You might end up choking on your food, and then what?"

Darius put the tomato in his mouth. He smiled. "So what did you do? Have someone check me out? That's fine. I have nothing to hide."

"Is that right?"

Darius picked up a roll, pulled off a piece, and tossed it into his open mouth. "That's right. It's like you said: Most things are stuff that can't necessarily be proven. The thing that's different between me and you? You're an Alabama legislator up for reelection later this year. And I'm willing to bet you that your opponent would pay dearly for what I'm able to give him on you. But I was thinking that I owe it to your daughter, who has been wonderful to me, by the way, when our paths have crossed, to at least allow you the first opportunity to buy the information that I have."

"Which would be?"

Darius flashed him a big smile. "My silence for starters. You see, your opponent would pay me for the information I can provide to pretty much take you out of the race for good. But you can pay me to keep my mouth shut and not give this piece of information that just may point folks in the right direction to learn everything they'd need to know about that bone marrow situation."

"And how much were you thinking of charging me for this 'service'?"

"Well, you know people have fallen on hard times these past few years. I have a family, as you've already learned, and we have bills mounting to the ceiling."

"Well, I hope you know I'm by no means a rich man." Lawrence took a sip.

"Yeah, I didn't think you were rich. But you probably do okay. I'm a fair man. I was thinking maybe you could give me a job with your campaign, one of those positions that pay well. I've never had a one-hundred-thousand-dollar-a-year salaried job before."

"So you want to work for me on my campaign?"

Darius cut off a piece of his pecan-crusted tilapia fish with his fork and shoved it in his mouth as he nodded. "That's a good start. After you win reelection, maybe we'll see where else I'd make a good fit. That's a fair deal, don't you think? This way, no money would have to come directly out of your pocket. See how I'm looking out for you already? Even *before* you put me on the payroll."

"Give me one bit of information that says you're worth a place on my campaign staff and my payroll. Otherwise, this meeting is over."

"How about Gabrielle Mercedes?"

Lawrence maintained his poker face. "And who is she that I should care?"

Darius's smile dropped slightly.

Just as Lawrence thought. Darius didn't have anything. All he was doing was fishing, although in truth, it bothered him that he would use bait that was close enough to truth to cause him to possibly take a bite.

Lawrence stood up. "Young man, let me give you a little piece of advice. I chew folks like you up and spit them out on a daily basis. Don't you ever try and blackmail me with foolishness again! Or I will not overlook your naiveté, and I will have you for breakfast, then lunch, then dinner. You need to be careful who you mess with. Because if you fool around and mess with the wrong person, trust me: You'll end up getting yours!"

Lawrence took out a fifty-dollar bill and stuck it in Darius's blue shirt pocket. "That should be enough to cover your meal. Oh, and the water? It's free." Lawrence patted Darius's pocket with the money in it. "Whatever is left over, why don't you use it to buy your children some ice cream as opposed to something for one of your women on the side?" Lawrence then leaned over and whispered in his ear. "And tell Fatima Adams the next time you happen to run into her that she was really smart to get out when she did." Fatima Adams was a woman with whom Darius once had a secret affair.

Lawrence patted his shoulder and strolled away without looking back.

Chapter 43

There is a generation that curseth their father, and doth not bless their mother.

—Proverbs 30:11

Paris had come to her parents' home for the third straight day in a row. On Monday, two days before, when no one was home, she'd come to the house and gone snooping in her parents' closet. Paris knew her mother kept all of their personal private information in a fireproof security box in their closet. Paris had located Imani's file and, more importantly, the information she was searching for—the name and current whereabouts of the person her sister had been a bone marrow donor for.

Then yesterday, Paris had taken Imani to meet Jasmine. Imani had been so appreciative of Paris doing that for her that today she'd invited her big sister to lunch, her treat, after a little retail therapy, of course. This was how Imani, so far, had spent her spring break. Imani was upstairs now in her room on the phone or the computer or whatever it was that she did after having bought some really cute outfits. Paris sat in the den with the television on waiting on her father to come home.

Getting to meet Jasmine had been much easier than Paris thought it would be. She'd called the facility to see if it was all right for the patient to have visitors at this time, giving the impression that she was someone close to the family. The woman who answered confirmed that Jasmine was *indeed* still there *and* receiving visitors.

Imani had told Paris how her father didn't want her going to meet the girl she'd been the donor for. He'd said they would see how things progressed and would possibly see about arranging a meeting at the end of the year. Paris saw how much this was hurting and frustrating Imani. But honestly, that wasn't the reason she had decided to do this.

Paris wanted to see the child that had moved her father to step out in the way he had done for her. She wanted to know who this little girl was and, more specifically, what she looked like up close. She wanted to meet the mother of this child to see if this was someone her father possibly had an affair with, ultimately producing an offspring that no one, other than the two of them, knew about.

Darius had told her what he'd heard on this situation. She and Darius had sort of set her father up. And her father had pretty much confirmed, as far as she was concerned, that *something* was going on. Paris just couldn't understand why her mother never questioned stuff the way that she did. Surely her mother had to hear what people were saying. Her mother had to know that it was at least *possible* that her husband, Paris's father, might not have always been faithful to his wife.

Of course, in her own world, she never thought Andrew would actually cheat on her, either. But she also knew: She would never say never. In the world she lived in, anybody and everybody were always suspect. During the height of an argument once, Malachi had told her that was a sad way to live—to never be able to trust *anyone* completely.

But Malachi was proof positive of what she was saying. Her suave, debonair, and most charming brother was flimflamming women left and right. Women believing they were the only one . . . his "main squeeze" (as her father would teasingly say in his old-school vernacular way), only to learn that they weren't. So, if her own father would cheat on her mother, and her clean-cut, church-going brother would cheat (although *cheat* was the wrong word to use in Malachi's case since he hadn't actually made a vow to anyone yet), then Andrew would certainly cheat if the right woman came along.

So when she told Imani she'd take her to meet the girl whose life she'd saved by choosing to be her bone marrow donor (fully aware that it was going against both her mother and father's wishes), she really hadn't expected to, once again, run into Gabrielle and her little doctor friend. But there Gabrielle was, hovering and protecting, just like she was the girl's mother or something. But Paris knew that wasn't the case. The mother's name was listed on the information Paris had located. Her name was Jessica Noble, a forty-nine-year-old widow.

But why was Gabrielle there? What did she have to do with this?

Paris had mentioned seeing Gabrielle to Darius when he'd called to check on her after she returned from taking Imani home. Paris wasn't actually expecting him to have any insight on this. But for now, Darius seemed to have become her willing accomplice, so to speak. She wasn't going to talk to Andrew about it. He was always so straight up about everything. And she *sure* couldn't talk to her mother. Darius seemed safe enough.

So she'd mentioned to him that she'd taken Imani to see the girl who had been in need of the bone marrow transplant, leaving out the part about Imani being a match, of course. She wasn't about to tell Darius *everything*. It was that trust factor thing again. Darius was charming and all, but there was something that wasn't sitting completely right with her when it came to him.

Darius had been a player that semester she knew him in college. He was as fine as he wanted to be, but he wasn't in her league. She'd learned earlier on with her stint with Cedric that she was more of a caviar girl and not the bologna sandwich type. Cedric was the last loser she vowed to ever give her valuable self and time to.

Cedric and Andrew had been friends. Where Cedric was lazy and a loser, Andrew had dreams and drive. When she met Andrew that first time at the club with Cedric, he wouldn't give her the time of day. He was more concerned with studying and doing the right thing than having a good time. She had been impressed that he was already in college studying to be a lawyer. Lawyers made a lot more money than losers, and Andrew was cute. She just didn't get how he could be friends with a do-nothing like Cedric.

So about six months after she kicked Gabrielle to the curb for messing around with Cedric (even though Cedric denied anything ever happened between them), she plotted to get some alone time with Andrew. It took some doing, but Andrew finally admitted she was someone he *would* possibly talk to, but that he didn't date women of his friends. She wasn't going to give up so easily. She cried on his shoulders about how Cedric and a friend she'd opened up her home to had stabbed her in the back by sleeping together. She didn't have to worry; Andrew didn't know Gabrielle. So he didn't know who she was talking about or that she didn't even care for Gabrielle. He didn't know that the only reason she allowed Gabrielle to live with her was to get a little money on the side, having Gabrielle pay half the rent (even though her father paid the entire bill) and using her to cook and clean.

But Gabrielle was so nice. And all of her friends liked Gabrielle. All they talked about was how great Gabrielle was. How beautiful she was. Paris didn't want to hear any of that mess. So when she suspected Gabrielle was having sex in her apartment, she knew it couldn't be with anyone *except* Cedric. She tried to get Gabrielle to confess, but Gabrielle acted like she didn't know what she was talking about. Paris could see that Gabrielle was guilty. She had the look of someone who'd been caught with her hand in the cookie jar. She just didn't want to confess her sins.

So Paris threw her out on the streets on her holy behind.

Paris's father didn't seem to have a problem with what she did. In fact, he seemed relieved. Her mother, on the other hand, thought that was an awful thing to do. Her mother told her she could have at least given her a week to find somewhere to stay. But to give her an hour was cruel, and Deidra warned her that if she wasn't careful how she treated folks, it was going to come back someday and bite her. But her father had approved of how decisive and direct she'd been. It was one of the few times she seemed to have done something that her father was pleased with. Malachi told her Gabrielle called twice as it was happening, leaving messages for their father to call. They both concluded Gabrielle must have been trying to get him to intervene.

But Gabrielle was gone. And she'd managed to get rid of Cedric, finally replacing him with Andrew after about a year of plotting and maneuvering.

And in the end, Andrew had proven to be a good choice. He was caring and a hard worker. In the very beginning of their marriage, he'd wanted to start having children. But she'd successfully convinced him that they should wait. He was easy like that. He didn't nag her about her never cooking or cleaning. He didn't say anything when she hired someone to come in and clean the house once a week, though he did balk when she told him she was thinking about hiring a cook.

"It's just me and you, Paris. We don't need a cook for just the two of us. Now, if we had children, then that would be a different discussion," he'd said after their first year of marriage.

Paris figured he'd said that to force her to have a baby. But she wasn't ready to have children yet. Then one year became two, two became three, and before she knew it, she was now finding herself trying to have a baby and unable to get pregnant.

Paris heard the garage door to her parents' house let up, then back down. She looked at her watch, got up, and went to the kitchen. She knew it wasn't her mother. Deidra was at Wednesday-night Bible study and wouldn't be home until around nine o'clock.

Lawrence stepped into the kitchen and saw her standing there.

"Hi, Paris. I thought I saw your car out there." He strolled over to her. "So what brings you here? Did you come by to see how your *boy* made out?"

"My boy?" Paris said, wondering what he was talking about. "What boy?"

"Yeah." Lawrence went to the refrigerator, took out a can of soda, and popped the top. He turned it up, then set the can down on the counter. "You know who I'm talking about: your boy. The one you tried to set me up with the other day: Darius Connors."

Paris's whole body stiffened. Her eyes began to blink fast. So her father knew she'd set him up on Monday. "I don't know what you're talking about, Daddy."

"Sure you do. You had your boy show up at the restaurant the other day as though it was some coincidence. The two of you acting like it was your first time seeing each other in a long time. Yeah, I fell for it in the beginning. I mean: Why not? People run into each other all the time. But then, he started strategically saying things to get a reaction from me." He shook his head. "I can't believe my own daughter would conspire against me like that." He went and sat down on the couch in the den.

Paris followed him and sat on the other end, away from him. "Okay, so maybe he and I had seen each other prior to him coming into the restaurant the other day."

"Seen each other my foot," Lawrence said. "You and he plotted together. And now you're trying to step your game up. But I'm going to tell you just like I told him a little while ago, right before I left him: I don't play that! I'll chew you up and spit you both out; I don't care if you are my child."

Paris frowned. "What do you mean when you saw him a little while ago?"

"Paris, don't play with me. I know you and him devised that whole little thing this evening. But you should know that I don't take kindly to blackmail. So you'd best be careful who you're messing with," Lawrence said. "You'd better get it through your head and get it through his head as well: I am *not* the one!"

"Daddy, I honestly don't have a clue what you're talking about."

Lawrence nodded. "Your boy Darius called my office earlier today. Told Mattie that he needed to speak with me, that he was a friend of yours, and it was imperative that he speak with me today. I'd just gotten back from a session in Montgomery, so you know I was tired. But with him mentioning your name, I returned his call. That's when he tells me that we need to meet for dinner. That he has some information that could hurt me and my family. Said he didn't want to discuss it over the phone, which I respect. But then he threatened me by telling me it was in my best interest that I show up or that I would be sorry."

"Are you sure it was Darius Connors?"

"I met him tonight. Oh, it was him all right." Lawrence stood up. "I'm telling you: You'd better be careful who you hook up with when it comes to me. I don't play when it comes to me and mine. I don't. I'll fight to protect what's mine."

"Daddy, I promise you: I didn't have anything to do with him calling you today *or* asking to meet with you. I promise I didn't." Paris was now standing as well.

"Well, I believe he and I have an understanding. And him trying to bring up your little ex-friend Gabrielle, whatever her last name is now, doesn't faze me in the least." Lawrence stared at Paris. "You tell him *that* the next time you talk to him. Then if I were you, I'd get as far away from that brother as possible. He looks and smells like real trouble to me. So if you didn't have anything to do with him calling me today, then he's using you to get to me. And I will hurt that boy—"

Paris touched her father's arm. "Okay, Daddy. I hear you. I'm sure this has to be some big misunderstanding."

Lawrence put his hand up to his mouth, then took his hand down. "Well, any misunderstanding is totally on his part. I assure you: I've made my position *crystal* clear. Paris, I have too much going on in my world for any foolishness right now. So if you're doing anything to try to get attention, you need to put that noise on hold!"

"Of course, Daddy."

Lawrence pushed his shoulders back and walked out of the room.

"Of course," Paris said with her hand to her mouth.

Chapter 44

Give, and it shall be given unto you; good measure, pressed down, and shaken together, and running over, shall men give into your bosom. For with the same measure that ye mete withal it shall be measured to you again.

—Luke 6:38

On Palm Sunday, five days after Jasmine had come home, Jessica was rushed to the hospital. It was Monday now; Tuesday would be Jasmine's ninth birthday. Jessica and Gabrielle had planned a nice little birthday party for her. But now Jessica lay in the hospital barely able to keep her eyes open.

Jasmine didn't want to leave her mother's side. So she and Gabrielle sat there for hours, waiting on Jessica to wake up the next time she'd wake up. When Jessica opened her eyes and saw they were still there, and she discovered that they hadn't been home since the last time she woke up, she insisted that they go home. She asked Gabrielle to call her lawyer and to let him know what was going on. "His business card is inside of that flowered box on the top of my dresser," Jessica said.

Gabrielle called Robert Shaw's office as requested and informed him that Jessica was in the hospital in critical condition even though she really didn't understand why this was so important to Jessica right now. Robert Shaw then did something that made her be even more confused. He asked her to come to his office as soon as possible. She had Jasmine. He told her it wouldn't take long but that it was imperative that she come today. He would be in the office for the rest of the day, so whenever she came, he'd make himself available to her. And if she couldn't come to him, he would come to wherever she was.

When she told Zachary about the strange conversation, Zachary told her he had an hour available and would be glad to watch Jasmine while she went to the lawyer's office. He could meet her at the hospital since Jasmine was insisting on going back now to be with her mother.

Gabrielle found the lawyer's office easy enough. Robert Shaw was a short man with a balding head who looked to be in his late fifties, possibly early sixties. He had a smile that instantly put Gabrielle at ease.

The meeting lasted all of twenty minutes, but the impact of what he'd said was life changing. Jessica had granted Gabrielle power of attorney over all of her affairs as well as her health care proxy. In addition, Robert Shaw informed her, Jessica had filed a petition for appointment of guardian for Gabrielle to become Jasmine's guardian in the case when she was unable to take care of her. Attorney Shaw had been instructed, upon knowledge of Jessica's health's decline, to begin the proceedings to make the petition for guardianship happen. And unless Gabrielle had any objections to any of this, he would begin as previously requested.

Gabrielle returned to the hospital slightly stunned. And what she saw when she got to Jessica's room almost broke her heart in two. Jasmine's head was lying on Jessica's bosom and Jessica's hand rested on Jasmine's head as she slept. Gabrielle looked at Zachary, who stood away from the two with his hand up to his mouth.

Zachary shook his head slowly when he looked into Gabrielle's eyes. She walked over to him, and he hugged her tight. Gabrielle had to be strong. She just wanted to gather Jasmine up in her arms and take all of the pain away.

After fifteen minutes, Gabrielle walked over to the bed. "Honey, come here," she said to Jasmine.

Jasmine held her head up. Her face was wet with tears. Gabrielle wiped Jasmine's face and smiled.

"I love her so much," Jasmine said as she cried.

"I know you do. And she loves you so much, too."

Jessica was trying to open her eyes. She then tried to say

something. She beckoned for Gabrielle, who moved her ear closer so she could hear what Jessica was trying to say.

"Did you talk to Robert Shaw?" Jessica said, barely above being a whisper.

"Yeah. I did."

Jessica tried to smile. "Is everything okay?"

Gabrielle tried to smile back. "Yes, everything is okay."

Jessica's eyes flickered like a light bulb preparing to blow. "Good. Tomorrow is Jasmine's birthday. Have to have a big party for her."

"I don't care about a party," Jasmine said, rushing to her mother's side. "All I want is for you to get better." Jasmine started visibly crying again.

"Zachary? Is Dr. Morgan still here?" Jessica asked as she tried to look where she thought he might be standing if he was there.

Zachary quickly moved to where she could easily see him. "I'm here."

"Can you take Jasmine out for a minute? I need to . . . talk to . . . Gabrielle." Her speech was becoming labored.

"I don't want to leave you, Mama. I don't want to go! Don't make me go. I want to stay here with you." Jasmine took her mother's hand and held it.

"I just need a few minutes . . . okay?" Jessica smiled as she closed her eyes. "Just a few . . ."

"Come on, Miss Jazz," Zachary said, taking her by the other hand. "What say you and I go down to the gift shop to see if we can't find something to cheer your mother up?"

Jasmine nodded, but didn't take her eyes off her mother. "We'll be back soon, Mama. Okay? We'll be right back."

Jessica nodded one time. It was as though that was all the energy she could muster now.

As soon as they left, Gabrielle leaned down closer. "You're going to be all right. You just have to keep fighting. You can't give up, not now. We've been praying for God's healing for you. Jasmine needs you." Gabrielle tried to smile, but her mouth trembled as she tried to sustain it.

Jessica shook her head. "No, I'm not going . . . to be all right." Her voice had faded now to a wispy whisper. "I've come to terms . . . that my healing . . . is not going to happen . . . on this side . . . of Heaven. But I want you . . . to do . . . something for me. I *need* you . . . to do it. I don't have . . . the strength left . . . to do it myself. But it must . . . be done."

Gabrielle could feel the tears making their way down her face. She wiped hard at them, determined not to let them win this time. "What is it?"

"First, I need you to promise me . . . you'll take care of my Jasmine for me."

"You know you don't even have to ask that," Gabrielle said, patting her hand.

Jessica closed her eyes and was silent. She was still for so long that Gabrielle thought she may have fallen asleep again . . . or worse. She saw her chest continue to rise and fall. She quietly released a sigh of relief. As soon as Gabrielle had almost decided to sit down, Jessica opened her eyes. Her eyelids had fluttered as she'd fought to open them.

"Gabrielle?"

"I'm here."

"Gabrielle, I need you to help me tell Jasmine the truth . . . about her birth. She needs to know . . . now."

Gabrielle began shaking her head. "I don't think she needs to be told that, not right now anyway. There's too much going on. We'll wait until you're better and get out of here."

"Yes, she needs . . . to know . . . now." Jessica reached like a blind woman, for Gabrielle's hand. She tried to squeeze it, but there was no strength left in her. "I need you . . . to help me . . . tell her. We need to tell her . . . before I make . . . my transition. I don't want her to . . . hold this against me . . . thinking I lied to her . . . all of these years. I need her to feel . . . like . . . I told her . . . the truth . . . myself."

Gabrielle placed her hand tightly over her own mouth, just in case the primal cry she felt forming deep inside her belly might somehow make its way up and out.

"Please. I need you to help me . . . tell her." Jessica's eyes closed once again. "All of it . . . including who you are . . . to her. She'll need to know this. She'll need to know that . . . she's not going to be . . . alone . . . once I'm no longer . . . here."

"But we can wait—"

"No . . . we can't. We've run out of time. And Jasmine needs . . . to know . . . just how much . . . she's loved." Tears were streaming from Jessica's eyes, pooling into her ears and past them. Gabrielle got tissue and wiped her tears away.

"Very soon . . . Jesus will wipe . . . my tears . . . away." Jessica tried to smile. "Gabrielle, you gave me . . . and my husband . . . the most beautiful gift . . . we could have ever asked for," Jessica said. "And now . . . reluctantly . . . but graciously . . . I am giving that gift . . . back to you. Live each day . . . with happiness . . . when . . . and wherever . . . you find it, Gab . . . rielle. I've discovered . . . through my years . . . of living . . . on this earth . . . that when we live . . . and we give . . . of ourselves . . . we find that . . . we never . . . actually die. Live . . . and continue to give. Promise me . . . you will . . . tell her . . ." Jessica was quiet again.

Gabrielle waited, fully expecting Jessica to open her eyes again so they could finish their conversation. Zachary and Jasmine returned thirty minutes later with a cute little brown, animated, get-well bear. Jasmine sat near her mother, cuddling the bear, waiting patiently for her mother to open her eyes so she could give her the present she'd so excitedly gotten Zachary to buy her.

But Jessica never opened her eyes again.

Chapter 45

Wisdom is better than weapons of war: but one sinner destroyeth much good.

—Ecclesiastes 9:18

Darius sent Paris a text informing her that the mother of the little girl that had needed the bone marrow transplant last year had died.

Paris just thought he was trying to get back in her good graces since she'd blasted him for meeting with her father behind her back. He'd explained the reason he'd done it. He claimed he was trying to get more information that might help her in her quest of learning the truth. After all, Paris was the one who initially posed the idea that her father had a little more invested in that little girl's welfare than mere concern. Darius had thrown Gabrielle's name in the mix just to see how Lawrence might react to hearing her name. After all, a little perturbed by it, Paris was the one who had mentioned Gabrielle was there when she and her sister went to visit the little girl.

As for him asking for a job working in her father's campaign (which he was the one who told her, since her father really hadn't clued her in on exactly what Darius had said or done), Darius said, "I need a job. Pure and simple. I need a way to take care of my family. They're closing down the place where I worked, and shipping all of our jobs overseas. I have obligations. You can't fault a good man for trying to obtain work." He then laughed and said, "You know what the Bible says. If a man don't work, he don't eat. Well, I was merely trying to get some work. And if you happen to have any clout with your father, I'd surely appreciate it if you'd put in a good word for a brotha."

"The way my daddy sounded, I don't think he'll ever even *consider* hiring you. He was livid."

"He might. If I happen to come across something that's of value or true interest to him, I can see him jumping to hire me then," Darius said.

But Paris had decided to cool it with Darius. She didn't like him doing things like that. He didn't even discuss it with her, he just did it. And if her father hadn't clued her in, she'd still be in the dark about it. It made her feel like she really couldn't trust him. She had issues with trusting folks as it was. But Darius was a smooth operator. And he'd made some good points, telling her that he only had her best interest at heart. And that if he was to get on with her father's campaign, it would give him more of an excuse to run into her more often.

She'd blushed when he said that, but acted as though what he'd said hadn't fazed her a bit. She merely said, "Just don't be doing anything like that again. I don't like the conversation me and my daddy had. Especially when I don't have a *clue* what he's chewing me out about. And now he's suspicious of me and you. He thinks we're in cahoots together against him."

Darius laughed. "But we are."

"We're not exactly in *cahoots* against him. We're just working all of this out and—"

"And we work better *together* than you merely doing it on your own," Darius said.

So (after almost two weeks of reaching out to her) here was Darius with this text, apprising her of something that she likely would not have otherwise heard. Jessica Noble, the mother of Jasmine Noble, who'd needed a bone marrow donor and miraculously had received one who matched perfectly, had died. Paris called Darius after she finished reading his text that briefly read, Jessica N, the lil girl's ma, died.

Darius was laughing when he answered her call. "You know, I was hoping you'd call soon. So . . . you still upset with me?"

"I wasn't upset," Paris said, scrunching her mouth as she spoke. He really did have some annoying traits about him.

"Yes, you were. You wouldn't take my calls or call me back. So you were mad still."

"Okay, about Jessica Noble? How do you know about this?"

"I told you that Gabrielle Mercedes goes to the same church I go to. She was there with the little girl today. I think the mother's funeral was yesterday. Pastor Landris called the little girl and Gabrielle up to the front so the church could pray for the two of them. The sad part is they say the little girl's mother died on the little girl's birthday. Can you imagine your parent dying on the same day that you celebrate your birthday? But Pastor Landris prayed a powerful prayer over both the little girl *and* Gabrielle."

"I don't get that. Why is she with Gabrielle?"

"I don't know. But from everything I was able to gather, apparently Gabrielle is her guardian now. Maybe she's planning on adopting her or something. Who knows?"

"Over my dead body she will!" Paris said.

"Wow! Listen to you. There certainly is no love lost between the two of you. I guess that means you must know all about her past life."

"What about her past life? What do you know about her? I just thought you said she went to your church?"

Darius chuckled. "You know . . . I could tell you all of this a lot easier in person. I'm not much of a phone person myself. Besides, I'm using up my minutes. So why don't you agree to meet me somewhere, and I'll tell you all about Gabrielle and her fascinating colorful past."

"It's Sunday afternoon. Cell minutes are free on the weekends. Besides, I can't. I have something to do," Paris lied.

"Oh. Okay. Well, when you're free, hit me up, and we'll see if we can't get together then. This information will definitely keep. Now keep in mind that when you call me, it might not be a good time for me. You know, I have this family thing going on and all. And my wife's been hovering over me a lot lately, so I have to stay closer to home more than normal. Of course, she and the kids are gone right now. They'll be gone for a few more hours. But now if I could get that job I asked your father for, then I would be a lot freer to come and go without her on me like white on rice."

"You do know that while you're going on and on about this, you could have told me what you know about Gabrielle. I don't want her getting that little girl."

"Well, the way you're responding to the news, it's like you already know. Let's meet for a cup of java or whatever you like to drink. I'm down for whatever."

"I knew Gabrielle when she and I were eighteen. We ran into each other about four months ago. And then, again, the other week."

"Well, I can tell you that what I know was *well* after she was eighteen. So let's say we'll meet at the Starbucks on 280 in about . . . twenty minutes?"

"If I was going to meet you, I definitely wouldn't meet you at *that* one. Too many folks know me at *that* one."

"Okay. Which one then? You name the place, and I'll meet you. There's a Starbucks in Trussville, one in the old Eastwood Mall area."

"The old Eastwood Mall area would work. I don't think I'll run into anyone who might know me at that one."

"It's not like we're doing anything wrong," Darius said. "We're just meeting for coffee to talk."

"Oh, I know."

"Okay. Then I'll see you in about twenty minutes."

"On my way out of the door as we speak," Paris said, then clicked her phone off.

Darius was there waiting when she arrived. He stood as she strolled in, then sat down after helping her with her chair. Oh, Darius was a smooth operator for sure!

"Okay, I don't have but about fifteen minutes," Paris said. "So tell me: What do you know about Gabrielle Booker . . . Gabrielle Mercedes, whatever was or *is* her name."

Darius grinned, showing almost all of his pearls. "Wow, who knew that there was so much bad blood there? Although, having personally interacted with her a few times myself, I can see why you might feel the way that you do. She thinks she's all that, but she can't hold a candle to you."

"Save the corny flattery for someone who'll fall for it," Paris said. "Just tell me what you know, and I mean don't leave anything out, either."

"Let me get us something to drink first. We don't want them throwing us out for loitering or not patronizing their establishment."

"Okay, fine. Get me a latte."

Darius nodded, smiled, went, and came back with their beverages.

Paris carefully picked hers from off the table where he'd set it. "Now quit stalling, and tell me."

He grinned. "Gabrielle Mercedes used to be a stripper."

Paris's eyes widened as she jerked back, almost spilling hot latte onto her lap. "You're lying! Now I know she'll go after someone else's man, because she went after one of mine. But stripping? A stripper?" Paris shook her head and primped her mouth. "Nah, I don't believe that for a minute. People will say all kinds of things about others. There's no telling what lies folks have said about me."

Darius leaned in. "Well, I happen to know for a fact that *this* is true. She was an exotic dancer who went by the name of Goodness and Mercy."

"Goodness and Mercy? And you know this for a fact? So what are you saying? That you saw her as Goodness and Mercy with your own two little eyes."

He took a careful sip from his cup. "Yep. You can say that I *may* have seen her with my own eyes. Although, I'd prefer we keep that between me and you."

"So what you're saying is that you don't want me to mention this tidbit of information to your wife?" Paris laughed.

"Well, my wife sort of already knows. Some bigmouth at church told it."

"Sounds to me like you attend a really interesting church. Gossipers, liars, and strippers, oh my."

"Oh, it just sounds like that," Darius said. "Pastor Landris preached a sermon sometime back on how even though we might be saved now, we're all still an ex-something. Of course, there are plenty of folks still wallowing in their wrongdoing.

But Gabrielle gave her life to Christ. She left the stripping business behind."

"And she's the director of the church's dance ministry? She gave me her business card that said that."

"She was. She's on a leave of absence or something, Tiffany was telling me. But she *is* saved and a new creature in Christ now. I told you: My pastor preached on that so we don't go there."

Paris took another sip of her latte. "What about you?"

"Me? What about me?"

"What are you an ex of? But I suppose more importantly, what are you *still* doing that you shouldn't be?"

He laughed and leaned in on his folded arms. "I'll make a deal with you. I'll tell you mine if you tell me yours."

Paris knew what he was doing. She wasn't going to fall into his little trap. She started playing with her hair. "So . . . Gabrielle was a stripper, huh? She's unmarried. And now you're telling me that an unmarried, former stripper has that beautiful little girl with *her*?"

"It looks that way."

"Well, it won't *look* that way for long. I'll be doggone if I'm going to sit around and just let something like that happen. Not on my watch."

"What do you care? It's just some kid who probably has more troubles than she's worth, especially after having a transplant."

Paris stood up. "Don't you worry about why I care. You just keep your eyes and ears open, and let me know what you hear where Gabrielle Mercedes is concerned."

He stood and gave Paris a military-type salute. "Ma'am, yes, ma'am!"

She grinned. "Stop that!"

"Just here to please you, ma'am," Darius said. They headed for the door. He leaned down, placed his hand in the small of her back, and placing his mouth right on her ear, he whispered, "Just *here* to *please* you."

Chapter 46

Dead flies cause the ointment of the apothecary to send forth a stinking savor: so doth a little folly him that is in reputation for wisdom and honor.

—Ecclesiastes 10:1

After Paris got home from her meeting with Darius, she called her father and asked him over. Andrew was gone; he'd left to go play golf as soon as he came home from church. So she and her father would be perfectly free to say whatever they wanted or needed.

She opened the door and gave her father a hug. They then went to the den.

"Daddy, I don't want to play games or beat around the bush. So I'm going to get straight to the point."

"That's fine. I like getting straight to the point. That also means that I can get back home in time to catch my basketball game that starts in about an hour. So what's up? You and Andrew still having problems?"

"No, this isn't about me and Andrew. It's about you and Jasmine."

"Jasmine? Jasmine who?"

"Jasmine, the little girl that needed the bone marrow transplant," Paris said.

"Why are we talking about *her*? If you'll recall, you didn't care to take part in the donor process. But as it was, things turned out just fine without you." Lawrence angled his body more squarely her way as he touched his fingers together like he was clapping with them.

"We're talking about her because I know the truth."

Lawrence chuckled and scooted back a little on the couch. "The truth about what, Paris? You're making no sense at all."

"Oh, stop it, Daddy! Just stop it! No one is here but you and me. Drop the act. We don't have time to play around. Look, I know that Jasmine is your daughter, okay?"

Lawrence's smile instantly fell as he drew his head back as in shock. "My daughter? Now you're *really* talking crazy talk."

Paris picked up a magazine off the coffee table, retrieved a photo she'd put there earlier, and handed it to him.

"What is this?" he asked.

"What does it look like, Daddy?"

He continued to gaze down at the photo. "Well, it looks like Imani and some girl that I don't know. Is this a friend of Imani's? What?"

"Does that little girl, that you say you *don't* know, look like anybody that you *do* know?"

"Not really. Why? Should she?"

"Daddy, look at how much she and Imani favor. Look at their eyes. They have identical eyes."

"Okay, so they favor, according to you," Lawrence said, setting the picture on top of the magazine. "What's the big deal?"

Paris reached over and picked up the picture. "The big deal is that this girl on the picture with Imani is the girl that Imani matched and was a bone marrow donor for. That's the big deal."

Paris watched as the coloring literally seemed to drain from her father's face. "Where did you get this? How do you happen to have a picture with *my* daughter and that little girl? How!"

"I have it, Daddy, because I took Imani to see her, and I took this picture of the two of them together. That's how I happen to have it."

Lawrence jumped to his feet. "You did what!"

Paris stood as well. "I took Imani to meet her."

"Who told you to do that?"

"I didn't need anybody to tell me I could do it. I told myself. You knew Imani wanted to meet her. You knew how much meeting her meant to her."

"Yeah, and I told Imani I would arrange something at the end of the year."

"Why, Daddy?"

"Why what?"

"Why did you want to wait until the end of the year to let my sister meet the person whose life she saved?" Paris took a step back from her father. "Why?"

"I do *not* believe you did that! You went behind my back and *deliberately* defied my wishes! You're practically sabotaging everything I'm trying to do, Paris!"

"Taking Imani to see Jasmine doesn't hurt you nor will it affect your reelection campaign. But you were definitely hurting Imani by keeping her away like you were doing."

Lawrence shook his head. "So you decided *you* knew what was best and took *my* daughter to do something *I* said I didn't want her doing. You completely disregarded my authority as her parent and just decided you'd . . ." He nodded his head. "And just how did you happen to find out where she was in the first place?"

"Why won't you say her name? It's Jasmine, Daddy. Jasmine. Her name is Jasmine Noble. And I'm not going to tell you where I got the information." Paris said it like a scared yet defiant twelve-year-old.

Lawrence nodded. "Oh, you don't have to tell me. I know how you got it. You were snooping around in our house again, weren't you?"

"You're just trying to shift the attention away from the *real* truth and what we *ought* to be discussing."

He looked at her with a cold stare. "And what truth is that, Paris? You think you know so much. What truth might that be?"

"The truth that you *are* the father. You're actually Jasmine's father."

"Humph! And exactly *how* did you come up with *that*? From some stupid photo you took? Because you say Imani and that girl favor? Do you know how often white folks say that all black folks look alike?"

"Stop denying the truth. Just admit it."

"Admit what? I want to know how you've come to this asinine

conclusion that I'm that child's father." Lawrence folded his arms. "That's what I want to know."

"Imani happened to be a match for her. Imani and Jasmine favor . . . a lot."

"And? That's it? That's all you have to be saying something crazy like this? The fact that my daughter turned out to be a match for that little girl. And because of that, all of a sudden I'm supposed to be that child's father? That's your brilliant deduction, Sherlock Holmes?"

"Look at her, Daddy." Paris flicked the photo at her father's face. "Look at her! Look at her and tell me she's not your child."

"Stop flicking that thing in my face. I don't need to look at it again. I saw it."

"Did you know that Jessica Noble died?"

Lawrence stopped, unfolded his arm, and looked at Paris. "She died? When did she die? Who told you that? From where did you hear that?"

"Oh, so you're going to tell me that you didn't know? You really want me to believe you didn't know Jessica had died, the mother of the little girl that you went all out for in order to find her a donor?"

"I promise you: I didn't know. Why would I? This is my first time hearing this." He sat down on the couch and appeared visibly and honestly shaken.

Maybe he really didn't know. Paris sat down beside him. It hurt her to see him shaken in this way. "You really *didn't* know, did you? So nobody told you?"

He shook his head. "No." He then looked up at her. "But there really would be no reason for me to have been told. I only met this woman once, and it was only after I started the campaign to help get a bone marrow donor for her daughter. I promise you, Paris: That was my first time ever laying eyes on that woman. And it was only that one time."

Paris gazed at the picture as she spoke. "I heard that she died about a week after her daughter went home. They say she died on her daughter's birthday."

Lawrence looked over at Paris. "Who told you all of this?"

"Someone in the know of what's going on told me." Paris didn't dare reveal her source. She knew how her father felt about Darius. After Darius told her, she'd checked on the Internet, doing a search on Jessica Noble's name, and verified she had indeed passed away. "I also hear that Jasmine is with Gabrielle Mercedes now."

Lawrence frowned. "She's what?"

"She's with Gabrielle Mercedes-used-to-be-Booker. Gabrielle has her now."

"Why would *she* have her?"

"I don't know, Daddy. I was thinking you would know enough to possibly shed some light on things. Maybe your investigative folks can find out why she has her. But I'll tell you this. I don't care how much you deny it. I believe Jasmine is your child. And I'll be doggone if I'm going to let my half sister be raised by someone like that woman! So if you're not going to do anything to save Jasmine from Gabrielle, then I'm not going to just sit around and do nothing, hoping for the best."

"I'm telling you, Paris. I didn't have an affair, a one-night stand, or anything else with Jessica Noble. I've never had sex with her a day in my life. I'm telling you: You're barking up the wrong tree. This doesn't concern us. We need to stay out of it."

Paris smiled. "Well, I'm going to do the right thing for Jasmine. If Gabrielle has custody of her right now, as I hear that she does, then it sounds to me like Jasmine doesn't have anyone to take her in. Therefore, I'm going to see about getting her."

Lawrence grabbed his daughter up by her shoulders. "I'm telling you, as your father, you need to stay out of this. Leave it alone, Paris. Let this go."

Paris broke from her father's grasp. "I'm not going to let that beautiful child be raised by the likes of Gabrielle Booker, oh, excuse me, I mean Gabrielle Mercedes. Jasmine would be better off with us. I'm married; Gabrielle is not. I have a college degree; Gabrielle doesn't. I can raise Jasmine up with the finer things of life the way I'm sure she's already accustomed to. Gabrielle doesn't have what we have. Jasmine needs someone who knows culture. Gabrielle doesn't know which fork to use when. I can introduce Jasmine to a world of beauty pageants and glitter, if she's interested."

"What about Andrew? Have you discussed this with him?"

"Not yet," Paris said. "But unlike you, who won't step up to the plate, even though it may mean your daughter will end up with someone substandard like Gabrielle, Andrew has a kind and good heart. And you can deny that she's your child until the cows come home. But in my heart, I know the truth. Andrew and I have been praying to have a family. Maybe this is God's answer to our prayer. Maybe God wants us to start our family by adopting Jasmine."

Lawrence rubbed the side of his head. "Let it go, Paris. Don't open this up. I can't afford a fight like this, not now. You know the media takes things and blows it up. They'll have a field day if you go after this child. For me, please, leave it alone."

"Daddy, all of my life, I've been selfish. I've only thought about what was best for me. Well, for the first time in my life, I'm not going to think about only me. I'm going to do something for someone else. Whether Jasmine is your child or not: *She* still needs a good home. Andrew and I can give her that home right here with us."

"You don't know what you're doing," Lawrence said. "I'm telling you: You don't know. So I'm asking you . . . begging you actually, as your father, leave it alone."

"Well, Daddy, you need to get going. I have a lot to do." She escorted her father to the door. "Kiss Mom for me when you get home." She pecked his cheek.

Chapter 47

And who is he that will harm you, if ye be followers of that which is good?

—1 Peter 3:13

"I'd like to come to your church for Bible study tonight," Paris said to Darius as soon as he answered his cell phone. "Can you give me the address?"

"Oh, so you're coming to our Bible study? Cool. Why don't I just meet you somewhere and you can follow me over there?" Darius said. "I'll tell my wife I have something to do and that I'll be coming on later."

"Listen, I'm not trying to get me or *you* in trouble with your wife. So just give me the address if you know it or I can just look it up."

Darius laughed, then rattled off the address. "So Paris Simmons is coming to visit us at Followers of Jesus Faith Worship Center for Bible study? Wow."

"Looks that way. And the name is Paris Simmons-Holyfield, with a hyphen."

"Okay, Mrs. Simmons-Holyfield with a hyphen. Is there any particular reason *why* you're coming to visit us?"

"If you must know: I'm hoping to run into Gabrielle."

"I see. So it has nothing to do with the great Word we get there? Well, I'll tell you what: If you'll park in section D and wait for me if I'm not there when you get there, I'll be more than happy to show you the general area where Gabrielle sits. You know how folks have an area they prefer more than others.

That will help make it a bit easier for you to 'run into her,' although I must warn you: She's generally with that little boyfriend of hers. Now it's her, that little girl, and her boyfriend."

"Her boyfriend is a doctor, isn't he?"

"That's what they say," Darius said with a slight singsong to his words.

"That's fine. I'm not coming to start any drama. I just want to let her know in person that I'd like to sit down and talk to her about something, woman to woman."

"Why does this not sound like it's going to be good?"

"I don't know," Paris said.

"Now, if you just want to call her, I can get you her phone number."

"I had her business card with her church phone number. I threw that thing away. No. I'd prefer to look in her face when I tell her some of what I have to say."

She and Darius discussed the time she should aim to meet him in the church's parking lot.

Paris arrived and saw Darius standing outside his car.

"Where's your wife and family?" Paris asked when he opened her car door.

"They're coming later. I told her I had an errand to run," Darius said. "Come on. Let's go in."

"Are you sure you won't get in trouble if someone sees you walking in with me?"

"We're walking into church. People walk into church alongside other people all the time. Last time I checked, it wasn't a sin to walk in church with someone other than your spouse." Darius laughed.

Paris kept space between her and him even though she could feel Darius making an effort to veer closer to her, "accidentally" bumping into her a few times. It did make her a little nervous that he was with her. When they got inside and he led her to the side where he indicated Gabrielle sat most times, she smiled at him. "Okay. Thank you. You can go find your family now. I can take it from here."

"Find my family?" He chuckled. "I have no idea where they'll be. My wife sits all over the place. It's according to what time she gets here. Most of the time she's late because of the children. That's when she doesn't just give up and opt to stay home."

They sat down and Paris tried to pretend she didn't know Darius, just in case anyone was watching them.

She really enjoyed Pastor Landris's teaching. She was shocked at how much he touched on things she was dealing with in her own life. He spoke about going on after disappointments, knowing that God has already gone before you and taken care of things before you ever even arrive.

"Even when things seem like they're going bad for you and cause you to wonder if God is actually listening to you, God is there," Pastor Landris said. "If you're going through something, you need to be praising God because it means one of two things. Either God has worked it out and this is for His glory, or God knows you can handle it and that you're going to come through. When things are at their lowest point, that's when you need to be looking up and praising the loudest. God will not put more on you than you can bear. God is there with you, whispering in your ear that you can do this; you're going to make it if you just hold on to His hand. You're stronger than you think. God is helping you work those faith muscles and you'll see just how strong, through His power and His might, you truly are."

After service dismissed, Paris almost hated to ruin the wonderful feeling she was having, following that message, to confront Gabrielle. But she had come here for a reason, and she was not going to be denied. She was going to carry out her mission.

She spotted Gabrielle and stood out of the way as the congregants filed out. "Hi, Gabrielle," she said when Gabrielle was passing by her way.

Gabrielle looked; bewilderment registered on her face. "Hi."

"May I speak with you for a moment?" Paris said. "In private?"

Gabrielle looked at Zachary, who was holding Jasmine's other hand. "I suppose. Sure." She let go of Jasmine's hand.

"We'll meet you at the car," Zachary said to Gabrielle, although it was obvious to anybody looking that he didn't want to leave Gabrielle alone with Paris.

Paris and Gabrielle walked out of the sanctuary over to an area away from the crowd making their way out the doors.

"Listen, I hear you have Jasmine Noble," Paris said.

"Yeah. You just saw her with me."

"Is this a temporary thing or what?"

"Personally, Paris, I really don't care to discuss this with you," Gabrielle said.

"Well, you may want to rethink that. You see, I think that beautiful little girl deserves a good and stable home. She's already been through so much."

"I won't argue with that. In fact, I absolutely agree with you."

"Personally, I don't think you're the right one to offer her what she needs. Not like what my husband and I can."

Gabrielle laughed. "Excuse me? You're kidding me, right?"

"No, I'm not kidding you."

"Okay, Paris, let's cut through the noise. What exactly are you trying to say?"

"I'm just letting you know up front that I'm planning on petitioning the courts to get Jasmine."

Gabrielle looked at her like she'd lost her mind. "You're planning to do what?"

"I'm going to petition the courts to get Jasmine, and then I'd like to adopt her."

Gabrielle snapped her head back. "Why? For what reason? I don't get it? You don't even know Jasmine. You have no association with her at all. I *know* this can't be you just trying to get back at me. Not even *you* can be that small and petty."

Paris lowered her head downward. "Small and petty? Is that what you think of me? That I'm small and petty?" Paris's voice rose slightly.

"Listen, I'm not having this discussion with you, Paris. Things are already in the works for me and Jasmine to be a family. So whatever you're calling yourself doing, you need to back off. I'm telling you . . ."

"Gabrielle, be reasonable, okay," Paris said. "Save yourself some trouble. Because I know you don't want to battle with me.

If it comes down to a court having to look at you and what you have to offer that little girl, and me and my husband, not even counting the weight I can summon with my father on my side, you're going to lose. That's a fact! And I don't want to go there if I don't have to. But your stint as Goodness and Mercy may well come back and haunt you, if we have to fight this out. I don't know what your role is in Jasmine's life, but I know Andrew and I can give her a better home than you *ever* can."

"As I said, I'm not having this discussion with you, and *specifically* not here. In fact, there's really nothing for us to discuss period! I don't know what you know or what you *think* you know, but I'm going to tell you: There's the other side of goodness that you know nothing about. Please don't make me go there. Because if you *really* want to see some *real* weight, then just wait until you see me with the weight . . . the glory of *my* Father"—she pointed toward Heaven—"on my side. That's the other side of goodness I'm speaking of; the Lord fighting my battle."

"Oooh, I'm trembling. The other side of goodness, huh? Well, don't let my beauty fool *you*, either. When I want something bad enough, I can get down in the trenches as well. But know this: I *will* be moving forward to get custody of Jasmine. So, we can do it the easy way, or we can do it the hard way. But I promise you: We *will* do it." Paris then turned and walked away. She was trembling, and not totally sure why.

But she had now, in fact, thrown down the gauntlet. Now she would just have to convince Andrew of how much she truly wanted Jasmine and to be sure that he was ready to fight right along with her.

Chapter 48

Behold therefore the goodness and severity of God: on them which fell, severity; but toward thee, goodness, if thou continue in his goodness: otherwise thou also shalt be cut off.

—Romans 11:22

Lawrence and William were in his office discussing the latest problem to present itself: Paris deciding she wanted to adopt Jasmine Noble.

Lawrence knew the truth that Paris *thought* she knew, but in truth, only knew a part of. Yes, Jasmine Noble *was* Lawrence's biological daughter. But not in the way Paris believed it was so.

Paris was convinced Lawrence had had an affair with Jessica Noble. Jessica was dead, as was her husband. And apparently there was no one to take their daughter, Jasmine. Paris didn't know that Jasmine was adopted, so her conclusion was that Lawrence had gotten Jessica pregnant and kept this secret hidden. Things would have gone on without a snag had the child not needed a transplant. And although someone other than a relative could be a match, Paris apparently wasn't buying that reasoning.

Lawrence knew that if things escalated and Paris pursued this, it would inevitably come out that Jessica had adopted Jasmine. That would surely bring only *more* scrutiny to all of this. Lawrence knew it wouldn't be long before Paris would start putting two and two together. If it ever came out that Gabrielle was the birth mother . . . well, it would definitely be like a glimpse of the full Armageddon to come.

He knew how Gabrielle felt about Jasmine. If she was willing to take him on to save her life, she surely wouldn't hesitate to do what she needed to do to hold on to her—now that she apparently had her back.

The only option he had was to stop his daughter Paris.

"William, we're going to have to do something to get my daughter's attention away from trying to adopt this little girl. If she were to get pregnant with her own child, I'm sure she would abandon this pursuit."

"I can't do anything about her getting pregnant now." William chuckled.

"I know that," Lawrence said. "I pray she gets pregnant. But if she doesn't, we're going to have to find some other way to divert her attention. If she tries to take this child from Gabrielle, then I've lost this election for sure."

"To be candid, you're already losing this election. You're thirty points down in the polls. When black folks found out you switched parties and became a Republican and that you're now spouting off Tea Party talking points, they're running from you like a man running from killer bees. And those Tea Party rallies with those racist posters being broadcast on television aren't helping matters."

"Well, let's just concentrate on one crisis at a time. You remember that last guy I had you check out for me?"

"You're talking about Darius Connors?"

"Yes. Him. Well, I need you to put someone on him and keep an eye out on both him and my daughter."

"Are you sure about this? You know you're always reminding me that Paris is family . . . that she's blood."

"I'm sure. I told Darius that he needed to be careful when he decided he wanted to play in the major league with the big boys. If Paris refuses to heed my warning, then you recall what they used to say when we were growing up."

William smiled. "A hard head makes for a soft behind."

"Yeah. She's grown now. So I can't control her the way I could when she was more under my thumb. If Paris won't stop on her own, then I'll just have to help her. And if she happens to fall on her behind in the process, oh well . . ."

"I'll get somebody on this pronto!" William left.

Lawrence looked toward the ceiling. "God, help me. God, help us all!"

Chapter 49

There is no fear in love; but perfect love casteth out fear: because fear hath torment. He that feareth is not made perfect in love.

—1 John 4:18

Having just left Paris, Gabrielle held it together when she got to the car where Zachary and Jasmine were waiting for her.

"Is everything all right?" Zachary asked.

She nodded and forced a smile. "Oh, yeah. Everything's fine."

"I remember her," Jasmine said. "She and her sister, Imani, came to see me the day I got to go home."

"Yes," Gabrielle said, turning to look at Jasmine, who was in the backseat buckled up. "She most certainly did."

"She must not have remembered me," Jasmine said.

Zachary backed out of the parking place. The lights in the lot lit up the car.

"Why do you say that?" Gabrielle asked Jasmine.

"She didn't say hello to me when she saw me. She acted like she didn't even notice or see me."

Zachary released a short laugh. "Oh, she didn't say hello to me, either," Zachary said. "I think her mind must have been somewhere else."

"Yeah, but, my mother says you're always supposed to speak to people you know." Jasmine got quiet.

Gabrielle tried to see what was going on with Jasmine. She could hear her sniffling. "Are you all right?"

"Yes." Jasmine sniffled. "I just miss . . . I just miss my mama."

"I know you do, sweetheart. But we know she's in a better place now."

"I know," Jasmine said. "She's with Jesus. But I miss her so much! I do!"

"I know." Gabrielle turned around and wiped the tears from her own eyes.

Zachary looked over at Gabrielle. He pulled the car over to the side of the road. Gabrielle smiled at him, jumped out, went and got in the backseat, and put her arm around Jasmine, who was crying hard now. "It's okay. I'm here. And Dr. Z is here. We're going to be here right with you. Okay?"

Jasmine nodded. Gabrielle buckled up in the seat next to her. Zachary pulled back onto the road.

When they reached Gabrielle's house, Zachary got out and came in with them. He stayed until after Jasmine was in bed.

"Come here," he said to Gabrielle, wrapping his arms around her as soon as she walked into the den.

Gabrielle couldn't hold it together any longer. She completely broke down.

"Oh, baby. I know all of this is hard." He sat down, pulling her with him. "Did that woman . . . Paris, isn't that her name? Did Paris say something to upset you?"

Gabrielle wiped her eyes and nodded. She pulled away from Zachary's embrace. "She says she plans on taking Jasmine from me."

"Come again?" Zachary said with an obvious edge to his voice.

Gabrielle primped her mouth a bit before steadying it. "She says she's going to petition to get Jasmine."

"What does she have to do with any of this?"

"I don't know," Gabrielle said. "I don't even know where this is coming from. Unless her father is putting her up to it, I can't imagine Paris wanting to raise a child that's not her own." Gabrielle released a short laugh. "In truth: I can't see her wanting to raise her *own* child. She's the type that would hire a full-time nanny while she sat there watching her fingernail polish dry."

"That bad, huh?"

"Unless she's changed from the person I knew." Gabrielle shook her head slowly. "I don't know *where* this is coming from."

"Okay. So tell me everything she said," Zachary said.

"Basically she said I wasn't fit to be anybody's mother, especially somebody like Jasmine. She made references back to my days as an exotic dancer. Oh, let me not clean up the way she said it: my days as a stripper. She indicated that Jasmine would fare better in a home with two parents as opposed to being with me. I don't know. Jasmine doesn't know her. How does she think it will benefit that child to have some stranger whisking her away to a home with people she doesn't even know?"

"I know."

"Jessica left her in my care. She did everything within her power to ensure Jasmine wouldn't suffer too much when she was gone," Gabrielle said. "I still haven't told Jasmine who I really am or the truth about who she is. I was supposed to. But with everything happening as it did and so fast; I just couldn't bring myself to do it then. Now Paris is here saying I'm not good enough to take care of her and she wants to take Jasmine away from me?" Gabrielle began to shake her head. "No. No. I'm not going to let her. I will fight her until the end."

"*We're* not going to let her," Zachary said.

Gabrielle smiled at Zachary. "Thanks for that. But this is my battle. I wouldn't dare involve you in this. It's going to be hard enough on me. I'll not let her drag your name through the mud. This is my battle."

"No, the battle is not yours; it's the Lord's." Zachary took her by both her hands. "And you're not going to fight this one alone because, as your husband, I'm not going to *let* you fight it alone. I'm going to be right there by your side every step of the way. Understand?"

Gabrielle frowned. "What?"

Zachary kneeled down on one knee. He reached into his pants pocket, pulled out a black velvet box, and opened it to a princess-cut three-carat diamond ring.

Gabrielle placed her right hand over her mouth and began to shake her head slowly. "Zachary . . ."

Zachary took her left hand and looked lovingly into her eyes. "Gabrielle Mercedes . . ."

Gabrielle started to cry with her right hand still covering her mouth.

"I love you," Zachary said. "And I want to spend the rest of my life with you as your husband and best friend. I want us to be a family: me, you, and Jasmine. In fact, I can't imagine my life without the two of you in it. I promise to love, honor, cherish, and, yes, fight for our love, every single day of our lives, if I have to. Gabrielle, whatever is in our past is in the past. And on *this* side of goodness, God's goodness, I would be honored if you would say yes to my proposal and agree to be my wife." He took the ring out of the box and set the box on the floor. He held the ring out to her as he waited for her to answer.

"Zachary," was all Gabrielle said as tears came streaming down. "But why? Why now?"

"Why now?" He grinned. "Well, because it took them a week to get the ring in that I ordered. Otherwise, I would have asked you last week. Now, will you *please* make me the happiest man in the world and say yes? Yes, you'll be my wife. Let's just forget about everything and everybody. The only people I care about what they think or feel when it comes to us, is you, me, and of course now, Jasmine."

"Are you sure, Zachary? Are you sure? Because I believe I'm in for the fight of my life if Paris decides to proceed with this as she indicated she would. You know I love you. I love you, Zachary. But I don't want to do anything that might hurt you."

Zachary stood up, pulled her up, and kissed her. "If that's true, then shut up with the commentary and say yes." He smiled, holding the ring up to her.

"Hmmm. I don't know." She shook her head. "If I shut up, then how can I *possibly* open my mouth to say yes? A closed mouth can't speak."

He grinned. "Gabrielle Mercedes, will you marry me?"

She looked at him hard, then broke out into a huge grin. "Yes!" she said. "Yes, I'll marry you!"

The next thing she knew, he'd slipped the ring onto her finger, and her feet were dangling in the air as he hugged her.

"Hey! Hey!" Jasmine's voice came through the loud laughing they were doing. "What's going on in here?"

Gabrielle dashed over to her and hugged her. "I'm sorry. We woke you up."

"Oh, I wasn't asleep. I always have a hard time falling asleep," Jasmine said. "So what are you and Dr. Z so happy about?"

Gabrielle looked up at Zachary, who was also grinning. He came over to them and, kneeling, took Jasmine by both her little hands. "I just asked Miss G to marry me."

Jasmine's face lit up. "You did? You asked her to marry you? For real? You really did?"

Zachary smiled. "I did."

Jasmine turned back to Gabrielle. "And did you say yes?" She held her hands together in a prayerlike pleading way.

Gabrielle was grinning hard now. "I did! I said yes!" She held out her hand, showing Jasmine her ring.

Jasmine started jumping up and down, then grabbed them both by their hands and started jumping up and down along with them. "Yay! We're getting married," she began to sing. "We're getting married." After about two more times of singing that stanza, she stopped and began rubbing her eyes with her fists and began to cry.

Gabrielle squatted down and hugged her. "Jasmine, what's wrong? What's the matter?"

"I was just thinking. I prayed and asked God for you two to get married. God didn't answer my prayer when I asked Him to heal my mother." She rubbed her eyes with her hands. "But God answered my prayer with you." She stopped wiping her eyes and suddenly broke into a humongous grin. "We're getting married! We're going to be a family! I'm so hap-py," she sang.

Zachary hugged her. "Me, too, Miss Jazz! Me, too! I'm so hap-py! Yes, God *does* answer prayers!" He stood up, looked at Gabrielle, winked, then hugged her. "God *absolutely* answers prayers."

Discussion Questions

1. What did you think of Paris and her relationship with her father? Her relationship with her husband, Andrew?

2. What were your thoughts about the whole Lawrence and Gabrielle situation?

3. Knowing what was going on with Jasmine, do you agree with Gabrielle's actions in her attempt to get a donor? What would you have done?

4. Do you feel what Gabrielle was doing could be classified as blackmail?

5. How did you feel about the revelation of Jasmine's father? Discuss the stage that set this, including Paris's treatment of Gabrielle.

6. What are your thoughts when it comes to Lawrence, William, and Paris? What word would you use to describe each of them?

7. Jessica Noble had her own health challenge. Do you think Jessica did the right thing from the time she learned about what was going on until the final thing she did? Discuss.

8. Mattie was a true gatekeeper. Discuss.

9. What did you think of the way Zachary helped Gabrielle, including getting her past Mattie that time into Lawrence's office? Discuss the confrontation in Lawrence's office.

10. What are your thoughts when it comes to these kinds of secrets? Are there times when something shouldn't be disclosed? Explain.

11. Discuss Imani and her role in shifting the dynamics of the story.

12. Do you believe Paris really wants to be a mother? Discuss.

13. What are your thoughts when it comes to Darius? Discuss the square-offs that happened between Darius and Lawrence.

14. Considering Gabrielle's past and what Paris feels she can do, who do you think is the best person when it comes to Jasmine? Why?

15. Discuss the night after Paris confronted Gabrielle in church and informed her of her intentions.

16. At the end, Zachary made his move. What are your thoughts?

Don't miss Vanessa Davis Griggs's

Goodness and Mercy

Available wherever books are sold

Turn the page for an excerpt from *Goodness and Mercy* . . .

Chapter 1

Come now, and let us reason together, saith the Lord: though your sins be as scarlet, they shall be as white as snow; though they be red like crimson, they shall be as wool.

—Isaiah 1:18

"If you're here today," forty-eight-year-old Pastor George Landris began, "and you feel there's something missing in your life. If you admit that although there are billions of people on this earth, you still feel like you're all by yourself—that sometimes it feels like it's you, and you alone. If you feel as though no one truly loves you. If you're fed up with being fed up." He paused a second. "If you'd like to be born again . . . you want to know Jesus in the free pardon of your sins. Then I want you to know that your being here today is neither an accident nor a coincidence. I want you to know that it's time for a change! You see, I've been told that the definition of insanity is doing the same thing over and over again but somehow expecting a different result." He shook his head slowly, then took one step to the side.

"Well, to that someone who's here today, your change has come. If you're looking for change, change you can *truly* believe in, then the Lord is extending His hand to you today through me. He's asking you, on *this* day, to accept His hand. I know I'm talking to somebody today. In your life, it's time for a change." Pastor Landris nodded as he narrowed his eyes, then ticked his head three times to one side as he smiled.

"Oh, I know we heard the word *change* a lot last year. We *talked* about change. Some of you even voted for change. Some of you voted for the first time in your life *because* of change. Well, on November 4, 2008, change took a step forward in these United States of America . . . a change that's *already* had an impact on the world. But on *this* day"—he pointed his index finger down toward the floor—"on this Sunday, January 4, *2009,* sixteen days before that embodiment of change is to be sworn in as the forty-fourth president of the United States, it's time for your own personal change. A change, a wonderful change."

Many in the audience began to clap while others stood, clapped, and shouted various things like: "Change!" "A wonderful change!" and "Thank God for change!"

Pastor Landris bobbed his head, then continued to speak. "For those of you here who are tired of fighting this battle alone, let me assure you that there *is* another way. And in case you don't know or haven't heard, *Jesus* is the way! He's the truth, and He's the light.

"And today—just as Jesus has been doing since before He left earth boarded on a cloud on His way back to Heaven, where He presently sits on the right hand of the Father—He's calling for those who have yet to answer His call, to come. Come unto Him all you that labor and are heavy laden. Jesus desires to be Lord of your life. Won't you come today? Won't you come? Come and cast your cares on the Lord, for He cares for you. Oh, yes, He cares . . . He cares. He cares. He . . . cares."

Pastor Landris extended his hand. He looked like someone waiting on a dance partner to take hold of his outstretched hand in order to continue the next step of a well-choreographed dancing routine.

Twenty-six-year-old Gabrielle Mercedes heard his words. She felt them as they pierced her heart. She doubled over as she sat in her seat. Quickly, she felt the warmth wash completely over her, starting at her head. It felt as though she was being covered with pure love and peace, as though buckets of warmth were being poured on her, the warmth quickly making its way down to her feet. Her feet heard the music inside of the words "Come and cast your cares on the Lord, for He cares," and they began to move, to tap rapidly, all on their own.

The music that played inside her was not the usual music one might expect to hear in church. It was music that no words she knew could aptly describe—angelic. Her body instinctively knew what to do; her legs summarily stood her upright. She hurriedly, but gracefully, started across—one–two, one–two, side step, side step—from where she'd been sitting, quietly excusing herself past those who shared the row with her. Then, forward she glided, with long deliberate strides down a wide center aisle—flow, extend, now glide, glide, faster, faster—toward the front of the church building's sanctuary. Everything happening before the right side of her brain was even able to effectively launch a logical and methodical discussion about any of this with the left side of her brain. She was moving forward, refusing to look back.

And when she shook the hand that continued to remain extended for any and all who dared to reach toward it, she didn't see the man of God's, Pastor Landris's, hand. All she saw was the Son of the living God called Jesus, Emmanuel, the Prince of Peace, the King of kings, the Lord of lords, the President of presidents. She began to leap—higher, higher.

And as she'd shaken Pastor Landris's hand, at least twenty other people also had come forward and stood alongside her. But she'd only felt the hand of God holding her up as she stood there and openly confessed she was indeed a sinner. She knew—without any trumpets sounding, any special effects, and any special feelings—that in that moment of her confession, she was saved. Saved by grace. Now.

Now faith is . . . now . . . faith is now . . .

And the feeling she did have? It was the Lord leading the dance of her life, whispering throughout her every being that she now only needed to follow His lead. She needed to allow Him to take her to the next step, and then the next one, and the next one, without knowing what the next step might be. Fully trusting His lead. *One–two–three.*

Oh, how Gabrielle loved to dance! But until this day, she'd never known the true grace in dancing. That amazing grace. God's amazing grace. The feelings she had now were a by-product of the new knowledge she possessed: the knowledge of knowing Jesus Christ in the free pardon of her sins. All of her sins, every single one of them, Pastor Landris was saying, were officially pardoned. She was free!

"Pardoned—your slate, wiped cleaned," Pastor Landris said to those who came up. "Your sins, totally purged from your record. It's as though they never happened. God says your past transgressions have been removed as far as the east is from the west, the north from the south. All of your sins—the ones folks know about, and yes, the ones only God knows. Gone. Gone! Whatever sins were in your past, from this day forward, as far as the Lord is concerned, they're gone." Those standing were being signaled by a ministry leader to follow her to an awaiting conference room.

"Hold up a second," Pastor Landris said, halting them before they exited. "I want you to say this with me: My *past* has been *cast* into God's sea of forgetfulness."

They did as he asked—some of them leaping for joy as they shouted the words.

"You are forgiven of your sins," he said. "Look at me." He waited a second. "And God is saying to you, don't allow anyone . . . *anyone,* to ever bring up your past sins to you again. Did you hear what I said? Don't let *anyone* use your past against you. If they bring it up, you tell them that it's under the blood of Jesus now."

The entire congregation erupted with shouts of praise as they stood to their feet.

Chapter 2

For I know the thoughts that I think toward you, saith the Lord, thoughts of peace, and not of evil, to give you an expected end.

—Jeremiah 29:11

"Do you have a Bible?" one of the ladies asked Gabrielle as they stood in the conference room where the new converts were taken after they left the main sanctuary.

"No, I don't. But I can buy one," Gabrielle said.

"Oh, we have one for you—a gift from the church." The petite woman smiled as she handed Gabrielle a six-by-nine-inch maroon Bible. "I'm Tiffany Connors. I'm part of the ministry that welcomes converts who come to Christ through Followers of Jesus Faith Worship Center. Our goal is to ensure that you have as many tools as possible at your disposal to get you started in learning all you can about the Lord. Pastor Landris insists there's nothing worse than having something new and either *not* receiving or *not* reading the manual that comes with it—oblivious to its features, benefits, and the instructions to operate it. And of course, any good manual contains troubleshooting information to help in understanding when something is not working properly, and what is needed to correct it. We believe there's no better manual for Christians—novices and veterans alike—than the Bible." Tiffany tapped Gabrielle's Bible twice, then held out her hand for a handshake.

Gabrielle glanced at the Bible she'd been given. She smiled at Tiffany as they shook hands. "I'm Gabrielle Mercedes, and it's a pleasure to make your acquaintance."

Tiffany tilted her head in a quizzical way. "Is Mercedes your married name?"

Gabrielle smiled. She wasn't offended or felt Tiffany was moving too quickly into her business. She knew exactly what was going through Tiffany Connors's head. It was what she encountered a lot since she'd legally dropped her last name of Booker and adopted her middle name as her last. Most people could tell by looking at her smooth brown skin; hair that was, without fail or excuses, relaxed every four to six weeks to keep it from going back to its natural state of afroishness; and a signature behind that defined many a black woman as a black woman (there always being an exception to any rule, as folks like J.Lo have proven) that she was not Hispanic, as her last name might somehow suggest.

The next logical thought was that she, being a black woman, must have married someone with the last name of Mercedes to have acquired it. She could have easily explained how she ended up with it, but didn't bother to. That would defeat the whole purpose of her having changed it in the first place.

"No, I'm not married, and I've never been married," Gabrielle said. She just happened to look down and realized she was hugging her Bible. She let her arm down by her side, along with the Bible she held in her hand.

"Gabrielle Mercedes. Well, it certainly is a beautiful name," Tiffany said. She glanced at her watch and grimaced. "Listen, I hope you don't mind my having to leave so quickly—kind of drop the Bible and run—but I have to go pick up my children from children's church so the workers there can leave."

Gabrielle smiled as she tilted her head only slightly. "Forgive me, but did you say children's church?"

"Yes. We have a church for the children. They call it children's church even though it's still part of this same congregation. There's also a teen church with activities geared specifically for the teenagers and their style of praise and worship. Today was my day to work in this ministry. And since Darius, that's my husband, didn't make it to church today, I'm the only one available to pick up my little ones by the cutoff time."

"How many children do you have?"

Tiffany appreciated that Gabrielle asked. She loved talking about her children. "I have three. My oldest daughter is Jade. She'll be eight this year. Dana, our middle daughter, turns six in a few months. And our son, Darius Junior, we call him Little D., just turned two this past November. He's in the toddler's section of children's church."

Gabrielle nodded. "That's nice of the church to have a children's church and a teen church within the main church. I only went to church a few times when I was growing up, although I went all the time when I was a baby up until I was about three. My mother used to take me every Sunday. . . ." Reflecting on her mother when she was too young (her aunt and others had constantly countered) to remember anything that had to do with her or anything else that may or may not have happened during that time caused her to discontinue, at least aloud, this train of thought.

Gabrielle smiled, pretending it was perfectly normal to switch topics and entire conversations in midsentence. "Suffice it to say, there was nothing separate for children or the teens to do in the churches I attended growing up. And the preacher where we *did* go those times mostly put folks to sleep. I mean, they would be sleeping good, too. Until he reached the end of his sermon and started whooping and hollering—startling babies, men, and old folks alike right out of their naps." She laughed. "I'm sorry. Here I am going on, holding you up when you clearly said you needed to go. Please, go on and pick up your children. And thanks for the Bible." She patted the Bible's cover. "It's beautiful."

Fatima Adams walked over to Gabrielle and Tiffany just as Tiffany was about to leave. "Well, hello. It's Tiffany Connors, right?"

Tiffany nodded. "And you're Fatima . . . ?" She frowned as though that would help her recall Fatima's last name.

"Yes, Adams. Fatima Adams," Fatima said as she politely shook Tiffany's hand.

"Well, Fatima, I must say that you have *impeccable* timing. I'm hurrying to get my children from children's church. Now I don't feel so bad leaving like this. Great meeting you"—she said to Gabrielle—"and great seeing you again," she said to Fatima.

Fatima turned to Gabrielle. "Well, hello there. My name is Fatima Adams, as I'm sure you just heard." She smiled and held out her hand to shake Gabrielle's, then suddenly leaned in and hugged her instead. "I just wanted to come over, introduce myself, and welcome you to the body of Christ, as well as to Followers of Jesus Faith Worship Center. We're so excited you've chosen to accept Jesus into your life. And believe me when I say that your decision is an eternal, life-changing, and life-saving one."

Gabrielle felt Fatima's hug had been sincere. Still, she quickly pulled away, and even took a step back. "Thank you. I'm Gabrielle Mercedes. And before you ask, I'm not married, so it's not my married name." She laughed a little. In truth, the hug had taken her a little off her stride. Gabrielle wasn't accustomed to being hugged. She hadn't been hugged much since her days with Miss Crowe, a teacher who had been a rock in her life. In fact, as she thought about it, the last time she'd actually allowed anyone to hug her, to really hug her, was the last time she'd seen Miss Crowe—some nine years ago. Right before that horrible accident that ended up dramatically changing both of their lives. Any other hugs didn't mean anything to her; they were merely perfunctory.

Miss Crowe was the only person who had really cared about her. She'd cared about Gabrielle's dreams and aspirations. Cared that Gabrielle was treated fairly and with respect. In a nutshell, Miss Esther Crowe had cared about what Gabrielle cared about. So, whenever Miss Crowe hugged her, she knew that Miss Crowe wasn't hugging her for what she could get out of her. She was hugging her because she knew Gabrielle needed it. After Miss Crowe was no longer in her life, she didn't want or care for anyone to hug her.

But she had to admit, there was something different about Fatima's hug—a hug that quite honestly she hadn't seen coming before it happened. A hug that felt rather sisterly, just one more thing she wasn't all that familiar or comfortable with.

Technically speaking, Gabrielle was an only child, born Gabrielle Mercedes Booker. Her mother and father were married before she was conceived. That was a big deal to her since it was the only thing she actually held over the four cousins she'd grown up with who could—and rightly so—be considered more siblings than cousins.

"Thanks for the information, but I hadn't planned on asking if you were married or not," Fatima said. "Not at this point, anyway. I wouldn't want you getting the wrong impression about us here."

In fact, Fatima had noticed the slight cut above Gabrielle's right eye. She couldn't help but wonder what the real story was behind that. And that pukey green, bright sunshine yellow, hot fuchsia, orange, and red scarf carefully tied around her neck didn't seem to match the classy outfit. Fatima pondered whether Gabrielle had possibly worn that scarf to merely cover up some infraction surrounding her neck. That cut above her eye had given Fatima plenty of reason to pause. And Fatima was leaning more toward some act of violence having been done to her than any act of love.

"Well, I wanted to come and personally welcome you to the body of Christ, as well as to Followers of Jesus Faith Worship Center," Fatima said, maintaining her upbeat manner. "I'd also like to give you my phone number and possibly get yours. That's if you don't mind me having it. With thousands of members, Pastor Landris wants to ensure any new people who attend here have at least one person they can easily reach, in case they need something or have any questions. A point of contact, if you will. And I am indeed delighted to say that I am your contact."

Gabrielle flashed Fatima a quick smile. *Indeed.* She'd caught Fatima's glance at the cut above her eye that honestly she'd forgotten was even there. And had she known she would end up going forward to be saved, ultimately placing herself visibly in front of other people instead of the come-in-and-leave-without-talking-to-anyone plan she'd originally had, she might have put off coming to church altogether. At least, until her impossible-to-hide-without-big-shades cut had completely healed.

Gabrielle touched the scarf she'd tied around her neck—happy now she'd chosen to wear it. Scarves were definitely not her thing. They were too old fogey for her. And she was not a scarf person. But leave it to her aunt on her father's side, Cecelia "Cee-Cee" Murphy, to give her something she didn't want but would later possibly need. The only time Gabrielle ever considered wearing a scarf was on her job, and only then if it was requested. Truthfully, even then, she didn't keep it on long enough for it to irritate her the way this one was beginning to do. She pulled at the knot to loosen it a little more, careful that it not become *too* loose and expose the black and blue bruises on her neck.

After leaving the building, she slid into her pearl-colored, automatic five-speed, V6, 2008 Toyota Camry Solara SLE convertible. She draped her off-white wool coat on the passenger's side headrest. She then placed on the passenger's seat her new Bible and the New Convert/New Member's Handbook she'd received from another person who came over right before she left the conference room. She cranked the car, turned the heat on full blast, and pressed a separate button to heat up her tan leather seat. The seat began to warm quickly. When she'd bought this car, that was one feature the manual spoke of that she thought she'd never use, especially living in the South. But on a cold day like this, she absolutely adored this benefit of her car.

Gabrielle reached for the Bible, retrieving the handwritten card Fatima had given her with her contact information along with a message she'd written. Gabrielle couldn't help but smile as she read it.

You are now a new creature. Those old things are officially passed away. It's time to let go of past mistakes made by you and even those made against you. It's time for you to walk in your godly call. If you need anything, have questions as you embark upon this new and wonderful faith journey, or you just need a friend, please trust me when I tell you that I'm only a phone call or an e-mail click away.

Fatima had included her home and cell phone numbers, as well as her e-mail address.

Following that were the words *P.S. Read Jeremiah 29:11.*

Gabrielle looked at the Bible and suddenly realized she'd never really opened a Bible before, and especially not to seek out a specific scripture. Those few times as a child she *had* gone to church, the deacons usually read from their Bibles while the congregation passively listened, and nodded with occasional amens. When the pastor stood and read his selected scriptures before giving his text, the congregation was neither required nor encouraged to open their Bibles and read along with him.

Even her beloved Miss Crowe, who had told her some things about God, had never opened the Bible or read anything out of it in her presence. Miss Crowe merely quoted a scripture when she felt the need.

Starting at the front, Gabrielle turned in search of a table of contents. Most nonfiction books contained one. Surely the Bible had to have one. Surely it had to.

She smiled when she found it. *Old Testament. Jeremiah. Page 1099.*